The Owl & Other Stories

John Auerbach

The Owl
& OTHER STORIES

The Toby Press

First English language Edition 2003

The Toby Press *LLC*
www.tobypress.com

ISBN I 902881 796, *hardback*

A CIP catalogue record for this title
is available from the British Library

Typeset in Garamond by Jerusalem Typesetting

Printed and bound in the United States by
Thomson-Shore Inc., Michigan

Contents

Preface: Saul Bellow, *1*

The Owl, *3*

The Black Madonna, *11*

My Captain and I, *45*

Cohen, *53*

Don Quixote and Other Jewish Memories, *71*

Durutti's Man, *101*

A Short Trip with Domenico Scarlatti and Elvis Presley
from Amsterdam to Paris, *125*

The Towage of the *Shomriah*: a Memoir, *153*

The Yellow Eyes of my Dog, *165*

The Longest Trip, *269*

After the Stroke, *281*

Entropy, *293*

Reflections on Life in the Last Decade of the 20th Century, in the Form of Letters to a Friend, by an Ancient Mariner, *301*

About the Author, *303*

Preface

John first wrote me because *Herzog* had given him some support in his late wife's final illness. He was grieving. We began a correspondence that went on for a couple of years before I actually met him. I think he came to the States first, and I saw more of him later when I went to Israel. On that first meeting I found out a little about him, but not the whole story.

I found him pert, deep, salty—seasoned at sea. I was amazed that he was so much at home in English, and such a Conradian. Like Conrad he was Polish by birth and a seaman. His English, for a Jewish Pole, was faultless. I was attracted by the conjunction: Poland, English and the sea. He was a great reader, which made him immediately sympathetic to me. He'd read Conrad, but not only Conrad. He was steeped in late nineteenth century literature, the Russians and the English.

I also immediately recognized that he was a born story-spinner. In him it was more than a flair; it was a passion—a passion with deep sources in his reading and his life. I was also attracted to the characteristic Jewishness of his story-telling. I have a very wide experience of this.

I immediately recognized traits of my family in him. My father, too, was a European who'd been everywhere and done everything. He had a way of speaking that grated on people and when he met someone from Lodz, he'd say, "Of course I know Lodz, I was there for three months!" My father was a restless man—he had to be to sail in so many directions at once. John, too, at one time. You can tell that his writing began in the long seasons at sea. His secret was that he was a man of letters, therefore incommunicable to most of his companions. That's in his stories, that he is hidden in the ship's company.

He should be read by all good readers because John is full of sympathy and never writes without strong feeling. He's not diffuse. Like so many writers of his generation he's given to art completely.

Why is he not better known? Known at all?

He was never taken up by the big shots. If I say he's a great Jewish writer he'll get thrown into the Jewish box. He's not just that. He wasn't published much? He didn't try very hard. He's a man without strategy who doesn't communicate much outside his stories. But there he has that gift of being able to communicate instantly with those whose antennae are prepared to receive rare frequencies. He's so used to living in dreams he doesn't have any ambitions.

Saul Bellow
Fall, 2002

John Auerbach passed away in November, 2002,
as this volume was in preparation

The Publisher would like to express appreciation to
Nola Chilton Auerbach and to Keith Botsford, for their
invaluable assistance in the genesis of this volume

The Owl

T he owl came from the night; possibly, when the ship sailed through the Strait of Messina. The owl came from the scented darkness of Sicily, or from the other side—the dry, parched darkness of Calabria. Or maybe even earlier, from the slopes of the volcanic island of Stromboli.

The ship passed Stromboli at eight in the evening, very close, the huge volcano cone blacker than the sea, blacker than the night. All of a sudden one side revealed itself illuminated by an eruption of fire; a shower of sparks burst into the air and some red lava and molten rock rolled slowly down. Maybe that was when the owl, scared, escaped from the volcano and found the ship.

The eruption did not last more than ten seconds. When the excited lookout (it was his first trip, he was an innocent young boy straight from the dreamy morning mist of some godforsaken kibbutz in the Lower Galilee; ejaculations, his own and of volcanoes, were still a matter of great excitement for him) stormed into the messroom and exclaimed, Come outside! Quickly, there, a volcano—fire, lots of fire, there on the port side!—only three of the crew rose slowly and went outside to see what was happening. The rest did not leave their places in front of the TV, on which they watched with interest Italian ads for deodorants, washing machines, aperitifs, shoes, and margarine: they have been watching these ads for the past ten days every day at the same time and the more they watch them the more they like them. Two other men in the mess did not interrupt their game of 'touch,' looking intensely at the cards on the table. They frowned at the noise the lookout boy made: it disturbed their concentration.

When the three that went out to see the volcano reached the deck, the fire sparks were already high in the sky and had joined other stars, and the lava had cooled off and was only a big pink spot on the mountain's slope, and the ship, steadily and constantly moving, was already at another angle from the island, so there was hardly anything to be seen except the night. The three men shrugged and returned, disappointed, to the little, warm, well-lit coziness of the messroom and to the happy smile of a pretty Italian woman on the TV screen. She was happy because she was using a very special washing-powder and her linen was whiter than that of her neighbor, but they compared their towels, and the other woman soon became happy too, for she also switched over to the washing-powder recommended by the ad.

But the owl was already on board.

2.

Next morning he saw the owl sitting on the lifeboat. It did not move when he came nearer. It was a large, beautiful bird, compact but without losing anything of its lightness, its feathers various shades of brown and gray and yellow. It had big talons and it looked at him with round yellow eyes, and it seemed to have a permanent sardonic smile on its face. There was no wind in the serenity of the early dawn, but the bird trembled.

He said, you got a lift with us, bird? Where to, big owl? and it rose with quiet dignity from its place and flew slowly, moving its great wings, to the top of the main mast. He saw it there, from the bridge, through binoculars, five hours later. It was difficult to watch with the glasses, his hands were not very steady these days.

3.

They caught the owl in the afternoon and brought it triumphantly to the messroom. A man held it with both hands, under the wings, out of the reach of the claws or beak, but the owl did not struggle. It looked straight forward with eyes unblinking and full of hate: only the two tufts of hair behind the ears quivered slightly.

"This is some owl, I must say," commented the bosun. "How strange! She did not move when I climbed up the mast, but she saw me coming: she did nothing."

"How do you know it is a she?" demanded the lookout boy aggressively. He had two deep scratches on his forearm, swelled with blood, and he displayed them with pride.

"Look between her legs," one man laughed.

"Maybe it's a domesticated bird," another suggested.

"Domesticated, my foot! Look at this," said the boy, showing his arm. "Look what she did when I carried her down the ladder."

"Back in the old country, I remember, I was a child then, villagers nailed an owl to the church door. They said it was a devil, a bad spirit."

"They used to do the same in Poland."

"Well maybe she is a bad spirit, she doesn't look nice."

"Look at these talons."

"Let the chief have a look."

The circle breaks to let him in: he stares at the bird in silence. He is the oldest man on board, almost twice the age of anybody else here. He has an old face and this face is now exactly opposite the owl's face.

"Well, what do you propose to do with it now that you've caught it?"

"Well, nothing."

He nods with contempt. "That's what I thought."

The owl turns its round head a little to the left, then to the right.

"What about letting her go?"

"Oh sure. But let's first play a bit with her."

"In the old country, they used to nail them to the door," this from the same big man with a black beard and moustache, and a balding head.

The chief engineer turns round abruptly, goes back to his cabin. "Let it free," he says over his shoulder, walking away.

"He hardly ever leaves that hole of his."

"Except when he goes down to the engine-room," the man with the black beard says, "to grumble, and to complain, and to scold; nothing is good enough for him. As if anybody needed him there."

"What do you want, he's drunk most of the time."

"He's useless, he's ballast."

"But he doesn't act drunk."

"No, but what he talks is bloody drunken nonsense."

"If he talks."

"That's right. Doesn't exchange a word with anybody for days."

"Hardly answers to 'good morning, Chief.'"

"A fucking old bastard: what does he sail for?"

"Same as you. Money."

"Shit! Somebody back home told me the old prick is rich—he knows him well."

"Is that so? Well, he seldom goes ashore to spend the money."

"What can he spend the money on, man? I'm sure he can't fuck any more and booze is cheap on board."

"Actually, he looks a bit like that owl, doesn't he?"

A wild burst of laughter. The owl moves from one leg to another.

"Sit quiet, bitch!"

"Upon my life, you're right: look at its eyebrows—exactly like the old man's."

"The question is, does a bird bring luck to the ship, or not?"

"I don't know."

"I worked with Italian fishermen once, they said a little bird does not bring luck. But we never had an owl on board."

"Well, what do we do with this fucking bird?"

"Lock it up in the paint locker, we'll see tomorrow."

"OK, that's a good idea."

Four of them walk with the bird the whole length of the ship on the dark iron deck, up to the forecastle.

The bosun puts the lock on the door and the key in his pocket. "Hope she won't shit on the paint pots."

"Or drink the thinner, she might get high on it."

"A drinking companion for the old man."

"He doesn't need any company. He drinks alone."

4.

The owl sits motionless on a gallon drum of red zinc chromate. The man, who has opened the lock with a skeleton key, leans with his back against the closed door and looks at the bird in the yellow cone of light that shines from his flashlight. He grins with satisfaction. He is still very dexterous as locks go: he maneuvers skeleton keys or pieces of wire in the locks, feeling the slightest pressures inside, the smallest resistance, his fingertips are very sensitive, the slight shaking of his hands does not impair his ability to deal with locks.

The owl narrows its eyes, and the man thinks, the light disturbs her, she does not like light, she sees well in darkness. That's why they caught you, stupid, he murmurs. Aloud he says, "Well, owl, time to get out of this stinking hole, eh, what do you think?" He slowly brings his arm close to the tin of paint on which the bird perches, and the owl takes two steps and sits down on it. The talons, with their needle-sharp points, pierce the thin overall fabric and dig themselves into his skin. A blood stain appears on the overall but the material soaks easily. "It's nothing, it's just some blood," he murmurs. "I know you can't help it. Still I know that you know that I'm on your side. Not with these hooligans."

With the other hand he turns off the electric torch and gropes in darkness for the door handle. Before he finds it, he thinks: Now I'm like a falconer—once I wanted to have a castle, a castle on a hill in a wood, with dogs, and horses and falcons. But this is a tramp ship's paint locker, and I lost that dream long ago, along with other dreams. And you are an owl and not a falcon. Let's finish with this sad business. His free hand finds the handle. Out on deck, he crouches low against the bulwark. The night is moonless and dark but the lookout or the officer of the watch on the bridge might see something moving on deck.

The owl turns slowly towards him, its flat face cut perpendicularly in two by the long black beak.

"You go now," he says. "The Calabrian coast is not far. Or you could go to Bari, or Brindisi. Wherever you want. Go, damn you. Be more careful next time."

The owl rises easily and the man watches for a second and a half as the big bird's wings move slowly and noiselessly in the air. Then the owl melts into the night from which it came. The man stares at the darkness a few moments more.

"I still have to put that lock on," he whispers, and goes back to the paint locker's door.

The Black Madonna

A point for consideration: the color of the story. It started in blackness—pitch-black, absolutely desperate—and dissolved in hopeless darkness. This full circle is not proscribed for reasons of harmony or aesthetics. The color is genuine, unpleasant as it is, and part of the story as well.

The blackness in the beginning was so absolute, so deep, that I cannot, even in imagination, recreate the improbable intensity of it. It enveloped the ship from all sides, it clung to its superstructure like tar. It muffled every sound, even the rhythmic thumping of the engine. Sometimes it seemed that the people on the bridge stopped breathing, because no sound was heard. And yet, when after endless waiting the pilot announced, "Steer one ninety-two now," the helmsman's voice repeated, like an echo in mountain wilderness,

"One ninety-two, sir."

"Steady."

"Steady, sir."

These voices seemed to emanate tiny flickers of light, but in between—periods of silence that lasted for ages—everything was submerged in that absolute darkness.

"Stop her."

The engine telegraph rang, and the engine stopped. But nobody on the bridge felt any difference; the ship could be suspended in the void on invisible wings, stuck fast in a dry dock, or floating noiselessly on the bottom of a fathomless depth.

Years of silence passed, and now the few people on the bridge, though busy and concentrating on their tasks, felt balanced on the verge of nothingness. It was out of the impenetrable darkness that a spell seeped in, blanketing their awareness silently but steadily. The captain was the first to shake it off. He coughed and said, "What next, Pilot?"

The pilot did not answer; perhaps, the captain thought illogically, he had simply disappeared after having got us into this mess. He had disliked the pilot from the first moment, when he saw him arriving in a whaler, rowed by four men.

"No," he'd said aloud, watching the boat through his glasses. "No, this can't be, Anno Domini 1960. Pilots do not come on board in rowboats anymore, not for a good forty years now. In Conrad's books perhaps, but not now. Not in a civilized country."

"They once called it *Ultima Thule,* what the ancients believed to be the furthest point north." The chief mate liked to display his liberal education at times, without stressing the other's ignorance too strongly; this could eventually make his captain angry.

"Never mind what they called it once," the captain said. "There are places much further north, decent civilized ports. And this is Northern Ireland, not a wilderness, and one has the right to expect normal harbor services here, pilots coming in motor-launches like anywhere else, and for sure in the United Kingdom. Look at the buggers."

The four men in the whaler pulled hard against the waves to bring their boat alongside the ship.

The captain dropped his binoculars and shook his head again.

"I wouldn't be surprised if he breaks his head trying to reach the pilot ladder."

But he did not: he jumped at the right moment, climbed the ladder with remarkable agility, and a minute later arrived on the bridge in his wet, black oilcloth, very stern, unsmiling, almost hostile. He warmed his big hands on a hot mug of tea, and his "thanks" was in such a low register that the steward was not at all sure if he'd heard it, and looked at him curiously.

"What is your draught, Captain?" he asked, when the ship cautiously entered the mouth of the river and the fog and the darkness grew thicker and thicker every minute.

"Eighteen."

He murmured under his nose.

"The pilot book says the river is dredged to twenty," the captain said defiantly.

"The pilot book," repeated the pilot. "We should not miss the tide."

"Scandalous," confessed the captain in a low voice to the chief engineer, in the chart room. "All this in order to load a few hundred tons of rotten potatoes, and probably to get stuck in this port for God knows how long." But there was no choice now but to continue creeping up the shallow and narrow river, under the guidance of this morose pilot, straining to see the buoys that marked the passageway. Or were they, too, the product of the imagination of those who drew this chart eighty years ago? And then their sons, perhaps, who added innumerable corrections throughout the years, just to prove that they acknowledged, reluctantly, the passage of time?

"What next, Pilot?"

The pilot shrugged; the captain felt the shrug, but did not see it. The captain's impatience, his rising anger, could be heard clearly in his voice.

"Well, Pilot, what next?"

The engine telegraph rang sharply when an invisible hand moved it from DEAD SLOW AHEAD to STOP.

"What a bloody entrance!" the captain said. "And this damned fog, on top of it. This beats the East Coast, London included, all right. I've never seen anything thicker than this!"

The pilot, barely visible, was a big man, very broad in his shoulders, or perhaps it was only the oilcloth that made him so big.

"What now, Pilot?"

His face, lit from beneath by the faint light of the radar screen, was a green mask. But the radar in fog was useless: it showed fantastic groups of islands, phantom vessels, nonexistent shores. In reality, there was only a narrow, twisted, and very long channel full of shoals and submerged rock invisible in the darkness. He was looking for a red light buoy somewhere ahead, and a few miles still further up, the port.

"We'd better drop anchor, Captain, and wait till it clears up a bit, perhaps till tomorrow morning."

"Drop the anchor!" exploded the captain. "I think we're already aground!" He spoke in a very loud, commanding voice, trying to shatter, if not the darkness, then at least the evil spell, to bring the whole thing back to reality. Others could be dreaming, perhaps, but he, the captain of a five-thousand-ton cargo boat on a normal voyage from one port to another, could not afford that luxury. He was consciously responsible to the owners, to the underwriters, responsible to the law. What the devil! If that moron of a pilot could not cope with the situation, he would, by God!

"Give full astern!" he shouted.

The bell rang again, and deep in the bowels of the ship, where there was no fog and no darkness, but always the bright light of neon lamps, and the glistening of well-polished, smoothly oiled metal, the engineer on duty reversed the big engine. As it picked up more and more revolutions, they, on the bridge, felt the slight tremor of the ship under their feet.

"Stop 'er!"

"We're not aground, Captain," murmured the pilot softly. "She's moving. And here's the buoy, we almost ran over it," he added. Incredibly, just a few yards from the ship's starboard side, a red eye blinked maliciously.

"See? I told you!" the captain said triumphantly.

"Sure," the pilot muttered, unperturbed. "Steer two-oh-seven," he told the helmsman.

"Two-oh-seven, sir."

"Dead slow ahead."

Once again in the chart room, the captain wiped his brow.

"Did you see that?" he said to the chief engineer, who studied the chart with his elbow on the table. "The fellow must be drunk! He does not listen, he simply does not listen! He ran her aground, I had to take the ship off! I only hope to God he'll bring her to the goddamned harbor!"

"It's not far now."

"And God be praised! I wouldn't like to have this lunatic on board any longer." Gradually, a few lights appeared ahead, dim outlines of some buildings, a silo, a few harbor cranes. The ship came alongside and was moored in silence. A few words of command were heard, muffled by the fog. Then: "As she is."

"Finish with engine."

"The fellow upset me badly," uttered the captain. "I wonder if I should offer him a drink, the bastard!"

"It's a cold night," answered the chief engineer. "You'd better do so."

The pilot unbuttoned his oilcloth, and a coat, and produced a battered wallet. From it he extracted two folded sheets of paper. "Will you sign these, please?"

The captain's anger subsided. He shot a sideways glance at the chief engineer.

"Pilot, better come down to my cabin. We'll have a drink. It's a cold night. Will you join us, Chief?"

The pilot looked smaller now; his oilcloth hung on the peg at the entrance to the cabin. He put his hands on the table and steadily looked at them, while the captain poured whiskey into the glasses.

"Soda?"

"No, thank you."

"You, Chief?"

"Straight, please."

They took a sip, and the captain cleared his throat. "It's a difficult passage you have here."

"When in the dark, and it is foggy, yes."

"I should say, there are plenty foggy days here, aren't there? And nights."

The pilot took another sip. "What are you loading here?"

"Potatoes, twelve hundred tons of them."

The pilot nodded. "It will take a week."

"A week!" exclaimed the captain. "Why so long?"

For the first time since he'd come on board, something resembling a sour smile appeared on the pilot's face.

"Shortage of labor," he said. "And then, the cargo doesn't arrive on time; they don't have the whole quantity stored here, you know."

"All right, but still," said the captain, perplexed. "A shortage of labor? I thought there was unemployment here?"

"The unemployed don't stay in this town." His glass was empty, and the captain poured him another drink. "They go away, to the Free State or to England. Very few men here."

"What about women?" asked the chief engineer; the conversation was boring him.

The pilot looked straight at him, and the chief received the first impression of his face. He was a middle-aged man, hollow-cheeked, with deep lines running from his nose down to the corners of the mouth. His hair was thin, his brow furrowed. This man has known lots of trouble, thought the chief, who prided himself on being a connoisseur of men.

"Women?" repeated the pilot thoughtfully, and immediately emptied his glass. "You'll find lots of women here. Perhaps more than you'd like. Or care for." He put his glass on the table and shoved the papers toward the captain.

"Will you please sign this?" he said. "I am afraid I have to go now. The town is lousy with women."

The captain and the chief looked up, surprised, and the captain signed the documents.

"Here you are, Mr., eh, Mr…"

"Halloran."

"Mr. Halloran, sir. You have to bring another ship in tonight?"

"Not tonight. Thanks for the drink. Goodbye, Captain. Perhaps I'll take you out to sea in a week's time. See you, Chief."

"A strange fellow," remarked the captain after the pilot had left. "And I can tell you already that I don't like this place."

"You haven't seen anything of it yet," laughed the chief.

"I am sure he was already a little tipsy when he came on board, and then three more drinks here. No wonder he won't bring any more ships in tonight, though he can stand his whiskey well, one must admit: he walked a straight line. What time is it?"

"Half past two," the chief said, standing up. "I think I'll turn in for a few hours."

"See you later, Chief."

First came the teenagers, thin and fragile, with bony arms and legs, and nervous smiles on their faces. Walking that thin thread that makes the difference between a child and a woman. They were giggling. They were whispering quick remarks to each other. They were hungry. They sat in the corner of the crew's messroom, pulling the skirts over their knees. Trying desperately to look ladylike in accordance with standards of behavior learned from the TV, movies, and teen magazines, most of them painfully aware of the clumsiness of their attempts, because after all this camouflage was removed, and a girl asked herself frankly: What did you come here for? to answer "for fun and company" would not deceive the conscience of even the most simple-minded or wicked of them. They all knew the answer: they came on board this foreign ship to get some food, to get whiskey, and to get laid.

They came in groups of three and four, as this gave them an

illusion of security, but even then they knew they'd be separated in the end, and each one would lie in another sailor's bunk.

Peggy, Helen, May, Rita, Cathy, sitting around the table on which seamen had played endless games of cards whilst the ship was underway. Now the seamen were having their supper, at another table, and the steward forbade them to invite the girls to sit with them. And so, eating their supper, they watched the girls, and made their choices for later.

"I'll take the redhead."

"The tall one, in the blue skirt, she's not bad."

"I prefer the yellow blouse, in the corner."

The girls fingered the foreign magazines they could not read, and stole glances at the plates on which the food was heaped.

"They are no whores," one sailor remarked.

"No, no. Good girls these. You don't have to pay them."

"Just give them a plate of chicken and chips."

"Later I'll take her for a dance. There must be some dancing in this town."

"First I want to dance with her in my bed. Pass me the salt."

A burst of laughter: the girls looked up. They did not understand the seamen's language, but they knew they were being talked about. They corrected their hairdos with small nervous gestures.

The chief mate stuck his head in the crew's mess, and watched the scene in silence.

"Who are these girls?" he asked after a moment.

"We invited them for a dance, sir," answered a seaman. They all laughed; there was no need to pretend.

The chief mate nodded his head several times. The girls blushed and each one of them tried to preserve her dignity, or what remained of it.

Outside it was dark and silent. The winches were not working, they had long ago finished loading the first one hundred and thirty-five tons of potatoes in coarse, brown sacks. That means seven, eight days, thought the chief mate. He was cautiously walking along the iron deck, which was covered with delicate, fresh frost. The powerful mercurium lamps, high on the masts, shed a bluish light on the ship and the quay.

The chief mate reached the forecastle and, stepping carefully over dunnage and cargo nets, made his way back aft. It was his night on board. He found a small, gnome-like old man in an oversized duffel coat near the gangway.

"You the night watchman?"

"Yes sir."

The man's face was wrinkled with a hundred creases, like a plate of shattered glass. He was hopping from foot to foot. It's cold, realized the chief mate. He went to his cabin, the first one at the entrance, poured a glass of whiskey, and brought it to the watchman.

"Here, drink this, it's bloody cold."

"Thank you, sir, thank you very much indeed." He downed the whiskey, and the mosaic of shattered fragments in his face filled with color.

"A fine ship this, sir. Last night I was on that Greek one over there, and could not get a glass o'tea. They chased me out of the pantry, they did."

He'll probably spend the whole night in the warm pantry here, thought the chief mate. "Keep a good look out, watchman," he said.

"You can be sure, sir. Thank you, sir."

The captain and the chief engineer appeared in the messroom in their best shore clothes, smelling of eau-de-cologne.

"We're going to see how things look here, we'll report to you tomorrow, so you'll know where to direct your steps in the evening," the captain said.

"Enjoy yourselves."

"We'll try our best."

"As far as the circumstances allow," added the chief engineer.

"This the watchman?"

The old man sprang to attention. "Yes, sir."

"Well, keep a good watch! Plenty of thieves in this harbor?"

"No thieves here, sir. People are too poor to steal."

"That bad? Well, we'll see. Good night."

The chief mate entered his cabin, drew the blinds and the curtains shut, took off his coat, and, sinking into his armchair, thought a moment about his captain. The captain loved normality, and hated everything that was somehow out of line. He should have been a clerk in a post office; unexpected things seldom happened there. True, adapting himself to his profession he has widened his definition of normal to include a lot of things that would appear most extraordinary to a dweller of towns: storms, calms, foreign shores. But anything beyond his previous experience, or the limits of his imagination and expectations, upsets him greatly, throws him off balance and makes him angry.

"That's why he blew up last night on the river," muttered the chief mate to himself, pouring himself a drink, and placing his shaving mirror against the bottle so that he might enjoy good company while drinking. I don't blame him, it certainly was dark there!

He touched his glass with that of the man in the mirror: *Prost!* How cheerful he was to be going ashore with the engineer! Everything perfectly normal: delays in loading—normal; cargo not coming in time—normal; labor shortage—normal. Now he'll get normally drunk and pick up a normal whore, and maybe bring her on board and have a normal fuck: he on top of her, and no fancy poses please.

The chief mate, contented with the smooth flow of his conversation, poured himself another drink, and suddenly remembered the old watchman freezing outside: freezing, my foot! The bastard was surely dozing down in the pantry. He decided to check, told the mirror he'd be back in a moment, and staggered outside.

The watchman was there, both elbows on the railing, contemplating.

"Everything all right?" inquired the chief mate in a loud voice.

"Everything all right," echoed the watchman.

The mate wanted to ask something important, but he forgot what it was the moment he opened his mouth.

"Did you see if the bosun went ashore?" he asked.

"No, sir. Nobody went ashore except the captain, the chief engineer, and later the radio officer with one motorman. All the rest have guests."

"What? The whores haven't left yet?"

"No sir. And they are not whores, with your permission, sir. They are just teenagers. Good girls, all."

"Come, come, don't tell me good girls are roaming the port and visiting foreign ships. What is this, the Salvation Army? Charity?"

"No charity. They come to get fed and drunk at the cost of being laid."

"Come in, have a drink. We'll leave the door half open so we can see if anybody comes on board."

Seated again in his armchair, and facing the gnome, the chief mate inquired, "What sort of town is this? It's the first time I am here."

"Majority are Catholics, sir. And five women to a man."

"That bad?"

"That bad. So the girls are all hot-pants, and they are hungry. And it is infectious, you know. You can have almost any woman in this town."

"I don't want any." The mate had had enough alcohol to slip easily into the role of a noble gentleman. Above all this. Couldn't care less about women.

"But there are very few men here."

Confound that watchman, the chief mate thought: Does he think I'm a queer or something? Well, he's had his two drinks, and that's enough, even for a cold night like this.

The chief mate stood up and the watchman, who understood the hint, got up, too, said thank you, and went out. The mate gave him a package of cigarettes.

Half an hour later, in his bunk already, he heard loud voices outside, and a woman in a burst of shrill laughter. The captain and the chief engineer were returning from town.

They've brought women with them, he thought, and suddenly felt very lonely in his big bed.

Noble like hell, eh? he said to himself. But you wouldn't throw her out of here now. Who would? It's cold! Well, maybe we'll take care of it tomorrow. Let them enjoy themselves.

He picked up a magazine, but couldn't concentrate on what he read. Then he fell asleep, and awoke only a couple of hours later, when he heard a knock on the door. He switched on the lamp and said, Come in, and was not at all surprised when he saw a woman entering: after all, he had been dreaming of women.

"The watchman told me this is the chief mate's cabin. Are you the chief mate?"

Hands under his head—he was sleeping on his back—the chief mate watched the woman with unblinking eyes. "Who are you?"

"Me?" Leaning against the door, she twisted her mouth into a leer, giving herself an attitude of jeering, biting, malicious irony. "Me? Mary Halloran is the name, at your service, sir. Not the Virgin Mary, to be sure, but Mary all the same. And on a running visit to the officers' staff on this here fine ship: senior officers only, mind you, the four of them: captain, chief engineer, second engineer, and chief mate. This here the right address?"

It was a voice full of mockery, and it had a ringing, metallic quality to it, which made it even less pleasant to the ear.

The chief mate, without changing his position by as much as an inch, scrutinized her closely. She was a good-looking woman, but not young; in her forties, he judged, making a mental note simultaneously, a good ten years older than he. She wore a plain black dress and a golden chain on her neck. She had a lean, eager face, with deep-set eyes and high cheekbones, and a very wide mouth; she had raven-black hair, probably dyed, he thought. She was unsteady on her legs, must have drunk a lot.

"What do you want?" he asked. The idea of moving aside in this big bed, and having her here, near him, with her heavy alcoholic breath, and unable to control herself in any way, made her repulsive for the present.

She smiled, and her grin became so wide that her mouth was a wound, a red slash across the lower part of her face. "A tiny little bit of whiskey, dear, that's all I want." She extended her hand, and with the forefinger and the thumb measured the quantity she wanted. "That much, and no more, it is no exorbitant demand, is it? Come on, don't be stingy, everybody contributed his part: the captain, the chief, the second engineer."

The smile froze on her face as she lost balance momentarily and caught the armchair to keep herself from falling. She made two uncertain steps, and slumped in the chair. Only then did she focus on the bottle and the glasses on the table.

"Oh, oh, see here: it is all ready and prepared, ain't it handy? And the mirror, let me look at myself: my, what a face!"

Suddenly, in a tone completely changed—sober, but with the metallic ringing still in it—she asked, "Are you going to drink with me or not? Make up your mind!"

The chief mate turned on one side, propped his head in his hand and, leaning on his elbow, said, "I'll give you no whiskey, lady. You're drunk as Lot."

"Aren't you a regular preacher. But you've been drinking yourself, haven't you?"

"I know when to stop."

In her black eyes there was now mockery, hate, desperation. "Listen," she said. "I won't bother you, if that's what you are afraid of. I won't jump into that snug, warm bed of yours. Not that I am a nun, mind you, but I've had enough of it, for the moment; I'm too tired. What I want is a drop of whiskey, and then I'm off home. Is it a deal?"

"Aren't there other ships in the harbor?"

All of a sudden she started to cry, noiselessly, big tears rolling down her cheeks.

"Right," he said, "we'll have a drink and then I'll bring you home."

"I don't need your assistance. I can manage myself."

"Like hell you can." He pulled on his trousers, and poured a drink for her and for himself.

"Health," he said, touching her glass.

"What's your name?"

"Jacob," he said. "Call me Jack, Mary."

"Health, Jack. You don't know what hell is."

"Do you?"

"Me? I spend most of my time there, except when in church," she added thoughtfully. Setting her glass on the table, she said, "I'm Catholic, you know. You too?"

"No."

"Only Catholics know what proper hell is, and Irish Catholics know best, because Irish Catholics are the best Catholics." Then, indignantly: "There ain't any justice: booze is flowing on these ships like water. You know what a bottle of whiskey costs in town? Guess!"

"I have no idea. Come, Mary, let's go."

She staggered to her feet.

"Where's the can?" she asked.

"Over there."

She went in, and turned the key. He heard water running—she stayed there a long time. When she finally came out, she was pale and composed. She had fresh makeup on. She managed a strained smile. "Really, there is no need to accompany me," she said evenly.

"I want to."

"I live not far from here."

"A lady shouldn't walk alone this late at night."

She looked up for a sign of mockery on his face, but did not find any: he was in earnest.

"A man might try to stop you, taking you for what you are not," he explained.

"There aren't any men in this town, only women. And how do you know who I really am?"

They were outside now, and he said to the watchman, "I'll be back very soon. If anything happens, wake up the second mate, by my order."

"Nothing will happen, sir."

The cold air stung his lungs, their breath was like thick vapor; thin ice cracked under their feet like broken glass.

The night was starless and absolutely silent, not a sound, except their steps on the cobblestones. She did not speak anymore and he kept silent. On the corner of the second street from the harbor, she stopped.

"This far," she said.

He let go of her arm and they stood facing each other, enveloped in the clouds of their breathing.

"Could I see you tomorrow?"

She started, surprised.

"I won't come to your ship again," she said.

"Unless you need whiskey very badly."

"Unless I need it very, very badly."

Standing so close to her, he found that her face was strangely delicate and fine now, clear cut. He framed it, with the background of the dark street (but omitting the cloud of steam), and hung it on the wall of his cabin opposite the entrance. The frame was thick and heavy, dark bronze, or gilded wood.

"I'll be waiting for you tomorrow, seven o'clock, here, on this corner."

"Don't let me wait, somebody could, you know, take me for what I really am, and pick me up," she said without bitterness.

"I'll be waiting for you," he repeated.

When recollecting this episode in his life, much later, the chief mate found many things inexplicable. Also, there were several blank spaces, which was rather surprising, for he had a good memory. He could not, for example, remember how many times he met Mary during his ship's stay in port. Torn shreds of their various conversations did not fit together, like pieces of a jigsaw puzzle: too many missing, others misplaced. Not that he was desperately keen on having the whole perfect and complete: as it often happens with men who have spent many years at sea, and experience a new encounter—with people, or with places—the vision of things past must be blurred to a certain extent. Occasionally these memories resemble a film on which only two or three exposures were taken.

And he did not hang her picture, framed, in his cabin.

But he remembered her well, in various situations: in the church, prostrate on the floor, before the cross. The chief mate sat upright on the bench, in the empty church, in which the only points of light were the two tall yellow candles lit on the altar.

He was not a Christian, but he had known many churches, and this one was different; even the smell was different. He sat there, very alien, and far more lonely than in any of the Mediterranean churches, feeling very cold inside, while Mary lay on the floor. He sat there until she rose, knelt beside the confessional, and confessed in a hoarse whisper. Later she sighed heavily: "What a bad Catholic I am, Jack." she said. "Here I am confessing my sins, getting absolved, and am told: go and sin no more, and even then I know as sure as anything that I am going to sin, and sin again. Absurd, isn't it?"

The chief mate was unimpressed. "Not at all," he said. "I never confess my sins to anybody."

"Don't you ever sin?"

"Oh, plenty," he said, laughing, "but I do not confess. Occasionally to myself. Even that, seldom."

She walked beside him with her soft, elastic gait, very feminine, holding his arm. "That must be terrible," she said. "I couldn't live without confession and absolution. But sometimes I wish I could confess directly to the Virgin Mary. With her I have always had better relations than with anybody else up there."

She was very adorable to him at that moment, and he stopped and kissed her on her mouth; this he remembered for a long time, even after he forgot how it was to be in bed with her. He remembered her words, the ramparts of the old fortress where they stood, the gusts of cold wind, and the taste of her lips: hard and fresh, like a wind in spring.

But Mary in his bed, on board his ship, was one of the missing pieces of the jigsaw puzzle, though she was passionate, and loving, and he remembered what she said later, already dressed. "I know what you're thinking about, do you want me to be very honest? All right.

Don't worry. I won't make love to any other man, as long as you're here. That's what you wanted to know, didn't you?"

"Yes," he said. He thought a moment and asked, "And what about your husband?"

"Leave my husband out of it. That is another story altogether. It has nothing to do with you."

"What does he do?"

She hesitated a second. "He is a seaman, like you. Please, don't ask me any questions about my husband; I did not ask you about your wife."

"I am not married."

"The better for you: so you, at least, do not commit adultery."

"Don't you love him?"

She had a trick of suddenly pulling on a mask of gross vulgarity, often brutal, and using it as a shield. "For Chrissake," she exclaimed. "Don't be that nosy! You won't have me telling you about every man I ever went to bed with?"

A minute later, repenting, angry with his answering silence, she added, "Much he cares about me…"

Whiskey was important. Whiskey was all-important. She craved it. She needed it in a different way than he did. She claimed it kept her alive. "I am half dead without booze," she told him.

"When did you start on it?"

"When everybody does here, seventeen, eighteen, I don't remember exactly. When did you?"

He shrugged. "When I started sailing, I guess. What does it do to you?"

"Gives me courage to live. And you?"

He thought a moment before answering truthfully: "It's the illusion of killing the loneliness."

"But it does not kill it, really, does it?"

"No. Nothing can kill it. But illusion is fair. We quickly learn to be satisfied with illusion."

"Sure, sure," she agreed with alacrity, eagerly. Touching her hair—it was not dyed, he learned—and moving her head in such a way that he saw her sharp profile. "Come on," she said, "let's go to bed. How many tons of potatoes have you still got to load?"

Slow as the loading proceeded, they were nearly finished after a week. The crew had the time of their lives: what little work there was to do was mostly interrupted by rain or snow, pouring endlessly from the low, overcast steel-gray sky. They sat in the pantry for hours, drinking coffee, and discussing the girls of the night before, and the night to come. Girls were plentiful as snow, rain and sleet. They did not cost money. They were on board ready to be had any moment. They lined the walls of the two dances in town: they walked the streets in twos and threes, asking to be taken, fed and put in bed.

Discipline became slack, then nonexistent. The bosun tried vainly to preserve some traces of his authority, but they knew there was the pale-faced redhead in his cabin, waiting, and he'd soon finish scolding them and run back to her, so they did not bother answering.

The chief mate was disinterested: the captain disappeared for two days, returned one evening accompanied by two giggling women and shut himself in his cabin saying aloud that he did not want to be disturbed. Late at night, one of the women, half-naked, walked the alleyway nonchalantly and finally landed in the chief engineer's cabin.

The gnome-like night watchman looked at all this with non-seeing, bleary eyes, then, turning his back and leaning against the handrail at the entrance, gazed for hours at the quayside, paved with heavy cobblestones, at the fog, sleet, at the night, despoiling the town with wet snow. The lamps were swaying in the wind, shedding feeble light.

In the ship's holds, sullen stevedores handled damp potato sacks, mute, waiting for the moment they could leave the dismal job and walk over to the pub at the corner.

In the messroom, two packages of newspapers from home lay on the table: for the first time in this ship's history, nobody bothered to open them when the agent brought them on board.

"This is insanity," murmured the second engineer. "This port has poisoned everybody. It has poisoned the ship."

They looked at him with blank eyes; they went to their cabins, to the girls and women awaiting them, thirsty for a drink, passive, resigned, complying with their destiny.

The whole town was deeply submerged in that cloud of resigned slumber. Parts of it were like any industrial town in the British Isles, the monstrosity of endless rows of identical houses with colorless fronts and big chimneys hitting out at one's eye. But even in those streets that appeared to be livelier, because of some shops and their window displays, the terrible apathy still lurked around every corner.

The chief mate, strolling occasionally through town, had conversations with a barber, at a newspaper stand, in two or three pubs.

People were sullen, sleepy, with a twist of disdain at the corner of the mouth. Their skin had a sick, grayish hue. He was struck by the lack of any noise in the pub; even drinking was done in silence. It seemed incredible all this had anything to do with religion, yet this was what he was told on more than one occasion.

But can this religious business effect people's everyday life to that extent, he wondered? This town is simply nuts!

Then he remembered how many allusions Mary made to things religious. Here, in this town, religion was not something to be taken care of on Sunday, only in church. It was everyday trouble, and all things were miraculously connected with it in one way or another.

"Catholics," snarled a Protestant shopkeeper, selling him a bar of candy. "You'd wonder, to hear how many people in this town live by orders from the Pope in Rome."

"The Pope," repeated the chief mate, a bit absentmindedly, as if he saw no connection.

"Yes, the Pope. In Rome!"

And on the same day, a cab-driver turned to him, and hissed: "They—the Protestants—they are foreigners here: a privileged, goddamned minority." Intensifying the hiss, he added: "They have no business here, do you hear?"

Their own ship, in spite of its silent occupation by local girls and women, seemed an oasis of normality. Vapors of hatred, suspicion and apathy dissolved before the entrance doors, the same doors on which he could read every time when coming back from shore: THIS SHIP IS AIR-CONDITIONED. PLEASE KEEP THE DOOR CLOSED.

He entered the officers' mess.

"Say, Mate," the captain said, picking his teeth leisurely, "this broad of yours, isn't she the same one who was here the first night?"

"No," said the chief mate indifferently. "It's a different one."

"They all look alike," sighed the chief engineer. "I've lost count."

"Talking of count, how much do they still have to load?"

"Eighty, ninety tons, no more. If it does not rain without interruption, we'll be ready tomorrow evening."

"Thank God," said the captain after a short silence. "After all, it was a bit too much of a good thing. I think everybody is getting fed up with being here."

"Bad weather ahead," said the radio officer. "Deep low moving eastward over Ireland. We'll get our share of the gale."

The captain shrugged. Handling gales was a normal part of his job. He cleared his throat. "Chief," he said, "keep the engine warm, will you? We might still sail tomorrow night. Mate, please take care that she be really sea-clear this time."

These were the first orders he had issued in seven days, and he felt strangely content about it.

Another strange thing was, the chief mate thought, that they never lacked subjects of conversation between them. They talked a lot, and yet they knew practically nothing about each other. Very often the subject was religion. She was religious in a queer way, she practiced it in her absolutely personal manner, as if it were her private religion, her own brand of Catholicism. "Mother of God or not, she was a woman first, and no mistake about it," she was saying, "that's why she should understand me better than the saints. And Magdalene, that one perhaps still better, and I sinning with a black pagan like you."

The chief mate, spread naked on his bed, grinned. Instinctively he looked at his olive skin. He took her hand and put it on his chest. Her skin was a dazzling white, almost transparent.

"This sinning business," he sighed. "Mary, I am afraid I'm too stupid to understand any of it, ever. Either you like it, and it's good for you, so there is no reason to regret anything, or not, and then you should stop it."

She looked at him with contempt, with pity, with sorrow.

"I'll tell you," she said. "Just stop bothering about it. There are several reasons why you are unable to grasp it: first, you are a man; second, you are a seaman; third, you are not a Christian; fourth, you are not an Irishman. Enough for you?"

He laughed aloud. "All right, all right," he said. Gradually, the smile vanished from his face.

"We're sailing tomorrow, Mary."

"I know."

"So this is the last night."

"Uhmm…"

"Soon you'll forget me."

"I will not; but is it of any importance to you?"

"We shall never meet again."

"One never knows."

Suddenly he had an idea. "Mary, can we meet tomorrow morning, say at nine, in town?"

"Why?"

"Please. I want to."

She hesitated: she was a bit annoyed. "All right, but you know I don't like it. One could be seen, we could meet somebody."

"Whom?"

"My husband."

"Your husband be damned."

He saw black anger in her eyes.

"Knock on this," she said. "Knock on wood." And, when he obeyed, she added, "Never say that again. I'll kill myself if anything happens to my husband."

"All right," the chief mate said. "I didn't say it, I never mentioned your husband. Good? Tomorrow, at nine, at the same spot where I left you the first night, OK?"

"This one is secondhand, sir," the jeweler said.

He balanced the tiny golden locket in his outstretched hand, pressed, and the lid snapped open. From her golden case, a miniature black Madonna with Child looked at him.

"I want this," the chief mate said.

The jeweler smiled. "During the war a few Poles were here," he said. "This seems to come from one of them, or their women. Apparently, they have a black-faced Madonna in Poland."

"I'll take it," the chief mate said. They stood silently watching the jeweler moving around stiffly, putting the locket in a small box, wrapping it carefully. The chief mate's eyes wandered over crosses, crucifixes, pictures of saints. Mary did not move.

He paid the jeweler and they went out.

"Good," said the chief mate. "We were talking about it yesterday. I know it's silly, but I don't want you to forget me completely. That is why I'm giving you this Black Madonna, to remind you of the black pagan."

Her eyes were burning when she took it from his hands, tore open the wrapping and put it on her neck.

"Thank you," she said. "Thank you again. Sometimes I shall pray for you."

They stood on the street corner, and wind came stealthily from behind the corner and hit them with wet gusts. There hadn't been rain since the morning, only wind, and a low, gray, menacing sky.

"I have to go to the ship now," he said.

She nodded. The chief mate thought that all the farewell scenes he knew from books or movies were hateful, and he wondered how this real one would come out. But his fear was unjustified.

"Go back to your ship, Jack," she said, "And I'll stay here. You are a no-good pagan, a bloody foreigner, and a seaman on top of all that, but perhaps a lot better than the others. I'll remember you, and pray to the Black Madonna to preserve you in good health. Bless you. Go now." She turned quickly and walked away with her cat-like, elastic gait; he waited till he could see her no more, till she disappeared behind the corner. Then he turned up the collar of his coat against the wind and went to the port.

Girls were running out of cabins still, two of them undressed, when the pilot came on board. He was sitting in the captain's cabin, silent, waiting for the ship to be ready to move. He refused a drink the captain offered him, and waited. Customs and immigration officers were rushing through the last formalities, agents and tallymen talked with the chief mate, the bosun was cursing two seamen who were late to appear at their post, aft. Finally, everything was settled, the chief mate buttoned his duffel coat, put on his working gloves, and knocked at the captain's door.

"Ready when you are, sir."

The captain rose. He was visibly relaxed and in good humor. "All right, Chief. Care for a drink? You remember Mr. Halloran, don't you? He brought us in a week ago. A week? It seems like a month, a year! What a lovely place you live in! Am I right, Chief?"

The pilot turned slowly and fixed the chief mate with his gaze. He had on the same old black oilskin, and there was something emanating from his face, from his deep-set eyes, a something the mate could not define, but the strength, the terrible force of this undefined thing was so powerful that he instinctively took one step back.

The captain sensed that something was wrong here and now, in his cabin, as if moving in the vehicle of time they had passed over some invisible hindrance, but being out of line of that mysterious magnetic field that spread between the two men, he could not feel its full intensity. He said lightly, "Shall we go up, Pilot?"

And the chief mate caught the moment that the pilot's eyes moved toward the captain, and said, "I am going for'd, sir," and left quickly. But as soon as the chief mate started walking on deck, he stopped short and whispered to himself: My God, My God. Mary Halloran's husband.

No, he thought in the next moment. Absurd! Where did you get that idea? You must be mad. He started walking again, slowly, forward.

Stupid, even if it were he, how could he know? All right, dismiss it altogether.

But he could not, and relaxed only when he heard the captain's voice booming through the loudspeaker: "Slack the head-line…slack…"

Aft, on the bridge, watching the last light of the day dying, the pilot waited till the ropes were in. He waited so long that the captain coughed desperately. God, the fellow is dreaming again, he thought.

But he was not sleeping. Halloran walked over to the engine telegraph, and put the handle on SLOW AHEAD. The ship started moving.

"We won't be able to take you down," the captain said. "You won't risk that will you?"

The pilot went out to the wing and looked at the sea. Long, oily waves were rolling the ship, reaching greedily for its bulwarks. No boat would come alongside in this weather; it would be smashed to pieces at the first attempt

He came back to the stillness of the wheelhouse.

"We'll disembark you in Belfast," the captain said, "it must be much quieter there."

The pilot grunted his consent grudgingly. "You can lie down in the cabin," the captain said. "It will take eight hours at least."

He did not answer. He leaned against the clear-view window and stared into the growing darkness.

They were completing a huge half-circle around the promontory, but as soon as the ship's bow pointed east, the monster lurking behind the corner attacked. The gale struck furiously, as though its only purpose were annihilating this ship, with its funny cargo of bagged potatoes and silly human problems, wiping it off the sea, so that no splinter remained afloat.

Both the captain and the pilot stepped back, as a huge wave crashed against the wheelhouse front. Cascades of water flowed down from the monkey island.

The ship shook and trembled like a man mortally hit, then plunged head down into an abyss. She had barely managed to straighten herself unsteadily when another monster wave fell upon her from the starboard quarter, submerging the decks, the bulwarks. The ship groaned and rolled on one side, trying to avoid another blow, in vain.

Water streamed swiftly onto decks, into passageways, like rapid, broad, mountain rivers. Then blow after blow followed, the incredible gale trying, amidst wild howling, to uproot the mast, to smash the superstructure, to tear the ship apart.

Above, through the gaps in swiftly running clouds, a moon was riding the dirty sky. But a little below these clouds there was no clear distinction between air and water. The wind tore sheets of water from the waves and sent them flying, pulverized, horizontally, like machine gun bursts, against the ship. Struggling incessantly, groaning and moaning, fighting hour after hour she made her way east and south.

The pilot remained on the bridge for some time, motionless, mute, looking through one of the front windows at the craze of violence outside.

His official role was finished; the ship was in the open sea, he was sailing now as a passenger. He looked at the other men on the bridge: the captain, the young third mate, the lookout man. They, too, kept silent. All of them seamen, and yet this eruption of elemental forces struck them into submission.

A beam of light lit the bridge momentarily, as the wireless officer entered and handed the captain a paper slip. He read it in the dim light of the compass light. Aloud, he said, "Gale force eleven. Not bad."

The pilot said, "We sometimes have gales like this here, in winter."

"Your bad luck, then," answered the captain tartly. "It will take us many hours till we reach Belfast. Don't you want to turn in, Pilot?"

"Very well."

The captain turned to the lookout man. "Show the gentleman the way to the pilot's cabin. See that they've put sheets and towels in. Good night."

He left the blackness of the bridge, and entered the well-lit alleyway.

Except for the violent rolling and pitching, the storm did not exist here. The polished floor glistened, the lights burnt brightly in their milk globes, and in the small cabin, the immaculate white sheets were spread on the bed. Here, with curtains drawn and the bed-light on, he was almost hermetically sealed off from the chaos outside. Halloran smiled. He took off his jacket and sighed deeply.

"Yes," he answered to the knock at the door.

"With compliments of the captain, sir," the steward said, putting a bottle on the table.

"Very considerate, very considerate," Halloran murmured. "Please tell the captain thank you. I am very obliged for his kindness."

"Yes, sir. Do you need anything else?"

"No, no. I am perfectly all right now." He tore off the wrapping and opened the bottle, and only in the last moment, when the door was almost closed behind the man's back, he cried: "One second, steward. Did you by any chance see your chief mate anywhere?"

"Yes, sir. They are all on the bridge: the captain, the chief, and the second."

"Could you please tell the chief mate to drop in here for a moment, whenever it is convenient for him, any time he is off-duty."

"Very well, sir."

The chief mate stood thinking in the darkness of the bridge. I am in for it. I should ignore this. I am not his servant, if he has to tell me something, he can bloody well come here. Bastard, he thought. Bloody son of a bitch. What an idiot I am, he thought the next minute. Why do I curse him? I'm the one who wrongs him and not the other way round. Besides, how can he possibly know about Mary and me? Absurd, nonsense.

And yet, he did not go to see Halloran immediately.

After he left the bridge, he had something to eat in the pantry, then went to his cabin and lay down in his bunk, but could not fall asleep. It's the bloody rolling, and the storm, he told himself. He knew well he was lying; he had slept in bad storms before.

He went back to the bridge shortly before four and had some coffee with the captain, who had just risen from the couch in the chart room. The captain had not left the bridge since they left port, but appeared to be fresh, not tired at all.

The chief mate suggested politely that he might have some rest in his cabin, but the captain laughed: "What for? You know that when things are on course I am perfectly fine. And I had a nice nap in the chart room, too."

"Then I'll be back in a few minutes," the mate said.

"All right, Jack, go ahead. And by the way, better have a look in on the pilot's cabin. We can't be very far now."

He knocked slightly on the door and there was no answer. The chief mate thought he might be sleeping. But when he entered, trying to make as little noise as possible, Halloran was sitting wide awake at the table, the bottle in his hand.

"Hello, Mr. Mate," he said. "I thought you weren't going to come. How is it sleeping with my wife, Mr. Mate?" Halloran continued. "Did you enjoy it?"

The mate stood silent, his face white and his heart pounding violently, as if all the blood were drained from his body and concentrated there, in that small spot in his chest.

"Don't feel complimented, please. You are not the first, and certainly not the last, Mr. Mate." Halloran crossed his legs, threw his head a little back and observed him closely. "Ships are still calling at our port; not too many, as you may have observed, but still, there are some, and Mary is not old. My guess is she'll reach a ripe old age."

The mate did not move. He felt his legs ice-cold and heavy, screwed down to the floor below. He responded to the ship's lurching movements with his body, but he could not shift from foot to foot. There was a bad, stale taste in his mouth.

Halloran poured himself a glass of whiskey, and took a sip.

"Have you nothing to say Mr. Mate? Remember, you are talking with Mary's husband! You are one of the family, so to speak! Doesn't it make any impression on you?"

If he takes out a razor and tries to cut my throat, I won't move, the mate thought.

"I wonder," Halloran said to the half-empty glass he rotated between his thumb and forefinger, "how it feels to face a man whose wife you have screwed twenty-four hours ago. I'm curious, and have had no experience in the matter till now."

He swallowed the drink and put the glass carefully on the table, still holding it.

"Terrible storm," he said, as the room tilted crazily. "Well, Mr. Mate, did you tell her you loved her? But Mary does not need it. I have to know," he explained, a second later, as if justifying his insistence.

"I am going to see her tomorrow if you disembark me in Belfast this morning; I mean, if you reach Belfast this morning. You won't believe it, but coasters like yours occasionally simply fall apart in such weather. Now I have nothing against your ship, God forbid, a sturdy, fine vessel; but it does happen occasionally. Every year it happens, in fact. They're found later, after the storm—a plank, a life preserver, a board, up on the coast. That is, what remains of them." He poured himself another drink, and smiled.

"I hope you are not offended that I do not invite you to share your own whiskey, but you are on duty, aren't you? Four to eight, is it? Well, I guess that is it, because this is the chief mate's watch on all ships, all over the world,"—his voice rose a little—"no matter if they are British, Turks, Yanks, Greeks, or Liberians. No matter what rag they are flying, four to eight is the chief mate's watch. So I don't want a drunk chief mate in charge of a ship in a bad storm."

There was the thumped echo of heavy thunder, as a bigger wave than all the others crashed on the decks. The lights flickered and dimmed for one moment, then burned with normal strength.

"Now me, I'm off duty, of course. I'm a passenger now. I am never drunk when on duty. But what I did want to say is this, Mr. Mate: I have bad dreams sometimes. One dream returns to me so regularly that I was thinking of consulting somebody about it. Perhaps a doctor. Or a priest, maybe. But each time I put it off; I say, all right, if it happens once more I'll go and see the doctor or the priest, I'll ask his advice. In fact, I'll tell you, since you are one of the family now."

"It goes like this: the whole North Channel, even the whole bloody Irish Sea, has dried up, to the Isle of Man, and far south, beyond the island, and I am wandering on the bottom of this sea, walking slowly, and looking around, and what do I see, but broken ships and skeletons of drowned sailors.

"Strange, no trace of dead fish, as would be reasonable, since the sea has dried up, but there are only heaps and heaps of sailors' bones and skulls, and broken ships, old—how d'you call them—galleons, and frigates, warships and merchantmen, coasters, trawlers, steamers and motorships, as far as the eye can reach. A strange dream, isn't it?"

Halloran closed his eyes, but caught the bottle with one hand when the ship started sliding down into another roll. He looked up again, and poured all that remained in the bottle into the glass. He smiled. "Eh, Mr. Mate? Can't you speak? Or did I scare you with my dream? Of course, your ship will reach Belfast some time, and I'll go ashore and catch the morning train home. Home," he repeated, licking his lips. "I'll tell you what Mary is doing right now, because maybe you're thinking of her. After all, I still know her better than you do, you must admit."

There was a knock at the door and a sailor's head appeared. "The captain wants you on the bridge, Mate."

The chief mate succeeded, with considerable effort, to move his tongue once again. "I'll be right there."

"I'll tell you what Mary is doing right now," repeated Halloran, unperturbed. "She is praying. She is praying to the Virgin Mary for this ship to arrive home safely; for me, for all the ships at sea to withstand this bad weather. Praying for herself. Praying, Praying. Perhaps even for you."

The mate turned, swung the door open, and ran away from the cabin. Halloran let his head drop on his chest, swept the empty bottle off the table and laughed softly.

"Where were you for so long?" the captain asked irritably.

"The pilot is drunk," he mumbled.

"Of course. None of this is his concern. I'm trying to get Belfast on the R.T. We should be there before long. This, right ahead, is the Bangor lighthouse, I should think."

"Belfast on the R.T., sir," said the radio officer through the window connecting the bridge with his cabin. "They'll put out a pilot boat as soon as we're in the bay. They say the sea is rather smoother there."

"Fine! Tell them we'll be there at—just a moment—Jack, check this position quickly, will you—tell them to hold on a moment…"

The mate went out on the port wing and took the bearing on the Bangor lighthouse, and another one, deeper in the bay. The moment he left the shelter of the wheelhouse he had the feeling that the howling wind wanted to tear his arms and head off. He returned, closing the sliding door behind him, stunned by the silence inside. He bent over the chart with dividers in his hand.

"Seven miles still to go," he said.

"Sparkie, tell them we'll be there at six fifteen."

The darkness outside was different from that in which they had been enveloped a week earlier, when entering the port. This, too, was impenetrable, but the black world outside the wheelhouse was boiling, exploding, being torn to chunks by the gale.

Gradually, as they entered the bay, the movements of the ship softened, it did not roll and pitch so wildly.

"Tell him to get ready," the captain said, without turning his head. "And send somebody to prepare the pilot ladder. Starboard."

The mate hesitated a moment. The first order might have been intended for him, personally. But he felt he could not face Halloran again. To the lookout seaman he said, "Prepare the pilot ladder on the starboard side and wake up the pilot on your way there."

The mate and the captain simultaneously raised their binoculars to the flickering of an Aldis lamp against the distant glow in the north. "That's them," murmured the captain, and put the engine telegraph on SLOW.

"Answer them, Jack."

The mate clicked the trigger of the lamp quickly.

"Stop'er."

The engine stopped, and the ship lolled for a few minutes in the invisible, dark water, like a dead whale. Mast-lights were lit and in their cool glare they could see from the bridge two seamen in oilskins on deck, struggling with the ladder. Then, into the cone of light, which cast glistening shadows on the surface of the waves, came a black, sleek motor cutter, dancing gingerly on the oily water.

"What? No rowboat?" the captain chuckled.

The door to the bridge swung open and Halloran entered. He stood a split second, silent, and in that split second the mate saw Mary Halloran as he had seen her the first time, leaning against the door of his cabin.

"Thanks, and good-bye, Captain. Bon voyage." And before any of them could answer, he disappeared. There was a slight crash as the pilot cutter bumped against the ship's side.

"Put a fender out!" shouted the captain, but the mate was sure nobody could hear him down below. He ran out on the wing and looked out.

Sudden panic seized him. He had an image of Halloran's body crushed between the ship's and the cutter's sides. He grasped the weather rail searching for him. After a while, he saw a burly figure in black, worn oilskin, climbing over the bulwark and disappearing behind it.

The sea was smoother by far here than outside, but still the launch was jumping wildly, its bulwark hitting the ship's side. Up and down it went, hitting and crushing to splinters a step of the pilot ladder. The mate's throat felt tight and dry, as he waited for the pilot's cry.

But it never came. He saw Halloran on the cutter's deck, entering the wheelhouse.

He's made it, thank God. Somebody lifted an arm on the cutter, and the next moment the darkness swallowed it.

"OK," he said coming into the bridge. "They're gone."

"Good. Let's get the hell out of this damned place."

"You know, I was afraid something might happen to him," the mate said. "He was drunk as hell."

"Put the course on the chart, Jack," answered, the captain. "It is remarkable how much liquor these Irishmen can hold. I wasn't a bit worried. I knew he'd manage it."

The ship, after its unexpected rest, now turned her head reluctantly to the east; she'd have to face the howling gale again.

"Half past six and no sign of dawn," muttered the captain.

But before they started struggling again, it seemed to the mate that, for the second time that night, he saw Mary's face in the white spray over the ship's bow.

"I'm overtired," he thought. "I'll be able to turn in, thank God, in an hour's time."

Kibbutz Sdot Yam, October 1968

My Captain and I

H

e drinks his Scotch straight. I prefer mine on the rocks.

Come to think of it, he drinks only Scotch or Campari, whereas I am almost totally indiscriminate with regard to my booze: vodka, brandy, ouzo, Scotch, arac, rum—anything with an alcoholic content of more than forty percent goes. He sniffs suspiciously before he touches the glass with his lips; I toss it off, vodka-like, whatever it is.

He also checks food first with his nose, lifting the plate quickly to his face. His nostrils quiver.

I start eating the moment the dish is in front of me.

We have our meals facing each other, for, though he is the undisputed master under God of this ship, we are equal in rank: were we to wear uniforms, each of us would carry four golden stripes on the sleeve.

It occurs to me as I watch him, concentrated as he is on cutting a piece of bread with a knife and dropping the square, precisely measured pieces into his soup, that our combined age is 105. The average for the rest of the crew is much, much lower. For that reason, the two other officers at our table respect our silence, and only occasionally exchange a remark in subdued tones.

The captain always finishes first, murmurs *bon appétit* and leaves in a hurry.

I wait only as long as it takes him to go upstairs to his cabin. The moment I hear the click of his door, I, too, get up, and go upstairs. In our respective cabins, we drink ourselves to death, separately, but equally.

I sometimes wonder how his drinking is: mine is a spiral staircase, with landings here and there.

I have many books in my cabin and when I reach certain landings in my drinking, I curse the books, sometimes in a whisper, sometimes in a normal, conversational voice, but never shouting.

The three books in his cabin are *The Stowage and Cargo Handling Manual*, *Nautical Almanac*, and the *Collective Agreement Between the Company and the Seamen's Union*.

I wonder what or whom he curses in the stages of his drinking.

We emerge from our cabins, often simultaneously, meet in the alleyways, on the bridge, or in the mess, exchange polite greetings in *sotto voce* and smell alcohol on each other's breath.

He does his job with the assistance of his executive officer, interfering mainly in matters of order and tidiness. The national and code flags are neatly arranged, the pencils sharpened, maps carefully stacked in the chartroom, ship's documents perfectly ordered in clean, transparent, clearly marked envelopes.

I have my first assistant running the plant, and on each of my five or six daily visits to the engine room I keep a sharp lookout that the place is tolerably clean, that no rags are wasted, and no oil and fuel are spilled; that the bilges be kept dry at all times. My calculations and papers are in good order, but by far not as precisely kept and calligraphically written as his.

I assume we both do our jobs adequately.

We both walk straight and do not behave like drunks outside our cabins.

How we behave inside them is our own private matter.

When inside, we keep our cabins locked.

Equal but separate.

We have been sailing on this ship together for more than six months and I do not think more than six hundred words have been wasted between us. The professional talk is restricted to the general outlines of the problem, then we transfer the matter: he, to his chief mate, I, to my second engineer. He gives his instructions to the chief mate in a low voice, in a voice so low that the poor man is compelled to say, "Excuse me, sir, what was it?"

He then repeats the sentence very distinctly, but in a still lower register, and a light of malicious delight blinks in his eye. I give my orders in detail, very often in too many details, to ensure their exact execution. My second, exasperated, often exclaims, "But Chief, I know how to do it! I've done it a hundred times!"

"OK then," I say. "Just don't forget…"

The captain is enthusiastic about conveying bad news, even if it's not true.

"We'll have a nice little storm tonight," he says, looking at me with his innocent, bleary, gentle eyes.

I walk over to the wall, look at the glass, and say, "The barometer has not moved."

I look outside, smell the air, check the sea, and say, "There won't be any storm, Captain."

He looks at me with just a shadow of irony in his eyes—those heavy bags under his eyes—and does not say a word. It's a hard competition: half of our lifetime is sea-time, and this, too, splits approximately fifty-fifty between us.

I discover, with hatred, in the mirror, that the bags under my eyes are as heavy as his.

The weather is lovely in the evening, the kind of sunset you can still occasionally see on Italian postcards, orange and clear, and I look at him triumphantly from the height of a landing in my spiral staircase. At this height, the air has a slightly pink color, I know it might change to red if I had three or four more, and I could then place both my hands on his heavy neck and press until his innocent eyes pop out of their sockets.

But I cannot reach him. He is on a separate plateau and moves in circles, or makes figure eights, as on a skating rink. He is too evasive. If he had two or three more, he'd stare at me, and burst inside. At the most.

He says, "We'll arrive there, let me see, against this current we won't make more than nine, let's say, at eight o'clock, and we'll drop the anchor. No chance they'd put us inside, not in this port."

I say, "Last time the pilot waited for us and we berthed immediately."

"An exceptional case," he says.

But when we arrive in port, at six and not at eight (for there was no current) and the ship is moored and fast at the quay, he says to me, "Shall we go ashore, to stretch our legs, and dine together?"

And I, leaning heavily against the railing of my staircase, say quietly: "Any time, Captain. My pleasure."

We walk close to each other on the waterfront street, the street afire with multicolored neon signs from cafes, bars and nightclubs.

It must have rained earlier, for the sidewalks and the road are wet, the lights reflect brilliantly on the smooth surface, and the smell of sea brine, strong here, is tempered by the sweet fragrance of trees in rain. The street is crowded, but there is no rush; some whores stand against the walls, others walk boldly on the street.

When we encounter a whore, he slightly raises his eyebrows and turns his head. His nostrils quiver lightly.

I stare shamelessly at her breasts, at her crotch, at the outline of the labia majora if she happens to wear hot pants, and the pants cut right into her slit.

He is above it, I am sure—no matter if he is skating full speed, tilted at an angle, the skates cutting a quick parabola on the dry, cracking ice—or stone sober, with that dull hangover ache behind his ears.

I am always beyond it, whether in the upper regions of my staircase, with multicolored (but usually purplish) clouds passing by my head, with purple gentle rain showering on my closed eyes; or down, beyond the lower border of conceivable misery.

We are going to eat now, in one of the waterfront street restaurants.

He will order meat—clean, please, he whispers toward the dark, smelly, pomade-glistening head of the waiter—with baked potatoes.

I will have octopus, crabs, shrimps, mussels, in heavy dark-red sauce, sharp with onion, tomato and garlic, pepper and salt.

He will have beer, transparent and clear; I will drink white wine, crackling dry and sour: I like to think that it was pressed out in soaked dark wooden vats from pale green grapes in the sweat and heat of a late summer afternoon, pressed out by the muscular legs of girls on a mountain slope.

We sit under the awning, waiting for the waiter to come with our food, silently watching the waterfront crowd crawl by, trampling the wet red, blue and orange lights on the dark asphalt, and perceiving, each in his way, the nothingness of the sea, very close, just behind the low sea wall.

Cohen

I n mid-September, the ship finished discharging in Istanbul and sailed in ballast to Salonika to load tobacco. On that short passage, I stood on the poop deck watching Greek islands conjured up from the sea, which was a silver panel, and disappearing silently to give place to other islands, promontories, pieces of land, solitary rocks.

Then from the upper floor of my engine room I looked on as the second engineer stopped the ship's engine, reversed it when the order from the bridge came—"half astern"—carried out several maneuvers as required, quite competently. I washed my hands when the final order arrived—"finished with engine"—and went up on deck. The ship was moored in the sun along a new quay in the harbor of Salonika.

Sapporta would send his men to take care of the ship's business, we knew it. When the last line is secured and the gangway lowered, several trucks with tobacco bales stand ready on the quay, and the port officials, customs, police, and medical authorities wait to board the ship like a group of eager schoolchildren, and a man is already putting a telephone on board.

All these are led by Sapporta's "man on the spot," who handles the whole business quietly but quickly; in ten minutes the winches start rattling, and the first tobacco bales are lowered into the ship's hold. He himself, after seeing to it that the signing and stamping of various documents proceeds satisfactorily, and that shore-leave passes are issued to the crew, comes down on deck to see that the loading goes smoothly.

"That's the way Sapporta works," says the captain in Polish. He always speaks Polish to me when in a good mood. "One, two, three,—and everything moves like a Swiss watch."

Sapporta's man, standing next to us, is middle-aged, thickset without being actually fat, and wears dark-gray trousers, a white shirt, and a blue tie. He has taken off his jacket: the heat is heavy. He has a round face with thick lips and a hooked nose, his eyes are hidden behind pale blue Polaroid sunglasses framed in thin silver wire. His round head is almost bald, but there is thick dark hair on his arms. There is a number tattooed on one arm. He has moccasin-type brown shoes on his feet.

"You should have said a Japanese watch, Captain," he says in Polish. "People have almost forgotten what a Swiss watch looks like." And when we exchange surprised looks, he adds, casually, "I can speak a few languages."

"Congratulations on your fluency in Polish," says the captain.

"Thank you. In addition to Polish I have English, German, French, Ladino, and Yiddish; also, some Russian. My mother tongue is Greek, of course."

"You mean, you were born here?"

"I was born here, my father, and mother, and their parents as well. And their grandparents, and theirs, all the way back to 1498."

The captain says politely, "That long?" The man looks aside. He leans over the hatch combing, to see if the stevedores in the 'tween-deck have pushed the bales all the way in, to the bulkhead. Satisfied, he lights a cigarette, cupping the match in his palms. He says, after the first puff, "Spanish and Portuguese Jews, you know. After the

Inquisition. The sultan admitted us to his empire, wanted us to settle down here, in this town."

We. Us. The captain is not interested in a Jewish history lesson. He wants no more conversation with Sapporta's clerk. He nods politely and leaves.

"My name is Cohen," Sapporta's clerk says into the blue. He takes no offense at the captain's sudden departure.

I walk over slowly to the other side of the hatch. The smell of tobacco is already over the ship, rich and strong; more trucks are standing on the quay waiting for their turn to unload. The drivers gather in a group, listen to Greek music on one truck's radio, smoke cigarettes, tell each other stories, laugh. Two white-uniformed men with pistols stand at the gangway, guarding. Precautions: it's an Israeli ship.

All of a sudden Cohen is near my elbow again.

"Your captain is not an Israeli, is he?"

"No. He's Polish. The mate is Yugoslavian. All the others are Israelis."

Cohen nods his round head, accepting the information. "Of Auschwitz I won't speak to you," he says, unexpectedly. Then, turning to the mate, he says: "These are the last three trucks we are going to unload with the shore crane. Then we'll dismiss it and work with the ship's winches only."

"In number two?"

"In number two, and in number four on 'tween-deck."

The mate leaves to give the necessary instructions to the deck hands, and Cohen says, "Books have been written about it. Lots of books. Too many books. Besides, my guess is you know something about it from your own experience. Right?"

"Right. But not in Auschwitz."

"Where?"

"Stutthof."

"Wait; was that somewhere near Danzig, Gdansk, as the Poles call it?"

"Yes."

"But you, yourself, where are you from?"

"Warsaw," I say, reluctantly.

He slips almost automatically into Polish. "Pan z Warszawy?"

"Z Warszawy."

Cohen starts annoying me a bit. But still he insists: "What street?" I tell him the street, the number, and the picture of a drab, gray, five-story apartment house emerges from a bottomless past, covers for one moment the huge, sun-flooded square in a new section of this Mediterranean harbor, trucks loaded with tobacco bales, cranes; a double exposure, one slide projected over another.

"Well, well," Cohen says in a suddenly colorless voice. "What a funny small world. I destroyed your house. Or what was left of it. Do you want to hear about it?"

I was not sure I did. I had enough disasters and absurdities to deal with, more recent ones. To dig out this one—of Cohen, demolishing the half-burnt house in which I had lived for the first twenty years of my life—would mean to add forcibly to that ancient-memories system functioning within myself, destructive enough as it was, working slowly but constantly, like diluted corrosive acid: like cancer. Why should I add to it, to increase its weight? It was in that flat that I saw the faces of my parents for the last time, and my sister, her head sunk low, sitting at her piano. But I left before they abandoned it for their appointment with death, before it was burnt. And later, much later, a Cohen from Salonika comes, and breaks to pieces what was left of it.

Without waiting for my final approval, he starts in at a brisk tempo.

"The Germans were here in April '41. Remember? Greece collapsed, the British withdrew to Crete; they were to lose it, too, not much later. First thing the Germans did was to round up the Jews: I was sent with thousands of others to Auschwitz in summer. Families separated, destroyed. The usual thing. Still—mind, you must know it, too—miracles do happen, even in concentration camps. I survived till Summer '43, and then they selected a group of two hundred Greek Jews and sent them to Warsaw, to work in the ruins of the Ghetto there, which was destroyed in the revolt of Spring '43; but this, again, you know better than I."

"I left before the revolt."

"But you know what it looked like after that, don't you?"

"I spent three days there after the war."

"Good. Then you know."

I felt tired of standing on deck in the sun and of Cohen's swift jumps from the Auschwitz death chambers to the ruins of the Warsaw Ghetto via tobacco bales stacked in the hold of an Israeli steamer in Salonika in 1974.

I say, hoping to finish this conversation, "So you dismantled what was left of my flat on Leszno Street, in Warsaw."

"Sure. We dismantled everything. They had a genius for organization, those Germans; a passion for it. There were bricks there, iron girders, lead pipings, brass fittings, furniture, clothing, shoes, kitchen utensils, hidden money, gold, jewels. Everything had to be sorted out, counted, loaded.

"Anything that could still be used in any way was shipped away to Germany. A job for many years; such an area, don't forget half a million Jews had been living there before the destruction!"

"And what did you do with my sister's grand piano?" I said, unable to bear the impact of the glare of the heavy, white sun. Tiny red flecks danced in the corners of my eyes; my face was oily with sweat. Cohen was unperturbed.

"A piano? Sure! There were pianos in the Jewish flats on that street. We stowed them in a separate place. A German officer came to inspect them. Those in useable condition were loaded on trucks and transported away. The others we were ordered to burn. We did. We did everything we were told: it was, you must understand, the best war job a Jew in those times could have dreamt of—of course, there was the strong probability that you'd be liquidated when it was over, but that was true everywhere, and there was enough work for years there. A good chance of survival, food, shelter! And the things we found there!"

Cohen lowers his voice. "The things that we did not hand over to the Germans—and mind you, it was instant death if they found anything on you—were the *mezuzoth* and the prayer books."

Some Jews cried, hiding them in their rags; Cohen did not. Was Cohen very tough? No. "I was," he searches for a moment in his several languages for the right word, and finds it finally in English: "I was numb. I just kept going."

I stack the story neatly on the shelves of my torture chamber and am ready to leave it at that. But Cohen is not yet ready. "It is too hot here," he says. "Come, let's go to your cabin, and you'll hear the rest of it. Ten minutes."

I agree reluctantly. I am not keen on listening to other people's troubles; I have enough of my own. It certainly is strange that we should meet after all these years, here, in a Greek port—a ship's agent and an Israeli seaman, and the bond between us; the ruins of a flat in Warsaw. Strange, yes, but not absolutely extraordinary: many echoes of the impossible twists and knots of human fate in those years reverberate till this day, more than a quarter of a century later. We enter the air-conditioned coolness of my room, and Cohen takes it all in: the furniture, the bar, the refrigerator, the desk, and the black-framed photograph on it. I know his eyes miss nothing. He belongs to that peculiar group of people gifted with the power of an instant and total perception.

I offer him a cold drink, and say, "So you dismantled the flat. OK. No hard feelings. It was thirty years ago."

But Cohen wipes his thick lips with the back of his hand, leans back in the chair, throws me one quick look, and goes on.

On the first day of August 1944, Cohen's group was working somewhere in the vicinity of Smocza Street. They had almost finished a wall, most of the bricks were no good, burnt and crumbling under the slightest touch, but there were two iron girders lower down, pretty straight, the fire had not bent them, and these the German foreman saw in the morning. He climbed on the mountain of rubble, touched the girders, mumbled, "Good iron," and said, "OK, take them out."

By four in the afternoon the longer rail slid down on the brick heap, crushing the bricks under its weight and raising a cloud of yellow dust. One of the Jews jumped aside at the last moment, saving his leg by a miracle.

"If it had happened, they'd have shot him," Cohen said. "Nobody would take a Jew to a first aid station or to a hospital. Replacements were always ready, in Auschwitz, in other places. Why do I remember this? Because on that day, at five o'clock in the afternoon, the Polish uprising started. And the same Jew was killed a month later, by a German shell."

Cohen is not a Jewish slave from Auschwitz any more. He is a member of the A.K. now, the Polish Territorial Army. He has a white and red armband on his sleeve and he helps the Poles kill Germans. "There are too many things for one man to remember," Cohen says. "It's not fair, these memories, don't you think? One can't live remembering and remembering, one should have a head like an oil-drum to keep all this garbage. That Jew that was killed, he was not even from here. From Corfu, I think. And why should I remember him? Because he was killed? Ridiculous! A quarter of a million people were killed in the uprising!"

Cohen fights the Germans with the Poles in Warsaw; he can be annihilated any minute, thousands perish, there is no light, no water, no food, and, finally, no ammunition.

The A.K. capitulates, but one of the terms of the capitulation on which the Polish commander, Bor Komorowski, absolutely insists, is that all survivors be granted POW status. He knows full well what would happen if they were classified as "bandits."

The Germans, who desperately need their two divisions elsewhere, agree—and Komorowski stands to attention, bare-headed, in a civilian coat, as the remnants of his "army" file by, into German prison camps. Cohen marches along. Passing, he looks at the stony face of the Polish general. This face, too, he will remember.

Cohen takes the advice of a Polish officer and declares himself an Armenian. "There were a few Armenians in Warsaw," the Pole told him. "Of course you could claim you were a Pole like the rest of us, but it is dangerous: that face of yours, and then, they could make us shower, or go for a medical examination, and then you're lost, you know."

Cohen thought of his young wife, from whom he had been separated on the railway siding in Auschwitz: SS men chased her away with sticks, her, and the two little kids, to one side. He was herded back with the group of men. Cohen did not want to live on; he was tired of life.

But the Pole went on: "There was one, I remember… he was called Petrossian. Big business with rugs on Stawki, near the river. Carpets. Buchara, Isfahan, Kabul."

"Are Armenians Christians?" asked Cohen.

"If they are," answered the Pole, "they don't look it. Sometimes our students beat them up during the annual October pogrom, by mistake; they thought they were Jews. But here, you have a chance. We only look for opportunities, don't we?"

When they start registering the prisoners, Cohen is Petrossian. Looking at the short, swarthy man, the German at the table frowns. He is not sure; he asks his superior, a morose SS man at the other table.

"An Armenian? Armenians are all right," he declares authoritatively. "Didn't you know? That's part of Turkey, and the Turks are officially neutral, but OK. Muslims. Saw a photograph of the Führer with that guy in the paper—what was his name, now—with a white round hat on his head—ah, yes Mufti. Mufti was the name. Actually, they are our allies."

SS man Behrendt warms up to something out of routine, something unusual. "If this guy is an Armenian, which he certainly looks like, he should not be with these Poles at all. He should be free. They must have forced him to join them. We'll ask him if he wants to join the Todt Organization."

Before the German at the table digests all this information, Behrendt himself gets up, smiling, and sticks his finger in Cohen's chest: "Armenian good," he says. "Poles pigs. No good." He spits on the ground.

"Armenian very good," he repeats. "Want nice clean uniform, good food, plenty? Work," he imitates a man digging with a spade, "work with hands, but good food, good comrades, eh?"

"Yes," Cohen says.

Saved by the picture of the Mufti of Jerusalem with Hitler—inspecting a unit of Bosnian Muslim volunteers—that flickered in the deranged mind of an elderly idiot SS man, Cohen rises in the hierarchy of Nazi Germany to the elevated status of "friendly foreigners"—Lithuanians, Slovaks, Latvians. He has never heard of Mufti Haj Amin, and if he had done, he'd never be able to establish the connection between the Arab and himself, except perhaps that of a most basic relationship, between a Jew and a pathological Jew-hater.

It is as round and as complete and as absurd as life in an absurd world; and it does not make the slightest difference where survival is concerned: survival is above absurdity.

Behrendt's promise is kept almost literally: he gets a clean, warm uniform, decent food, and within a fortnight is shipped away with his battalion to Norway—a country of whose existence he has been virtually unaware. Here, in winter, the day lasts only a few hours, then deep darkness envelops the world. But the port in which they work is well lit by strong electric lamps; only when the wailing siren announces the arrival of British or American bombers do the lights go out. This happens every day.

The unfathomable idiocy of Jewish fate! The madness of the Jewish God!

Cohen from Salonika, in the khaki uniform of the Todt Organization, is loading broken tanks, irreparable guns, boxes, and crates into the holds of old steamers in Bergen: war material and loot. Pieces of furniture. A grand piano appears again on the stage; a crazy Nazi officer wants to save it for himself.

Sometimes it pleases this mad God to light the fantastic fires of the Aurora Borealis in the black sky, and to spread them like fiery curtains from horizon to horizon—a symbol of the absolute and final defeat of any reason, of any logical context—to celebrate the confirmation of insanity.

Images of his former life flicker occasionally with lightning speed through the mind of a bewildered Cohen. They do not stay there long enough to linger on. But he sticks to one, with enormous effort: he, a boy in Salonika, beginning to read the Torah under the stern eye of the rabbi: "In the beginning God created the heaven and the earth. And the earth was without form and void; and darkness was upon the face of the deep. And the Spirit of God moved upon the face of the waters...."

The Spirit of God! That's how it was once, in the beginning—*tohu va'vohu*, without form and void—and this is it now, for certain. This is where he has arrived.

The siren wails again, the lights go out, and stronger than the blizzard's howl, the droning of the bombers makes the darkness vibrate. Darkness upon the face of the deep; and the Spirit of God.

Cohen-Petrossian presses his body against the wall of the shed. Then the bombs start falling.

"Do not disregard this Spirit of God. The thing is," Cohen says, "we should not try to figure out what it looks like, where it is, and how it acts. Just accept the idea that it exists."

Of course it does, for how else could you explain the order, two months later, following which Cohen's group is taken away from Norway and moved back to Germany?

Somebody gave the order. Ten thousand orders were issued on that day, deciding countless men's destinies, and one of them included Cohen's movements and fate: out of the *tohu va'vohu* of Norway in winter, back to the *tohu va'vohu* of Central Europe.

To follow the once more victorious Germans, across Luxembourg and Belgium, to keep open the supply roads through which would roll fuel for the advancing tanks, munitions, food, supplies. When Cohen, shivering in the severe weather of December '44, keeps shoveling the snow away from the winding roads in the Ardennes, a very young, rosy-cheeked German commander tries to cheer the battalion up: "One more effort, lads, a bit more, and we're over the hill. It will be warmer and more pleasant when we reach France again, especially the South of France." Marching back to their quarters after a fourteen-hour work day, their shovels shouldered, Cohen and two other Greek-Jew-Pole-Armenians keep singing with the whole company: *Es geht alles vorüber, es geht alles vorbei…* ("everything passes, everything goes away…")

Never were more truthful lyrics adapted to a marching song. For the Spirit of God wanders restless upon the face of *tohu va'vohu*, nobody knows where, perhaps it settles down like a tired bird for a short rest in the dugout of an unknown Yankee general, one McAuliffe, in the town of Bastogne, who, when confronted with a German demand for immediate capitulation ("you are completely surrounded, your situation is hopeless, if you reject this ultimatum you and your troops will be annihilated…") bites his cigar, spits, and says, thoughtfully: "Nuts."

Then the Spirit of God flies away on another of its manifold errands, but the German offensive collapses on the incomprehensible stubbornness of an obscure American general and his soldiers. The Battle of the Bulge is over, forgotten are the dreams of the blue skies of Southern France. *Es geht alles vorbei…*

Cohen knows little about all this (he heard that story much later) but he is moved once again across a Germany that resembles more and more the ruins of the Warsaw Ghetto, to the second station, after Auschwitz, of his European Odyssey.

In Dresden now, he experiences another kind of hell on earth—there are such a variety of hells—and after Dresden, further north, northeast, and south.

And then one day the Germans are no more and the Russians are there.

Cohen accepts a Coke from my refrigerator but refuses categorically anything stronger than that, not even a beer. "From those times. Can you imagine the amount of alcohol used by the Russians on the occasion of our liberation?"

"Yes. Russians liberated me, too."

"Well. Then you know. And a refusal to drink with them—to

Stalin's health, to Rossokovsky's health, to the tank brigade's health—could cost you a bullet in your head. Since then I haven't been able to touch alcohol. You drink?"

"Yes."

"Well," his black eyes move quickly and I know that he is acutely and perfectly aware of everything that goes on in this room, "You must have your reasons for it."

"Yes."

He keeps silent for a minute, then glances at his watch.

"I'll finish my story now, with your permission."

"OK."

Millions of people displaced by the madness of war move around now; some west, others east, rumors are spreading about transports being organized to bring people home. Yet it does not seem as if a transport will take Cohen and his two comrades to Salonika. They decide to move in the general direction of Greece; in the west the war still rages.

One day they find themselves in Lublin, which is full of refugees and survivors of all kinds, along with Polish and Russian soldiers, and Cohen, very practical, inquires about a Greek consul, a Greek representative. But people approached with such a strange question give him a quick glance and move swiftly away without answering. Cohen, indefatigable, is not discouraged: he keeps asking.

Finally one man, in a long, worn raincoat, with a thin ash-colored face, tight skin, and colorless eyes, listens carefully. He licks his lips and scrutinizes Cohen and his companions.

"A Greek consul?"

"Yes, yes, a Greek representative, to help us get home."

"A Greek consul?" the man repeats.

"Didn't I make it clear?" Cohen says politely, but with an undertone of impatience. "I can repeat it in another language if it is more convenient for you."

"In what language, for example?"

Cohen smiles: "In Spanish, Greek, German…"

"In Spanish, in German," the man repeats slowly, "and where do you come from, comrade?"

That was the first time in his life that Cohen was addressed as "comrade," and he makes note of it. It also makes him slightly uneasy.

"From Greece, I told you."

"No, what I mean is, now."

"Now? Vicinity of Dresden."

"That's in Germany, isn't it?" the man gestures in a western direction.

"It seems so."

There is a strange expression on the thin man's face, a grin, almost a smile, were it not for the long perpendicular line running from his left nostril down past the thin lips, almost down to the receding cleft chin. He says: "That's all I wanted to know. I arrest you. You are a bunch of spies."

Cohen and the others are too stunned to react. They stand motionless, staring incredulously at the man, as he takes out of his pocket a small metal whistle and puts it to his lips. A few minutes later, five militia-men with short-muzzled Russian automatic rifles escort them to prison.

Little attention is paid to the Greeks in the tiny classroom, used now as a provisionary prison for Germans, Poles suspected of being members of the A.K., and some real Vlassov men, for there was a spectacle going on in one corner: a former SS man had succeeded in cutting his veins with a piece of glass, and the crowd watched with interest as he bled to death.

He was dead by the time the guards broke in and dragged him out, leaving a large pool of blood on the floor.

"Did it quickly," somebody remarked.

"Experience," another one added.

"Experience? Bloody amateur work," one of the Vlassov men said disdainfully.

Next morning Cohen was brought before a judge.

"I have very little time, and very much to do," the short, dark man in a buttoned military tunic explained. He glanced at the papers on his desk. "I know everything about you. You are spies, it is as clear as the sun. We have already disposed of dozens like you, and they keep sending us more. What I want to know is the name of the man on the American side that sent you, and where you hid your radio equipment. If you tell me this, you may save your skin. If you refuse, I'll have you shot before noon, all three of you. I state it clearly, to save time and trouble. Speak."

Cohen looked at the man behind the desk with his piercing black eyes, and at the other one on the portrait, above him, heavily mustached, glancing down with what seemed to be a benevolent smile. This portrait was flanked by two others: a man-lion face, with a genius' bulging forehead and a heavy beard, and a bald man with a goatee, his chin stuck out aggressively.

"We have no time," the judge said apologetically. "The war is still on, and this is a revolutionary tribunal."

"We are no spies," Cohen said. "We were in Auschwitz; we are just refugees now, Jews from Greece."

"Aha! And how do you come from Greece to Auschwitz? And from Auschwitz to Dresden? And where did you learn Polish?"

Cohen felt all of a sudden very tiny, impotent, and extremely tired. He could not recollect being more tired during the whole war. "This," he sighed, "is a long story. Has the military tribunal time and patience to listen to it?"

The judge drummed with his fingers on the table.

"Guards," he said, "Leave for a moment. I must investigate this prisoner alone. Watch the door well from outside."

The soldiers shouldered their rifles and shuffled out. The judge got up behind his desk and beckoned Cohen to step up nearer. "Say *Shma Yisrael.*"

Confronting Marx, Stalin, and Lenin, Cohen closed his eyes, and said, "*Shma Yisrael, Adonay Eloheynu, Adonay Ehad.*"

Something broke in him. Tears burst suddenly from under his eyelids and rolled down his cheeks, burning the skin of his face. He opened his eyes, and wiped his face with his sleeve. The judge sat down and scribbled a few words on a piece of paper. He opened the drawer and put a small rubber stamp on the paper.

"Go now. Remember, don't ask any questions of anybody."

Cohen took the paper and moved to the door. Before opening it, he once more turned round and looked at the short, swarthy man standing under the three portraits behind the desk. "*Shalom*," said Cohen.

"*Shalom al Yisrael*," whispered the man.

Cohen gets up. "The rest," he says, "is not even absurd. It is simply stupid, an endless repetition."

He looks down at me. "I started everything from the beginning after the war."

"As if nothing happened? With what?"

"With nothing. I married, have two sons. Good boys."

He looks now directly at my desk, at the photograph in the black frame, and then straight into my eyes.

"I told you all this because I demolished your house in Warsaw. I had to explain."

"I understand."

"And you, too, started anew, from the beginning, after the war?"

"A few times."

"But we must, isn't it true?"

I said, "It becomes more difficult every time."

He turned his head again, and asked in a very low voice, "And this last time? When?"

"Half a year ago."

He was silent for a long time, then spoke again. "That Jewish judge in Lublin gave me the best advice of my life: not to ask unnecessary questions. I follow it to this day whenever I can. So I ask you no questions. But the starting anew is a must, an absolute must. You see that, don't you?"

But I saw nothing. At that moment the whole world, with the air-conditioned stillness of my cabin, the noise of the cranes and winches outside, with the huge asphalted square and the trucks and the railway wagons, and the immense pale blue Greek sky above it whirled around me, and when I opened my eyes again Cohen stood in the doorway.

"Start from the beginning, with nothing," he mumbled. "Never ask questions. The Spirit of God over *tohu va'vohu*. Good luck to you. *Shalom*."

Then he was gone.

Don Quixote and
Other Jewish Memories

Will you forgive me some indulgence in memories? They are the real fabric of my life and sometimes I suspect I am more involved in them than all the people I know. Immune to any control they come and go, these memories; capricious harpies, they drag me into the past, then throw me back into the present, disregarding all the rules of time.

Don Quixote is again on the agenda, for some reason.

The book had only twenty or thirty pages, in big print, with crude, full-page color illustrations; I was a boy of five or six. Naturally, there was a windmill, and a very thin, funny-looking man with a lance; also a short fat one, behind him, riding on a mule. Every Saturday my grandfather came to visit, and I, shifting my eyes from the book and studying him from the side, noticed, with a mixture of horror and wonder, how alike they were: Reuven, my father's father, and the funny man in the book.

Grandfather wore high, peasant-style boots; the leather shone with oil and smelled very strong. He was tall, lanky, his stiff beard was white, spare, and he had a bulging giant's forehead. It was frightening, the resemblance, for had not my mother explained to me that the man in the picture was mad? Could it be that Grandfather Reuven—he owned and ran a tombstone factory and was a rational man—no, it could not be. Anyhow, I loved him immoderately. He balanced me neatly on his hard knees while we looked at the illustrated supplement to the daily paper, and said, now let's see who these guys are. It was sheer bliss to clutch his large hands with big strong veins and to touch the stiff wiry hair of his beard with my cheek. I used to explain to him who those guys in the paper were.

No, he could not be mad. He would not charge windmills on the plain, mounted on a gaunt horse. Not my Grandfather Reuven.

Conversations behind the door: conversations of people unseen. But that was in another life—or was it?

Crouching in the warmth of the bed under the blanket, I heard my parents talking. They spoke in low voices, probably for fear of waking me, but their voices rose and fell, and my heart rose and fell.

"He sold it all, I tell you," my father said, "and bought Ashkenazy's second-hand bookstore. In its entirety."

"Old books?"

"Yes."

"My God. What will they live on now?"

"He gave some money to Mother. He said it's enough to live on. He said the ancient books are worth ten times as much as he paid for them."

"Worth? To whom? Good God!"

"He has those bundles of rubles. Thousands of rubles. He says the Bolsheviks will fall soon and we'll be able to live like princes on that Czarist money. It will be exchangeable."

In a whisper, my mother said: "He's mad. He's lost his wits."

After a long silence—my heart stood still—a still lower whisper: "I don't know. I'm not sure."

Then, only the rustling of sheets. No more talking. My head

throbbed. Reuven, mad? Like the funny man who fought the wind-mills? And I loved him so much. I loved him so much it choked me with despair. I kept asking, "When is Saturday?" and my mother answered, "Soon, the day after tomorrow," or, "Tomorrow, tomorrow he'll come." One Saturday he failed to come, and the Saturday after that. "Grandfather is ill," they told me.

Then, one day, they took me to his house, and in the middle of the floor was a long box covered with black cloth, a golden Star of David embroidered on it, and Grandmother, tiny, her face eroded by tears, said, "Say goodbye to Grandfather, child. Grandfather has died."

This was my first encounter with death, with the death of someone I loved more than myself. Many others were to come, but I knew nothing of it, had no premonitions, and was in pain only because something I thought belonged to me had been taken away. Nobody had asked my permission.

Some very old, very heavy books appeared in our house, and I was sitting on my high stool at the table and a book was spread out in front of me so huge that it covered the whole table.

"This is the Bible, with illustrations by Gustave Doré," my father said. I looked for a long time at the Egyptian army drowning in the sea. I put my tiny, colored Don Quixote on the open Bible, and looking at the knight sprawled in dust, with his broken lance, asked, "Did he die? Like Grandfather?"

Father laughed, but I sensed insincerity in his laughter. "Of course not," he said, "he just got hurt, but he soon recovered, and had many, many other adventures."

I felt sorry for the wounded knight, for my dead grandfather, and for the drowning Egyptians, and decided that when I grew up, I, too, would have many adventures.

2.

When you don't see the people talking, the conversation, overheard, has a different taste, like a cigarette smoked in the dark. Two men are talking just outside my window and I cannot help hearing them. I recognize the voices: one is the security officer, Shaul, the other, the new deck cadet, Avinoam. First trip.

They stand the security gangway watch, probably ten to twelve, or ten till two, I'm not sure which. I myself am exempt from this duty. They walk slowly from the gangway a few meters aft, and back, talking. My windows are almost opposite the entrance to the ship's accommodation. I keep them open but draw the curtains. It's raining outside, but not cold.

In the beginning, Avinoam explains, there was the newspaper ad from the Ministry of Transport. A young man with a jacket slung over his back, staring at a freighter in port. A kit bag at his feet. Underneath, in capital letters, the caption: WHERE TO? And beneath that in regular print: Be a naval officer. Travel all over the world and get good pay. Then came further details and addresses of the recruitment offices.

"What struck me most," he says, "was how similar we were. This man in the ad and I, even when seen from behind. We could have been twin brothers. Our shirts had the same pattern. The jeans were the same. It could have been a snapshot of myself minus the kit bag and the ship in the background. I had hardly ever been in a port, but I often walk with my jacket slung over my shoulder like that in winter, when you go out thinking it's going to rain and then you feel too hot in the jacket, you take it off, and throw it, you know, over your shoulder and hold it by the collar with your left hand."

"And what did you do back home? I mean before you saw the ad," asks Shaul.

Listening to his voice outside, I remember his face: pale and serious, light olive skin and a young, short, coal-black beard. All these kids looked like biblical prophets when young, I thought. Once, on Independence Day, in the good old days, the military parade started with eight young sergeants, all with beards, marching briskly abreast with submachine guns slung over their chests. The crowd went mad for them; young, armed prophets.

But this one must have been a baby at that time. Will his beard, fifty years from now, be wiry and white? Has he anything—anything at all—of the other man's personality, opinions, inclinations? No, no, these things only ripen with age. Don Quixote embarked on his adventures in his late forties: you don't even know what it's all about till you're forty.

"Oh, I'm a banana man," says Avinoam. "Back in the kibbutz, as long as I can remember, I worked in the banana plantation. Always. As a schoolboy, before the army, after the army, and then in between reserve duty. Did you know a banana is indestructible? You cut it down, root it out, burn it, plough through the fields, do anything you want, the banana stays. All of a sudden a bright green impertinent sturdy leaf, all rolled up, starts growing defiantly, and grows and grows. Funny, isn't it?"

"Must be boring as hell."

"You get used to it," Avinoam answers. "You get used to everything. If it weren't for the war, maybe I'd be walking in the banana grove right now, in sweaty work clothes with a machete in my hand."

"What war does to people," Shaul says. "Where were you?"

"Paratroopers, in the south. We crossed on the first night."

"Arik Sharon's men?"

"Yeah, and you?"

"We threw that bridge across. That's where I got wounded."

"The next night, after us. I got it. We couldn't have been far from each other."

"Sure."

A silence now behind my window, filled with the soft rustle of Italian rain. They must be lighting their cigarettes; I can hear a match being struck. Then, Shaul's voice, low and quiet. "Many killed from your kibbutz?"

"Four, one on 'Chinese Farm', two in the Golan, and one pilot."

"Yeah."

"It rains all the time here, not like back home."

"Yeah. Back there it was raining fire."

"It sure was."

I know they're leaning against the wall of the deckhouse now, smoking cigarettes, looking at the rain, and they're both back there, on that October night in the Sinai. Two years ago.

Shaul interrupts the silence. "The ramp gave us some protection," he says. "I mean the breach in the ramp. But on both sides of it, man, that was something. Such concentrated fire! Artillery, katyusha rockets, tanks, God knows what! And the machine guns, to finish off what was left. You crawled low under those pontoon bridges, and you knew that if you left that breach, you disintegrated. Nothing could survive that firestorm.

"My knees were shaking. I was too busy trying to control the shaking to think about anything else. And you know what? I couldn't control it. I put a lot of effort into it. I gave it everything I had, but I couldn't control my bloody knees. A guy next to me put his face in the sand and mumbled something, or ate sand, I don't know, I only saw his mouth moving constantly. Then I thought, God let me be killed instantly and stop seeing, stop hearing, stop trying to control, stop feeling, stop thinking. Get killed, but not crippled. Not wounded."

"Well, you got wounded after all," chuckled Avinoam.

"Yes, I got it. A sublieutenant crawled under the pontoon, and I saw his teeth chattering. I didn't know him from before. He wasn't from my unit. I saw him for the first and last time in my life. He screamed, What's-the-matter-with-our-boys? Wh-wh-what is the matter? People are waiting for that fu-fucking bridge-br-bridge, there, on the other side! Under fire! What the hell, are you waiting f-f-for? And he jumped out, right into the open, and stood there. It was a pure miracle, the fire didn't touch him."

"And then," said Avinoam, "you got that bridge across."

"And then," Shaul said, "we rolled that pontoon out, into the open, and into the canal, stumbling, cursing, falling, getting up again, we got it into the water, connected it with the other pontoons. Then I was hit and it was over for me. And you?"

Again Avinoam chuckles. "Well, I was on the other side. We crossed in rubber boats. I dug a hole for myself, and waited for your bridge. We didn't know how and when, but it stood to reason that there had to be a bridge, sooner or later, for the tanks and for the heavy equipment. We couldn't attack without it. That's what they told us. The next morning the tanks started coming, across the bridge, and we moved, too."

"I was already in the hospital by then."

"Where were you hit?"

"Here. And here. Big shell fragments. And one here, a small small splinter."

Looking at the town square in the rain, they smoke silently.

"It will be two years exactly, tomorrow," Avinoam says.

"A lot of guys were killed in that war."

"U-huh."

"This security watch, just between us, is bullshit."

Shaul answers, "In a small town like this there's not much of a chance they'd try anything. But in the big ports, you'd better watch. Who's supposed to relieve us?"

"Moshe and Saadia."

Silence.

"You know, after all that, I went back to the bananas."

They laugh now, both of them.

"Indestructible, right? Like you said."

"But I didn't stay long. Couldn't find a place for myself. Did this and that, then again a couple of months in the bananas. And then, I saw this ad in the paper. I thought, why not try it? It couldn't be any worse than the others, right?"

"No it couldn't."

Again a silence, and then Avinoam says: "A lot of good guys were killed in that war. An awful lot."

Then they fell silent.

3.

I get up very early in the morning and go ashore. The ship is moored right at the town's main square. One side of it is open to the sea. On the three remaining sides are very old houses, and narrow streets paved with large stones climb the hill on top of which the church stands. In the middle of the square is a war monument. The statue of a very slim youthful goddess of victory with small breasts leans forward with extended arms and glistens darkly in the rain. The artist's model must have been young. Perhaps he had no money to pay a full-sized woman to model for him. Or perhaps he just wanted it that way. Under Nike's feet is a white stone, and though much of the lettering has been erased by the weather, I can still read:

I prodi figli suoi cadutti
nell'ultima guerra mondiale,
gaeta
Col. Prisco Orgoglio
e con rinnovelata fede....

That should mean "with renewed faith," I thought. But this was in 1919. I wasn't born yet and had no faith. I had faith later, only to lose it—definitely—still later.

At the base of the monument stand four ugly heavy mortars, one in each corner. The rain has washed the monument and the mortars clean, and tall pine trees and palms sway slightly in the wind. There is much rustling of leaves, and the raindrops glide from Nike's wings and breasts, and from the mortars.

The square is empty aft that hour. A black dog crosses quickly, a Vespa roars by. The neon sign RISTORANTE is turned off, but the two others, BAR and TABACHERIA still shine in red letters.

Then it stops raining and the sky is the color of mother-of-pearl and the church on the hill catches the first rays of the rising sun and blazes red for a few minutes. After a while the sun hides behind the clouds and the church becomes pale yellow and sad. The two Bourbon kings in front of the church, Maximilian and Ferdinand, and the young Nike among the alpine mortars brace themselves for more rain. I return to the ship.

4.

I have a strange aversion to people who never turn off the radio in their cars. They just switch off the engine and walk away, so that when they come back and start the car the radio starts talking immediately. My boss, driving to Haifa with his wife, gave me a lift as my car was out of order. The minute he started the engine the announcer said that the American astronauts had landed on the moon. I said I preferred the moon goddess to a moon rocket, and was given a contemptuous look. My boss, driving, looked in the rear-view mirror to check if I was serious. I was.

His wife snapped, "Nonsense. At least they've done something. They got there, to the moon. You think it's easy? It's an achievement. Moon goddesses are words, what do words achieve?"

"They sometimes transmit beauty, if they're good words," I answered. "Beauty and truth: words sometimes reveal truth."

He started to say something, then stopped. He was my boss, even if you took into account the special relationship between us. We once pulled nets together on board a deep-sea trawler, but that was long ago. Now he was running a shipping company, and I was an executive, responsible for seeing to it that the ships ran smoothly, that there were no technical problems. That was my job as supervisor. It was also, I realized, the peak of my career on that level, I could hardly go higher.

But now, on the way to Haifa in the same car, and after that look he gave me in the rear-view mirror, I knew what he thought: could I be trusted with the job while harboring such loony ideas, preferring moon goddesses to moon rockets? Why, one day I might prefer the Flying Dutchman to a modern, diesel-engine-propelled freighter, and what would happen then? In my office the shelves were loaded with bound volumes of *Motor Ship, Ship's Maintenance and Repairs, Tankers and Bulk Carriers, Lloyd's Annual Report*, and instruction books on all kinds of machinery. But he knew that at home there were none of these. On my private shelf Cervantes was king, while on the supervisor's desk, John Lamb's *The Maintenance and Running of a Marine Diesel Engine*. I knew both volumes almost by heart; this Lamb was every marine engineer's gospel, and if you lived according to it, you would keep your crew constantly in the engine room, because the chapter on "Preparing the Engine for Work" comes right after "The Cooling of the Engine after Work." Lamb's slaves never saw the sun or the stars, except maybe through the skylight, if the chief engineer was negligent enough to let them lift their eyes for a second. So this Lamb was the right stuff, Cervantes was positively not, and my boss had his justified suspicions.

I don't imply that this was the reason, but it might be one of the reasons that I found myself in a ship's engine room once more after three years as an executive. In any case, my boss didn't protest very violently when I submitted my resignation some years ago.

Sailing again was good if you loved the sea as I did, had a decent crew, and a first assistant that could be relied upon. But on this old ship, I had a very questionable first assistant, and it was so badly undermanned that I had to keep watches myself: not much of a pleasure at my age. So I had little time for anything else, except, naturally, in ports like this one where you stayed for days and days and days.

5.

One morning, the day after we arrived in Taranto, a block of houses appeared on the horizon. As it rapidly came nearer we saw that it wasn't a skyscraper laid horizontally, but an American aircraft carrier. It could have been the renowned and malicious wizard Merlin in disguise for all I knew. (I was, on this day, on Chapter xxi of *Don Quixote*.)

The vessel entered the outer harbor slowly but under its own power, and a swarm of tugboats came out of port and started maneuvering it into position. They moved around nervously and then took the carrier's lines and moved cautiously and slowly. You could feel how nervous and tense the tugmasters were, but nothing of it showed, you just felt it, transmitted on invisible waves. Then the anchors were dropped and the carrier became a permanent feature of the landscape for the next ten days.

Its cranes lowered big motor launches and boats, moveable bridges swung out, and yellow helicopters rose from its flight deck. The deck was so crowded with planes it seemed impossible for any craft to land there, but the helicopters always came in safely. Unlike the helicopters in my head, which always crashed.

Over the decks, over the planes and bridges, towered the ship's funnel and its complicated superstructure, many stories high, adorned with all kinds of radar aerials, antennas, and mysterious gadgets of electronic equipment. Some of the radar pans rotated permanently. Motor boats kept coming and going all the time, and in the evening much of the ship was floodlit. On the side of the funnel the number 67 appeared, so bright it must have been visible miles away. In the aft, lit from below, you could read the ship's name, in letters four feet high, across the ship's whole width: *JOHN F. KENNEDY.*

The next day, *Kennedy's* children flooded the town. They came in swarms of three, four, or five hundred, on shore leave, in civilian clothes, a few of them wearing blue sweaters with the name *John F. Kennedy* written in white. The natives were perplexed: this port had served the Sixth Fleet frequently, and they were familiar with American sailors, but the crew of the atomic carrier was a special new breed, and the Italians eyed them with suspicion.

They were white, brown, yellow, black, but only a few of the blacks had Afros; Afros were on the way out in 1975. Some had inexpensive cameras, others carried portable transistor radios, some smoked big straight cigars, and still others were just tall, clean, crew-cut boys, walking the streets with hands thrust into their pockets, staring at the girls and looking quietly at the shop windows. They behaved well; the MP patrols swinging their long nightsticks had little to do.

Quantities of American goodies found their way onto the street. Tough little boys approached cars stuck in traffic jams offering cartons of Marlboro, Kent, Wrigley's gum, Hershey's chocolate bars.

And still the townspeople, the inhabitants of this place in southern Italy, continued to stare at *Kennedy*'s children as if they were from outer space.

A strong wind blew along the Corso Italia, across the bridge, and down along the edge of the Little Sea, the Mare Piccolo. Old people met the wind with severe faces, accepting it as inevitable. *Kennedy* was also inevitable, and so were the churches in the Old City, where you could find a haven in the still darkness and rest your eyes on the mild light from two candles, with figures of Christ or the Madonna between them.

But further up the street, the houses of the new town gave little protection from the wind; there you would meet stern carabinieri in splendid uniforms, elegant, glistening chrome-and-glass bars, fresh flowers under crumbling monuments, put up once in the name of glory, the glory of a fallen hero or of the homeland, or of some illustrious regiment possessing chivalry and courage. All past now, swept by this chilly autumn wind.

You would meet a clear, fresh-faced kid from the *Kennedy* trying to grasp—in a calm, reserved way—the meaning of it all: of a post office, say, occupying a decrepit palace from the beginning of the last century, complete with gray columns and stone giants supporting the gate. Little boys, appearing from nowhere, attacked him: "Hey, Jack, you gotta cigarettes, Marlboro, Kent, Camel? Pay good money. Plenty lire. Want to meet my sister? Very clean. No? No nothing?"

The *Kennedy* boy would gently shake his head and walk on. In Italian, in dialect, the little boys abused him, called him an idiot, a queer, a sissy, an imbecile.

6.

You don't sit down in bars in Italy; there are no stools provided. You just stand there and sip your drink, rubbing elbows with people who have dropped in for an espresso or a capuccino.

I have a brandy, Vecchia Romana, Black Label, and the man

next to me has a milkshake. It took a lot of time and effort to explain to the bartender what he wanted, but the bartender accepted it as a good joke, laughing a lot, and throughout the long process of preparing the milkshake, keeping the other two bartenders informed about what he was doing. It was a great joke with them, but the American boy was very polite and patient. When his drink was ready, the boy, his reddish hair thinning visibly in front and cut very short in the back, sipped it innocently.

"What is it you're drinking?" I asked.

"A milkshake. What about you?"

"Vecchia Romana. A very good brandy, as good as any French brandy."

"Never heard of it."

"These guys here laugh at me," he said, after a moment. "I know it even though I can't understand what they're saying. But it really is a nice drink, even though they can't make it the way it should be made. But I don't blame them. Even on board they don't make it like back home."

"Where are you from?"

"Bixby, Oklahoma. You've never heard of it. A small town south of Tulsa. You know where Tulsa is?"

I knew Tulsa, improbable and incredible as it seems. Thirty-five years ago I knew a sweet girl whose name was Tamara. We used to take long walks on the wooded banks of the Vistula, holding hands or shyly kissing. She talked a lot about her older sister, Helen, who had emigrated to the States four years earlier, married, and settled down in Tulsa, Oklahoma. Very soon she would send papers and money for Tamara, and her mother, and they too would go to America. And what would I do then? Stay in Poland, and cry for my lost love? No, I was ready to follow Tamara to the moon, to hell, if necessary. I'd find a way to get to Oklahoma.

In the end, Tamara stayed in Warsaw—the money and the papers didn't arrive in time—and was slaughtered by black-uniformed Latvians or Ukrainians a few years later. And I, well, I was here now, in a bar in Taranto, having a bitter-tasting Vecchia Romana. Best regards from Oklahoma. I still remembered snapshots of Helen, round-faced and smiling, leaning out the window of her house in Tulsa.

I wouldn't tell all this to the boy with the milkshake, whose elbow touched mine: no use spoiling the drink for him. Instead, I asked him what his job was, and he said, "Oh, I'm a radar technician. And what do you do?"

"I'm on a tramp ship. Engineer."

"Where are you from?"

"Israel."

"That's Palestine, isn't it?"

"Was once."

"You like this town?"

"Like any other town in southern Italy. Yes, I like them. It's not like Naples. We spend most of the time in Naples. I can get a milkshake in Naples any time I go ashore. Here I have to tell the barman how to mix it, step by step. Very primitive. And not very cooperative, either."

"Well, you're strangers here."

"In Naples they like us."

"You can't be liked everywhere."

He finished his drink, and reflected, his face pale, clean, and open. "No," he said, "you can't. It's a pity, isn't it?"

"It is," I said. "But that's how it is. Accept it," I added, thinking of Tamara and her sister Helen.

7.

In Taranto, I used to go with the chief mate to the cargo office at the end of the dock. There he would ask politely but persistently why our ship wasn't being loaded, and the foreman, who didn't look like an Italian but like a Pole or a Russian, would smile his bashful smile. He would look at the papers on his table, tap his pencil, and talk at great length about how three of the four large cranes were out of commission and were going to be repaired, maybe by tomorrow afternoon. (They were fairly new cranes and there was no reason why they shouldn't be working properly.) Or else it was a strike of customs inspectors down at the plant where the flatcars loaded with steel coils came from.

"So why are the other ships in port being loaded?" asked the chief mate.

"The three other ships are *bandera nazionale*," said the foreman, "customs has nothing to do with Italian ships taking steel to Ravenna or Palermo or La Spezia. But your ship is export. You can't load without having the papers stamped by customs, and the customs men are on strike."

If it wasn't cranes or customs it was the wind which was too strong. Or else a strike by the locomotive drivers. Sometimes the chief mate would lose his patience. His nose became red, then purple, and he would begin shouting. "I don't understand what's going on!" The purple from his broad nose would spread upward and cover his forehead. I worried about him.

"Zalman," I finally told him, "let's go back on board. If the locomotive drivers are on strike, we can't do anything about it. Nor can the foreman here. They're on strike, Zalman. They want higher wages, or maybe less noisy locomotives."

"What language are you speaking?" asked the foreman with genuine interest. "Is it Hebrew?"

"Yes, it's Hebrew."

"Modern Hebrew, you mean?"

"Extremely modern," I said. "Zalman, come. It's no use sitting here."

So Zalman would thank the foreman for his explanation and we would leave. That night, I knew I would go to town by myself to get drunk.

8.

At a certain point it became obvious to everyone that there must be a mysterious connection between the inexplicable delays in our loading schedule and a pending claim against our ship by a certain tugboat company. They wanted a bond of several thousand dollars to be deposited in one of the major Italian banks until the case came to court or a compromise was reached out of court.

The company claimed that two tugs had assisted our ship when it shifted from one anchorage to another while the ship's engine was out of order for five or six hours. The tugboat company did not want to deal with us directly, but only through their lawyer. The captain informed the main office in Haifa, and waited for instructions, and meanwhile the ship stood idle.

A ship staying too long in one place defies the purpose of its existence. Everybody and everything connected with it becomes infected by this terrible malady of idleness. The crew—whose relation to the ship is symbiotic—is the most exposed, and therefore the first to suffer. Two of the men had accidents and were sent home by plane and only one replacement came back. Two others got sick and had to be sent to a hospital. Others were sulky, quarrelsome.

When the captain knocked at the door and proposed that we go together to the agency so that he could show me a real Godfather, I was a bit reluctant. But then I thought it might be interesting. I like the captain and saw that he wanted some support in dealing with the Mafia; he was in real trouble. So we went together, the captain with his elegant attaché case, I with the Suez Canal, the Nike statue, and all the rest in my head.

The agency dealt mainly in tourism. There were modern counters and travel posters on the walls: Morocco, Tunisia, and Spain. Three or four clerks sold plane tickets and gave information, and a tall girl with a large but thin nose and white imitation leather boots was in charge of the money. "You can change dollars here, you know," the captain said. "They do it gladly. No questions asked. No receipts. The girl does it."

We crossed the outer office with its steel and glass furniture and bright posters and went through a doorway to a back room with a high, vaulted ceiling. On the walls hung two ancient maps, one of Taranto, the other of the Adriatic Sea, and an artist's rendering of the passenger liner *Italia*. To the left behind an old-fashioned desk sat Mr. Cellini, smoking a cigar. He was a corpulent man with a large face that was red after his morning shave, an iron-gray mustache, and iron-gray hair, combed back carefully from his receding forehead. He had very light blue eyes, the blue of an early spring sky in Italy, eyes which were as elusive and restless as the birds in this sky: always in motion, they never rested for long on one spot.

It was warm in the office, and he took off his jacket; a frightened boy ran up, took it from him, put it respectfully on a hanger and placed it in a closet. Mr. Cellini then began telephoning, sitting in his silk shirt with broad black suspenders over his ample chest. There was a dense atmosphere around him, an almost visible aura, heavy with centuries of inherited, feudal power, undisputed, autocratic, and so vast that it seemed to take a special effort on his part to sit there in that modest chair as the owner-director of a mere travel agency. In this disguise he behaved like a benevolent, half-amused Greek god in a simple mortal's body.

And where would the most excellent chevalier of La Mancha fit into this, I wondered, sitting in this vaulted office and observing the *padrone* talking on the phone? He would not. He would only watch the show, if he were hanging here on the wall somewhere, in a dark portrait by Velásquez or El Greco. With a sardonic smile. With contempt. Because the show he would see from his elevated position would be Sancho's show. Measured on the scale of sheer human dignity this could not be on Don Quixote's level of understanding. At his best Mr. Cellini—and no matter if he was the all-powerful *padrone* my captain and I imagined him to be, or just a low-grade crook—could only act a very dignified Sancho. Watching him talk on the telephone, floating in his self-inflated solemnity, which, after all, is a trademark of the managerial class, anywhere, in any country, I tried to reconstruct his mental processes for myself. In vain. Still, the spectacle was fascinating. At a certain moment, the muscles moved in Cellini's large face, pulling the skin into a grin: the corners of the mouth would lift on both sides, and the lips part slightly, revealing long rows of small, square, yellow teeth. There was no doubt: he was smiling. And the smile, which was exactly like the permanent expression of big reptiles in a zoo, chilled. The captain, sitting at my side, shot me a look and shivered. Cellini's assistant, too, fixed his eyes on his boss who, during this whole performance, was speaking in the local dialect and making it sound as dignified as Latin. As long as it lasted, he was as near as he could be to shedding his Sancho personality; but the power of his "stinking pride of degradation" almost pushed him out of there like gas accumulating in a bottle of a fermenting liquid slowly forcing the cork out. At this point, I imagined, Don Quixote in the portrait would have frowned, perplexed.

But then he quit smiling, and it was over. He replaced the receiver, relit his cigar, and puffed on it. It was then that I did what I was asked to do, performed my act of great courage, asking, "Would you think it possible, Signor Cellini, that there is any connection between the tugboat company's claim and the delay in the loading of our ship?" "Connection?" he said, his eyes running from one corner of the room to another. I only prayed that they would not land on me, and that he would not smile; that would be too hard to bear. But he did not.

"We are in southern Italy," he said curtly. "Is there a connection, you ask? I do not know. Still, being where we are, this, too, could be possible."

He returned to his papers. It was his assistant now who spoke in a very low voice on the phone to the shipping company. "Your cargo is not ready yet," he said. "They say perhaps the day after tomorrow."

The assistant, Mario, was also out of place here, like everybody else. And where did he belong? The answer is simple: on horseback, with a fur hat, with a short, thick bow in his hands and feathered arrows in his quiver. For me, he could only be a Tartar.

Naturally, I had seen Mario's picture on horseback with a fur hat, in the very remote past, in one of the ancient leather-bound books for which Grandfather Reuven sold his factory. A Russian painter produced this masterpiece, as far as I could remember. The picture of the knight himself I saw that same evening, in the office of the tug company's lawyer. The *avvocato* sat, facing a wall lined with heavy volumes. Light from a bronze desk lamp flowed onto the top of the desk. The rest of the interior was in semi-darkness.

"And who is the creator of this beautiful painting, *avvocato*?" I asked as soon as we were seated.

"This? An unknown master of southern Italy. The portrait is of one of my ancestors, of course. We are a very old family in this town. As to the claim, gentlemen, kindly note that we do not propose to place your ship under arrest, or prevent its departure. We only want a bond. And the arbitration, whenever it takes place...." His voice drifted away.

From the semi-darkness above, this little crook's ancestor looked at him with stern disapproval. The white ruffled collar was hidden in front by a triangular black beard; the nose was thin but powerful, straight, the eyes black and burning. As the lawyer rambled on and on, and the captain kept nodding to indicate his attention, I had a real urge to interrupt with apologies to ask, "Do you know, by chance, what your illustrious ancestor's trade was?" But I restrained myself: I have studied the art of restraint, I know how to do it. I doubt now that the man in the portrait was this lawyer's ancestor; he might have bought the picture in an antique shop. He was one of Sancho's breed.

Now he alternated between ill-concealed threats and plain ass-kissing. He pleaded, he tried to persuade, he pressed. Only when the captain, in despair, said, "But I told you, I must have my owners' authorization, from Haifa, and I hope to get it by telegram tomorrow," did he realize that all his efforts were in vain, he'd been wasting his time on the wrong people. Then he became nasty. He offered us cigars, which we refused, and said, "Well, if that's the case, I am sure everything will be settled to our mutual satisfaction. And how is the general situation in your country at present? *Siempre guerra*, eh? Always, always war. How sad!"

"We have bad neighbors," said the captain.

Go fuck yourself, *avvocato*! You are, no doubt, one of those whom Don Quixote called a "monstrous and proud crew"—the merchants of Toledo—and, later on, a "coward brood, slavish crew."

What do you know about my country and my people? Always war, you say with your crocodile smile, sadly; a young man, "progressive," I see a copy of *L'Unité* on your desk, with photographs of Yasser Arafat and Farouk Kadoumi on the front page, and from the smirk on your face I understand that you approve of their views. You, too, long for a "democratic, secular state in Palestine." Perhaps like Byelorussia or Cuba. Or maybe like Vietnam, Angola, or Lebanon. I cannot know how far your tastes run, but there are, alas, a lot of choices. The world is full of democratic, secular states, they sprout like poisonous mushrooms after rain. The future belongs to them, you calculate in your small, dark, sleek, handsome head. And in addition to that you hate America, whose symbol, the nuclear carrier, at this moment befouls the waters of your ancient, noble harbor. You dislike and pity and look with contempt at the *Kennedy* kids roaming your streets. They're like stupid babies, you think, compared with your compatriots with their long history and the traditions of this ancient peninsula.

"Imperialism," you mumble. "Colonialism, expansionism, you and your American allies...." Crowds of young, active, progressive semi-intellectuals like you repeat the same phrases, *avvocato*, all over the world, every day. But I can look quietly into your eyes. What can Arafat or Kadoumi teach me about a "democratic, secular state" that I do not know? What can they teach me at all? And even you, *avvocato*, so aware of the history and pride of the generations of your forefathers—the pride and dignity which you, a modern man, discard as anachronistic—even you cannot compete with me on this level: my ancestors wrote books of philosophy while yours were still living in the woods dressed in animal skins.

So shut up, *avvocato*, and return to your dirty business; your quixotic ancestor, in a heavy gilded frame, spits down from above on your pomaded head.

9.

One day at the breakfast table the chief mate told me: the *Kennedy* is gone. I went out on deck to check; the huge vessel had disappeared.

It must have sailed at daybreak or during the night, and now only the fact remained: Kennedy was gone. Thirteen years earlier, during intermission at a concert in the elegant Concertgebouw in Amsterdam, an excited hat-check girl came up to me and said, "A terrible thing has happened! Your president is gone."

"My president?"

"Yes, Kennedy. He was shot dead in Dallas. They just confirmed it on the radio! You're an American, aren't you?" She spoke in a high voice, other people heard, and the rumor spread through the well-dressed crowd like a ripple on the surface of the sea. Outside, in the drizzle of an Amsterdam evening, boys were selling extra editions, with two-inch headlines: KENNEDY SHOT DEAD.

Then the intermission ended, and people started flowing back to the concert hall. We left. I was not an American and Kennedy was not my president, but I could not go back to listen to Chopin's Etudes, played by Rubinstein. A picture from my childhood book of a man sprawled on the sand, his lance broken, floated up and dissolved: "Is he dead, father? Like grandfather?"

Something turned over in me and then settled down again, and I knew that what they called an "era"—perhaps a small one measured on the scale of human history but still, an era—had come to an abrupt end. Many things would be changed now, I thought. They were.

In Taranto, thirteen years later, with the nuclear carrier gone, standing on deck in a vaguely gray Italian morning, I felt that on our tiny scale, here and now, something would change also.

"Zalman," I told the chief mate, "they'll start loading today: perhaps we'll sail tomorrow."

"Of course," he said quietly. "The foreman already told me so this morning. The bond was deposited, yesterday, by wire."

Like a ripple on a smooth sea. My children called such a sea, before the ripple came, the Sea of the Dolphins. Sometimes we would go fore, to the ship's prow, and watch the bow crush the solid, heavy surface into a trough of white, sparkling crystal. With the long rake of the bow you could also see the reflection down below, like in a dark-blue mirror, of your own head, your body leaning over the protective rail. Then, out of the deep, four, five, six dolphins would appear, like torpedoes speeding on a parallel course with the ship's hull, sometimes touching it at great speed, rubbing lightly against it: free, parallel, and very powerful. At an invisible signal they would break from below the surface, jump in perfect unison a meter or two in a graceful arc, showing a black glistening body in the air, then turn before falling back into the sea, to show for a second a long white belly, always on an exactly parallel course with each other, like a group of superbly trained acrobats, powerful and compact. At another secret order, they would turn left or right, and suddenly plunge into the deep from which they had come, disappearing quickly in ever darker blue, purple. This was the dolphins' sea, the enormous stretch of smoothness and harmony and calm, with a fair chance of a school of dolphins appearing from nowhere and vanishing in the same mysterious way.

But sometimes the dolphins would not come, and you would sail, cutting the satin surface for hours or even days, until a secret force ruffled it, tiny ripples appeared in patches here and there, the surface broke into patterns: then a puff would come, a mere breath of wind, hardly deflecting the smoke of your pipe from its straight, perpendicular spiral, but strong enough to dissolve the magic: and the Sea of the Dolphins would be gone.

On a quiet night, we sailed from Taranto to complete loading in Genoa.

10.

You make a passage through the sea and you keep functioning on all levels, an act of equilibrium not to be lightly dismissed. Helicopters keep crashing in your head, mostly at night, but sometimes during the day as well, with an ear-splitting shriek of torn metal and great explosions of flames. Your heart pumps more quickly for a few seconds, then you quench the flames and go on, proceed, as it were, going up a few steps, or down, until you can check with a steady eye the exhaust temperatures of each cylinder on a remote-control pyrometer in the bright light of the engine room, watched anxiously from the side by the engineer and/or the motorman on duty. You register the difference between cylinder number two—305°C—and cylinder number six—325°C. You know then that the helicopter flames have been temporarily extinguished again and you make a remark to the other man about this or that. Or you make a joke or admonish him, according to your mood.

You continue your short walk in the engine room—because you function correctly on this level now—noticing, as you pass, that the upper half of the lubricating oil separator looks like the space helmet of the men who have landed on the moon. The sight glasses are like visors, but there are no eyes behind them, only black lubricating oil. You go quickly past the turbine, because the shrill, extremely high-pitched noise it makes—eight thousand revolutions per minute—can be damaging to the ears; it is this noise that has made you half deaf already, for you have listened to it for many years without protecting your ears with special earphones. Now the law orders them to be worn in the engine room, but you do not comply with the law, because you think in your conservative simple-mindedness and with mulish idiocy, How can I hear a wrong noise in the engine if I have these mufflers on my ears? And they increase your claustrophobia as well.

You open the lid of the thrust bearing and see muddy oil flowing heavily there among the pads, and you think about the clear stream of water breaking in furious tiny waves on stones and pebbles in a wood, somewhere two thousand miles north of here and thirty odd years in the past. You put your hand on the rough cast-iron casing of the bearing to ascertain the temperature. You do not trust the thermometer mounted there for you have seen too many thermometers showing wrong temperatures, and you notice that the man who last painted this casing with cream-yellow paint did a lousy job of it, smeared it on impatiently, whereas the oil painting over the *avvocato*'s head, in semi-darkness, with its somber clarity, made you suck in your breath. Of course, the painter did not have to chip away the rust first, he painted on canvas, but this motorman, or oiler, or whoever the hell he was, didn't bother much about the rust either, he just smeared over it with his brush.

95

You close the lid of the thrust bearing and touch the gland of the propeller shaft (bent over halfway because the shaft tunnel isn't high enough to stand upright). Then you return on the other side of the engine, past the boiler, past the turbine, compressors, generators, checking them as you pass, and well aware that they look as they should but also like something else: like patterns on a tapestry which do not belong to the design, but exist only in your head, but nevertheless exist, and if you try to persuade yourself to the contrary, they periodically but persistently return to remind you they're here and no use denying the fact. The same with configurations of flowers or books or even ashes and cigarette butts in an ashtray, or the easiest and most obvious one of all, the clouds in the sky. Popular, too: many people notice them, many have written about them. Therefore, one should not make fun of anyone who sees giants instead of windmills: giants are there, for sure, though I myself saw Calvary crosses with crucified people on them, or helicopter blades. But this is my very private vision.

Now, having assured myself that the generator, as a generator, runs smoothly, I send a friendly wave of the hand and a smile to the engineer keeping watch and climb the stairs up out of this engine room, and continue to sail on a fresh, rippled, dolphinless sea, heading north toward Genoa, which should be the last port on this voyage.

II.

Merchant ships are sent over the seas to carry cargo from one country to another, but mainly to make profit for their owners. Remember this. The profit factor has an overwhelming influence on the lives of ships and crews; all other considerations are almost meaningless. It is of no interest to a good Greek ship owner in what condition his ships and seamen are in as long as they make the passages according to schedule and as long as the cargo arrives dry and in acceptable condition. The tendency is to reduce everything not directly connected with profit to an absolute minimum: minimum safety conditions, minimum crews, minimum wages. Minimum spare parts carried and used.

Our Israeli ship owners always looked up to the Greeks, seeing them as shining examples and ideals. Saving at any price was the motto of this company, and nobody dared to laugh at the joke that sometimes the cost of saving rose sky-high, and a certain confusion resulted. But the principle remained unshaken.

Now, if the basic philosophy of your life is Marxist in any form, you'll direct your efforts toward reducing the profits of your owners, thereby increasing your own. My friend, the company boss, would hotly deny this, saying you can find a compromise, a golden mean, between your yearning for profits and all other valid considerations. I said nonsense, either you're a virgin or not, there is no middle course here.

The donkeyman knocked at the door, a sheet of paper in his hand. "I haven't got enough overtime this month," he says. "It says only ninety-eight hours."

"But that's exactly how much you worked. I have the copy of your form here."

"Don't you understand that overtime is the biggest part of my wages? I have to support a family!"

"But I can't approve payment of hours and days you haven't worked!"

"With all due respect, chief, you don't know anything about it. You come here for one or two trips, and want to change the world."

"On the contrary, I don't want to change anything."

"Every chief signs these overtime sheets, it's normal procedure, the office knows about it! And approves of it."

"Willingly?"

"No, but they have no choice. They're bound by union agreements; somebody has to run these ships."

"But how can I pay you for what you didn't do? Tell me, how!"

The donkeyman is clever, he sees there is no sense discussing these matters with a man who doesn't understand the simplest facts of life. He collects his overtime sheets and goes away, and will gladly spread the news that the chief is soft in the head. But I'll be damned if I pay for work that wasn't done. Let the crooks in the office find some other, cleaner way to compensate people for the low wages they're paying.

But one fault of mine is seeing people in other contexts, in other situations than the ones in which I encounter them. It is a strange deficiency that spoils my ability to deal with reality. While this donkeyman discusses his overtime with me, here and now, I see him also—in spite of myself—at home, with his wife, laughingly explaining to her: Look, I had that strange old fool this trip, making a fuss about overtime. They take him on once or twice a year because he was one of the company's founders or something, an old-timer, a real relic, and a kibbutznik on top of everything, which means he hasn't the remotest idea what money is.

She does not exactly know what to do with this information, and says nothing. He says, never mind, I'll add what's missing here on the next trip.

Now that he's gone I enjoy the solitude of this tiny cabin: the sharp, smoky taste of the Scotch, the sweet, slightly metallic flavor of the tea, and the bright clean light of the fluorescent tube over my desk. Clearly, I enjoy sailing more than arriving, I always love being underway, suspended, in passage. It is smoother, easier, when you are underway: the tensions are located at the arrivals and departures.

I also like to think that in this moment, in this tiny spot of space and time, between the past and the future, there are seventeen-thousand-six-hundred-twenty-seven ships sailing in the sea, which means that the same number of my colleagues, my counterparts, whom I'll never meet or see, exist, act, do, think, feel, laugh, read, drink, dream. This secret knowledge is conveyed to me through very special waves, passing through the sea and penetrating easily through the iron shells of the ships' hulls.

Perhaps there is even a direct connection between this ability of mine to see the seventeen-thousand-six-hundred-twenty-seven engineers now, before the glass raised by my hand reaches my lips, and the clear picture of my donkeyman, engaged in intimate conversation with his wife, three weeks from now. But however it may be, it comes to me naturally, without any effort on my part. Along the same lines, I can, looking at next year's car model, glistening with chrome, see it rusted and dented, hardly more than a heap of broken metal, in some backyard or in an automobile graveyard, just two or three years from now.

One day, thirty years ago, in March, I saw a hundred Flying Fortresses in a clear sky, glistening like small silver flowers, flying in one long line, heralding liberation. A few years later, somewhere in Germany, I saw the same planes, partly covered with torn tarpaulins, their paint peeling, and the asphalt strip on which they stood covered with litter, empty cans and cigarette boxes, pieces of paper, and tall grass growing out of the deep cracks in the runway. The sky was gray, it was drizzling, nobody was looking at the Flying Fortresses whose past was glory in the sky. I asked an old man, squatting in a tin hut at the end of the runway, in shabby civilian clothes, unshaven, drawing on a cold pipe, what's going to happen to these planes? And he looked at me with colorless eyes, shrugged, and said, what do you expect? Scrap.

Perhaps the memory of the glory persists. Not always in war monuments and history books; perhaps, rather, in books of knight errantry. Or simply in human memory: in your skull and mine.

Durutti's Man

Publisher's note:

Originally composed in 1963, *Durutti's Man* was re-written during the summer of 1967, after Auerbach consulted Robert Graves for advice. The latter wrote to the author in September:

"I'm glad you approve of the *Durutti's Man* alterations… I think it's a very good story indeed." [underscoring in the original] —M.M.

Among the Spaniards who frequented the Café Catalan in the old harbor of Marseilles, Jose Fernandez kept aloof. He was not justified in doing so by reasons of social standing, or by any special qualities of his character or personality; in fact, he was very much like all the others, handicapped, if anything, by his scarred face, in which only one eye shone.

But Fernandez was a Durutti man—he had fought with the famous division and remained at heart a passionate and idealistic anarchist—and this gave him a feeling of superiority over his companions in exile, none of whom could lay claim to such a glorious past. Of course, outside this little group hardly anyone remembered now what or who Durutti was; in the apocalyptic spectacle of the Second World War, the memory of a small local civil war fought on the Iberian Peninsula was blotted out completely, its hundreds of thousands of victims forgotten now as people shed fresh tears over tens of millions slaughtered in a great conflict where the dimensions of misery and suffering surpassed all imagination. And what, after all, were Guernica and Madrid in comparison with the ashes of the cities of Europe, which even now, in 1948, were still warm and smoldering?

Fernandez was intelligent enough to understand this. He and his comrades bore their old grief and sorrow quietly and with dignity, they did not take part in the macabre discussions and quarrels which were so very much in vogue among certain people in these first after-war years, the subject being: who suffered most?

Still, sometimes he wondered how short human memory was, and how easily things were forgotten; for, after all, it was on the cities of his country, and nowhere else, that the planes were tested, those that would later reduce Europe to rubble.

Fernandez had only fought with Durutti for half a year, but he felt that those six months had contributed something permanent to the pattern of his behavior and thinking, something that had become an organic part of him and which, he felt, would stay with him until he died. He wore the memory of the Durutti days like others wear decorations and medals. But medals and distinctions were not known among the Durutti men, not even officers' badges.

Sometimes Fernandez calculated: there are hundreds of millions of people in the world, but only three or four thousand were fortunate enough to have fought with Durutti. I am one of them. With that awareness, a proud glint would light up in his right eye, his only one. The other was glass.

He had lost the eye, alas, not in the fight against the fascists, but on the barricades of Barcelona, in the dark days, when, within earshot of the Franco offensive, the defenders of the Republic fought each other; when the Durutti men were forced to resist the communist traitors, who, on orders from a foreign capital, wanted to disarm them.

Fernandez was evacuated from the hospital before his wounds had healed and followed the tragic track of thousands of refugees who would not accept fascist rule and preferred the bitter exile of France.

Once safe from fascist persecution and imprisoned by the friendly French in a concentration camp, Fernandez had the opportunity to examine his ruined face in a cracked mirror in the camp's lavatory. Initially, he was deeply shocked by what he saw: a very pale face, with two deep parallel scars running from the left cheekbone to the corner of the mouth, where the fragments of the bomb were clumsily extracted by the surgeon in Barcelona. But the worst was the place where his left eye had once been. In its place there was a half-healed cruel wound covered with moist, black, lashless eyelids. The scars and the closed eye gave his face a permanent sarcastic grin, though he felt far away from grinning.

In fact, he remained a somber man throughout the many years of misery that followed this first tragic confrontation with his face, and this permanent gloom, combined with a strange melancholic and bitter pride, became the most outstanding features of his personality. One would almost certainly use these adjectives, when asked at random to give one's first impression of Fernandez: gloomy, melancholic.

His compatriots reserved a certain special respect for this strong, grave, taciturn man; usually occupied by the hard struggle for daily bread, consumed by never-ending nostalgia. They had no time to make a thorough inquiry into each other's psychology. The Spaniards in Marseilles formed a very loose group; only memories linked them, and memories get worn out with time, like clothes. Occasionally they met, exchanging greetings and useful information: where and how one could earn a little money, or find a better living.

It was on one such occasion that Albino, the *calderettero*, told Fernandez to come on Monday evening to the Café Catalan, and to pass the word on to others he might encounter that there might be a well-paid job for quite a number of them, who, like Albino and Fernandez, were seamen by profession.

"What sort of job?" Fernandez asked.

But Albino could not tell him, and Fernandez thanked him for the information and said he would come, for certain.

This, he thought, came right in time, for in fact he had already been looking for a job for several days, after having been paid off a month earlier from a fishing cutter. They were smuggling cigarettes and other merchandise from Tangier; Fernandez quit the job when he discovered among the cargo some crates with well-oiled submachine guns. He did not know who was selling them, who the buyer was, but he did not like it, and paid off.

"You yellow?" jeered the skipper, handing him the money.

Fernandez did not find it necessary to answer; he gave the man one long look, whereupon the skipper's thin smile disappeared gradually, like a moon entering eclipse. Fernandez still had money to keep him for some time, but a job now became a rather desirable thing, and he was glad he had met Albino.

2.

The meeting took place in one of the back rooms of the Café Catalan. Had the faded and worn wallpaper been able and willing to speak, it would have been able to relate extremely interesting stories about all kinds of strange business negotiated there. It could have told about women, narcotics, stolen goods and forged papers and money that had changed hands; and, because, after all, all business and activities can be traced back to the human beings who pursue them and are reflected and conditioned in their thoughts, passions and personalities, the wallpaper could, narrating in a cracking, tired voice (old wallpaper always has a tired voice) present us a dazzling gallery of the strangest people ever encountered.

But the wallpaper in the back room of Café Catalan could not speak; it could only listen patiently, and that is what it did this time too: it listened to a speech delivered by a Greek gentleman to a group of Spanish refugees.

A Greek. Fernandez scrutinized him gloomily. Apparently a Greek must have his fingers in every illegal job. This one was very polite with them, taking, however, utmost care not to lose his air of aloofness; silently stressing by his dress, voice, and behavior that he belonged to another class than they, even if he was talking business with them. Lopez was with him, the mate, and Captain Gonzaga, a picture of a Spanish gentleman, a black tie glistening on a shirt of impeccable whiteness, a checkered suit beautifully ironed, as if taken out half an hour earlier from the window of a tailor's shop. The steel-gray, thin hair was combed carefully on his head, the mustache well trimmed.

A strange man, Captain Gonzaga, Fernandez thought. Whatever made him stick to the command of the Republican destroyer and then go into exile, instead of enjoying the easy life at home? In 1936, Gonzaga, a professional officer of the navy, and a gentleman, did not even hesitate for one moment—so it was related—when he decided to fight for the Republic. He had nothing to win on the Republican side; his natural place was with Franco. Nor did he have any illusions about who would win the war: he was quoted freely as saying that the Republic was lost. Some people in Barcelona whispered that Captain Gonzaga was a defeatist, a nasty and dangerous word at that time. But he fought bravely till the very end, and nothing could throw a shadow of suspicion or bring into doubt his unswerving loyalty to the Republic; as a commander of a destroyer he participated in the famous battle in which the cruiser *Jaime 11* was sunk. Why did Captain Gonzalez not join Franco's men at the outbreak of the war, or later, as many other officers did? He would probably have risen to the rank of a vice-admiral or so by now. He had a small estate near Seville, he was a gentleman, always properly dressed, shaved and combed, always aloof from the people under his command; yet he remained faithful, scuttled his ship, and went into exile with the others. Why?

Fernandez remembered now that Yera, a little, wiry fireman from Almeria, who seemed to know every bit of gossip in the country, once produced a story, according to which Captain Gonzaga had had a very romantic affair with a woman placed much higher than he in government service, in the Ministry of Defense in Madrid. Hopelessly in love, Yera had said. *Allors, cherchez la femme.* But Fernandez would not believe this; it could not be the real reason. Gonzaga remained an enigma for him. He turned his attention to the Greek.

"Men," he was saying, "Captain Gonzaga and Señor Lopez here have told me about your honesty and bravery. They assure me that better seamen cannot be found anywhere, and I trust their word implicitly. I want to entrust you with a delicate job, and utmost secrecy is necessary in order that it may succeed. Now you, as men of honor…"

He spoke for a quarter of an hour before buying drinks for everybody and giving them some money in advance. Fernandez shrugged. All he understood from it was that they were to sail a ship loaded with illegal immigrants past the British blockade to Palestine. Rodriguez, the lame donkeyman, asked what would happen if they were caught by the British. There was nothing to be afraid of, explained the Greek. The possibility of their being captured was extremely remote; should it, however, occur, by some unpredictable and impossible accident, an imprisonment of a maximum of several months in a British camp in Cyprus would be the worst that could be expected. No other questions were asked.

Fernandez signed on almost without hesitation. He wondered if the Greek knew that a man from the famous Durutti division was among the seaman whom he had just now employed. The pay was really generous and Fernandez had no objections to the job. He had been doing illegal things often enough; he had even developed a little private philosophy about it; the world was built and run on illegality. The first condition was that it had to be done on a large scale, only then would it work smoothly. The second trick was, of course, not to be on the losing side, and not to get caught. Take Franco: he had been highly illegal until he won, and there he was now, perfectly respectable and acceptable, recognized and given honor by all.

Then there was, naturally, the personal and delicate question of individual conscience. Either what one did did not interfere with one's quiet sleep at night, or it left one with an unclean, coppery taste in one's mouth. It depended, too, on how much imagination one had; if you sailed with smuggled cigarettes, for example, you could hardly imagine anybody wronged by it; on the other hand, crates with guns were not good, because one could easily see, after closing one's eye, dead people, mutilated corpses, tears and pain. Fernandez had seen enough of it in his life. In this business, paradoxically, one usually saw things after closing one's eye, especially if you *had* only one eye, he thought bitterly.

Now bringing people where they wanted to go anyhow could not do much harm to anybody, could it? He thought, and closed his eye; the coppery taste did not come to his mouth—the job seemed clean as far as he was concerned. These and similar problems occupied Fernandez's mind during the flight form Marseilles to Stockholm. The Greek had them transported by air: assuming that you are honest men, he had said, and that you'll do your job as befits men and Spaniards, I, too, am not saving on expenses to provide maximum comfort to you. This was new for all of them, never having flown before.

Fernandez looked through the window at what looked like huge exploded packages of cotton wool. Sometimes a shred of landscape could be seen through the holes in the clouds. Once during the flight he went to the men's room and found it agreeably clean, glistening and equipped with lots of gadgets he did not know. In the mirror on the wall he saw his grinning face, his dead glass eye, and the scars. For some reason, which he was not able to explain, he looked at his reflection longer than necessary, and all the time he looked at himself there was a queer dizziness in his head.

"I am flying over the clouds," he whispered. And again: "I am flying."

3.

It was bitter cold when they arrived in Stockholm. The cold was crisp, clear. He compared it with the frost of Austrian mountains on a winter morning, and decided quickly, no, there was no resemblance: a Mediterranean frost always bears a nucleus of hope for burning sunshine, a tiny hope, but so potent that one could not ignore it. Here, there was none of it; the rising sun—if it rose at all—would be high, shrunken, cold. Steam rose from their mouths with every breath. Hard, crisp snow covered the sidewalks.

At the hotel, the captain talked to them. "We are here legally; your seaman's books have been stamped by the police and your visas are in order. Besides, in this country, I have been told, one can live a hundred years without coming in contact with the police. But I want to remind you that our job should not get too much publicity, or even a little publicity; in our own interest, let's make ourselves as inconspicuous as possible. Avoid contact with authorities of any kind, and concentrate on your job. The best thing is not to get in touch with anybody. Journalists are another danger: one wrong word from one incautious mouth and we've lost our job and our money, let that be clear to you. And don't forget we are, after all, only a bunch of stateless men; we can be deported from here much easier than we have been admitted. Accommodation has been provided for you in a small yard, where we'll have to do the refitting of the ship; the less you leave that yard, the better for you. That's all. Tomorrow you'll see the ship."

One look at the ship, next morning, made them burst out laughing in unison. It was an eerie sight. She was an ancient excursion steamer with a huge funnel and a perpendicular stem, which for the best part of the past thirty years had been plying the lakes and fjords near Stockholm. Her plates were paper-thin; she seemed hardly fit to sail now even on an inland sea, let alone on an ocean voyage.

The Jews had purchased her—most probably with the help of the same Greek gentleman who had hired them in Marseilles—and wanted to refit her in such a way that she might accommodate no less than twelve hundred persons, and then sail to Palestine.

Fernandez was assigned to help building the accommodation in the ship's interior, and, along with several other men, was shown a huge pile of planks in the yard. They were instructed to build berths that were two feet wide, six feet in length and a foot high; this was the allowance per person. Fernandez felt embarrassed; this was hardly a place to live.

"We have to put twelve hundred people in this," said a tall Jew who seemed to be the boss of the entire enterprise.

Fernandez stood in silence for a full minute. Then he shrugged and went to work. But cutting and fitting the boards and planks he could not stop thinking of the people who were ready to sail in this ship. They must be strange, he thought. Or, just very ordinary: his mind produced a vision of the endless caravan of his own people, moving north toward the French border after the Republic collapsed. He thought there must be something in it, something more than a casual glance can take in. Call it human folly, something absolutely unpredictable that makes people travel, sends them wandering, not always in search of food, to the confusion and despair of those who guard frontiers, issue laws, forbid trespassing and impose heavy penalties for violating those laws. A deep furrow creased Fernandez's brow from intense thinking, and when a bunk was ready and he was starting to work on another one he would whisper to himself: I wonder who will sleep here?

In the evenings he would take a stroll. The streets were bright with the cold light of neon and strong arch-lights, glistening with the shining enamel of cars, with huge glass-plated shops, bars and restaurants, clean and white with snow that did not melt; clouds of frozen breath escaped from the mouths and nostrils of passersby.

He noticed that they were clad in solid, warm clothes, they had serene, satisfied faces, and neither hunger, nor war, nor great suffering had left their traces on them.

To Fernandez they looked very innocent, pure.

He noticed, that most 'bars' were places where only milk was served in various forms; later, he was told that there was a partial prohibition on alcohol in this country, that a bottle or so of spirits was issued monthly to every adult over twenty six. Wine was not prohibited, but was so expensive that only the rich could afford it. The wholesome food, plenty of milk, a clever and efficient government, and a great amount of social security and freedom made the Swedish people happy, he was told; a whore was not to be seen on the streets.

They are very much like babies, he thought, and felt compassion for them. They were ignorant of what passion was, or what a man with a shattered face felt; if ever brought in on the secret they would die from the very shock of discovery. He pitied them in their quiet luxury, in their order, in their efficiency and health.

Something is wrong here, he mumbled under his nose, walking through the bright streets, feeling decidedly uneasy in these surroundings. Weren't they bored to death? The people and the towns he knew were different: Barcelona, Madrid, Seville, Marseilles, Tangiers, various harbors of the Mediterranean he had visited before the war. These places were seething with life, day or night, and their inhabitants drank, made love, hated, fought, laughed, cried—most of these activities, if not all of them, carried out in public, on the street. In stark contrast, here they seemed to be subjected to only the mildest of feelings: a polite smile instead of hearty laughter, sympathy instead of love, a silent disapproval instead of hate.

Milk instead of wine.

Fernandez shook his head; something was wrong here.

And apparently, something was. At this time a very strange thing happened in Stockholm. On a Sunday evening, a small bomb exploded in the waiting hall of the Central Railway Station. Nobody was hurt, and no damage resulted, but in a town in which the loudest noise heard during the last hundred years was the backfiring of a car engine, this was something. The newspapers had their headlines, the police investigated, with no result: nobody was arrested. At the end of the week the excitement was dying down, and the forthcoming match between Norway and Sweden occupied the front pages of the papers. Then, again on Sunday, another bomb exploded in a post office. This time, two people were slightly injured and the tension in Stockholm rose sky-high. It would be a gross understatement to say that crime had been totally unknown till then: there were thefts, some murders—mostly with a sexual background, suicides. All these statistics compared favorably with other big European cities. They were explicable. The motives of the crimes were greed, lust, melancholy, sex. But the average Swede could not grasp why anybody would place bombs in public places. Meanwhile, only the newspapers profited; they knew well how to take advantage of the Sunday bombings.

IS OUR POLICE FORCE INEFFECTIVE? asked one paper in two-inch lettering across the front page. MADMAN, ANARCHIST,

FOREIGN AGENT? asked another. WHO IS THE MYSTERIOUS SUNDAY SABOTEUR? WHERE WILL THE NEXT BOMB EXPLODE?

It exploded in a telephone booth in one of the beautiful squares of the town, destroying it completely. No victims.

The citizens of Stockholm were stunned. The chief of police asked the public to help in the search for the dangerous lunatic; every suspicious person, especially those carrying packages on Sunday, should be reported immediately to the nearest police station. Armed patrols were increased. Still, next Sunday, another bomb exploded, and a week later, another.

4.

Fernandez and his colleagues in the small shipyard knew nothing of it. They were busy, conscientiously continuing their work of refitting the funny, impossible excursion steamer and preparing it for her first and last sea voyage; she was not intended to do more than this trip, the boss told them. He appeared three or four times weekly in the yard, exchanging a few words with the engineers and occasionally with Captain Gonzaga. He usually then made an inspection of the ship, stopping for long minutes in one place, as if day-dreaming, or walking slowly like a sleepwalker, the worried, melancholy look never disappearing from his face. Then he would nod several times and sigh deeply, as if he wanted to say this is it, alas, and nothing can be done about it.

Fernandez had a feeling of sympathy for this tall man with sloping shoulders, and he always had to fight the impulse to approach him and say, "Cheer up, comrade, things are not so black as they seem to be. I've seen worse ships than this sailing the sea."

But he never did; after all, who could say what was really troubling the man?

The day of sailing seemed near. According to the numbers painted in red over every bunk, she could accommodate 1175 passengers. Surveying his work, Fernandez hoped the voyage would not last long, for the interior of this ship resembled closely that of a slave ship, the model of which he had seen once in the Nautical Museum in Marseilles.

One day, bunkers arrived, several trucks with coal, and the next day a gentleman brought a Panamanian flag, which the bosun promptly hoisted on the flag post astern, without unnecessary ceremony, in quite the same way he hung his warm underwear to dry after washing.

That evening, during the meal in the crew's mess, Fernandez heard that they were supposed to sail the following Monday. Then he started on his daily stroll.

It occurred to him that he might try to buy a French newspaper. In fact he was feeling a little ashamed that he could live, like the others, for more than a month without an inkling of what was going on in the world. A foreign paper could surely be obtained at the Central Railway Station, and Fernandez moved slowly in that direction through the transparent, violet dusk. Halfway there, at a busy crossing of a main street, he saw a large newspaper stand. Its walls were covered with journals, magazines and papers from around the world. He hesitated; if he bought his paper here, he could return to the ship, it would shorten his walk by an hour. But Fernandez did not want to save time, he had too much of it. He enjoyed his walks, unless his feet were too cold. Standing on the corner and hesitating, he caught a glimpse of a woman's head among the papers. He came up nearer. The girl, sitting inside, lifted her head and smiled at him. Fernandez smiled back: she was very young, she had fair, glistening hair, merry eyes and a short nose. She wore a yellow sweater and looked very clean and fresh, as if she had, that very moment, stepped out of a bath. She said something in Swedish and Fernandez shrugged helplessly, and said, in French, "I want a French newspaper." He felt that, incredibly, he was blushing. She looked up at him, concentrating, trying to understand. Several people approached, bought local newspapers, and Fernandez pointed hastily with his finger at *Le Monde*. She leaned out of the window, unhooked it and gave it to him. She accepted a paper note he handed her (he had no idea how much it would cost here), and returned him some coins. Fernandez lifted his hat and left, carrying his paper.

He felt strangely contented, as if he had succeeded in some important enterprise. A minute later he stopped to scold himself: like a little boy, upon my honor! And what makes you so glad, you idiot? He was ashamed to admit to himself that it had been a long, long time since a human smile had been directed at him, intentionally.

"I will never return to this place," he said aloud, to punish himself. "If you want a paper, buy it at the station."

Next evening he went directly, and without hesitation, to the kiosk, to buy *Le Monde.*

On the third day she asked him if he was a Frenchman—that much he understood—and he denied it proudly, telling her, no, a Spaniard. España, he repeated a few times, pointing at himself, and then he added: But not Franco. Vive la Republique! And the blonde girl burst out in such lovely, warm laughter, and gave him a smile of such radiance that he expected the snow on the pavement around the kiosk to melt right away. But the frost was strong and the snow did not melt. Fernandez pondered whether he should tell her that he was one of the Durutti men: that would earn him new respect in her eyes. The doubt never crossed his mind that she might never have heard the name, or that she might not have known there had been a civil war in Spain ten years earlier. In his shyness, he decided not to mention his glorious past for the time being. There would be time for that later. At that thought he stopped, catching his breath with a hiss, realizing that he was actually unconsciously planning further encounters with the blonde girl from the newspaper kiosk.

Yet on his way back to the ship he stopped in a bookshop and purchased a booklet of Swedish-French dialogues. Also, that very evening, Fernandez locked the door of his tiny cabin and looked in the mirror for a long time, studying his face and wondering how repulsive it made him to people. In any case, he personally had grown accustomed to it.

On Saturday night, the Jewish boss arrived with two other men, whom Fernandez had never seen before. They made a minute inspection of the ship, assuring themselves that everything was in order. Then it was officially announced that they were to sail on Monday, at eight o'clock in the morning, for Marseilles. The first thought that crossed Fernandez's mind was: two evenings more, and he had so much to tell her!

But when he saw her a couple of hours later, he discovered that the barrier of language between them made close contact all but impossible. With the help of his booklet he stammered a few words, blushing terribly all the time. She understood what he said, but laughed incessantly, probably because of his pronunciation; her head, tossed backward in a paroxysm of laughter, with golden hair flowing in waves over her shoulders, was the loveliest sight Fernandez had ever seen in his life. He, of course, could not understand her answers. He asked her when she finished work, and if she would go for a walk with him afterward. She listened, her mouth half open, then burst out in laughter again.

"No, no," she said. "I work late."

"I shall wait, even till morning."

"No, no, I cannot do this."

"And tomorrow?"

"No, no," she said, and never stopped laughing, like mad.

It occurred to him that she might be afraid of him. Laboriously, he started looking for the necessary words in his booklet.

"I am a seaman," he said. "But I am an honest man. Very honest. An anarchist. Understand?"

She dried the tears from her lovely eyes, and shook her head. "No. No, not understand."

Anyhow, he was glad she had stopped laughing at last. Perhaps she was not laughing at his pronunciation, perhaps she laughed because of his face.

"Good bye," he said. "I am sailing in two days. But I will come tomorrow to say goodbye to you. And then, I will return one day." She was serious now, more serious than he had ever seen her before.

"Good," she said. "Good. Come tomorrow. But sure?"

5.

Roses are very expensive in Stockholm in winter, and not every florist kept them in that season. Fernandez ran through all the main streets, until, finally, he found what he wanted, in an exclusive hotel shop.

"Roses," he said. "Red."

"How many?" the women asked, and scrutinized him with an unfriendly look.

"Plenty."

"They are two krones apiece." She raised two fingers to make him understand.

"I did not ask you how much they are," snapped Fernandez in Spanish, and added in French: "That's all right. Wrap them well."

"No," he added, watching her arrange the flowers. "Close the upper end of it as well." It would be silly to walk with these flowers through the streets, better if they looked like an ordinary package.

After emptying his wallet, Fernandez emerged from the florist's carrying something that roughly resembled a well-wrapped oversized mandolin.

He did not know yet what he'd say to the girl in the kiosk; his thoughts were confused. Dense snow started falling from the black sky, and he hurried through the whirl of the white flakes, brushing away, from time to time, from his brow and lashes a flake that momentarily obscured his vision. He had a strange feeling of unreality, walking in the snowstorm, clutching the flowers in his right hand, and the misty swirl of snow round the street lamps added to this feeling. They'll wither in this frost, he thought, and increased his pace.

The resemblance to a dream sequence increased as he drew nearer to the kiosk. She would be there, waiting for him. What would she say when she opened the package with her long, trembling fingers?

He crossed the street, and entered the cone of light that flew from the window of the kiosk. He caught a glimpse of golden hair and stopped, to make the wonderful feeling last longer. Thus hypnotized,

Fernandez did not even see who the two pairs of strong arms that grabbed him brutally from both sides belonged to. He turned his head violently and struggled to free himself, but in vain. The men dragged him toward the black car that waited nearby, its engine running. He wrestled heroically while a third man removed the flowers. Even in the absolute surprise of the assault, Fernandez noticed that he did it in a strange way, not touching the package at all, but twisting his hand to the point of breaking it, till his fingers were forced by the intense pain to loosen their grip.

In one terrifying fraction of a second, he saw the girl leaning out from the window. In her eyes, in her face, there was no surprise, no compassion or sorrow, but an absolute lack of expression, as if she were looking at a customer asking her for a paper. He opened his mouth to shout, to call her name, and then he remembered that he did not know her name. She drew her head back inside, still no sign of recognition on her face, and only then something snapped in his will to resist, and the policemen pushed him effortlessly into the car. It started moving immediately, with great speed, the siren howling, the illuminated blue letters POLICE visible clearly even through the curtain of dense snow.

The man sitting near the driver turned, shone an electric torch straight into Fernandez's face, then directed it at the package of flowers resting on the third policeman's lap, and said, "If it isn't him, my name is not Lindquist. This time we've caught him."

The man at the desk tapped its black surface with his fingers, smiled wryly, and said, "Fine, Inspector, that's it. You are lucky this man is what he is: a stateless seaman. He cannot even complain, you understand—no consulate, no embassy. I doubt if there is anybody at all who cares if he is under arrest or not. Well, you can just tell him, sorry old chap, it was a mistake, and send him on his way."

"I'd like to smash his bloody face," Lindquist grinned comically. "He ruined my chance of becoming famous."

The man at the desk laughed.

"Don't make it uglier than it is. It was his face, mostly, that brought him all the trouble."

Lindquist nodded sadly.

"His face, the package, but, above all that silly goose from the kiosk with her idiotic babbling about anarchists; when she told her story here yesterday, even you were almost convinced we'd got the Sunday Saboteur."

"I guess the roses were intended for her; they must have cost him a fortune."

A policeman entered, carrying a tray. On it was a cup of coffee, rolls, butter and jam, and a packet of cigarettes. He put it on the table before Fernandez, who sat there, like a statue, motionless.

The three men observed him with interest.

"Eat," the chief inspector said. "That's your breakfast."

There was no sign that Fernandez perceived what he saw or what he heard.

"Eat," Lindquist repeated. He was a big, bulky man with a broad face, and he really felt a bit sorry for Fernandez. "Have your breakfast, and then you can go. It was a mistake, we are sorry, we had to keep you here overnight. Now you can go. You are a free man. Libre, you understand?"

Fernandez blinked with his only eye and got up.

"No breakfast? No eat?" asked the chief inspector.

Fernandez turned to the door.

"Wait a minute!" Lindquist said. "Wait. Here are your things, take them."

Fernandez returned to the desk and collected what they had taken away from him in the evening: cigarettes, a box of matches, his seaman's book, a handkerchief, a pocket comb, the belt from his trousers and a faded, worn, military document, which they had not bothered to study thoroughly enough to discover, in the right lower corner, the signature of the division commander, Durutti.

Without saying a word, he turned once more to the door and went out.

Whatever made Captain Gonzaga make his decision was a great puzzle for Fernandez. No doubt, he thought, the men who had arrested him an evening before must have telephoned from the police station, after having assured themselves that his papers were in order and that he was not the man they were after. The address of the yard and the name of the ship were in his seaman's book.

But, according to tradition, to reason, to Fernandez's experience, Captain Gonzaga should have sailed at the fixed time without giving a damn about a miserable sailor who had missed his ship. He could and should have sailed, and he could have completed his crew easily at the first port of call. Beachcombers, stranded seamen, and bums of every kind were the easiest article, obtainable in any port.

The fact was, he had waited for Fernandez without even knowing if he would finally appear. How long had he intended to wait for him?

Fernandez thought about this while standing in front of the captain, who sat behind his desk delivering a long speech. The two officers were also present, sitting to the left of the desk, Lopez playing with his cigarette holder, the second mate looking stubbornly at his shoes. A Swedish frontier police official sat patiently on the right side, waiting till the captain had finished and he could put the official stamp on the ship's papers and let it sail to hell. And beside the captain stood the tall Jew, with the usual, sad expression on his face. All of them listened—or pretended to listen—to the captain's moralizing tirade against Fernandez. It was a long speech delivered in beautiful language, and he had time to think of various problems. No doubt it was strange of Captain Gonzaga to have waited for him, and now to talk for half an hour. But he had behaved strangely before, and Fernandez remembered wondering in Marseilles what had made captain Gonzaga stick to the Republic.

Perhaps, Fernandez thought, the Jew had persuaded him to wait. The Jew had a good face, though sad.

Fernandez sighed, and stepped from foot to foot. The speech seemed to draw to an end, the captain's voice rising now.

"You realize, of course, that you brought dishonor and disgrace

on us all through your idiotic and thoughtless behavior. "Hombre"—
the captain pounded his fist on the table—"how many times have
you been told *not* to get mixed up with the police here, under any
circumstances? How many times?"

How strangely people act and react, Fernandez thought. You
can live a thousand years and you won't know what makes them
really tick.

"Answer, hombre! Have you nothing to say? Absolutely nothing?
They said you were kept at the police station, that you were arrested
by mistake. What mistake, for Christ's sake? Explain!"

Fernandez sighed. The captain was not really angry, he knew.
He was making all this noise for the benefit of the others, and, probably, to maintain his reputation as a tough commander.

"Fernandez! Wake up! Answer! Have you nothing to say?"

Fernandez looked through the window of the cabin; snow was
still falling. He licked his lips.

"No, señor," he said finally, with conviction. "Nothing to say.
No, señor."

At sea, January, 1963

A Short Trip with Domenico Scarlatti and Elvis Presley from Amsterdam to Paris

1. An Explanation about Madness

"The real problem," Izi said, "is to convince them that we have every right to make alterations in these ships. They are our ships, aren't they?"

My real problem, Stephen thought, is to preserve sanity. Or to fend off madness. Or, at least, to prevent them from noticing it.

"We have to push it through forcefully," continued Izi, "in Paris, now."

He, for example, would be the last one to notice madness, Stephen thought, unless I stop resisting and give in to an intense urge to clasp my hands in front of me like a cradle and make a perfect headstand, yoga-style.

Even then, he'd look at me in bewilderment, confused, and say, reproachfully, why are you standing on your head, Stephen? People are looking at you! Then he'd try to put me down, gently, back on my feet. No, the practical approach: first put him on his feet so that he looks like everybody else, with his head up and his legs down, then ask him what made him stand on his head.

Izi was suspicious with Stephen, uncertain, cautious.

"And this is the real problem," Izi repeated.

Sanity and madness, that's the real problem, Stephen thought, or, normality and madness. Because, I, so far, have no proof at all that what they call normal behavior is equivalent to sanity. But his problem, with which he had been living for twenty years, was only how to conceal his madness.

Stephen could consider himself successful. Nobody would say categorically that he was mad: a few inquisitive ones, those who were more watchful or observant, would suspect some slight deviation from normal standards, but nothing more serious than being an outsider. So what? After all, nowadays so many nonconformists were running around, not to mention the young ones with long hair. Not enough to put one before a Court of Inquisition, to crucify, or to burn at the stake. Ha! Not even enough to put one in a mental institution, he thought with real pride. A success, an achievement, to be able to keep up a façade like this, in spite of the huge effort it required. Sometimes it made him very tired.

Just imagine what would happen if, sitting at a conference table, in some shiny office—he was visiting many offices lately, and participating in several meetings with pathologically normal people—just imagine, what would happen if he bowed his head, snapped open the little door in his forehead with a click, and poured out its contents onto the table!

He chuckled, and Izi, who was drumming his fingers on the table, looked up with sleepy eyes. They would jump up in panic, turning over their chairs, leaving their papers, rushing to the door, jamming it in wild flight, in a desperate attempt to escape from the crawling, sparkling, crackling, explosive heap on the table.

They were sitting in pale Dutch sunshine on the Rokin, in an outdoor café, and Izi was planning the journey to Paris, where the next meeting was scheduled in a couple of days, while Stephen was alternatively ogling the girls passing by and looking at the clouds piling up over the roofs. In between digesting these two visual impressions he was thinking about what Izi was thinking of him. He must be mistrusting, and a little bit scared, too, sensing instinctively that there was more of Stephen than came to the surface; something like an iceberg, three-fifths submerged. But it must be only a sensation, no real awareness or understanding. Izi was indeed not too happy when they appointed Stephen as his partner and companion in this deal, but then he was assured that Stephen was an excellent engineer, and his strangeness had nothing to do with his professional qualities. When you are ordering ships abroad for millions of dollars you need somebody who knows a little about a ship's machinery.

As to the girls, one in ten had something special, by the grace of God, and unidentifiable: whether it was the smooth slimness of leg, the softness of shoulders, or the celestial harmony of the line between the ear and the chin, a perfection of the geometrical form up to that point where it stops being geometrical and starts being an artistic concept, he could not tell. But one out of ten girls had it.

The remaining nine were scanned furtively, and the resulting saving in time put to good use watching the yellow cumuli; soft, huge pillows over the pointed roofs of Amsterdam's seventeenth-century buildings.

They were developing from the inside out, on the same principle on which the petals of a rose opened: the movement out and generally upward, accompanied simultaneously by a change of colors, from dark-gray to light yellow, but the ripeness was unaffected by the pastel tint of the color. Always a full body of flesh to that kind of cloud, no matter how delicate the color. Now there were also others, of course, wisps of cloud, shreds, torn off, detached and independent of the main body.

He lowered his eyes, slid them quickly over the green dress and round hips of a passing girl to the pillar plastered with advertisements opposite. Tonight: Horowitz playing Scarlatti. A bit lower, a pale green, flat, two-dimensional face with long sideburns and an open mouth with foot-high black letters across: E L V I S.

"There is no reason why we shouldn't go by train this time," said Izi. "We've got plenty of time."

"Sure. Why shouldn't we go by train? I've gotten sort of tired of flying."

"That's it." Izi was almost happy: his companion was making normal conversation. "They've got a fantastically comfortable train, I've heard."

"Yes. The Trans European Express, the T.E.E. they call it. Let's take it."

"Probably cheaper than the plane, too."

It was cheaper: it was low and red. Stephen was scared of it at first. The immobility and silence frightened him, because trains should be associated with hissing steam, huge wheels and rods and pistons as yet unmoving but pregnant with latent power or hidden fury. Black oil glistening on all parts, a harnessed beast waiting for the moment of release.

Not this train: a sleek low form of red metal, absolutely silent and dead. It looked as if it would never move; it looked like a child's wooden toy. No wheels were to be seen. And when Stephen and Izi were sitting in comfortable armchairs, facing each other, the train started moving with such a gentle motion that they did not notice it at all during the first few seconds: no whistle, no slamming of doors, no tension, no excitement. Simply, the newspaper stand on the platform started sliding backwards. The big electric clock, a few people, all seen through the huge window, moving backwards. No rambling of the wheels on the rails, no droning of the locomotive.

2. Travelling Through a Tunnel: *Andante Moderato—Allegro—Andante.*

After a while, when the black of the tunnel had surrounded them completely, Stephen opened his eyes wider and saw the big fat cumulus spilling over the triangular roof of an old house in Amsterdam, the front of the house decorated with gilded ornaments, and a deep, dark chasm exactly in the center of the cloud. The girl in the green dress stood in the middle of Elvis' face: it looked as if she were emerging from his open mouth with fleshy lips. The house, tall and slim, shrank under the weight of the cloud, but Elvis grew perceptibly larger. Small electric bulbs placed at intervals on the walls of the tunnel projected Izi's mobile face for a fraction of a second. Horowitz started playing Scarlatti's sonatas. The red T.E.E. shot out from the darkness into dazzling daylight: the voyage Amsterdam—Brussels—Paris had started.

Elvis, as aesthetic impressions go, was definitely and irrevocably ugly. Lucky for him that the passing girls filled the huge cavernous cavity of his mouth, for even this mouth was more like a gaping wound than a normal orifice. The girls were chatting, smiling, some bashfully, some insolently, and a few of them, provocatively. Between Stephen and Izi, a snowfield: a table covered with white cloth; discreetly interwoven in the fabric, barely visible in the pattern, the letters T.E.E. Cheaper than the plane. Slower, but cheaper and more comfortable.

"Four hours," said Izi.

It was running very smoothly, with such great speed that it did not seem to move at all. The landscape was running backwards, the flat endless fields of Holland and Belgium, canals, barges, solitary and pathetic lonely windmills.

"They'll put it that way," Izi said, "to show you what a great favor they're doing us. What the hell, we've paid for it, these are our ships, and we can have them the way we like them, eh, Stephen?"

"Yes," Stephen said.

"As I told this guy in Amsterdam, listen, mister, don't teach me stability please. I'll show you how you can build them without that raised quarterdeck, I told him."

A ship with a raised quarterdeck does look a little like a hunchback, that's true. But that doesn't really make any difference, except from the aesthetic point of view.

"We can also save on other things: you don't really need that fresh water generator in your engine room, do you?"

"I cancelled it," Stephen said, and disappeared.

For, finally, the wheels made the kind of music and rhythm he had been waiting for, and he was greatly absorbed in the Sonata in D Major. Also, he disappeared from the conversation about the fresh water generator, because he was now Alexander Dubcek, deep in discussion with Husak.

"There is only one thing against you, comrade Dubcek," said the other man, without raising his voice. "You have betrayed the Revolution, that is all."

He did not actually smile, but there was an indication, a hint, that an ironic smile would flower now, easily, behind the steel-rimmed glasses.

In contrast, Dubcek's smile came spontaneously, and he did not try to hide it. "Gustav," he answered, not trying to hurt the man, though he knew the other disliked being called by his first name except by the closest members of his family; he called him Gustav because he had known him for so long and because there was a slight trace of maliciousness in Stephen after all.

"Gustav," he answered, "the statement you have directed at me has been uttered innumerable times throughout human history. It has been repeated so many times that it would be deprived of any meaning had it had any meaning in the beginning. But it did not. I can only remember one instance when it was justified, more or less: Durutti told Walter, in 1939, in Barcelona, 'You have betrayed the Revolution, comrade.'"

Barcelona was a sunny place: huge, and harsh, and raw, with paralyzing, dry heat lying on it like a thick slab of glass.

"Ever been to Barcelona, Izi?"

Izi looked up with small eyes and was again suspicious. He could not help being suspicious when talking with Stephen.

He nodded. "Yes, why?"

"Nothing, just thinking about Barcelona."

Izi relaxed a little bit, enough to allow himself a smile. Husak smiled, too.

"I know what they are saying about me. But everything that is going on here and now, in this country, and everything that has happened to you personally is the result of your betrayal of the Revolution," he said. Wiping off the smile, so that his face changed instantly into one of an ascetic, a state prosecutor, or a prophet, he added severely: "Not that it makes the slightest difference in human history, what happens personally to Alexander Dubcek."

"Perhaps it makes a difference to the human condition?"

"The human condition is an integral part of human history."

"Exactly the contrary!"

"That is the basic issue; that's where all your misconceptions originated."

"We discharged bagged cement in Barcelona," Izi recollected, "and stayed there for three days. I went to see the bullfight, it was fun."

Madness may not occur suddenly, like an explosion. Sometimes it grows gradually, perceptibly, through a certain period of time, an incubation period: in this particular case, let's say, five years. It's only that the awareness of it hits one as a sudden discovery, and from that point on one tries to fight it, or to hide it. He had chosen to hide.

He'd seen the bullfight there, and found it fun. The bull—massive, solid, though from the distance it was only a black spot—on legs like steel springs, unpredictable and immensely evil, and the multicolored matador performing a bizarre dance around the beast. Izi found it fun, and Stephen forgave him, riding on a high wave of magnanimity.

3. Suspension of Qualification

From the beginning of this shipping business they had spent quite a lot of time together. Izi said once, "All the philosophy I need in life is supplied to me in absolutely sufficient quantity and quality by the Levite."

After remembering that, it was easy to forgive him that funny sweating bull in Barcelona, with bloodshot eyes and flies buzzing around its wet hide.

Late in his life, Stephen suspended the qualifying of other people; in other words, he refused to say: this is a clever man, and that a stupid one. He discovered that judging, or dividing in categories, was only a game of linguistics, devoid of meaning. He was proud of this discovery, because he had made it long before he ever heard the name Wittgenstein.

Fat, grazing cows were moving backwards behind the windows of the train, without raising their heads.

"…to assure the proper functioning of everybody's mind."

It should be stated that way, and warranted, like in a Bill of Rights, or a Constitution, or a Covenant.

Yes, very nice wording this, but what would the parties be to such an agreement? Stephen could only see one, pathetically inadequate to sign covenants, or agreements, always desperately searching for the second partner for signatures, for assurances, so that the pact could be valid. He shook his head sadly: Alexander Dubcek had no more chance than a snowball in hell. He returned from Dubcek back to his present physical position, and felt sorry that Dubcek was not sitting now in the comfortable compartment of the swiftly running Trans-European Express, on its way from Amsterdam to Paris-Nord: he would be sitting quietly, staring through the window, or, perhaps, reading a paper. But there, in the part of world in which he was living now, it became more and more common practice to simply declare a man insane, and consequently to put him in an asylum, which precluded any chance of travelling. It was more decent, more elegant, and more rational than shooting, which they practiced before, and just as effective.

A man in an insane asylum was as harmless as a dead one.

Three cheers for normal men!

Since he had suspended judgment, he would never qualify Izi as a stupid man. There were no doubt certain deficiencies in the workings of his mind, but all well within the limits warranted in the nonexistent Covenant, under the paragraph in which "the proper functioning of everybody's mind" was solemnly promised. Together with other promises, naturally.

You always wanted to sign, he said to himself, to Alexander, but there is no partner to such agreements. Why the whole future was built on men like Izi; standardization, normality were the condition sine qua non of the very existence of the human race; cases like Stephen's could be the result of a biological mutation following an atomic explosion. Or, the result of a brain tumor. How could he know he didn't have one? Blurring of vision would be one of the first symptoms, it said in a popular medical book.

If such was the case, he was safe still. Nothing of blurring with him, for sure. But what about distortion of vision? Yes, that distortion which he preferred to call madness for lack of better definition, and which on the one hand permitted him to see things Izi was seeing, and often in the same way (they agreed on many technological and financial matters concerning the construction of ships), but also to see much more, a lot more, simultaneously or consequently. That was the point.

This conversation took place in a modestly furnished room of Alexander's flat in Prague, a green table lamp spreading soft light on their faces, and on the shelves crammed with books, mostly paperbacks. On the lowest shelf, near the radio, stood a cheap plaster replica of Nike of Samothrace, six inches high. They were selling these copies outside the Louvre, Stephen now recalled, and at the same moment could smell the scent of falling wet leaves, the smell of autumn. As for Scarlatti, the little Sonata in A Major fit into it like a suddenly-found piece in a jigsaw puzzle.

This Nike, headless and maimed, was all ready to fly at the top of the wide staircase, with a terrible rush of huge wings, he remembered.

Avoiding the face of the man opposite him, which suddenly became unbearable, Alexander rested his eyes frequently on the little replica: not that it could bring him much respite, the tiny plaster thing; he really was lost.

4. *Sonata in A Major*

Once more saddened by Dubcek, and riding this fake noiseless express train with huge windows, through which he could leisurely observe things running backwards—fields, animals, windmills, canals, houses, and people, all running backwards, and disappearing, swallowed by nothingness—Stephen was more relaxed now. His companion, Izi the sea-captain, devoted himself to the absurd pastime of reading a newspaper, which made Stephen almost happy, in spite of the persistent melancholy of Dubcek.

Time was rushing backwards, together with all those other things, but he did not worry, he knew from previous experience it would stop somewhere and spill you out, such things are almost inevitable with you, aren't they?

But the woman, whose turn was coming now, was not. In fact the last thing you could say about her was that she was conventional: in fact, she was extremely unusual. A very rare woman.

The first storm of the year, hatched out in the enormous heat of several *khamsin* days, was gathering on the fringes of the village, and kept creeping around it from all sides, groaning softly, rambling, flashing noiseless bursts of light: from the south, over to the west, to the north, and again from the south, like a jungle animal, lurking in darkness, circling its victim before striking, before the lethal jump.

Right above, the night sky was still clear and serene, but this pool of velvety dark-blue was shrinking steadily.

Listening to the voices of the coming storm, they lay silent, prone, for a long time. Only when the first heavy drops fell on the roof, they sighed, almost in the same moment, a deep sigh of relief.

Then the first gust of wind hit the house, and the woman spoke.

5. In Darkness Where the Skyscrapers Are

"I forgot to tell you," she said, "that I love you: in heartlessness, in lowness, in daylight, and in the darkness. I love you."

Then, "Hold my breast," she whispered, in the warm, soft darkness saturated with her scent, the mixture of her perfume and the natural smell of her body. "Hold it," she said, and he, obediently, cupped her right breast in his extended hand, and thought, what could it be to her, what could it mean lying like this, all cuddled and glued to him. What is it, he wondered. Security? Tenderness? Sex? Perhaps animal, biological, atavistic things, deeper than sex and tenderness.

The woman almost purred, like a cat held on your lap in front of an open fire, stroked and caressed.

The night went on and the storm raved and howled outside, shaking the fragile windows and doors of the building. Squalls came and went, heavy sharp drops hitting the roof and splashing in puddles. But Time was cheated. He once looked at his watch (he held the breast with the other hand) and the phosphorescent dial showed ten minutes past two; four hours later it was half past two; and still later—an eternity later—it was three o'clock. That was it then, he laughed silently, it was so simple no one had ever discovered it before, this stone of wisdom, the Great Silly Mystery. It was absurd in its simplicity, shedding the chains of time, the rough area around the nipple and the nipple itself, alternatively soft like a petal, or stiff and taut, the woman purring noiselessly in the warm, scented darkness.

5a. Variations on a Theme

Holding one round breast in his hand, and suspended in timelessness, he now remembered the nights in Ravenna: immense and low, blood-red from the glow of burning gases blown out from invisible smoke stacks, huge, fierce commas of fire, trembling and bright, commas of fire in the invisible print of night. The raw pungent smell of refineries and petrol industries; flashes of light and fire, an ideal stage-set of decorations for a modern Macbeth. And the witches? Of course, there were witches, and harpies, and furies, but he was keeping them back now, they could do nothing to him now; he was momentarily immune.

Holding—with real piety now, as one holds a holy relic—this round breast, barely touching it, he was inside the churches of Ravenna, and the guide was pointing with his flashlight at the glistening mosaic, somewhere in the high, suspended cupola. This cupola was, in fact,—it occurred to him suddenly—like the breast he held, but experienced from inside, with somebody's flashlight illuminating the mosaics. These were gold and dark-blue, in some parts gold predominating, in others dark-blue prevailing, very much like the Passacaglia in C Minor. Yes, certainly like this. The guide, an old, tiny, wizened man, played with his electric torch, the Passacaglia on the mosaic representing Christ as a shepherd with a lamb in his arm. The light spot moved from Christ's huge liquid eye to his golden crown—but all the time on the inside of the cupola, of the church's curved, convex ceiling—and then returned to the lowest registers of the illuminative deep, deep blue of the night sky. Serene night, surrounding Christ and his lamb in a Ravenna church, flames of the petro-industrial plants raging outside. And he, holding the round, smooth, soft breast in his hand moved his fingers an inch down, to the spot where the curvature started, where this miraculous globe grew out from the flatness of the skin.

He felt the rhythm, the pulsating of blood under the woman's skin: regular, reassuring. Gusts of wind and rain were coming, wild, unexpected: blasts of fury, bordering on madness. But the tiny vein on her temple (he touched it experimentally with his lips) lived its own, steady beat. Constant, unchanging.

For a while he continued in that closed, solid ring of awareness, of realities: the cupped breast, night over the port area in Ravenna, the mosaic in the church, Christ's eye, the Passacaglia, pulsating blood. A solid ring, suspended firmly in the storm outside. "Darling," he said, "we shouldn't quarrel about whether Scarlatti should be played this way or not. You'd say, this is not Chopin, it's Scarlatti. Sure, Horowitz was a great artist, nobody would question it, but he shouldn't play Scarlatti this way, all this pedal work. Banal, that's what it is, you'd say, that's how things become banal." She kept silent, and he left the reassuring, safe abode of a defined circle of thought, and moved recklessly on.

About quasars and pulsars, mysterious sources of energy, in the universe, hundreds of thousands of light years distant from here, emitting radio waves, pulsating, spreading them in all directions: sometimes caught on the parabolic antennae people have erected here.

The vastness of it, and the sudden perception of his mind's limitations, did not scare him. He looked left and down, at the perfect curvature of the breast, at the lovely roundness of it, the little globe, the substance of it, smooth, satin-smooth, skin and nipple, so lovely; and then back to the quasars. The poverty of the mind was evident, one need not go out to the universe to make oneself sure of it; already the failure to realize what was a universe, without a beginning or an end, and the lameness of the human thinking machine: what a miserable, poor device! And people so proud of it!

Sitting at his desk in the classroom, he copied the sign the teacher had drawn with a piece of chalk on the blackboard: a horizontal figure-eight.

"Infinity," said the teacher. He looked at the blackboard and crossed his hands behind his back. The noise of the street below was coming through the open windows; it was a warm day in spring, but he felt a great chill spreading from the blackboard with the small white figure in the middle of it.

"This," said the teacher, "is infinity."

He looked at the class with his expressionless eyes, "Any questions?"

Silence.

"Good," said the teacher, "so you know now what stands for infinity."

"What are you laughing at?" she asked.

He gently stroked that beautiful globe with the pink nipple, bent his head, and kissed the breast. "Infinity" he said.

"What?"

"Infinity. Quasars, and pulsars, and whatever they are."

"And earlier. Where were you?"

"The churches of Ravenna. Ever been there?"

She shook her head.

"A fascinating place," he said, putting his arm under her head and feeling its weight in the hollow of his arm. "A haunted place, very strange in its beauty."

"What else?"

"Bach's Passacaglia. And Scarlatti's sonatas, as played by Horowitz, about which we were quarreling."

"So what about them?"

"How sweet they were, I thought. Better, closer, greater than those pulsars, which can be perceived only by mathematics. But mathematics is an abstraction by itself, of course."

"And Scarlatti played by Horowitz?"

"Great God, no! No abstractions, they. The most real things in the world, if we don't mention your breasts, which are Reality itself, and..."

He stopped abruptly in the middle of the sentence. The human concept of time was basically wrong, he thought. They were comparing it to a river, a stream, always flowing, always moving. But time was not like that at all. Time was immobile, like the black surface of a tar pool. People were frantically thrashing in it and thought the sticky dark substance was in motion. Every movement required effort, that's the reason why tar...But she did not like that picture, it annoyed her.

"You are sick in the head," she said. "You should exchange your head."

"Yes. They should have shops for exchanging heads, or places like they've got for exchanging old books."

"For renewing heads maybe."

"No. At least mine you cannot repair or renew; you could only exchange it for a new one."

"What is yours like, inside?"

He thought before answering, part of him listening to the fury of the storm outside, another part always aware of the touch of the woman's breast.

"I'll tell you," he said. "It is like a skyscraper. In the late night hours. Can you see it? It's standing in a long row of other skyscrapers, in the hot night of a huge metropolis, in a world of skyscrapers. Some windows are lit, most are dark. Inside, elevators are speeding up and down; empty, naturally, running smoothly and quietly on well-greased steel cables and black iron rails, from which oil is dripping.

The elevators stop on some floors and pass others without stopping. Whenever one stops, the automatic doors slide open. Nobody goes out, nobody comes in. The elevator stands, its doors ajar, facing the long, empty corridors. After twenty seconds, the doors shut with a click, and it moves: up, or down, it is of no importance at all. There are thousands of rooms on each floor of the skyscraper. Some are empty, others are filled with papers, files, books; one room on the 23rd floor is full of Scarlatti's music…"

"Played by Horowitz?"

"Never mind; the door of this room is buttressed with mattresses, so that the music won't escape to the corridor, where it would be torn to small pieces and blown away by the wind that is sweeping the floors.

"The number of empty rooms is frightening: sometimes a room that was jammed full with all kinds of garbage, or with huge heaps of loose pages, becomes empty in a second, as if by the touch of a sorcerer's wand." He laughed in a whisper.

"You wouldn't believe it if I told you what impossible things you'd find in some rooms; you wouldn't believe how empty those empty rooms are. There is no sense of confusion in general. The elevators move systematically, according to some secret schedule, but what is the schedule? On the seventeenth floor, just opposite the staircase, is the huge, liquid, dark-blue eye of Jesus from the church in Ravenna. Lighting? It is a diffused, soft light, but cold and steady; and no lamps are visible. One floor is full of mirrors; they extend the corridor into infinity; and I think that on the highest, the uppermost floor, there is no ceiling and no roof. A horizontal figure-eight, huge, black, immobile, covers the whole thing. And on the opposite end, down, deep, deep down, there are cellars, and these, too, are full of rooms, and alleyways, and corridors."

He came to a halt abruptly, and she did not say anything. Feeling her back with his breast and belly, he tried to match his breathing rhythm with hers. For a few moments they breathed in unison, but then it did not work anymore. She was breathing faster.

"Tell me about the cellars."

"What?"

"The cellars of your skyscraper," she said.

"No," he answered reluctantly. "Those are mine exclusively."

"Tell me about them."

He shook his head. "You wouldn't like the things that are going on down there. It is only for me."

"What color are they?"

He again timed his breathing with hers. The storm outside seemed to subside; silence was moving on, swallowing ever bigger pieces of vocal space; inevitably, like a glacier sliding down a slope, but much quicker, rapidly.

"Gray," he said. "No, not exactly gray: the color of wet pavement, the color of ancient tombstones in a very old cemetery, where all the lettering has faded, and only a crumbling stone remains. The elevators have to stop there too, now and then, you know."

She is unpredictable enough, hasty enough, bad enough, to cry out, "Crap, bluff, shit!" and to jump out of bed, to run out, to disappear in this overwhelming, conquering silence, in the void, in infinity, unless there was something to stop her, something stronger than herself.

Who am I to judge it? he thought. What does her skyscraper look like? Perhaps it was as buzzing with the frantic movement of thousands of faceless people, crowding the elevators (which may be running at top speed), rushing through the corridors, bumping into each other as mine was ringing with deadly silence. It is all hers, and she would refuse to share it with anybody; her body, yes, this she would share, willingly, as she does, but not her skyscraper. Those not rich enough to possess one get a one-story house, or a mud hut.

He chuckled silently: the old guide with a face like shattered glass looked at him steadily with bleary, empty eyes, his torch pointed at some distant corner of the mosaic, meaningless. Old age, senility. To measure the amount of one with a special instrument, with infinity: you could put a scale on the lower arm of the horizontal figure-eight starting at the intersection of the arms.

To measure the height of a skyscraper; the emptiness of its corridors, the speed of its elevators, or the multitude of its crowds; to measure the sweetness of Scarlatti. The vastness of the black-red night over Ravenna. The white foam boiling under a ship's bow when she makes her way through the sea.

No sound was heard now: everything had come to a terrible standstill.

Just then she stirred. "Hold me tight," she whispered. "Hold my breast. Make love to me."

5b. Finale

With his heart regaining its normal beat, he held her still, gently, and tried to remember, but nothing came back. An uncertain, feeble, diffused light started seeping through the curtain. In this weird illumination he could see her pale face sleeping, relaxed, serene. A cock crowed: far away a heavy truck passed, a bird made an uncertain noise. The curtain moved slightly in the breeze. What was it all about? Where was the night?

Lazy, sweet fatigue overwhelmed him, he closed his eyes. I cannot hear her breath, he thought, otherwise I'd try once more to breathe in unison.

6. The Letter

In the morning, when he was still asleep, she left. When he woke up later, he found a note on the night table, saying:

I love you:
in daylight,
in tiredness,
in sadness,
in lowness
in heartlessness.

7. Confession

What was so tragic about Alexander was the inevitability of it: it was like being a needle, pulled by a huge, horseshoe- or sickle-shaped magnet. It drew him with an irresistible force; even the woman could not save him from it, not with her note, surely.

It occurred to him in a flash that the initial connection that had brought the tragic involvement in that matter was madness, a momentary awareness of his own madness sparked by Izi's innocent remark, beginning with, "The real problem is…"

Caught in that magnetic field, and unable to resist or escape, he was standing in a great hall facing the members of the Assembly seated in countless rows of chairs. Somewhere in the first row, Gustav was sitting, two fingers of his left hand supporting his temple, waiting for him to begin.

He had been called upon before this forum, to recall his sins and errors, to strike his breast in public, and to cry *Mea culpa. Mea maxima culpa*! To renounce. To regret.

But to promise improvement in the future, to better his ways, this was not required of him, because he would never be given the chance. Firm belief in the irreversibility of Time and History was an integral part of the Sanity of this congregation, as opposed to his Madness, to the emptiness of his skyscraper.

He only had to repent in public, and to vanish: even his memory would be erased.

The hall was roofed by a huge cupola—it was an old palace—and Alexander, both hands placed firmly on the pulpit, raised his eyes upward, over the rows of seats, over the gallery, but in vain, there were no mosaics on the curved ceiling, no dark blue and heavy gold of the Ravenna churches; not even any allegorical figures flowing miraculously on clouds, or magnificent robes that were like clouds, nothing of it, just creamy convex space, freshly painted or white-washed.

Whereupon Stephen, still undefined, still, like proverbial Sisyphus, stronger than his fate, looked down again at the crowd waiting silently for his self-accusing confession. Ripples of whispers rumpled the smooth surface of the sea. Alexander tried to recognize people he knew in the front rows: and all of a sudden, he realized, with a shock, that none of them had a face—where their face should have been, there was a flat white cardboard surface, row upon row of white planes, extending far into infinity, dissolving under the shadow of the gallery, and higher, on the gallery itself. Stronger in his defiant silence than before, Stephen waited for his salvation.

I can wait for a thousand years, if necessary. Into infinity, if necessary, and beyond. And they will wait, too, until they rot, until green mould covers the cardboard of their faces.

That was it then. And meanwhile?

A strong breeze rumpled the sea. That's where salvation was coming from.

Stephen now looked straight at the smiling eyes of a sailor with a short black beard, a thousand wrinkles in the corners of his eyes, gazing at him, and smiling incessantly. There! Smell that wind! Here you can still live! The surface has not been affected at all!

It was on a terrace, in some port, and the terrace ended abruptly, and below, and very near, almost touchable, was the sea, running white-foamed little waves, a strong wind whipping it up and whistling in their ears: it was a year or so after the great war, and ashore everything lay in evil-smelling ruins, towns and villages and people, even those who had survived. Cripples, and hunger, and huge cemeteries, filth and rot. But the sea was running strong and alive, unconcerned about all this.

"See?" the sailor asked, still laughing with his eyes and with his heart. "See that? Come on, let's not waste time here, let's find a ship, and sail for the salvation of our souls, and to hell with all the rest!!"

He did, then.

He smiled now, the same crooked smile, though all that had happened long before the madness started, long before Dubcek, long, long ago. But the memory of that strength, of that wind and the sea, remained.

"What is it?" Izi asked.

"Nothing. I was thinking about....was thinking about the sea."

"You'd like to sail again?"

"I think I would. What about yourself?"

Izi scratched his head and looked out the window. "I don't know. For a trip, now and then, yes."

Stephen licked his lips, there was a taste of salt on them, from those times, probably.

"You know, we hold all the cards: it's our money, we're the owners, and they can't interfere with the planning of our ships, those bastards in Paris," Izi said.

I can't blame him for not giving a damn about Alexander, Stephen thought, marveling at the fantastic performance from the working of a genuine one-track mind. I wish I had one, instead of that maze of tracks, running on several of them simultaneously, often in opposite directions. Take that fake train: it couldn't run at the same time from Amsterdam to Paris, and from Paris to Amsterdam, could it? No, but it could possibly run in a circle, and the passengers wouldn't even notice the difference. At some time it must have crossed the frontier, perhaps in France the tracks were not in the best condition, or the rails were worn out, because it was rambling now, making metallic, ringing noises, and the wagons were swaying slightly. The engine whistled at a crossing, and this shrill sound, and the rattling of the wheels and the swaying of the wagons brought to them the awareness of great speed, the rush of that short red train pulled by a powerful diesel locomotive.

"It's making good speed now," Izi remarked, "we should be in Paris at noon. I sent a cable in the morning, somebody should be waiting for us at the station. When did they say the meeting was?"

"At two in the afternoon."

He was prepared; he had his notes, his calculations, and he would quote numbers, when necessary, kilowatts, and Hertz units of frequency, tons of deadweight, dollars of money, and revolutions of shafts.

Alexander Dubcek, pale and silent, left the podium, stepped

down the stairs, and walked along the aisle. A fly could be heard in the hall, but there were no flies here. Exit Alexander and the alleged betrayal of the Revolution: revolutions of shafts were more effective, and he usually knew how to control them. But for that, the time would come later, in Paris, at two. If the time came.

Because now there was already the suspicion that this train was really running in circles. It had always been like that: if you thought even for one split second of something, if it crossed your mind, it left a trace there, like a tracer bullet; and later it might happen, it might happen, it was like giving an opening, a chance to evil fate.

He looked out the window, suspecting, and found confirmation of his fears; he could see the engine, the train was running on the periphery of a huge circle. He chuckled. "I think we're going backwards, Izi."

Izi lifted himself from the armchair, he was a heavy man, short and stocky. He chuckled, too, and remained standing at the window, his back to Stephen. "A wood," he said. "We're entering a real forest."

It had no real meaning. The geographical position had no meaning, neither had Time; but this still had to be proven. The forest was certainly not in his line now, but if the train was really running in harmonic circles, he'd find himself in Rokin soon, in an outdoor café, watching clouds. Imagine Izi's surprise!

But neither Amsterdam nor Rokin were in the line any more: the reason for that might be the falling dusk, slow, heavy and violet, which for itself as it was might be perhaps acceptable, were it not for the electric lights, sharp and antiseptic, which they turned on the moment it started darkening. Elvis' face became even more ghostly, dark, rotten, ghoulish green, but the crowds jamming the sidewalks became thicker, and now formed a solid, multicolored curtain between the people sitting in the café and the advertisement pillar.

Stephen sighed with relief. The dusk relieved him from Elvis, and he could go on, to another night, not in Ravenna, but it was still in Italy, in another town: a huge piazza on a dark winter night, absolutely off-season, with no tourists and no crowds at all, the place cold, wet, abandoned, almost surrealistic in its emptiness. He had sat down, absentmindedly, on a wet wicker chair in front of a closed café. The cathedral shone with a dull, milky light, as if the stones themselves emanated it, or it might be a reflection of the moon behind a veil of vapors, for no external light was used; they were saving electricity on such evenings.

He was sitting there alone in this great famous square, as if on the bottom of a huge aquarium, expecting great fish to swim over his head at any moment, to pass, moving their big fan-like tails in a slow, graceful motion. They wouldn't disturb him, he knew. They'd just swim from the portico of the museum on one end of the piazza, where tormented, bearded giants with bulging muscles were supporting the balconies and galleries on their arms and heads, past the campanile, to the cathedral front, where they'd disappear among the bronze horses with blind eyes, and come back, swimming restlessly like fish in an aquarium do, casting a black shadow on him in passing.

Knowing there was no danger from the fish, he followed their movements peacefully, but with interest. One could live down here, he thought, among the fish, unperturbed: just an observer, in green. Let them pass.

"Ever fall overboard, Izi?"

Izi stepped back from the window and sat down again.

"Can't recall I ever did. Why?"

"I mean, ever fall in the water? Under water, where fish swim?"

Izi dismissed this.

"I say, Stephen, that reminds me of something. As we have no fresh water generator since you cancelled it, perhaps we'd better make a fresh water tank in the afterpeak, what do you think, eh?"

Purpose is a great thing, he thought, purpose all-embracing, all-justifying, all-explaining, all-encompassing, shining and remote, but always there: purpose in terms of which everything can be understood and explained.

So would Alexander, as Husak, catching the opportunity and using the occasion, was quick to observe. Yes, the same Dubcek who stubbornly refused to repent. But history was moving onward, in one direction, with a Purpose, and toward a purpose.

Like Izi's mind.

Like this train, unless it was running in a circle.

A ship's bow, crushing the water in an ecstatic storm of dazzling white foam, served no purpose as far as the sea was concerned, because after it had passed, the sea would quickly close again, and no trace would be left.

8. Emerging from the Wood and Reaching the Destination

From between the two green walls, the train shot out into the bright sunshine, and Izi and Stephen blinked their eyes.

"Of course, one could do that," admitted Stephen amiably. "You could also convert one of the double bottoms into a fresh-water tank."

Izi shook his massive head. "Nope. A ship must have a minimum of ballast. Stability, you understand?"

"If that's the case, use the afterpeak, I don't object," agreed Stephen, and became a restless fish in an aquarium. Pressing his nose to the invisible glass wall, to meet somebody's giant eyes glued to the partition on the other side turning back, and swimming frantically, only to meet a glass wall again a few seconds later. But what else can you do, after rejecting the Purpose? What can save you, except an explosion in the aquarium, which would shatter the glass walls?

"You sure you're well, Stephen? You look pale and you're sweating like hell. It's not that hot in here."

Smiling feebly, Stephen nodded.

"You sure? You know, we should arrive there in top condition, it might be a tough discussion there after all, with those bastards in Paris. They'll try to pressure us, their reputation is at stake. You know what, Stephen? I'll call a waiter. You want a glass of water or something?"

Izi pressed a button and waited, and, following his example, Alexander pressed the button of the elevator hard, trying to stop it from steadily moving down, toward the ground floor and the cellars of the skyscraper.

"Rosen is the worst of the whole gang, the son of a whore," Izi said, waiting for the attendant. "He will never forgive you, canceling that fresh water generator."

"I also put an auxiliary switchboard down, in the lower engine room, and moved the starter of the auxiliary lube oil pump near to the maneuvering stand," added Stephen.

"There! That's what makes them furious! They didn't want any improvements or changes."

The elevator came to a stop without the slightest shock, and the doors slid open noiselessly.

"Messieurs?"

The gray-haired attendant in white jacket bowed politely. His face—the rugged, worn face of the guide from Ravenna—was immobile.

"A glass of cold water for the gentleman. And, while you're about it, bring me something to drink, too, a bottle of orange juice, please."

"Immediately."

The open doors of the elevator faced an endless corridor, gray and silent. Alexander hesitated: he was scared to leave the well-lit cubicle. But he knew that if he didn't, the doors would close noiselessly, and the elevator would move. Up? Or down?

Which of the countless closed doors in the corridor led to the Assembly hall, where, row upon row of people with cardboard faces were waiting for him to confess his betrayal of the Revolution? How could he decide? The old guide appeared again, with a tray, bottles and glasses.

"Nu? You're better now? You looked as pale as death before. Phooey, look what shit they serve here as orange juice: this liquid was never even in the vicinity of a real orange, all goddamned artificial stuff."

The train rambled over crossings, tore with fury onto bridges, through small tunnels, above towns and villages and auto roads, through shreds of open country, with a little green here and there among some miserable trees and dying shrubs, whistling and moaning.

"It must be near already. Suburbs of Paris."

"Are you nervous?" asked Stephen. "Don't get excited, we'll settle everything to the organization's complete satisfaction, as the phrase goes."

"Why should I be nervous? All the cards are in our hands. Say, Stephen, you sure you're well?"

"Never felt better in my whole life."

Hearing only his own hard footsteps, he walked through the endless corridors. Sometimes a door half-opened on the side, and a thing of beauty could be perceived in the time-space between two steps, such as a golden cumulus cloud, a purple flower, a wall of dark-blue mosaic, the curvature of a woman's breast, the sequence of five notes (in A flat minor) of a sonata, the smell of a strong sea-wind.

But he did not stop on his way, because he had to go on.

Only that. Nothing more, just that, walking on and on.

Nothing else made any sense, and certainly not that silly red train that was just pulling in slowly to the station.

It came to a stop like a child's toy that had been wound up with a key, and the spring ran out, and there was nobody to wind it up again.

"Come on, come on," urged Izi. "What are you looking for?"

"The key, to wind it up again."

"What key? Come on, Stephen, let's go."

The doors of the train opened automatically. Carrying their little suitcases, they stepped out.

But then Stephen was alone again, and it was a different station, very big and empty under the arched glass roof. The diffused light filled the vastness of it and there was only the red toy train with a big key on the top of the engine, and Stephen with his small suitcase walking with measured-steps across the platform (paved with octagonal gray tiles) toward an iron post with a white placard on it.

He stopped near to it, and read the message in big black letters:

NO MEETING WILL TAKE PLACE AT 14.00
THERE WILL BE NO MEETING AT ALL.
ALL MEETINGS ARE CANCELLED.

Stephen laughed softly in the infinite vastness of the station.

Kibbutz Sdot Yam, November 1969

The Towage of the
Shomriah: a Memoir

S ometime in the early fifties, I towed a trawler called the *Shomriah* from Mersin in Turkey to Haifa. I was the skipper of a fishing boat, a trawler, with very few qualifications for the job. I had never been a skipper before, knew very little about fishing. I had some experience of the sea, but that was all.

I was very young, as was the country. Almost everything in it was amateurish. I was no exception.

Times were difficult for Israeli fishermen: domestic fishing grounds were barren, so there were two alternatives; to go south risking encounters with Egyptian coast guards or planes, or north to Turkey. Being caught there meant having your boat confiscated and spending some time in a Turkish prison; these had a bad reputation.

I had a good steel boat and a crew of five able-bodied and willing men. They told me to sail to the Turkish coast to fish.

I tore the map of the eastern Mediterranean out of an old, thin, child's atlas to see where Turkey was, and we sailed. This was before the time of real sea charts. But we already had radio-telephones and reliable echo sounders.

I went to sleep about halfway out and the men took turns at the wheel. I tried to sleep as much as possible on the way out. I knew that once we started trawling there would be no more sleep. I told them to try to steer a straight course and wake me if anything unusual happened, to watch the temperatures on the pyrometers in the engine room, and if in doubt that anything were unusual or not, to wake me.

They were a reliable gang of men.

They shook me when the lights of Mersin showed up faintly on the horizon and the echo sounder showed a steady thick line of seventy fathoms. There was a mild breeze from the west, but the night was really velvety, the sky bright with many stars and a broad patch of the Milky Way. I rubbed the sleep from my eyes and went up to the wheelhouse. I opened the throttle and we launched our first net, which had been prepared on the poop deck.

Now they went to sleep and I remained alone at the wheel. We trawled straight west. I jumped down on deck and put my hands on the trawling cables and felt the net skimming the bottom of the sea seventy fathoms below the surface. I made some strong coffee for myself. I brought the hot mug into the wheelhouse and once more checked on the echo sounder to see if we were keeping a straight line of seventy fathoms. Everything was okay. That was our first net and if we had any luck there would be this night, the following day and another night and maybe another half-day until we filled our cold storage with catch and started homeward.

Under water anything can happen, even if the area is considered clear: your net can be entangled in some hidden obstacle, a rock or submerged log, and if you didn't spot it immediately and stop trawling, you could lose your net or your whole gear—Hercules lines, steel cables and otter boards. The utmost alertness was called for—no dozing off for even two minutes! I did not find it too difficult to stay alert.

Almost all my memories are dominated by the smell of the sea. There are, of course, the harbors, which are worlds in themselves as smells go, for each port has a smell of its own. But now I am speaking of the sea itself, which has a strong odor, fresh, salty, iodine-like, deep, dark, luring and in a mysterious way, sexual. On a trawler, it pervades the bodies of men, sticks to their hair and clothes. It came now with increased strength from the net, which we recovered from the depths of the sea after three hours, what we called the 'sack' floating on the surface till we dragged it onto the poop deck and emptied it there. The catch wriggled, pulsating, the inhabitants of the sea bottom unaccustomed to the air and light that was now killing them, beating their tails and twisting their bodies in death throes, and still following their basic instincts, trying to swallow each other. Huge groupers with red bladders protruding from their mouths like tongues, two or three enormous sting rays, powerful and slimy octopuses and shrimps, strange crabs, spiders, sea stars graceful in their beauty, little sharks and sea serpents and a multitude of fish of every possible or impossible color and shape and form.

The men sat in a circle around this heap of catch, sorting the fish into flat wooden boxes according to their size and type. The poop deck was scrubbed and washed with sea water. I turned off the powerful lights. All this time another net was already in the water, again harvesting the sea bottom. Now the men went below to catch two or three hours of sleep and again I was left alone in the wheelhouse looking at the feeble compass light overhead and occasionally switching on the echo sounder. I rather liked this solitude although I had to fight my yearning for sleep. But this was the routine: once in the fishing grounds, the skipper never leaves the steering wheel, in our case for three days and three nights.

I was aware that I was not completely alone within the fifteen mile radius; there were other Israeli trawlers in these waters. I heard their conversations on the radio. I knew all the skippers by their first names. Some were comparing catch, fishing grounds, gear; others were simply talkative, chatting, gossiping like old women.

Tonight most of them were lower than we were, to the north and northeast. I did not feel like talking. Our catch was relatively good and I didn't want any competition in our spot. We still had one more day of fishing in addition to the present night. I was looking forward to the moment when the last box would disappear into the ship's hold, the net spread for drying between the two masts, the otter boards stowed, and the long trip home would commence.

I played a little with the tuning dial on the radio and listened to the forecast. It was not good—a prediction of strong southwesterly winds—and I yelled back at the radio, "You're telling me? I have it here already!" Indeed the Southwestern started blowing and I closed the wheelhouse windows. But the somewhat stronger sea had not yet interfered with the trawling. I was tired but knew I had to wait at least eighteen hours till I could get into my bunk. During those long hours at the wheel I learned how to accept a situation which cannot be changed. Young as I was, it was an acute awareness. The war years were still sharp and fresh for me. Then, each day I had concentrated on coping with my false identity, with the foe within myself, and with the immediate, hostile surroundings. One wrong word, even one instance of behavior that didn't quite 'ring right' would have meant disaster.

Now, as a skipper of a fishing trawler, I felt an imposter, but I didn't have to deal with a false identity. I was I, and this ego had no need to act.

The problem was the weather, the sea. Human relations were in general friendly and I was always elated by the unlimited freedom of movement, freedom of choices for action. It was the prize of the sea, and so I was tranquil while trawling at night.

Toward morning, I heard the skipper of *Shomriah* calling. His engine had broken down. He was drifting and asking all ships in the area to tow him to Haifa.

By noon he was desperate: so far no boat had offered to tow his ship. In the afternoon the sea was high and some skippers said it was their last net, they were going home. The skipper of the *Shomriah* could be heard again. He cried, "Guys, don't leave us here!"

Someone answered, "Don't worry, Menachem, somebody will take care of you. 'Strong heart!'" which meant, in our slang, take courage.

"'Strong heart' is all very well," said Menachem bitterly, "but some people have black hearts."

The wind was blowing hard now; the Mediterranean is an inland sea but has a well-deserved reputation for violent storms. The great Conrad had already noticed that "the cradle of the craft," as he had called it, "is often subject to fits of ill temper comparable to outbursts of sea fury of great oceans." Big swollen rollers tossed the ship. In the moonlight I saw the white foam topping the crest of black waves.

Menachem called for help again. Standing on the deck some of my crew listened to the radio conversations, and someone remarked that it would be crazy to tow him to Haifa, that in such a storm it would take at least two days to do it. Another man added "they have no business working here in Turkey with that stupid boat of theirs." *Shomriah* was an old wooden boat with an ancient Ansaldo engine that would break down every other day. It was true, they should have stayed in Haifa Bay. But here they were, helpless, two hundred miles from their base.

I disliked Menachem. He was a fanatical ideologist with a big mouth that often babbled nonsense. He looked like a barrel on short stumps of legs, topped with carrot red hair on his head.

We continued to trawl, and then a strange thing happened.

I chanced to glance at a book I found under the echo sounder, the Nautical Almanac for the year 1945. I must have seen the book there a million times, every time I touched the echo sounder, and yet somehow never registered its presence.

It must have been bought in the early fifties when they sailed the boat from Holland to Israel. A piece of furniture, undusted, fitting snugly under our Bendix echo sounder. Inside were long columns of numbers probably indicating the positions of celestial bodies for every day of 1945. The book was obsolete. For some reason it made me angry to find a book I had not noticed for a year and I was about to throw it overboard when the book fell open to an appendix titled *Some Useful Suggestions for Mariners*. There I found the following item: "When towing a disabled vessel an anchor chain may be successfully used, the anchor itself in the middle of the distance between the vessels."

The *Shomriah* was drifting, Menachem frantic. He was as amateurish a skipper as I, perhaps even more so. My men were standing at the steps to the wheelhouse. I said, "We cannot abandon them here. Very soon they'll land on the beach in Mersin and the Turks will dump them in jail for fishing in their territorial waters." The men looked at me in silence. I picked up the phone and told Menachem we would tow them to Haifa. "At last!" he shouted, "somebody with a bit of conscience. I knew it would be a *kibbutznik*!"

I didn't feel like entering into a philosophical discussion on the connection between being a kibbutznik and having a conscience. "Prepare your anchor chain. We'll tow you on it. And turn on your projectors so that we can see where you are and what foolishness I am about to commit."

It took two hours until we had the *Shomriah* in tow with the anchor chain, with the anchor dangling in the middle as a shock absorber. It didn't leave the water for the next fifty hours.

Menachem asked on the phone, "How did you know about the chain and the anchor?" For a moment I considered telling him about the almanac and finally answered, "Menachem, it's elementary. Towage is always done this way."

With all the threat and danger it poses there is exhilaration for the seaman who has to face a storm at sea in his fragile craft. Challenging the awful forces of nature is always unique, cannot leave a man unmoved.

The wind was now certainly at least Force 9 and we were somewhere between the Anatolian coast of Turkey and Haifa, towing an old wooden boat with a fairly good catch in our own hold. At night, we couldn't see the mountains of Cyprus; everything was hidden by rain squalls and the impenetrable darkness of the storm. On the left, also concealed, was the Syrian coast. We saw little except the great waves rising like mountains above the ship, valleys torn out from the water by the wind, their slopes attempting to separate our ships when they were on the opposite side of the slope, to shake them apart violently, to tear them apart. And we had the anchor chain connecting us, with *Shomriah's* anchor in the middle.

The storm had many faces, and my moods responded to each. The sky cleared miraculously for a few minutes, the wind chasing the bulky wall of clouds somewhere to the east, and immediately a few strong stars shone on the turbulent sea; there was a surge of optimism and confidence. Sure, I thought, we'll get the *Shomriah* back to Haifa. I was ready to tow the boat to Honolulu if necessary, to tow her forever.

A squall came, and hard rain and hail banged on the roof of the wheelhouse and its windows. I looked up; we were entering a corridor of thick darkness. The stars disappeared, sheet lightning closed the space ahead with ghostly bluish light, thunder rolled overhead. Now the waves were molten lead before its boiling point, heated in a crucible heavy and oily, but they changed quickly to angry little dogs, attacking the body of the boat from all sides, as though they wanted to destroy it, as though it were a living thing. Perhaps it was. I could hear it groaning and moaning, protesting the onslaught.

Now keep a cool head and be realistic. The reality is that you are somewhere between Cap Andreas and the Syrian coast on the course to Haifa. How far to Haifa? You don't know but it shouldn't be very far now and the Stella Maris lighthouse has a range of some thirty-five miles. You have a good steel boat and a crew of very good men. Why not climb up on the mast and have a good look from above for the Stella Maris?

The rain stopped and I climbed the mast. Right astern was the feeble mast light of the *Shomriah*, but straight ahead was the swinging lighted arm of Stella Maris. I counted the periods of light and shouted to the men below "Guys, we did it! We're home!" A couple of hours later we circled the buoy at the entrance to the harbor. I looked at my watch. It was three hours past midnight. The towage had taken fifty hours, even more than I had thought. The silence of the port was stunning after so many hours of the turmoil of the sea. A huge shore crane crouched humming over a bulk carrier, a predator, a spider devouring a smaller specimen, sucking its blood. We leave the *Shomriah* at the fisherman's quay and I shake hands with Menachem, who says nothing, and I don't like him any more than I did before.

Finally he says, "Let our respective treasurers discuss the financial aspects of this story, shall we?"

Our two trawlers belong to kibbutzim and both Menachem and I are used to the fact that money is dealt with exclusively by the treasurers. I nod. Now we unload our own catch to the waiting truck. Someone cuts off the engine and again the silence stuns us. It feels as if our hearts have stopped beating.

I drink coffee with the five men of my crew and go out on deck again. All the port's lights are on and a powerful beam of light passes overhead.

I feel enormous relief and something more than that. It takes a few minutes to realize what it is, then I know, the greatest satisfaction a man can realize: a job well done. I go down to the cabin and lay myself in my bunk. I am very tired and happy and hope to sleep a long dreamless sleep.

I sleep almost twenty-four hours and the next evening I am summoned to the kibbutz secretariat. I am told that I was wrong to tow the *Shomriah* to Haifa.

"Your catch came too late for the morning fish auction and is a heavy financial loss," said the secretary.

"And you certainly damaged the engine of the boat with that uninterrupted towage of almost three days," added another member.

I said, "I took care that the pyrometers were checked every four hours and the temperatures were always normal. And isn't the engine of a deep sea trawler built for such a purpose, to drag a heavy net and gear on the sea bottom for hours and hours?"

"This is a different thing."

"How different?"

"Different."

"Why didn't other trawlers offer to schlepp this disabled *Shomriah* home?"

"I told you, we were the last to leave the fishing grounds."

"At any rate it was a wrong decision, a mistake. Please don't do such things in the future."

I said, "You mean you were serious when you told me I should have left the *Shomriah* there, drifting in Turkey?" I got up. "If I had to make the same decision tomorrow, I'd do it again," I said.

The members of the secretariat were silent and a man said, "Look, the skipper of the *Shomriah* certainly had a big problem there, but the moment you started towing them, they became your problem, right?"

I said "Right. And in spite of everything that was said here, I think I solved the problem the right way. Anything more you have to say to me?"

They were silent and I left.

An Afterword:

The "I" in the story of the voyage of the *Shomriah* is not the John Auerbach who wrote it. I am now a man in his mid-sixties and the inevitable passage of time did not leave me unscathed; it has damaged me in many ways.

Still, a violent urge persists to relive the wonders of that trip, to feel on my cheeks the lovely sea breeze that became a real winter southwestern storm in the Mediterranean, to perceive with my inner eye the dark tunnel from which the storm came, and once more feel the courage, the faith and the unshakable conviction that I did what had to be done.

The Yellow Eyes of my Dog

The day the war started, they walked on a field. The field had been ploughed through, deeply, a few days earlier, and things were being found. Only a few people were really interested in the coins, old oil lamps, and pieces of pottery, although the kibbutz was practically sitting on top of the ancient town, and antiques abounded, with everything from marble columns and statues to coins and beads and gems.

But he and she kept looking for and finding old things, and they were always fascinated by them, each for different reasons.

What they shared between them was the wonder of relaxation, the sudden disappearance of nervous tension, which came with the very slow walk, eyes fixed on the ground, and silence all around interrupted only by birds, and the occasional rustling of leaves on the trees around the field when wind rushed through them.

The dog loved it for still other reasons; she ran in a wild gallop, in great leaps, chasing an imaginary hare, long ears swept back, the tail stiff, all four feet together to be stretched out in the next fraction of a second to the maximal extent. Sometimes, she would run up to them, her long thin tongue stuck out, mouth open as if she were smiling, eyes glistening, her nose black and wet, begging for approval, for a pat, for an encouraging word.

"The coin that you found yesterday," the man said.

"What about it?"

"I cleaned it: you can read the inscription. One Severus, Emperor, Augustus, etc., etc."

"What about him?"

"There were two or three of that name. Fought battles, killed other people, were killed. One of them committed suicide."

"Well?"

"I look at his face on the coin, try to find out which one it was. Imagine the sound of his voice. What the women he loved look like. What he thought."

She smiled. "It is a beautiful coin, but you know I don't particularly like these faces. Faces can lie, you know. I prefer those things made by men: tiny designs on pieces of pottery, on oil lamps, inscriptions…"

"And how this coin was used," he continued. "Who paid with it? Where? For what? What was bought with it? Food? Women? Slaves? In a shop, in a brothel? Entrance to the games?"

"…primitive jewelry, gems, small patterns, beads, that kind of stuff," she said, her eyes firmly on the ground.

Just then they found the lamp: he spotted it first and called her without touching it, leaving it as it was, almost a part of a lump of hard earth on the side of a furrow. She cried out loud and her face lit up with pleasure as she delicately picked up the pale-yellow piece of pottery, a complete oil lamp, seventeen or eighteen centuries old, with a clear inscription on its rim.

They removed the dirt out of it carefully, holding it in their hands, looking at the proud imperishable beauty of it from all sides, happy and excited.

The dog came running, and stood, panting, looking at them with round, golden, questioning eyes.

"We won't find anything more today," he said. "What extraordinary luck!"

"Let's go home and clean it properly and look at it. What a lovely little lamp it is!"

They had their coffee later, at home. The lamp stood on the table between them.

"Do you believe it was left there for all those centuries for us to pick it up and to bring here?"

He thought before answering.

"Yes," he said. "Yes, I believe it."

"What is it? Destiny?"

"You can call it that."

"Let's have some very good, old, music," she said. "To celebrate. I love that lamp."

"You cannot have music as old as the lamp. Besides, there is no music on the radio today, it's Yom Kippur."

"I forgot. So tune in to the BBC. Let's see what they have."

He touched the button.

The dog, exhausted, sighed, and let his head sink to the floor.

From London, a stiff British voice: *"Large scale fighting has broken out today between Egypt, Syria, and Israel."*

"What, what is that?"

"Put that beautiful lamp away, darling," he said. "It is very bad news."

2.

"Too old, they said."

"Too old?"

"Yes. Somebody explained: the computer automatically rejects everybody over forty-five. A punched card, that is. You know what such a card looks like?"

"An IBM? Or similar to that? Yes. I've seen them."

"Well. This is a modern army run on computers. Over forty-five: out. The computer rejects you."

Stepping over the dog, which for some reason had stretched herself out on the cool tiles right across the entrance to the bathroom, he enters and strips quickly. The pullover, the shirt, the trousers. He throws them over the plastic toilet seat. Crowded, this goddamn place, tiny. The undershirt and underpants. Then, impatiently, aggressively, almost threatening, he watches the angry man in the mirror. On his neck, on a golden chain, a good luck trinket is dangling. Much good luck. Old. Too old.

The head he skips. The head is of no importance.

But the arms are still strong, the skin is smooth, and there is no decaying flesh under it. Not an inch of fat. No pot-belly, a lot of body hair from the waist down, on the legs, in the groin. Not too old. He is functioning exactly like he did five, ten years ago, Muscles on the legs. Tendons.

He prefers not to look at the eyes, they are perhaps the oldest part of him. Of everybody.

Relaxing, in resignation, he puts his clothes on.

The eyes, for sure. That is why the computer rejected him.

When he's dressed again, carefully avoiding the searching eyes of the man in the mirror, he draws the curtain over the window. Blackout. There is war outside this bathroom. The dog stirs when he steps over her, lifts her head. Looks at him with yellow eyes and yawns. What teeth! White, long, sharp, curved: pink tongue, black throat.

"There's a war on, you know," he says, and the dog wags her tail. "You don't know anything," he tells the dog, filling his glass, and refilling it once more, he adds: "A bloody war. You do not know anything. You are not old enough, probably."

The dog keeps beating her tail against the floor, and the man says, pouring another shot from the rectangular bottle: "But Wittgenstein says that even if we understood the language of dogs we wouldn't understand what you say."

The dog becomes longer, leaner, sharper, after the fourth glass, and just as he starts understanding the dog's face, the dog's fate, the dog's facts of life, the siren starts wailing for an air-raid alert.

He carefully puts the glass on the table, and, after a moment of thought, fills it once more from the bottle. The rise and fall of the wailing stretches the dog elastically, she expands (in length only) and shrinks, and follows the noise with pricked ears.

"We're not going to the shelter, dog. We have experience in going to shelters. Remember never to go to an air-raid shelter or to a cellar during an air raid. You can add it to your doggish life principles. Unless you have a very compulsive urge to die in togetherness."

Outside, in the falling darkness, the siren dies very slowly, sliding down for ages to ever lower registers. Sinking in thick violet shadows. A dying animal. Nothing has changed. A slight breeze moves the trees. The short-shorn carpet of the lawn, soft under your feet, and cool. Pleasant. He takes a few steps, remembers all of a sudden that he is too old, and sits down on the porch, the dog in front of him, pushing its tail, its behind against his chest.

"You want to be close, you want to be together," the man murmurs. "You are a pathetic dog. You'll have to find your own war rules."

The thinnest possible slice of a moon and two or three stars: except for these, the sky is empty and transparent. Not out of such a sky the Riders of Apocalypse. But people are dying right now in a flash of fire, in a roar of explosion, in convulsions of pain far from here: not on this lawn. Not in the radius of his vision. Too far to be seen or smelled. A Polish proverb teases him but he cannot remember how it ends, he is drowsy after four or five glasses. The all-clear sounds. It is difficult to know when to stop, when to continue. The art of balance. Disillusioned, he pats the dog's melancholic head. Too tired. Too old.

3.

More about the dog.

She'd a middle-sized dog, one of a litter of ten, which is a bit of an exaggeration even as animals go, and even taking into consideration the commandment of our Holy Scriptures to be fruitful and multiply. The dog's mother must have taken it too literally.

Surprisingly, most of the puppies survived and were adopted by respectable kibbutz families. The only visible mark of their kinship with each other is the head, a pointer's head. Apart from that they were as different as only dogs can be, a multitude and variety of forms and colors: short-legged, bow-legged, elongated and short, black and brown and white.

There were five males and five females in the litter and they accepted each other when meeting later on kibbutz lanes and lawns, by a quick smell-check, a nod, and a tolerant indifference—not unlike their masters, the kibbutz members.

This female dog, this bitch, is long-eared and friendly-faced like the rest of her brothers and sisters, but unlike them she has long legs and a very proportionate body and an active and sensitive tail. In fact, she has almost all the characteristics of a pure-bred hunting dog, which she is not. She has eyes with long lashes. The eyes are mostly yellow, but sometimes they change color and become gold, or golden-green. She responds to the name Mississippi.

She accompanies her man and woman when they walk in the fields, looking for ancient things.

4.

Crew list. This is a trip on behalf of the Ministry of Defense. Consequently, it is an all-Israeli crew

1) Zeev Benyamini, Master
2) Hanan Shalef, Chief Mate
3) Dan Shavit, Second Mate
4) Aharon Weinreich, Third Mate
5) Adam Ben Yakov, Chief Engineer
6) Meir Orfi, First Engineer

7) Gedalia Offenbach, Second Engineer
8) Haim Pasternak, Third Engineer
9) Albert Cohen, Electrician
10) Paul Seltzer, Radio Officer
11) Aharon Palti, Bosun
12) Moshe Zavadski, Carpenter
13) Moshe Chaimi, A.B.
14) Eliezer Rosen, A.B.
15) Steve Levy, O.S.
16) Jacques Rubin, O.S.
17) Ran Amitay, M.man
18) Giora Caspi, M.man
19) Victor Rosenstreich, Wiper
20) Israel Damari, Cook
21) Alisa Weingarten, Stwd.
22) Chana Ben Shmuel, Stwd.
23) Efraim Gold, Utilityman

Signatures: Frontier Police, Ministry of Transport Security

5.

The whole country is smothered by blackout, but the port is one big blazing Christmas tree, the quays flooded by projectors, the ships with powerful mercury lamps, clusters of lights hanging over gangways: an explosion of light in darkness. The nearest explosion was two or three hundred kilometers away, along the Canal, where a thousand guns blazed a line of fire. There, soldiers on both sides were running amidst a rain of projectiles or driving in armored vehicles, or ducking into dug-outs and strong-points, their heads low between their knees. Cunningly, diligently, they were trying to kill each other and escape destruction themselves: that night saw many deeds of hero-ism performed.

The dog blinks her yellow eyes, momentarily blinded by the

ship's lights, and tucks her tail between her hind legs. She is shivering and refuses to climb the steep gangway. He takes her like a baby, and carries her aboard. The smell of the dog's hide is in his nostrils, the tenseness, the charged nervousness of the animal; once he puts her on the iron deck, she seeks refuge between his legs.

The Syrians must have achieved a breakthrough, and a deep one; they are racing through the Golan Heights with a phalanx of tanks the likes of which the world has never seen before. The radio spoke of *absorbing* battles, *absorbing* the shock. That must have cost us many men. Hundreds, probably. The same in Sinai. Why did they let them cross that bloody canal? Admittedly, it is not very wide. He recalls seeing the soldiers on the other side, in baggy pants and undershirts. Fifty, perhaps sixty meters. Not a real barrier. On our side, tourist buses were coming and going daily. People took snapshots. The idea of standing on the shore of the Suez Canal was first weird, then funny, and finally there was nothing to it. Everything extraordinary to it evaporated in the desert heat. The Egged Bus Cooperative put up station signs, as drab, cheap, and lousy as anywhere in the country. A soldier sprawled in a wicker chair, legs outstretched, the rifle propped against a stone, yawning. But they should have bombed them when they were crossing in their rubber boats, or whatever they had. Or, when they built the bridges. One can never know what went wrong. We will know, later.

The dog doesn't care, she is looking for a place to hide. But he cannot explain to her, only reassure. He scratches the dog's head, and she quickly licks his hand; a hot, rough tongue.

She had wanted animals in the house, had pressed. He had opposed, mildly, in the beginning, liked the order and cleanness that with dogs were impossible to maintain. But he started liking her quickly. The helplessness, and the supreme dependence, the eagerness to cooperate, to be "good", to be loved, scratched, petted, nursed, won him over.

And then there were the dog's eyes: a secret, an enigma. The longer you looked at them, the greater the fascination. Kipling thought an animal could not bear to look into human eyes for long, it had to turn away. He sees that this is nonsense. They sit opposite each other for long periods of time, fifteen, twenty minutes, looking steadily into each other's eyes. Frozen in complete immobility, but eager; far more than curious.

The ascent toward understanding would come only later. After the third, fourth glass. Some whores in Amsterdam's famous windows sat as motionless as this dog. Unmoving eyes. Others knitted or read comic books, but the real ones could look you in the eyes for ten minutes, and the eyes were as cold as cobblestones in winter. Try and understand! He laughed. The dog's eyes were never cold.

He opens the cabin door and the dog is too scared to start searching, smelling. She jumps on the sofa, and stays there, trembling.

"This is your cabin, Sippi, with a nice sofa. I know it well."

He distributes the few things he's brought with him between the closet and the drawers. He did not lie to the dog, he knows the cabin well, he knows the ship, has sailed in it on occasion. When he was not yet too old. The black surface of the desk, the lamp, the telephone, the tiny bedroom, the well-lighted bathroom, they are all reassuring.

"Feel at home, dog. We're sailing together in this war. I'll get a life jacket for you."

He opens the door of the bar, and is satisfied to find a bottle of Scotch, a bottle of real Russian Vodka, and another one of gin, and glasses. Everything is as it was six, eight, ten years ago. Once more repeating the pattern of one's life: always exciting, nostalgic, and a little dangerous. He is confident now, and gives another boost to his confidence with a quick, double shot of Scotch, turns to the dog, who, from the sofa, follows his every movement, and tells her in a low, strange voice. "We'll return from this trip together, you and I. You'll see."

And the dog, straining to understand, and failing to understand, beats feebly with her tail on the soft cover of the sofa. Because she's been addressed.

6.

The cook is dead drunk.

The cook is permanently drunk. Once, he had an agreement with the captain: he was allowed to be dead drunk four times on a normal trip of six weeks; nobody would bother him on those days, and in between he would cook meals for the crew no matter how wild the storm outside was and how badly the ship was rolling or pitching.

But that was long ago, and the captain with whom he had that agreement was gone. The captains and the crews have changed, but he has remained, year after year. Drinking daily, nightly, more and more, sometimes with other men, but mostly in his cabin, sitting in his cabin on a small imitation leather sofa and talking in a low voice to himself or to the monkeys on the postcards. There were several of them pasted on the wall, in color, and over his bunk; he had collected them long ago, and sometimes they talked back to him, made grimaces. Occasionally, when he lay down in his bed, they jumped around, swinging on their tails and shouting.

There was also a calendar on the wall, printed by Ancora Ship Chandlers and Ships' Suppliers in Antwerpen, on which the cook crossed off the passing days with a pencil, and right over the washstand, a front page from another calendar, from back in '67, which he'd gotten from a ships' laundry—"quick, efficient service"—in Liverpool. On this front page was a naked, smiling girl, in profile, holding a huge plastic flower. Her left breast, visible, had a perfect pear shape, but not much more was to be seen because of this plastic flower, sticking out of a pot; she was clinging virtuously to its stiff, plastic stem.

The cook sometimes looked at her with a bleary eye when shaving, but in his normal state of drunkenness he preferred the monkeys.

They met in a narrow alleyway on the main deck where the cook was on his way to his cabin, bouncing off the walls like a billiard ball. Strange that he should recognize him in the dim light, and so drunk. "You sailing with us, aren't you? I thought so. Come to my cabin, let's have a quick one. When war starts, the old-timers come back. Not before. Believe me, there's hardly anybody left to sail with, they're all kids."

The monkeys grinned from the walls. The cook swept away a soiled white shirt and some dirty socks from the chair.

"Make yourself comfortable. Ever drink bourbon? They didn't have bourbon in our day. But then, you remember, Courvoisier was one dollar fifty. Now it's five, in a plastic bottle!"

He touches the fancy bottle suspiciously, presses it with his thumb. Plastic, no mistake.

"To our health."

The bourbon, cool and smooth. More refined than the Scotch? "Let's have another," says the cook as he pours. "I brought a bottle like this last trip to my old man, in Jerusalem. He always gets his booze from me, he's never short of it. Good man. You know, he had four shops in Sana'a, and he owned a village, a whole village there. Would you believe it? And what he does not know in the Torah isn't worth knowing. He knows it by heart. Every morning, a glass of this. Here, have some more. At eleven, again. And when he gets up after his afternoon nap, he starts serious drinking. And then he sets out on his tour to visit his grandchildren."

"Good bourbon."

"Have another one. Of course, when we finish this, we'll have to return to Walker. Or to the Moscovskaya Vodka. Did you know we have several cases of it here on board? Bought in Rotterdam last time. A dollar fifty a bottle. If I knew there'd be war, I'd have bought more. But who could know? Those whores fell on us so suddenly."

"You keep the slop chest on this ship? Sparkie used to do it."

"Not this Sparkie. Too bloody lazy. I have been selling slop chest for almost a year. On percentage, I do it. Have another one."

His father had a village in Yemen, but this drunk, small, wiry man of an indescribable age was born in Jerusalem: he has eyes like burning coals, almost smoking, cheek bones protruding like a Genghis Khan warrior, and thin arms surrounded by thick, knotty veins. Hair like black iron wire. Quick wits and short temper.

In Jerusalem, he tells stories of far off countries he has visited and the old man listens quietly, with silent skepticism, nodding slightly and sipping the booze his son has supplied. This, the youngest one, has always been strange: praised be the Lord, the others are all right: one, a butcher, the other, a shop owner, and still another one, learned, a clerk in the town hall. The youngest one, this seaman, has never married. No grandchildren from him. From the others, yes, plenty, the Almighty be praised.

"I brought along a dog with me."

"A dog? To sail with you?"

"Couldn't leave it at home. War."

"I'll give it a bone now and then. Food is no problem on board, you know."

"Yes, I know. When are we sailing?"

"At eleven tonight, a few ships together. That's what they usually do in war."

"I know, I've sailed in wars before."

"Believe me, I couldn't care less, but it makes me angry that those sons of bitches fell upon us on *Yom Kippur*…Where are you going? Have another one."

"Last one. I've got to see the Captain."

"Haven't seen him yet?"

"No. First I came to see you."

"I am glad you're sailing with us. There are three or four guys you can still sail with. All the others are just kids. Have another one."

"Later. I'll go and see the captain now."

"Don't worry about your dog. It'll be all right."

"Thank you."

7.

He thinks: If this ship is sailing out into the vast darkness of the night in order to bring back washing machines, refrigerators, transistor radios, TV sets, flashy cars, and all the other junk that Israelis have learned to love so much between the Six-Day War and this one, I'll jump overboard, I couldn't stand the shame.

The big engine warms up slowly, picking up revolutions, sending deep vibrations into the ship's hull, into everything and everybody on board. On the dials of manometers and thermometers the needles quiver, climb very slowly, surreptitiously. Higher up; over the huge body of the main engine, pipe exhausts, rods, rails tremble, the thin structure of this surrealistic cathedral, reaching up toward the invisible skylight somewhere four stories up. White neon lamps flicker quickly, plenty of light here always. And the roaring noise of motors, engines, generators, quickly revolving discs, impellers, crankshafts, metal against metal. Add to this the trembling of the floor plates on which he is standing: and the smell of hot oil, hot fuel, hot iron, exhaust gases.

Again, as once upon a time, his engine room.

They were right, he thought. Too old. Too obsolete. Outlived your times. Also this ship, this engine. They wanted to sell it, they were right. Of course it was still functioning, but with conscious effort.

She, laboring in ballast, to achieve her twelve, twelve and a half knots: he, handicapped by so many years, tying to continue living among people and events and modes of behavior he could not understand.

The fuel oil booster pump pressure is a bit on the low side. Perhaps when they change over the day tanks it will rise. Otherwise, everything seems to be strained but normal. As normal as he, he thinks.

Okay now. The plant is warmed up, running smoothly. He can leave them alone now, they're on their way out, a blacked-out ship, a stupid precaution for they could be tracked and stalked on the radar. No news of mines or submarines in this war yet. He plans to listen to the news bulletin at 01.00; it must be still very hot there, on both fronts. What quantities of weapons they've thrown in, great God, the Russians gave them everything.

He thinks, I am a colonialist, militant, imperialist, aggressor. An Israeli lackey of the FBI. In addition to all that, a Jew. And of course, to top off the list, too old.

He slowly climbs the stairs out of the engine room wishing to see what the dog is doing, closed in the cabin with her fear and uncertainty. He turns the key and the dog jumps with wild joy, throws her paws on his chest and looks at him with unbounded love in her loving yellow eyes.

8.

"Whatever you do, wherever you are, you cannot stay out of it. It's not a question of ideology, I tell you. Pure reason and good sense, that's all." The radio officer puts his hand on the books. "I tell you, this man knows what he is talking about. He is a simple, clever man." Paul is trying to sell them Uri Avneri's book, his concept of a political solution for Israel, for the Middle East.

Oh, no, he is not stupid or naive, this radio officer. He has known him for some years, they have sailed together. Ashore, he has also seen some of Sparkie's women, and knows in what circles he traveled at home. Aboard, he is a very competent radio officer, and he has what Conrad called "ability in abstract," what we now call intuition, the unknown quality that makes a good doctor, a good engineer, a good barber or a good waiter. Yes, he has it, Paul. But like all young people—almost all, let's say—he also has a keen feeling of injustices committed and looks for solutions; naturally, on the Left. Even if it is only Uri Avneri's solution.

"He should try to improve his *Olam Ha'zeh* magazine instead of writing books nobody reads," says the electrician.

"*Bul* has put him out of business," remarks the cook. "The girls are sexier and more naked."

"Idiots," replies Paul quietly. "All you ever think about is cunts. You," he turns to the cook, "are possibly too drunk to ever think of cunts. Booze has flooded your brain. Uri produces *Olam Ha'zeh* only to make money for this," he says, picking up a volume.

In the game of poker in the recreation room, Sparkie wins constantly. It could be that he swindles—he is absolutely capable of it—but nobody can prove it. His partners—the cook, the electrician, and the third engineer—have respect for him, fear him. Is it synony-mous? Must a man be feared in order to be respected?

It is odd, he thinks, that a man who has read Taylor's *Primitive Civilization* would bother with Avneri's book. But it is a fact.

"Two cards for me."

"One more."

The cook shakes his head. "No."

Sparkie takes the bank again, rubs his hands. He is in high spirits now. "You too,"—he turns directly to him now—you can profit from this book. You are not too old for that yet, even though you are an old, cynical whore."

"Thank you. I have enough to do without it."

"When I finish parting these dopes from their money, you are invited for a drink in my cabin."

"Thank you again. I never refuse that kind of invitation. Later you can come to mine, and we'll continue."

"Discussing Uri Avneri?"

"Drinking."

Paul shakes his head. "You've become a real alcoholic, eh?"

"None of your business."

"Of course not. I just remarked. Who's dealing? You? OK, here we go…"

Playing cards, watching TV, listening to the news, drinking. But the ship continues on her course, steadily: the sea is smooth, and the weather is lovely.

He gets up and goes to his cabin.

9.

Great God, Saul, he writes to a man he calls his friend, how I hate these Russians in the Kremlin! I hate them so much that I am scared of the intensity of my hatred. The hatred becomes personal, pathological, to the point where the mere sight of Brezhnev's arrogant, swollen face with his phony Mephistophelian brows, or that of Podgorny, sour, stony—I bet he is suffering from piles or constipation—causes the muscles in my stomach to contract, and puts the germ of a nauseating headache in the left part of my skull.

Trying—with enormous effort—to subdue it, to deal with it in a more rational way, I realize that they are only the most refined product of a long evolutionary process: the dehumanization of human beings. Humans shedding their humanity. Coming of age. A full circle. The brazen cynicism is still an important part of their equipment. In later stages, it will be unnecessary. A super-apparatchik will be able to say, 'Yes, I do lie: so what, why shouldn't I?' But meanwhile, they and their followers, whose name is The Millions, can still only be hypocritical and hide behind denials, claiming virtue in the scale of the values they keep in deepest contempt.

'Dehumanization? Lies? Us? Nonsense! Idiocy!

'On the contrary, we are the real outposts of humanity in the disintegrating world of colonialism, imperialism, fascism. The dignity of men, of working men, equality, this is what we are after. The freedom of the human race from inequality, from racial prejudices…'

Saul, do you remember their 'Peace Congresses?' The Dove?

The dog sniffs and whines in the lowest possible register, barely audible. She puts her left forepaw tentatively on the letter. But there is no place here to walk, he explains patiently, softly. There are only iron decks and deep darkness outside.

Inside, too, for that matter.

He looks regretfully at the last lines of his unfinished letter: freedom of the human race. That is why right now the ship is gliding smoothly on the black sea, Soviet tanks and guns are spitting fire, roaring, and scores of missiles are chasing Israeli planes.

"This," he tells the dog, "is what I would call perversion. Do you have such a concept in your dog's vocabulary?"

She sadly withdraws her paw, and with a human sigh, her body curled, settles down on the sofa with her long head on his knees.

Brezhnev has dogs, he has seen pictures of the man with his hunting dogs, brutal, alert faces, the raised shotgun. "You, too, look like a hunting dog."

But she has never hunted in her life. "And you never will. Not as long as I live. But now I must go, and you stay here."

Desperation. Pleading. To no avail: a drink is an absolute necessity, otherwise it'll be too sad, too tragic. And not alone, please. Do you understand? That's how weak we are, on occasion: not with the mirror, not with you, dog, human as you are, but with Somebody else. With Paul, with Albert, with Meir. With anybody. Why? I cannot tell you that. But I need it badly. In order to survive till tomorrow.

The problem with the stones on the shore is that the moment they are dry they cease to be multicolored stars fallen from the sky and kissed by the sea, and turn into dull, ordinary pebbles.

"Albert, this is the best thing the Soviet regime has produced so far."

"Smooth as hell."

"You simply don't feel it when you're drinking, no hammering in your head next morning. Dangerous, too, because you don't know when you've become drunk. *L'chaim!*"

"So what?"

"Well, you have to stop some time."

"This," he says, "is the problem of all problems: to stop or not to stop. Hamlet dealt with this."

"Who?" the cook asks, filling the glasses once more. "We once had a Norwegian mate, on the *Har-Sinai* it was, who never stopped. Drunk from the beginning of the trip to the end."

"Like you?"

"Me? Have you ever missed a meal on this ruddy ship when I'm around? No? Okay, so don't talk!"

The cook becomes quarrelsome. This stuff gives you a shot of energy, it feeds the fuel to your brain cells, gets them moving again when they get stuck in the mud of hopelessness, of apathy, but it also releases things you have kept under control before. The Yemenite becomes aggressive, and generous. They know, too, how to tease him; the electrician specializes in it. He always mentions Israel's arch-foe, Makhlouff, a cook on another ship of the same company.

"Now, Makhlouff, whenever people came to his cabin to drink, he knew how to entertain them."

"Sure," the first engineer immediately cuts in, "sure, but that was Makhlouff! What wasn't there on the table? Everything: cold cuts, sardines, lox, all kinds of olives, nuts…"

"Canned oysters, roast beef…"

The cook tries hard to listen to these lists indifferently, but his olive skin becomes a shade paler and his teeth are clenched. He cannot hold his ground against it for long.

"Sure, but that was Makhlouff! The same Makhlouff who once said that if he'd been a member of the right party he'd now be the chief supply officer of the Israel Defense Forces, at the rank of general. As it happened, he always voted for Begin, and retained the rank of sergeant."

"Sergeant or corporal, with Makhlouff there were always good things on the table."

"Wait here, all of you: I'll bring you something from the fridge, something that goes with this vodka, you bastards."

The cook returns loaded with smoked ham, jars of olives, canned mushrooms.

This is insanity, he thinks. An insane way to spend the war. People are spilling blood right now, moaning in the agony of death; you are spilling vodka with oysters. But this is a munitions ship, and that serves as a justification. Always trying to justify, to set straight, to find compromises with your stupid conscience. Growing gloomy. This is not a soul-searching session, is it? Fortunately, a motorman sticks his head in, calls him down.

Under the floor plates of the engine room another pipe has broken. An old ship; pipes burst frequently. And now, in ballast, with all these vibrations. Pointing flashlights, they look at the pencil-wide stream of water gushing under great pressure. They look at him anxiously. He nods quietly. "Nothing can be done for this at the moment. Try to bind a rag around it, though it won't hold. Pump bilges every hour. Don't cover this."

Back to cook's cabin? Not necessarily. Into the dense night

outside. The mast light a wandering star. Faintly seen the forecastle, the decks, the rigging. A hundred miles to the south, invisible, the African coast. Try to breathe in deeply, to catch any smell of Africa. Because the breeze comes from there. No. Nothing. If you pass nearer, you can get it: raw, dry, a very special smell.

Back to the news on the radio, at midnight.

In the cabin, the dog curled under the blanket beats a tattoo of wild joy with her tail. Her man has come back.

10.

More than half the crew is asleep now. Others are on watch: two men in the engine room, two men on the bridge. Four men are playing cards in the messroom, but they, too, are sleepy, and they are going to finish the game soon.

The ship moves quietly in the darkness, the darkness filled with winged demons. St. Anthony's temptation: voluptuous women with thin mysterious smiles on their pale-golden faces; rosy bodies beneath transparent veils in creamy and rosy gardens bathed in diffused light, as if the sunrays could not penetrate the mist or low-lying clouds.

St. Sebastian's martyrdom: the arrows in his body sharp, deep. The light is failing. In turbulent waters, monsters lurk: glassy eyed, clad in slimy scales, with sharp claws and spines on their backs. It is impossible to say if it is the hand of providence that keeps the ship on its course, or the fantasy of a demon. One descends countless steps, looking with suspicion left and right, thin mists rising from below, passing swiftly behind the window panes of the high-flying jet plane, and one loses one's ambition or ability to plan, just to be ready for the next surprise, to react or to be transported…

"Sorry to disturb you. Are you awake? Get up, please."

"What's happened?"

"It's not good: there is a warship alongside us."

"What warship?"

"That's it, we don't know. She won't identify herself: she just keeps demanding from us: WHAT SHIP?"

"OK, I'll be up in two seconds."

The dog looks at me with a huge question mark in her eyes.

"Stay here. If anything happens, I'll take you with me. Stay, stay where you are. Good dog."

The warship is blacker than the night. It is alongside, and only a distance of thirty, forty yards separates the two vessels. The red, malicious eye of an Aldis lamp starts blinking again. In flashes, the faces of the men on the bridge appear suddenly dark red, tense: W-H-A-T--S-H-I-P?

"They have been doing it for the past fifteen minutes," says the captain.

"Did you answer anything?"

"Nothing."

On the table in the captain's cabin, there is a dark-green bag, heavy with big iron pieces, containing secret codes and papers, ready to be thrown overboard if they try to board the ship.

"How far are we from their coast?"

"A hundred miles, at least."

"It could be a NATO ship," somebody suggests in the darkness.

"It could. It could also be Spanish."

"Or Algerian."

Sparkie, in shorts and undershirt, tries frantically to get through to Haifa.

"Close the bloody door to your radio station: they can see the sweat on your face even without binoculars."

"I got it," he says, listening to the Morse crackling in the loudspeaker. "I got them. Wait, they'll stand by for us. They can do nothing for us here."

W-H-A-T--S-H-I-P? W-H-A-T--S-H-I-P?

"I'll wake Meir, Captain."

"OK. Shall we answer: Greek ship, Naples to London?"

"Perhaps, no, wait a moment longer. We are so far from any territorial waters that they really have no lawful basis to stop us."

Just then the ship, black, menacing, starts sliding back slowly and places itself just behind the ship's stern. Then a huge projector is switched on and floods the whole superstructure with blinding white light.

"Now they can read clearly what ship and where from," says the captain. On the stern, welded with steel stripes, are the ship's name and the home port; they have been covered with a thin layer of gray paint, but are visible enough. No more guess work for the warship. The projector is turned off.

"They are probably waiting for their instructions."

"Probably."

This is the last word spoken on the bridge.

For the next ten minutes the ship quietly sails her course, the warship following in her wake, one ship's length away. Then, the distance starts growing. The warship has slowed down or stopped. They watch its blacker-than-night silhouette diminishing, ever smaller and smaller, through binoculars. Then, already barely visible, she turns slowly and sails south.

The captain unpacks the canvas bag.

"A drink?"

"Two drinks."

The captain's cabin is a comfortable well-lit room, it could be a living room in an apartment ashore, one does not feel one is aboard a ship in this room.

"Six days before we sailed from Ashdod," says the captain, "my wife gave birth to a son."

"To your son's health, the first toast! *L'chaim*!"

"When that ship stayed with us for ten minutes," he continues his monologue, holding his glass with long fingers, "I thought it would take a damn long time till I see my son, my first-born, again." He laughs.

"They wouldn't intercept us like this, I knew it, I knew it," murmurs Sparkie.

"Did you really think they'd take us to Algiers?"

"Never mind. *L'chaim*!"

In Algiers, in another time, in another world, because the man was then a boy of fifteen; in the evening, violet shadows flow down the streets toward the waterfront. The setting sun sets a thousand windowpanes afire. In the harbor, an old felucca with a half-furled red sail swings slowly on her anchor. A black freighter sails slowly out, its siren deep, hoarse. The world at peace, the world's heartbeat slow, regular.

On the Kuneitra–Damascus road hundreds of tanks open a hurricane of fire and explosions. Dead soldiers in khaki lie on both sides of the road.

The dog beats on the sofa with her tail: the man is back.

"Mississippi, we almost sailed to Algiers." The dog, in a frenzy of happiness, licks his face with her hot, rough tongue.

"I don't know if they'd let me keep you with me in the prison." He submits for a full minute to the dog's caress. "Enough now. Enough! Ah, dog! How little you know about this world of ours." She crawls under the blanket in search of ultimate happiness.

"As little as I know about yours, dog."

The ship sails serenely westward.

II.

Enter Eliezer Rosen, able-bodied seaman.

A dramatic entrance, and immediately he has the stage to himself.

Actually, he entered much earlier, before the ship set off for this trip. He signed on in accordance with the law. He is not interested in the war. He is not interested in anything very much except in Eliezer Rosen. He is so magnificent in his isolation that he really does not care at all about the audience or the other actors. He is glad that he is sailing away from 'that madness' at home because he has heard, naturally, that there is a war on.

Pressed by other seamen, he says reluctantly, "I do not understand anything about politics. I am a seaman, I do my work if they pay me in accordance with union contract wages. By the way, there's a bonus for dangerous cargo: munitions or weapons."

He does his work for the first two days, chipping rust on the main deck with a scaling machine. On the third day of the trip, Eliezer Rosen is sick. The second mate, responsible for the medicine chest, reports to the captain. "He cannot work, has almost passed out, and is having difficulty breathing."

The captain is worried, moderately. He would like to have his crew healthy, but on a ship, sailing in ballast, the absence of one AB does not impose much of a burden on others: nor does it impair the ship's seaworthiness in any way.

"Take his temperature in the evening and tell me how he is." Eliezer has no temperature in the evening, but complains of severe pains in his chest. The stewardesses bring meals to his cabin, but he does not eat. In a quiet but clear voice he asks to be left in peace. In the morning, his eyes are closed and he answers the second mate's questions with moans: he does not speak.

Although radio silence is imposed, the captain decides to get in touch with MEDICO, an international organization giving medical aid and advice to ships on high seas. Accordingly, a telegram is sent, listing the symptoms of Eliezer's sickness. The answer arrives within a few hours. "Complete rest recommended. The man should be hospitalized as soon as possible."

In the evening there is a knock on the door, and Mississippi lifts her head and glares with wide-open eyes.

He says, "Sippi, quiet! Sit down, captain." There is a definite sympathy between the two men, and the dog relaxes.

"I am in trouble," says the captain, "would you do me a favor?"

"Anything that can help you. A drink?"

"No, thank you. Later. Would you mind going with me to Eliezer Rosen's cabin and having a look at him?"

"Let's go."

It's a good cabin. Originally when the ship was built it was destined for the cook. It's spacious, has only one bed, an imitation leather coach, a formica table, a washstand separated by a curtain. There are two pictures on the wall, a calendar, and one old *Playboy* pin-up. Eliezer lies quietly, prone, with closed eyes.

"How are you, Eliezer?"

No answer. His face is ashen-white, a four day stubble covers his cheeks and chin.

"Would you like a cup of tea?"

A moan.

"Do you still have pains in your chest?"

No answer.

"Eliezer, open your eyes, we want to help you."

He very slowly draws up his eyelids, looks at the ceiling over his head. The two men bend over him trying to look straight into his eyes, but they find that he is not there at all. He is somewhere far away, and certainly feels no pain.

Outside, he told the captain, "One cannot be sure, but I think the man is very high."

"High?"

"Yes, high, on drugs. Check to see if he's got hypodermic needle tracks on his arm. You know where to look for them, don't you?"

"Yes, I'll check, right now."

He returned five minutes later. "Plenty of holes there, he must be on the real hard stuff."

"What do you intend to do with him?"

"Exactly what MEDICO told us: to get rid of him as soon as possible; to hospitalize him in the first port."

Next morning, Eliezer feels well enough to come to the messroom to have his breakfast. He throws a woolen blanket over his shoulders, like a poncho, and on the spot earns his nickname: Blanketman. Somebody at the table tries to joke with him, but Eliezer snarls and looks at him in such a way that the joker turns pale and the smile vanishes from his face.

"We should warn the men not to joke with him," says the third mate. "He is not a greenhorn, he is a real old-timer. I sailed with him two years ago. They flew him back from New York to Israel."

"What happened?"

"Nothing much: he opened the chief mate's skull with an iron spike. Nobody ever joked with Eliezer Rosen after that."

His social status is secure and elevated. When the cook prepares an impossible lunch for two consecutive days (it is a minor miracle he cooks at all during this period, drunk as he is) and the crew presents the captain with a letter of protest, Eliezer's signature is the first on the list, before that of the bosun and the carpenter.

His is the best seat in the television room, and he instructs others where to sit so that they don't disturb him. Occasionally he bestows a favor on somebody, condescending to play a game of backgammon or cards. He benevolently instructs young crewmembers about their legal rights; he has the last word in discussions about overtime and special pay. He does not work, since he is officially sick, and spends long hours in his cabin, lying in his bunk. At other times, he haunts the ship's alleyways, mess, recreation and TV rooms, the blanket always on his shoulders, disregarding the fact that the ship is well heated.

He is, it turns out, a clever man, not the doped moron he appears to be; there's an inner logic to his behavior, he's capable of calculating, and knowing exactly how to make his way in the world in which he lives. "Far more successful than I have ever been," I think bitterly.

12.

Darling,

My days during the first ten days of this trip have usually started at seven. That's when Mississippi scratches my face, and says in a whine: 'I have to go out!'

I take her on the boat deck, and after running for ten minutes with her nose close to the floor, she finds the exact spot she has been looking for, crouches, and pees there. It is not always the same place, and watching her every morning during this ritual, I wonder what it is that directs her choice.

After bringing her back to the cabin—she is reluctant to return, she apparently enjoys the fresh morning on the sea as much as I do—I go down to the pantry and bring my first cup of coffee to my cabin: you know that I am absolutely incapable of starting a day without it.

Only then do I shave and shower and go down to the mess for breakfast. At the table there I meet the chief mate, first engineer and, usually, the captain. We talk business for a quarter of an hour or so, and then I go down for my first daily inspection of the engine room.

Having spent many years of my life at sea, I am accustomed to sleeping well on ships, but during this trip I have had difficulties falling asleep and keep waking up during the night at irregular intervals.

I then turn on the radio, and try to catch a news broadcast. Listening to the news has become an obsession. In the beginning, almost everybody on board was victim to it, but for most the intensity of the malady wore off the further we sailed from Israeli shores; by the time we approached Gibraltar, the majority were satisfied with the news as typed daily by Paul, the Sparkie, who listens to a special broadcast from Israel for ships at sea once daily. My case is different. Even after ten days I can easily spend an hour turning the knobs of a radio. The Voice of Israel is out of range at this distance. I listen to Italian, German stations, to the Voice of America, to the BBC. *It's amazing how many ways the same news can be dished up! What unbelievable tricks can be performed with words!*

Here's BBC *Radio 4: '...the assumption might well have been made that Presidents Assad and Sadat were simply seeking to defer the major coup by the Israeli forces which, in accordance with Israel's usual policy, might have been expected to follow the heavy diplomatic setback of Austria's recent concessions to the Arab guerillas...but initial Arab and Soviet claims that the new war in its present form and on its present scale was started by Israel are simply not credible and have not, in fact, been very seriously sustained...'*

An example of cool objectivity, isn't it? What proper wording! BBC *English, or the Queen's English, I have never mastered it completely, it is not my mother tongue, after all. Envy. Regret.*

And yet this configuration of words, these 'might have been' constructions, leave a bad taste in my mouth when repeated aloud. To my ears, they sound like a false note, like a dissonance. Is it because I have been trained to listen most attentively to the wild music of an engine room, and to discover any abnormal sound?

No, it is definitely not a problem of sound. One day the BBC *reported that, according to a communiqué issued in Damascus that afternoon, Syrian warplanes had attacked Haifa, that the oil refineries and the port installation had been hit and set afire. No other European station found it necessary to repeat that nonsense. Apparently they learned something about Syrian war communiqués during the Six Day War, when they reported that they had bombed Tel Aviv, Haifa, Netanya and Naha-riya, even though not one bomb fell on these towns in 1967.*

An American with a nasal twang reported a few hours later that the news from Damascus about the air attack on Haifa seemed to be 'the product of oriental imagination.' But the BBC *did not retract, even though they had a special correspondent in Israel who certainly checked immediately and found that the Syrian claim was simply a brazen lie.*

I've just been called—I will continue later…

13.

The sky at sunset is sloping downward, like the roof of a tent, and the land from both sides is closing up, forcing the ship to the tent's corner, sailing toward Gibraltar.

More and more ships are going on converging courses, all toward that narrow mouth of a funnel, as if the tall rock on the right side were drawing them like a magnet.

Even more careful than before the night encounter with the warship, they keep to the northern coast, ever nearer to the Rock.

He stands on the boat deck, beneath the bridge, where all the crew not on duty are gathered, passing one pair of binoculars from hand to hand, exclaiming that they can see the canons now, threatening under the low sky that is the color of a rusty iron plate. Enormous flat slopes, smooth slopes of concrete: inside, they say, this whole giant rock is hollow like a honeycomb, or like an anthill, drilled through with tunnels, corridors, galleries and alleys: underground buildings.

He prefers to see it as the Glass Mountain from the fairy tales he listened to half a century ago near the big, black kitchen oven.

The hero climbed on, with bleeding fingers. Grimm, no? German folklore always seemed to be a bit cruel.

It would be difficult to negotiate Gibraltar's smooth surfaces at that angle. They most certainly have lifts inside, many automatic lifts and staircases. Interesting, how this mountain must look inside; it could probably be broken open by an atomic explosion. He paces the deck slowly, counting the ships: nine, ten, fourteen, two submarines as well.

A magnet mountain, yes, he remembers the primitive woodcut well, too. Planks flying loose from that ship, and big nails in the air like arrows, and the sole sailor in the middle of the picture averting his head in fear and despair: he'll drown in a moment. The book was heavy, with a thick, hard cover, and there was a thin engraved metal plate on it: *The Universe and Humankind*, in Russian. The pages were of thick, glistening paper. He once cut his finger on a page.

"Watch out, child, you can cut your hands badly with paper." How odd.

Mississippi, excited by the vicinity of land, by the smells perhaps, runs around the deck, suspiciously watching from under the life boats, her tail tense, her lips and the tip of her nose twitching slightly. Now the opening toward the Atlantic looks more like the door of a furnace, big orange and red streaks flowing from the sky downward, westward. Ships are also coming in from there, and fanning out in all directions of the Mediterranean.

But in his head, there are shadows of associations concerning the furnace doors, and he leaves the deck, whistling to the dog to follow him. The electrician calls out to him. "Come over to see me later. I have a fresh bottle, we'll try to catch the 21.00 German news."

The first mile-long wave of the ocean swell rolls the ship very gently when they start drinking. "What shall we call this? It can't be an aperitif," says the first engineer.

"The occasion is evident. Entering the Atlantic!"

"We always used to…"

"Quiet now, vodka is not good when warm," says the cook. "Let's get started."

14.

Along the coast of Portugal, along the Spanish coast, going north, starting at the diagonal of Biscay, under a sky of milk: under Salvador Dalí's sky, low below the crucified Christ's feet on a smooth sea, breathing very slowly and regularly with Atlantic swell.

One day a short message in code arrives: Proceed to Kiel Canal. The captain does not keep it secret, and it has a cheering effect on the crew: Kiel Canal may mean Copenhagen, perhaps Sweden, or even Finland. Even Eliezer puts the enormous weight of his experienced opinion into the discussion and confirms gravely that yes, Copenhagen is OK. Gothenburg is still better, though more expensive.

"To enjoy life as a seaman," he explains to three young sailors, "you must have money, and lots of it. Remember. Without money you are nothing but a bum in a port."

He still walks around with the dirty blanket thrown over his shoulders. You see him everywhere and at all times. He asks the captain respectfully for sleeping pills; he cannot sleep nights. He still does not work and answers the question 'How do you feel' with a gloomy look.

The ship is to enter the English Channel this afternoon, and visibility grows worse every moment. The radar is on constantly, and the captain now stays permanently on the bridge. First fog patches, and then a blanket of fog, solid and dense, descends on the sea. The traffic, as always in these waters, is very lively, on both sides of the separation zone. Ships going northeast keep close to the French coast; the southbound near to England. But these are only recommendations, not rules, you can expect at any time to encounter a ship which, for reasons unknown, including the captain's mutinous temper, sails against traffic.

And then there are the ferries crossing the Channel from France to Britain, from Britain to Holland. Hovercraft. Fishermen. Yachts. All this, in visibility limited to three or four hundred yards, requires a very watchful captain on the bridge if you want to make a safe passage. For this reason, the captain of this ship stays on the bridge for twenty-four hours and more, and has his meals brought up to him.

When the passage is finally ended and the ship starts sailing the buoyed routes of the North Sea, the captain tells him—his eyes inflamed a little from two sleepless nights—"I have started my master's career on the wrong foot: things keep happening to me…"

"Nonsense! You're leading the ship beautifully. And she's in ballast!" It is no simple matter, an empty ship on such a voyage.

"No, no," he interrupts gently. "Bad luck on this trip: there was this warship, and now—please don't tell anybody—this morning I found the ship's strongbox empty."

"How much?"

"Three thousand one hundred and fifty-four dollars."

"When did you see it last?"

"Before we sailed, on the evening of the departure."

"Where was the key?"

"In the key closet, in my bedroom."

"You have suspicions?"

"Naturally."

I thought a moment, and said, "No. I don't think he is cunning enough for that. Nor daring enough. Look, it takes a lot of guts to come in to the cabin, to go to your bedroom, to find this key. To open the box, to replace the key, knowing all the time that you may be back any moment."

"He knew I'd stay on the bridge while we were in the Channel."

"Did you check well? Perhaps you misplaced it somehow? Put it in another place?"

"I've checked ten times."

Together, they turn everything upside down in the cabin. Nothing. The money is gone.

There was morphine in the same box, but some of it is left: the captain does not know how much.

"If I were in his place, I'd take this stuff before the money."

"Maybe he couldn't be sure what it was?"

He now pictures Blanketman cautiously entering the captain's cabin, looking all around, looking for the key—he is an experienced seaman, he knows where to look for it—opening the strongbox, taking the envelope with the money, closing the box, replacing the key. He shakes his head. "Captain, I'll bet you it's not him."

"Accepted. A bottle of Scotch? OK. But who else?"

"You have to make a general search."

"Of course. Before anybody leaves the ship. And I'll call the local police to assist us. But if we load tanks and guns, it will be complicated."

"Are we loading tanks?"

"The message came this morning. Proceed to Bremerhaven. Keep it between the two of us, OK?"

"OK. But I'll tell Mississippi."

"Good. She can know."

"I am sorry, Captain. You don't deserve this, so help me God."

He smiles, smiles bashfully. "What the hell, it's apparently part of the job; but they never teach you things like that in nautical school."

"No, they don't."

As if nothing had happened, the ship sails on, from one numbered buoy to another. There is much talk on the radio and television about an armistice, Russian and American pressure, Russia's unlimited supplies to the Arabs, and American airlifts to Israel.

"Sippi, I doubt if we'll arrive in time with these tanks. This barge is running at twelve at the best, it took us fourteen days to get here, takes two or three days for loading, fourteen days back…"

"It's your business to give her more speed. And what about those bones you promised me this morning?"

"Silly dog, I can't give more speed than this old coffee mill is doing. As it is, the exhaust temperatures are already too high. And I talked to the cook about those bones, he says he'll prepare them for you, but after we threw that second bottle through the porthole, he must have forgotten. I'll remind him, don't worry about it…not on meat and bones alone…aren't you sorry for that man, and this his maiden voyage as captain, with all these troubles?"

"You forget I am a dog, after all. And bones and meat are very, very important for me. I am totally dependent on you, as a supplier. If I go to the galley and steal them, what would you say? You'd beat me blue. Isn't one thief enough on a cargo boat of this size?"

"Who is the other one?"

"You've already had four shots of Scotch now, it is only ten o'clock in the morning."

"Three."

"Four. You forgot the one before shaving. An eye-opener you called it. So you had four shots of that stuff, and you're talking nonsense already: I did not steal those bones, so don't talk to me about the other thief."

"Sippi, did Blanketman steal the money?"

She looks at him reproachfully and keeps silent.

In desperation, he takes another quick one. It gives him courage. But at lunch, he looks at Eliezer with different eyes. It is still the same Eliezer, he has not changed at all. He asks, after lunch, "Captain, are you sure you'll be able to hospitalize me in Germany?"

The captain assures him he'll be taken to the hospital immediately, without asking him how he knows about Germany.

"I still have pains in my chest, here, you know, Captain."

"I know."

The pilot vessel is lit like a Christmas tree in the estuary of Weser, a river mouth so wide that you don't see the shores at all. It looks as if the pilots wait for you in the middle of the sea. And the sea itself becomes gradually very rough, the wind is rising and howling. But nobody cares: they've made it, a trip of two weeks minus one day, and they launch a small motorboat from the pilot vessel, which is less than half a mile from the ship now.

He and the dog go to the bridge as the pilot climbs up the

ladder. Standing in the alleyway with the dog, he tries to decide if the pilot could have been a young sailor on a Nazi submarine thirty years ago. "You just can't tell, Mississippi. You just can't tell, a human face is a most effective mask."

"Two and a half hours up the river, you'll probably load weapons or munitions on the American pier," says the pilot casually. "Two other Israeli ships were already there."

But before the entrance to the lock, there is a short conversation on the VHF phone between the pilot and somebody ashore, in German, and after gently replacing the receiver, he says, "We're dropping anchor here meanwhile, Captain. We have to wait."

The rattling of the anchor chain, engine slow astern, then stop, then: FINISHED WITH ENGINE. Sudden silence after thirteen days of constant thumping. The ship swings slowly on the anchor with the tide. The pilot puts on his raincoat.

"Goodbye, Captain. Here is my boat. Thank you."

That same evening, they announce an armistice on the front between Egypt and Israel.

15.

Consider it an atavistic return to the womb: the ship was born here, somewhere a bit further up on the shores of the same river. The river was as dark brown as it is now, with dikes on both sides, naked willows along the banks for miles and miles of hopelessness.

Under a low gray sky, swarms of crows circle overhead. Nearer to the river mouth, there were seagulls, big and sharp-eyed, screaming out their insatiable hunger, fighting furiously over every scrap of food in the water and carrying the fight into the air, tearing a piece of meat or fish out of each other's beak. Flapping their huge wings.

But now they are in the crows' territory, slower and more sinister than the gulls. They sit in silent rows on the naked branches and occasionally send one of their band for a reconnaissance flight over the river. When the messenger spots something worth his interest, he announces it to the others in a piercing cry. Then the whole flock makes its way swiftly over and the fight for the chunk of food starts, as ruthless as that of the seagulls.

At a bend in the river they anchor, where there is more space for ships passing to and from Wesermünde, Nordenham, Brake, and Bremen, all of them further up the river. Fourteen years ago, he was present when they put this ship together from iron plates somewhere in the vicinity. He went over to the shipyard every morning breathing small clouds of steam in the cold air, walking quickly on the frozen ground to keep his feet warm.

Not too old, then. A young man. The supervising engineer. He climbed the scaffolding, watched the German welders, riveters, mechanics, carpenters, all of them working as though possessed, for the *Wirtschaftswunder* was in full swing, life was becoming better every day, and the cosmic disaster of 1945 was sinking quickly into oblivion: but one had to work harder and harder. That's what they were told, and they obeyed, a disciplined crowd. The supervisor, the Israeli engineer, could look on, it did not make them self-conscious, they had nothing to be ashamed of; the quality of their work was high. He stared for long minutes at the raw iron frames, newly installed machines, motors, pipes. He hardly exchanged a word with anybody. Sometimes he took off his woollen gloves and spread the plans and drawings he carried in a black leather portfolio.

It rained. It snowed. The naked trees around the shipyard gesticulated wildly with their branches in the wind. He climbed the wooden ladder up from the iron mausoleum that would become an engine room in a couple of months.

His head always bare, he walked over the ship; a 'reparations' ship. Later, he would sail in this ship. In the evening, when it was dark outside and the port was bathed in the cold glare of powerful lamps and the flare of electrical welding exploded silently all over the place, he buttoned up his coat, and walked back to the little town, where he had hired a room in a *Gasthaus*. The electric stove was on, but the room was naked, clean, sterile, like a monk's cell. He turned on the desk lamp and checked the lists again, the drawings, specifications, instruction booklets.

Downstairs, in the inn, white lace curtains at the windows, the shipyard workers would start drinking their beer around nine o'clock. There were two movie houses in town, but they were mostly frequented by teenagers, kids conceived more in desperation than in love during the war years. The older generation preferred the television, or the pub.

They drank beer and relaxed, and talked, in this white-walled cozy warm room, and later, becoming nostalgic or romantic, or mellow, they would start singing, and these songs, together with the beer vapors, would rise up to his room.

They were very correct, very civilized, they greeted him with respect: "*Jawohl Herr Ingenieur, haben Herr Ingenieur wohl geschlaffen?* Not too cold for you?" This from the big buxom blonde-haired, blue-eyed proprietress of the inn. "In my room it is nice and warm." A long, unblinking stare.

To hell with you, you bitch: I'd rather freeze to death than sleep with you. Reading Graves' poems for relaxation, to neutralize the roar of German voices and the smell of beer and wurst.

"And you haven't been here since then?" asks the electrician.

"Yes, many times with ships. But it's different than living here."

"Times have changed," says the first engineer. "Here, take these olives, they go well with whiskey."

The cook, tired of his monkeys and happy that he has human company to drink with, declares: "I've always liked German ports. What is important to people like me is that they don't dis...discro...disc..."

"Discriminate," the first engineer helps him.

"That's it. Against colored people. On the contrary. Their girls like screwing with Negroes, Arabs, Spaniards. A dark skin, even not very dark, just like mine, and you're in business, boy."

"Most of the nightclubs in Berlin are owned by Israelis."

"A great asset for us."

"Sure. And their broadcasts in this war are more favorable to us than the French or the British."

Back then he wasn't drinking yet. On the desk beneath the lamp in the *Gasthaus* stood a framed photograph of a woman. Poetry was effective. But the woman had been dead for a long time. People were giving him all kinds of advice about how to live, people with good intentions: one very old man with a beard, somebody's grandfather, came up to him, put his slightly shaking hand on his arm, and said, "In accordance to what is written, one must forget." And gradually, in accordance with the old man's advice, he forgot. Forcibly. The problem that remained very acute was how to fill the vacuum.

"Give me another one," he said. "By and by we'll eliminate all this."

Laughter. A standing joke between them, but still good for a laugh; once they drank somewhere with the crew of a Cuban freighter, which was well educated politically. Asked about conditions in Castro's land, they'd answer: "Poverty? Well, there is still some poverty here and there, but by and by we'll eliminate all this. Whores? None. No prostitution. Well, there are still some, but by and by..." and so on. They kept asking them absurd questions just to hear that lovely phrase, and later it became an integral part of the ship's slang.

"Here we are back in good old Germany. We'll see what they'll give us."

"It's the Americans that give us, not them."

"And what does it look like ashore now?"

"I hope we'll get to see for ourselves in the morning."

"*Inshallah.*"

Undressing in the cabin an hour later, he tells the dog, "You'll get ashore tomorrow." Her ears move a little. "It will be nice to stretch your legs a bit, heh? I'll take you to a park or something, where you can run a bit." Now she beats with her tail on the sofa.

"Don't get involved with any German dogs please. Fraternization is one thing, but...you're an Israeli dog, aren't you? A *sabra*, born there. You know that in wartime we don't hold any grudges, we love each other very much. Even that dog-hunter; nobody would think of bringing him to the kibbutz now. He is probably mobilized, somewhere on the road to Damascus or in Egypt now, not shooting dogs, I assure you."

And that woman who thinks keeping dogs is a bad bourgeois habit, to be abolished in a kibbutz society? They never change, war or peace. They have been so brainwashed, so indoctrinated, that nothing ever changes in them. She fulfills the stereotype and strives with her whole being to live up to this stereotyped standard: hardworking, social, clean, severe, no make-up on her face, no fancy clothes, do your knitting, clean your apartment, have a tidy garden, take care of your husband's clothes, listen to the news, believe in Golda and pray for the children on the front. A woman in war. A worker-woman. A kibbutz woman. Hair tied up in a bun on the back of your head, if possible.

"Enough of this poison for tonight, dog. Let's take another shot of that other, merciful poison, and we'll turn in. A busy day tomorrow."

16.

Nothing of the sort. The ship swings on her anchor and seems to be forgotten by all. Ships are passing in the river—Greek, British, Indian, French, Dutch, Polish—all of them with pilot on board, heading to Bremen, or in the opposite direction, to the sea. Small boats pass close by on their business. Barges. Tugs. Twice a motor launch with WASSERPOLIZEI in white letters sails around the ship.

"That's what we were running for like mad? And now they let us wait!" the chief mate says. "Once they sent us out from Haifa on Passover Eve, when everybody in the country sits down to the Seder. They sent us to sail full speed to Thassos, to load iron ore. We begged, we protested, we asked them to postpone the sailing by three hours, but nothing helped. We sailed out, and had Seder at sea. When we reached Thassos we dropped anchor there, and stayed on anchor for ten days and only then started loading."

"But this is war, man!"

"Cease-fire, since yesterday. They don't need your tanks or guns anymore."

"Like hell they don't."

"Fact is, they're letting you rot in this river."

"Patience, boy, twenty-four hours haven't yet passed. They can still come in the afternoon, and the whole night ashore is yours."

The cook walks around nervously, like a big cat, already in his shore dress. Mississippi looks at the river banks, brown, covered with patches of meager grass here and there, her nose and tail high, quivering slightly, high-strung: lifting her left forepaw, running from port to starboard and back. Temptation.

Patience. He pets her back but this has no effect on the dog's tension now.

At five in the afternoon a tug comes alongside and brings three visitors on board: two Israelis and the German agent's representative, a young man with a honey-colored beard and reddish hair.

The two Israelis sitting in the captain's cabin are exactly the opposite of each other; one is loud and enthusiastic, the other, quiet and detached, has said just two words against the torrent of his colleague.

"So I loaded these two ships with goodies, and got them out. You are the third one. You've fixed security watches as they should be, Captain? Not that it matters much, I've got several Negro MPS as well. Now this is the plan: you'll put in the day after tomorrow, in the morning, and will load."

"Have you brought any newspapers from home? We haven't seen a paper in two weeks, you know."

"Israeli papers?" the other man looks surprised. "No, we haven't got any papers with us. I have some at home. But we talked on the telephone with Tel Aviv today and everything is all right."

"Very sensitive munitions this, you give it one strong look, and whew! up you go…You're the chief, aren't you? Well, you'd better disconnect the electric current to your holds altogether, we don't want any shorts there, do we?"

"I have a sick man on board, he has to be hospitalized."

"We'll talk it over when you're in, Captain. As we said, you'll get in in two days."

"If there isn't a problem," says the other man quietly.

"Yes, there is a slight chance of a problem, but I hope that in the end everything will be all right and smooth and you'll load your stuff."

"I also have a case for criminal investigation."

"Now, in war?"

The quiet man says, "Look, Captain, let's leave it till you are moored alongside, OK?"

The redheaded German does not say a word. He polishes his fingernails.

Then, they are gone and the crew in the messroom starts complaining vociferously about the lack of any launches ashore.

Eliezer shifts the blankets over his arms. "According to the contract, boats for service, for shore-leave, should be provided when the ship is anchored outside the port."

"Clever sea lawyer that you are, you should know that the ship hasn't been cleared yet, not by the medical authorities, not by the police or by customs. Anyway, what good would it do you if we had a service launch ashore, Eliezer? You can't go ashore, you'll be brought straight to the hospital in an ambulance."

He looks up at the captain, their eyes meet, and he says softly, "I am not speaking for myself, Captain. Just for the men."

Ten minutes later, facing his dog—who has suddenly became completely apathetic, curled in a semicircle with her long nose between her hind legs, eyes closed, and sighing an almost human sigh (where did she learn it?)—he is glowing with quiet satisfaction. He has made the right decision, then: not too old, in spite of the computer. They won't be bringing television sets and washing machines, they'll be bringing munitions.

Simultaneously, he knows deep in his heart how wrong this approach is, how egocentric, and how unimportant this consideration is. Did you sail out to prove that you are not too old? No, I sailed to bring military supplies. But other people on board do not seem to care much what the ship will carry on her way back. Are you more patriotic than the others? No, I don't think so. But I do care a lot about this country. I have no other. I am happy if I can contribute, even in the smallest way, to winning this war. You must win it? We cannot lose it: and I cannot lose it, personally: to be a candidate for the Final Solution once in a lifetime is enough. I swore then I would never, ever, be a candidate again. The whole issue is very simple for me."

The captain pages him. "Come to the bridge immediately, please, it is the agent on the telephone, but his English sounds so German that I can barely understand."

On the VHF the agent is panting with excitement: "*Um Gottes Willen*, Captain, I told you that you must disappear from here immediately, do you understand?"

"Tell him I must get orders from other authorities than he."

The agent becomes frantic, hysterical.

"At once! You must sail now, now! I'm sending you a river pilot in half an hour!"

"I don't understand anything of it," says the captain quietly.

"Neither do I."

"But is the engine ready?"

"On ten minutes notice."

"OK. Let's wait and see."

They look at the promised land of Bremerhaven behind the lock gates, behind the barren dikes, where the glow of the town already lights up.

Then, again, the name of the ship is called on the phone.

This time it is another voice, from another place, and it speaks Hebrew.

"Captain? I am sorry. Please follow your agent's instructions, we can do nothing against it. Very sorry. You'll sail to South Wales now, to Swansea, it is not far from Port Talbot, Bristol."

"I happen to know where Swansea is," says the captain, red with anger.

"Well, *bon voyage*, then."

From the darkness of the river another pilot arrives, wet in the drizzle. He is a big, burly man who takes off his duffel coat, removes an evening paper from its pocket and spreads it on the chart table.

"Well, gentlemen," he says, "because of these two pictures I now have the unpleasant duty of taking you out to sea."

What a scoop they scored, that photographer and reporter: In the white glare of mercury lamps, a whole train of flatcars is coming up to the freighter. On every flatcar there are two self-propelled guns or tanks. The other picture shows other tanks on board the ship. And finally, the article. He translates it from German, and they listen.

The ship is sailing slowly down the river it has come up yesterday, towards the sea, the pilot giving quiet orders to the helmsman, which the man repeats in a clear voice. "One hundred twenty-five."

"One hundred twenty-five."

"Steady."

"Steady."

"Midships. Full ahead."

"Full ahead, sir."

Over the past few days, the citizens of this town were surprised to see railway transports of tanks and artillery being unloaded and put hastily aboard the steamers along the quay. This could easily be seen by any passerby on the street. However, on the other side of the fence, armed American military personnel motioned the onlookers to move on. Our correspondent, taking pictures, was surprised by two MPS, *who jumped over the fence and took both him and his camera into custody...*

"Steer two eight one. Half speed."

"Half speed."

"Steady as she goes."

"Steady, sir."

...Only thanks to the quick intervention of our police was our reporter released. The pictures he took are reproduced above. The Minister of the Interior has already lodged a vigorous protest this afternoon with the American officer in charge of military supplies... The Ministry

announced that no military supplies would be loaded from German ports to any party participating in the war in the future.

"Full speed, please."

"Full speed engine."

We think that our American allies and friends here should be reminded that although they are welcome guests in this country, this is still German territory, a sovereign and independent state...

"Strange, isn't it? They don't write anything else?"

"No. There's football on the inside page, and a shortage of oil."

"No foreign news?"

"Yes. France declares neutrality. The Soviet Union issues a warning.

"Twenty five, thirty years, it's a short time, isn't it?"

"I remember," says the electrician, "one German woman swore to me that the Negroes in the American zone raped as many women as the wild Russians in their occupation area. 'No difference,' she said. 'War turns people into beasts,' she said."

"When was it?"

"Then, after the war. I was a kid. In '46."

"It's an independent country now."

"Sure it is."

"Two hundred sixty. More to Port."

"More to Port, sir."

"How much have you got on the compass?"

"Two hundred fifty-five."

"Steady so."

"Steady, sir."

"Still, it is strange that they should make a scandal about it. They could have loaded it elsewhere, in a place where a nosy reporter wouldn't come."

The cook arrives on unsteady legs, in his best dark-blue suit. "No launch ashore?"

"We're sailing, Yisrael."

"Sailing? Where?"

"To England."

He looks at us with uncomprehending eyes, tears off his tie, and says, "You're crazy, all of you! The whole bunch!"

He staggers out, mumbling. Then comes Eliezer. "I won't be hospitalized here, Captain, sir?"

"No. You'll be hospitalized in Britain."

"I don't feel so well, sir. I'd prefer to go ashore here, sir."

"We are out at sea, Eliezer. The river pilot leaves in half an hour."

He looks around, looks at the darkness of the sea outside, and pulls the blanket tighter around his arms. Without another word, he turns around and heads to the TV room.

There, you can see for a fleeting moment a snapshot of our own ship as she appeared, anchored, a few hours ago at the Bremerhaven roadsteads. Also on the screen are images of tired, bearded young Israeli soldiers, 'somewhere on the Egyptian front,' cleaning their weapons. Weary. Cut to the handsome, clean-shaven North German TV announcer: "The guns are silent now."

But his theme tonight is different: he is busy with that persistent foul taste in his mouth, which obstinately resists all attempts to wash it away with Scotch.

"Evil is obscene and stinking, Mississippi."

The ship is stopped for a moment, the pilot must be leaving, I should go and ask him to leave his *Norddeutsche Zeitung* for me as a souvenir. Inertia prevents me from getting up: what do I need that rag for? To brag later how they chased us out?

"Dog, I did not say Hannah Arendt was wrong with her banality of evil: but the main thing about evil is not banality, but obscenity. Take it from me. This applies to Eichmann's crime, which is genocide, and to all other crimes, even down to such small, insignificant pieces of shit like the expulsion order for this ship.

"Genocides, dog, means evil on a very large scale. We've had plenty since that transportation officer sat in his glass cage in Jerusalem. We've had Congo-Katanga, Biafra, Bangladesh, Vietnam,

Burundi, South Africa, and Brazil (where some people on trial claimed honestly that they did not know killing Amazon Indians was wrong)—to mention only the most important ones.

"How about it, Mississippi? Obscenity plus banality, eh? And if it is true we're sailing to Britain, they won't even let you ashore; the British are very strict about it. It's a criminal offence if I take you ashore. But don't worry, I will. I will. Even if it is only at night, and only in the port. We'll find a place for you to run, and to pee and shit like a dog should. People shit into each other's faces daily, and you're just an innocent dog."

17.

Sailing back the same way they've come, spotting the same, numbered buoys in opposite order, was like walking back from a visit where the person you were looking for wasn't home. Or, perhaps, did not want to see you. In any case, the door was closed, nobody answered.

Mercifully, the sea was quiet. When it is as quiet as now, it is difficult to imagine a real gale, with huge steel-gray waves rolling and crashing down on the decks. Naturally, its only obvious purpose is destroying, annihilating you and whatever funny vessel you happen to be in. That's the treacherous part of it. Looking at this smooth water now you cannot believe the potential of fury hidden in it is real. But that's how the sea is, and it is silly to accuse it of treachery.

It is the human lack of imagination that is to be blamed. He has sailed these waters in war and in peace, but what is it now? The guns are silent, but he can still see wisps of smoke rising from the hot gun barrels; and the acrid smell of burnt things, burnt bodies still in his nostrils. It takes no effort to recreate these in his imagination, but a storm on this quiet sea, hardly.

And still they do not know what had happened there, at home, who has been killed and who has been wounded, only that there have been many. They sail in the shadow of this war, it is with them the whole time, the sun is in hiding and the color all around is dark bluish-gray in daytime, blackness at night.

Another pipe has broken in the engine room and he silently watches water streaming in the bilges.

"Never mind, we still have a day or a day and a half to go, we'll manage somehow. We can rig another pump to deal with it; in port we will take care of it."

"And if they don't let us in, like in Bremerhaven?"

"Then we'll say we have emergency repairs, they have to let us in to fix it."

The crew is more nervous now, seventeen days at sea, the tension is high. Only the necessary words are spoken. The continental TV set is covered with a blanket, the British one is turned on. The Middle East war is not very much on their minds, the oil crisis, the energy crisis is, but this is very relative indeed. Watching the little box nobody would deduce this nation is in any trouble at all: for hours and hours you can watch football matches and an international gymnastics contest for women.

Women is an exaggeration: the East European teams, with Russia leading with several first places, stars young girls of eighteen, seventeen and even fifteen. With their young children's bodies, they perform incredible feats of balance and equilibrium, fantastic jumps and somersaults defying the laws of gravity. The public is wild about them. Then, the leading girl of fifteen twists her ankle in a jump, and loses precious points.

The camera eye follows her like a magnet, keeping the close-up of her childish face for all to see, biting her lips as she goes down the aisle, and finally, when the trainer, a stern-faced matron, whispers into her ear, tears rolling down her cheeks. Words of reproach? Encouragement? You nasty little bitch, is that what we taught you to do? Is that what we spent years and tens of thousands of rubles on, for you to lose first place? To cry in front of all these foreigners? Or, perhaps: Hush, Olga, child, it's nothing, it could happen to anybody. You're wonderful, it's just real bad luck. We have to accept it, my dear...

A strange thought occurs to him, that maybe it was he who, looking at her in the recreation room of this Israeli ship, sailing west

now, but on a very definite mission to bring weapons and/or munitions—to fight the weapons and munitions sent by the same country
that has sent this girl to perform gymnastic feats in Britain—he, who
put the evil eye on her, causing her to slip in that fatal jump. He, with
his own bleary eye, covered with a thin film of booze, and so full of
hatred for the rulers of their country and all that they stand for, for
the perverse and evil symbolic and dialectic of the Soviet State, that
it extends, irrationally, to everything, even things as remotely connected with it as this girl. He had, after all, cursed her aloud with
chosen curses in the several languages he speaks, hating to see the
USSR at the top of that list, hating it more than seeing Czechoslova-
kia or East Germany or Hungary up there in the second, third, and
fourth places.

If she were told he had given her the evil eye, she would be
perplexed, this girl, and the stern-faced matron would say, What
nonsense! Does he think you are a primitive child of a backward
nation, and believe in magic?

And to her he would say, Yes, Madame. I have not the slightest
doubt but that you and that child belong to a very backward nation,
in spite of your so-called achievements: Sputniks, rockets, the Moscow
Metro, sophisticated weapons. As for magic, you are too stupid to
understand anything about it.

Naturally, she would pay no heed to what he said, but she'd
throw him as hateful a glance as the one he'd hurled at her teen
acrobat; Communist women know how to look at you straight on,
and with furious hatred.

The man with the blanket, Eliezer, says aloud: "I wouldn't mind
raising that Russian girl on my prick tonight."

And then it comes to him in a flash, that he has placed himself
in the same camp with Eliezer: a sign of equality between Blanketman
and himself: Shipmates. Jews. Sailors. Israelis, both. This makes him
still more furious, and he looks around for somebody to drink with,
but the cook is playing poker for cigarettes in the messroom and the
first engineer and the electrician are busy in the engine room and

the chief mate is on watch and the captain is on the bridge. That leaves only Mississippi, but it occurs to him that she does not really like to watch him drinking. She sits straight upright, like a man, her back to the sofa.

"Things are very bad indeed, dog," he reports to her as he refills his glass. "They chased us out of Germany like a bad man boots out his dog. I've never done that to you, have I? I hate the Russians, which you can well understand, but I hate a lot of other people and things as well, and this makes living a difficult business. What makes me so bitter, for God's sake? For instance, I think it's ridiculous, obscene in fact, this BBC television offering hours upon hours of football, sport, and millions of people finding interest in it. Glued to the idiot-box. Do you realize that back home, on our kibbutz, there is a man who seriously believes that having, or not having, a television in the room of every kibbutznik is the balance between equality and inequality, that it is of paramount importance for the whole future of the kibbutz. A Hamlet: to be or not to be—reduced to TV. Now, would you believe it?"

The dog puts her long snout on her front legs.

"Don't take it to heart," she says after a long pause. "You are taking things far too much to heart. Too dead serious. Too much Camus, and Kafka; and Beckett. Don't be so serious: take things easier, that's all I can tell you."

"Thanks for the advice." He knows he cannot conceal the contempt in his voice. "That's what I expected. I knew you'd say that. And stop trying to charm me with those goddamn innocent eyes of yours. Eyes are for lying, you know. And I am old enough to recognize fake sincerity and innocence there. In dogs and in people. It's better to build a wall just behind the retina, like our Blanketman does. Ask me no questions and I'll give you no answers. And if you do ask questions, I won't give you any answers, either."

But later, in bed, they reconcile. It is cold now in the cabin, and she creeps in under the blanket, to feel him near her. She keeps his feet warm in the process. Symbiosis.

18.

Coming to the bay in southwest Wales is like landing on another planet.

Ah yes: but they say a dog has no real memory. You cannot punish her today for what she did yesterday. You can only pretend about the complexity, you can only anthropomorphize your dog to a certain limit. Past this limit, both of you are helpless. The dog can only look at you and you can only shrug. These are the frontiers of the contact, impossible to exceed, like the speed of light.

The bay is quiet, with black water. This quietness spreads out on the surrounding hills, perhaps carried on the back of a tidal wave in prehistoric times, leaving the air of strange tranquility permanently ashore. The sediment of solid, pre-war times is there, too, something that predates two world wars. The ship enters the ancient lock slowly, and on the embankment long rows of silent anglers keep their steady eyes on the line. The ship has come from beyond their system, and they aren't keen to meet these space-travelers.

But the first man who jumps aboard, one of the mooring party, a squat, middle-aged sailor, catches him by the button of his coat and murmurs, "I am not an Englishman, I am Welsh. I am sorry the British Government declared an embargo, and that they refuse to let you load the spare parts for the tanks they have sold you. You can only load steel here, solid Welsh steel."

And then the ship is moored in the quietness of the inner port, a very big port but with few ships in it, no trace of the feverish activity usually associated with a harbor. In the cold, still, afternoon air, blue smoke rises from the chimneys of cottages on the gentle slopes of the hills. Further up, there are rows of identical, tidy, old-fashioned houses; the smoke makes a simple, slightly melancholic music in the air.

South Wales.

Her Majesty's immigration officers are cool and polite. "Mind you, sir, that your dog does not go ashore, there is a heavy penalty for that offence. And the Customs people are correct and absolutely incorruptible."

"Oh, they are very strange, very sweet people," says the electrician. "Wait till we go to the Flying Angel Mission for Seamen, you'll see."

Paul shakes his head, "Queer, very queer people. They have not woken up yet."

"You mean they haven't heard about Uri Avneri yet?"

"Last time they heard about your Palestine was when Allenby rode in to Jerusalem on a white horse."

The mode, the air of a place, infects even the foreigners' behavior.

"Ah," the captain explains to the agent, "we have, unfortunately, some trouble on board: one man must be hospitalized, and even before that, there was a case of theft. Could we please have a representative of the Law on board?"

And so, until the Law arrives, the crew stays on board. It is now nineteen days that they have not stepped on terra firma. The gentle hills are alluring. In the evening, the Cork ferry booms mournfully, and heavy gloom descends on the countryside and the docks.

Fuck the Law, he says, and puts a collar on the dog's neck and takes her ashore.

How strange to look at the rusty side of the ship from the outside. The dog tugs impatiently on the leash, pees against a bollard, sniffs on the quay, her nose touching the ground: lots of alien, unknown smells. It is cold and wet, and a halo forms around every yellow lamp. The dog and the man shiver and return on board to the warmth and light of their cabin, but the man draws aside the curtains and stares through the window. There is something fascinatingly beautiful in the ugliness of the place. Some women are made this way, with ugly features and yet enormously attractive just because of it.

Pressing his face to the cold glass, the man loses his way in thought, as if his mind were numbed by the inertia of the outside world. The dog has no problems at the moment: she crawls under the blanket and falls asleep immediately. He detaches himself from the windowpane and goes to the pantry for a cup of coffee.

"Tomorrow, perhaps tomorrow, we can phone home."

"Sure, first thing ashore."

"I am afraid to phone home," says the chief mate, "afraid to ask who's been killed."

"Same here."

"Maybe we shouldn't?"

"Phone? We must."

They are very far from their country now, further than the distance that can be measured in miles or in weeks of absence. If it were Bremerhaven, they'd be much closer. But this place somehow has managed to remain in the early years of the century, has refused to join in the mad rush of time that has swept the world and their country with it.

The last bottle of vodka is opened; the cook is mysteriously elated about it: "We've finished sixty bottles of the stuff, five cases, in nineteen days! Not bad!"

He gets up and goes upstairs. This, too, is a way to spend the war: some are fighting, others are waiting, and still others drink sixty bottles of vodka.

We'll load steel here, he thinks, and we'll sail home. What have you brought? Steel, billets. As usual, eh? Sure. Steel in the lower hold, generals in the 'tween-deck.

"Will you go again next trip?"

"No. Unless there's war."

19.

Early in the morning, a gray Jaguar brings a uniformed police sergeant and two plain-clothes detectives: CID, they murmur, by way of introduction.

The sergeant is big and homely, with a protruding belly, and one of the detectives has an impressive black mustache. The other is tall, with a very white face. Drinking beer slowly, they listen quietly to the captain's narrative. When he has finished, there is a long silence. Then the sergeant clears his throat. "I understand, Captain, that in your opinion the theft occurred during the ship's passage through the English Channel."

"Correct."

"Could you tell us how far were you from the English coast during this passage?"

"Well, we were sailing northeast, and the traffic in this direction goes near the French coast."

"But how far would you estimate were you from our, from the British, coast?"

"Ten, fifteen, twenty miles."

"Of course. Well, you see, the point is, that if the money was stolen at that time, you were outside British territorial waters."

"No doubt about it."

"Then I am afraid we cannot help you. You were outside the limits of British jurisdiction."

"Beer," says the captain in Hebrew, "is not enough. Put a bottle of Scotch on the table."

"I was just about to do that. Let's work on them, otherwise they won't help us at all. I'll tell them there is a man I suspect."

"OK."

Half an hour later, the detectives, slightly bored, but a lot more sympathetic, agree to cooperate.

"But remember, Captain," the sergeant emphasizes, "this is Israeli territory, and officially you are leading this investigation, not us. The suspect, naturally, does not have to know it. Kindly call him in."

Eliezer enters the cabin, and he has no blanket on his shoulders. He is absolutely unperturbed, barely throws a glance at the policeman, looks at the captain.

"Eliezer, you will finally be hospitalized. But before this, I must tell you something. The ship's cash has disappeared. We are going to do a body search on every crewmember going ashore, and we will search in the cabins as well. As you are the first man to go ashore, to the hospital, we'll start with you."

He nods quietly. "Yes, sir. You can start with me. I understand. I have nothing against it, sir."

Eliezer, the captain, the chief mate and the two detectives go to Eliezer's cabin. Standing outside in the alleyway with the sergeant, he expects any moment an explosion of violence from inside. But after only a few minutes, the door opens, and the mustachioed detective asks for a plate from the messroom.

"A plate?"

"Yes, a big plate, please."

And then, five minutes later, they all file out. The chief mate holds the plate in both hands, and the plate is full of greenbacks.

"You found it?"

"Every cent of it."

"Well," Eliezer says, "Well, you don't have to search any more. To tell the truth, I wanted to return it the day after I took it. Because you were so good to me when I was sick, Captain. But I couldn't find the key anymore, you probably kept it in your pocket after the money disappeared. In fact, Captain, you shouldn't have left it in the key-box in the first place. A grave mistake on your part."

Later, on the captain's desk, they count the money: three thousand one hundred and fifty-one dollars. The detectives looked amused.

"Well, Captain, you've got your money back."

"Yes. I want this man repatriated immediately, and handed over to the Israeli police."

"That might prove difficult, sir. As far as I've heard there are no vacant places on planes flying to your country, and bookings have been made several days in advance. Anyway, he has to be brought to London first—under police escort, of course—eight hours by rail."

Eliezer sits in the messroom with a face like a large flat stone, a blanket on his shoulders, and eats his breakfast. The chief mate tells him that, by Captain's orders, he is forbidden to go ashore.

He accepts this information with a short nod, and puts another spoon of sugar into his coffee. Nobody speaks to him, and he eats his meal leisurely and serenely. Then he lights a cigarette and returns to his cabin.

20.

"A Hitchcock landscape," says the electrician. "But it is not far. A ten minute walk."

They continue on the desolate dock road, under bridges and cranes, in the evening drizzle. The lampposts are spaced a few hundred yards from each other. Grass sprouts from between the railway ties and on either side of the cobblestone road. A Greek steamer with all lights out: a dead ship. Two or three trawlers which look as if they have not been out to sea for years. The water in the docks is bottomless, ink-black.

He walks along with the others in this Gothic fantasy, thinking the landscape is absurd, a Hollywood set for a movie. But it is not a movie set, it is real, like the sign: *Flying Angel*. Flying is extinguished, or the neon tubes burnt out; Angel—in ghostly blue—stands clear against the black, cloudy sky.

He gets his surprise in the entrance lobby: Dalí's Christ of St. John of the Cross. The others cannot understand his excitement.

"Take it easy," they tell him, "we'll get the phone calls through all right."

"It is not the phone call. It's this picture; the reproduction of it is on my desk at home."

"And this is the original?"

"No. The original is in Glasgow, that's where I bought the reproduction years ago."

The captain and the chief mate look at the picture critically. "What do you like so much about it?"

"The landscape below, and the shadows of the man on the cross."

"*Oy vey*. That man and those who believe in him and his symbol haven't done much good for guys like you and me."

"No. Heavens knows they have not. But he was a Jew, a *sabra* like you."

"No doubt, no doubt." And after a pause: "The landscape is nice, but I've seen better. Who painted it?"

"A guy called Dali."

"Come on, boys," says the electrician, "I want to phone."

"Where did all these guys come from? I saw hardly any ships here!"

The club is filled with seamen: Greeks, Turks, Chinese, Malays, French, Norwegian, British. Some play billiards, others watch color TV, still others talk or sit at the bar.

"You can't get anything stronger than beer here. Twice a week, there's a dance. The girls are from good families, volunteers all: yes, also those that serve at the bar. You are not supposed to date them. I've been here twice before. Last time in '69. No, '68 it was, in December. But it's another priest now that's running the place."

"And you didn't date the girls?"

"Of course we did, silly. The old priest wasn't very strict about it. Later they came on board, the women."

"Come, I want to phone."

"They also have a library here, and a souvenir shop."

The *Flying Angel*: a place of light and warmth in the chilly darkness of the docks. Or, a resting station in between your ship and the town, which had more and better points of illusory lights and warmth to offer: pubs, restaurants, movie houses, dance halls. But some seamen stay here on their way to town: it is still a mile to go, and one illusion is as good as another. Might as well kill the evening here.

"The landscape is all right, but it is unreal, too peaceful. It is war now!"

"Not everywhere."

"Come, I want to get to that phone, damn you! Stop staring at that fucking picture and let's go to the office!"

The new priest, dark, young, bespectacled, shows no surprise at having Israeli crew here. He understands their need to phone home as soon as possible. But they tell him from London that all lines are busy, you know, reverend, there is this war going on in the Middle East, the correspondents must report, send messages, the world has to know what is going on there; besides, there are many Israelis living in London, they want to speak with their relatives, all the lines are booked for the next two or three days…

He speaks in a low voice on the telephone, but a thick vein, pencil-thick, shows on his forehead, across it, from the base of the nose to the beginning of his scalp.

"Yes, but these are seamen, they have been at sea the whole time, they must get information from home, you understand, don't you? By the way, what did you say your name was? Oh…are you Welsh by any chance? Yes? Ha! Ha ha! Well, I'm Welsh, too, of course, listen, you must get that connection for me, will you? It is terribly important…"

You couldn't have a conversation like this with an operator back home, in Israel. Somehow, after Independence, and the beginning of arranging life in our country, we forgot the operator; the telephones are automatic, aren't they? And when you succeed in reaching an operator, he, or she, is actually offended. Brusque, tough, short-tempered.

And this Welsh priest is talking to a Welsh woman somewhere in the Foreign Exchange in London. Romantic crap, trying to convince her to give him priority on a long-distance call to Israel. For his seamen, he says, because some of them have sons or brothers in the army, in their air force, you know. So they have to know. Yes? Tomorrow, at eight sharp in the evening, our local time. Aren't you sweet! Very good. Very good, my dear. Thank you, thank you indeed!

He turns his beaming face toward us. "Tomorrow," he says. "Tomorrow, you'll talk to your families. Is there anything else I can help you with?"

21.

Late at night they are shifting the ship, for some reason, to another quay. It takes an hour of the night, this operation, ferrying across the blackness of the pool, water so intensely black that it brings to mind tar, even in its consistency. Styx.

Then they pass the lines, first the bow, then the stern, everything very silent in the cold night air; one could think the voices are absorbed in this chilly fog like blood in a sponge, no shouting or calling.

On the bridge the pilot, giving orders in clear sotto-voce, says finally, "That'll do. Captain, would you ring down for FINISHED WITH ENGINE please?"

He shakes hands with the captain and on the way out stops for a moment at his door. "A nice, tidy ship you have here."

"Step in for a moment. Would you join me for a nightcap?"

"And the dog?" He pats her long head and the dog does not bark or growl, she sniffs at his hand for a second, and licks his fingers.

"Answers to the name Mississippi."

"Is that so?"

"Take off your coat, it's warm in here."

He is a little hesitant, this heavy man, well into his fifties he must be, but you can feel he accepts the invitation with gratitude.

"Well, just for a moment."

"You still have ships to move tonight, or is it the end of your shift?"

"No, no. No more ships. I'll walk home now."

In Europe, pilots have cars waiting for them at two o'clock in the morning. Also, he thinks with a tinge of bitterness, in Haifa and in Ashdod, before this war. That we learned quickly; these people here are still more innocent. The pilot will walk leisurely, his hands deep in the pockets of his greatcoat, his head hung low, through the Hitchcock landscape, to his home.

"I have a dog, too," the pilot says. "A terrier, a male. She can smell him on me."

The bottle of Scotch on the table between them, glasses raised in their hands, he adds: "I live with my dog."

This, then, they have in common.

Oh, what a lot of things they share! And they did not know

of the other's existence an hour earlier. He thinks, we just suspected it, like we hope for the existence of other civilizations in the galaxy. We'll probably never meet again, but I'll be a tiny little bit happier with the knowledge that this pilot exists, does his work, drinks, and then goes back home to his dog. I'll be a bit richer for that. The age, the profession, and the solitude that goes with it like a shadow. Half a century of life.

And there is an equal load they do not share; each has his own, particular package, custom-made for his own private perusal; burden, sediment.

"How is it down there?"

"I don't know, we sailed on the third day of the war. At that time things seemed to be rather grim. But tomorrow I have a phone call booked, then I'll know more."

"Do you have anybody in the army?"

"A son. With the air force."

The pilot fingers the stem of the glass.

"You, there's only you and the dog?"

"Only the dog. My wife died three years ago. No children. But I have this dog."

But there is the bottle between them, and it is almost empty an hour later.

Few words are spoken, but a certain equilibrium has definitely been reached, and both men know they can face the day tomorrow. The Scotch helps them in a gentle way to quiet the impatience of their hearts. The pilot's face is a shade redder when he gets up, but he is steady on his feet. He puts his big paw on the empty bottle.

"Well, this is John Barleycorn," he says.

"He is a friend indeed."

"A great friend. But you must respect him."

"Oh yes. We do, we do. Shall I help you to the gangway, pilot?"

"No, thank you. I'll manage by myself. I am all right. And thank you once more." He goes away, with an unhurried step, a burly hulk of a man.

On the quay he pulls up the collar of his coat, thrusts his hands in his pockets, and walks home without looking back even once.

22.

He cannot sleep. It is three o'clock and he turns in his bed this way and that. The pilot should have arrived home by now.

The phone call tomorrow. That priest has fixed it. Strange priest. How do they manage without women? But he must be Church of England, which means that they can marry, can't they?

It was in another country—where was it?—ah, Sicily. Yes, in Sicily, near Palermo it was. A monastery so beautiful, so serene, that you could imagine…well, perhaps after a certain age. Fresh, fragrant air, a small fountain, cool, playing in one corner; marble, twisted, delicate columns, flowers. Contemplation. Our Lady in the Heavens. Our Lady of the Flowers. But this was another country, another world, the Mediterranean. Here it is far north, it will still be dark at eight in the morning, and it is already dark at three in the afternoon, and in between it is also dark, a slightly lighter shade, and cloudy.

And even with that, the place has an enormous poetic force of a most peculiar kind. Remember *Under Milkwood*? The music of it?

"Who?"

"Dylan Thomas, of course, the Welsh poet. It was once produced at home, in Hebrew translation."

"Was it? I seldom go to the theatre. Movies, yes."

"No, they haven't made a movie out of it yet. They could, I guess. Why not?"

"I'd like to have a woman right now, here."

"No whores in this town. But perhaps you can meet a nice, clean half-serious girl who'd go to bed with you."

"I want to have a good meal in a restaurant. I'm sick of our cook's grub. Let's go to a Chinese restaurant."

"Let's go to a pub."

"Let's go to the movies."

"Let's go back to the *Flying Angel*."

"Let's go back to the ship and sleep. Or watch television."

"What are they doing at home now? Crying over the dead. Mourning the boys killed. You'll know, tomorrow at eight."

Yes, we have this phone call tomorrow. We must know and are afraid to know. I wonder if she walks alone on that field now, looking for things? Sleep, come. Oh please, come, sleep. I need you badly.

23.

Night descends again on the Welsh town and port.

Street names and ads are in two languages here, English and Welsh. They are different, the Welsh, perhaps in the similar meaning of us being different. As we were. As we are still: the Jews, not the Israelis. Strange language, twisted history, alien customs. Perhaps this is it.

Only with us it is more extreme. They are regarded with a certain ironic amusement; eccentrics in a queer, tiny nation, like the Basques, or the Scotch. But we are dangerous, or at best, a nuisance, and have always been so. The world would be relieved if we disappeared one day from the surface of this planet.

But who, exactly, is this 'world'? The crowds applauding the Soviet girls? Or perhaps the young Arab—and his audience—who appeared on television the other day reading a statement issued by OPEC. He was the official speaker for the organization. He said that the sanctions imposed earlier by the Arab countries on the members of the European Community would be eased somewhat in December, in view of the correct stand these states took during the Israeli-Arab war. Holland, he announced, would be an exception, because of its friendly attitude to Israel and to Jews in general. The sanctions would continue to be enforced against the United States.

The Arab speaker had a handsome face, with a meticulously trimmed mustache. He was serene, but also elated in the awareness of his immense power. Four or five European reporters stuck their microphones as near to his face as possible. A big crowd of journalists in the hall, tense, silent, taking notes; they hang on every precious word that escaped the speaker's lips. The Arab sheikhs are the world's Supreme Court now, in which the other nations' conduct is judged. They tell the French, the Germans, the British, what is right and what wrong. They deal out justice.

Supporting Jews, nay, being neutral, is wrong, explains the young Arab. You must condemn them, as you traditionally have. Do we have to remind Europeans of their history?

Well, that'll mean less oil for this one, a bit more for the other, none for Holland. Cheese-heads were always a stubborn race, and far too easy-going. Therefore, may their cars stand near the curb, motionless, may their flats remain cold in the bitter European winter, and may their industry stand idle.

The Germans, however, were again correct. So were the French. They disliked the Jews.

Thirty years ago, the Arab bowed very low and kept repeating yes, *effendi*, anything you say. Libya was a strip of yellow sand with the skeletons of Rommel's tanks sticking out of the dunes (but they attacked us on *Yom Kippur* with several times more tanks than the total number that participated in that famous El Alamein battle). Thirty years ago nobody had ever heard of Abu Dhabi, and the King of Egypt carried out the orders of the British High Commissioner.

But the world today? Standing on all fours, whining, their tongues thirsty for a drop of oil. They wait for a word of mercy from the dark-skinned young man and he tells them what is right and wrong. Well, that is the world for you, amused with the Welshman and repulsed by the Jew. Because we are different: most people dislike the different. Even in your own kibbutz, those who do not conform are, at best, distrusted. There is something wrong with you if you aren't like the others, if you don't accept the warmth of togetherness.

Like the Dutch. Why shouldn't they issue a simple proclamation, like the others, saying the Arabs are right, the Jews—wrong? What is this obstinate, rebellious spirit?

And why does this priest in the *Flying Angel* spend hours trying to get the Foreign Exchange in London again, for his Israeli seamen? The Welsh woman there must be gone, for there is a long delay, but in the end they get the connection, and for three minutes each one of them hears voices from Israel, four thousand miles away.

They listen to these voices and anxiously watch each other's faces. Then they go, the whole group, to the big hall, sit down around a table, and drink strong British beer.

Three men from Singapore play billiards, walk around the green table with long cues in their hands, stalk the white balls on it. They exchange a few words, monosyllables. Totally absorbed in the game.

"How many?"

"One dead, one badly wounded. They cut his arm off. And at yours?"

"Very bad. Three or four killed. She did not want to tell me. Then I said, Woman, that's what I am phoning you for from this hole thousands of miles away."

"Any people I know?"

"Yes. Zaro's son."

"My God."

"The other one was killed in the Six Day War."

"Let's get the hell out of here."

"Where do you want to go?"

"Back to the ship of course. I feel like getting dead drunk."

The chief mate was not with them when they did the drinking during the voyage before. He is a sober, competent type. Even-headed. Silent. Now he wants to get drunk. It is not that simple, my dear.

You cannot just take the bottle and drink yourself unconscious and go to bed. Tomorrow you'll have an impossible hangover, and that's all you'll get out of it; you won't even forget the killed boys. John Barleycorn is a good friend, but you have to respect him.

He has a last look at the sunless landscape at the bottom of Dali's picture. It is very serene. He thinks he'll probably never be in the *Flying Angel* in Swansea again.

"Reverend, you did a great deal for us. We want to thank you for it. We won't forget it."

"Don't mention it."

"We Jews are troublemakers."

"You always have been, ever since Jesus the Jew from Nazareth was born."

"Even before."

"Most likely. But think where the world would be without those troubles…"

24.

"Two things," the captain says. "First, we finish loading tomorrow. We take only half of the cargo here, then we sail to Rotterdam, and perhaps to one more port still. We'll load something there. Second, we can't get rid of our friend Eliezer here. They twisted it this way and that, found all kinds of excuses, there were no places available on the flights to Israel, and so forth and so on, and, well, we have to take him to Rotterdam. We have no choice."

"What does he say?"

"Oh, he says he is basically better, but he certainly would like to be repatriated."

"By plane?"

"Naturally. I'll tell you, I certainly have had enough of Eliezer Rosen, and I invite you to a gorgeous drinking bout when we finally get rid of that bastard, but since we recovered that money I can't help feeling kind of sorry for him."

"It is strange, isn't it?"

"It is, and it is a terrible weakness, I know, which I can ill afford in my job."

"Don't talk nonsense, you did fantastically well dealing with him. And you know you can regard this trip—up to now, touch wood—as a personal success, an achievement."

"Never mind that. Of course I sent a letter to our Haifa office, telling them the story. And I duly logged him in the official logbook; and still I really do not know what this compassion for him is."

"I feel the same way. But don't worry, his sea-career isn't finished yet. He'll get out of this business, and I bet you'll find him on another ship one day, perhaps with another company. He'll be a bosun by then, or a carpenter at least. People like him are successful in life."

He sighs heavily. "You know what? I'd like to see my son."

The ship moves out. She must never stay in one place too long; this is the condition of a ship's life, from the moment she slides down the slipway and nods in gratitude to the launching lady on a gaily decorated platform—he had this experience within his memory, too, and the woman who, smiling, accepted this nod of the ship's gratitude was once his wife—till the day she's moored at the wrecker's quay, and her crew abandons her, making space for people who'll do the dismembering job. In between these two dates, restlessness is the essence of her being. Like solitude is that of humans.

He has lived these moments of arrivals and departures on board many, many times. Later, when too old (what a phrase!), he watched ships arriving and departing in port, going into the unknown and coming back from a trip, tired, the faint smell of places and seas still clinging to the iron plates.

This departure, he explains to the dog, standing in the stern of the ship, is to be cherished. Like every memory of this trip. It is unlikely, dog, that we'll have many more departures in our life. On this trip, perhaps two more. If we are lucky, there will be other trips, but only a chance in a million that we'll depart from Swansea, Dylan's home port, again. Who knows? But we have always loved chance. Gambling: a more complete freedom of choice than that of a roulette table is hardly imaginable. That is why I love it so much, not to mention the fascination of watching the croupiers' faces. The main thing, however, is the delight of free choice, of freedom.

It was the worst possible weather: snow and rain and wind, but Moshiko was insistent. "Come! Come! It's tonight! This is the night of our luck! Come!"

Running through the abandoned streets, bent in half against the fury of a wind that threw sleet in their faces, he kept repeating to himself, "Insanity! Insanity!" But they never slowed their wild rush.

In the great entrance hall they stamped their feet, laughing, brushing away big patches of snow from their shoulders. The white-haired hall porter in splendid livery looked on with unconcealed bewilderment. Armored knights lining the walls stared suspiciously through closed visors, neck-guards slightly raised, leaning on their swords. It was as real as a dream.

Then you get rid of your wet raincoat, enter the gambling room, as magnificent as anything in that old house. One glance at the green roulette table—the gamblers, the croupiers at the periphery of your vision—and you throw your chips on the table just as the croupier murmurs *rien ne va plus* and you watch the little silver ball run against the rotating wheel.

Sixteen, says the croupier calmly and taps with his rake on your chip: plain. You nod slightly, and he pushes the money toward you. You've won. You get a lot of money; you almost miss Moshiko coming back from another table, carrying in both hands a stack of chips. Enough, he says, enough. One throw, and it's enough for tonight: didn't I tell you? Let's clear out of here, otherwise we'll lose everything. Out, they were, ten minutes after arriving, each richer by a couple of hundred dollars than they were before. A childish joy.

Money, he thinks, is not important. For Eliezer Rosen, yes, but not for him. Never was. Freedom of choice, freedom of movement, freedom of decision—yes. Always. The number one conflict in his twenty-five year association with the kibbutz. Money, in the kibbutz, in spite of half-hearted official denials, is all-important. This is what the true Marxist ideology has come to in practice, after all is said and done.

Hey, you want to settle your score with the kibbutz right now, at the end of October 1973, during a fragile armistice in another bloody Jewish-Arab war? On board an Israeli freighter, originally sent out to bring military supplies, weapons and munitions, but frustrated in that mission, somewhere between Swansea, southwest Wales, and Rotterdam, the Netherlands? Is this the right time and place?

Money is the driving force in everybody, he thinks, because money gives power, money buys televisions and stereos, and transistors, and that's what they are after. Even on a kibbutz.

Stop it. Might as well stop your fucking thinking machine for a while, it would be good for you. The captain says we'll stay in Rotterdam for several days, you can do some maintenance work on this ship, to keep her going. Take your mind off of these riddles, puzzles, and knots in your head. His hand reaches for a sheet of paper. He writes in clear, big, block, letters.

LIST OF WORK TO BE DONE:
  EXCHANGE EIGHT EXHAUST AND INLET VALVES ON THE
    MAIN ENGINE
  REPAIR BROKEN PIPE ON THE STARBOARD SIDE
  REPAIR BROKEN PIPE ON THE PORT SIDE NEAR THE
    COMPRESSOR
  OVERHAUL THE LUBE OIL SEPARATOR
  RETIGHTEN THE GLAND OF THE RUDDER BEARING
  RETIGHTEN THE GLAND OF THE STERN TUBE
  MAIN ENGINE: THREE LOOSE CHOKES AND HOLDING
    DOWN BOLTS TO BE RETIGHTENED.
  CARTER CONTROL: REPLACE BROKEN SCREWS ON THE
    CARTER DOORS... ETC, ETC, ETC.

Enough work for a week or more. Prepare order of spare parts for the main engine and for the generators, prepare order for supplies...

You have plenty to do. Discard all the other stuff. Do your work, and in the evening go and enjoy yourself like all the seamen in the world do. Like Eliezer Rosen. Be a normal person for a while. Please. Try your best.

"You too," he turns violently to the dog. "Stop acting goddamn human! You're a dog, aren't you? Be a dog! I'll bring you a bone, and I'll let you run around. And then, go to sleep! Aren't you happy?"

25.

Rotterdam is a good place. As an organization, it works with remarkable efficiency. Hundreds of ships come and go. The buses, the railway, the metro, run on exact times. The phones work faultlessly. The streets are clean. The fire brigade, electric service, the police, everything is as it should be, and helps to run the place smoothly.

"In Rotterdam," remarks the captain, "you have a feeling that nothing has changed. Not in the sense of Swansea. Swansea is timeless, suspended in limbo at the beginning of the century. But not Rotterdam. Here they proceed from year to year with business as usual, with normal progress. We are expected to move forward, aren't we?"

"I don't know."

"What do you mean you don't know! Progress is a normal process of living. That's what they're doing: keeping ahead of others. The biggest port in the world. Every year more ships and barges. Every year more cargo, new improvements. That is how things should be!"

On the quay, huge vehicles like giant science-fiction insects are carrying forty-foot containers, red lights rotating constantly over every wheel, every wheel the size of a man, and the man, tiny, sits up above in the glass cabin with a closed circuit television set and radio telephone and panel of electronic gadgets. No second is wasted, no movement superfluous.

"In Haifa," the electrician remarks, "the same container carrier has one light instead of four and works at a quarter of the speed of those here."

"Very efficient, very progressive. As if nothing happened."

He sighs. "I do hope they'll be as efficient in handling Eliezer."

They are. The day after the ship's moored, the agent's man takes Eliezer away. "Come, you're flying home this afternoon. Your ticket is ready, we have a place reserved for you on the afternoon plane."

He is not upset or excited. He does not say hello or good bye to anybody. They watch him from the ship, loading his bags slowly, systematically into the agent's car. He buttons up his coat and they drive away.

"Listen," the captain says, "you, and you, and you. Come with me. I want to drink to it. I want to drink to getting rid of that son-of-a-bitch who brought bad luck to this ship, and that I don't have to be sorry any more for that miserable doped-up bastard. Come!" The captain pulls the cork out of a cognac bottle and fills the glasses.

"Well," he says, "here's to the end of the Eliezer Rosen affair."

There is a commotion outside. Raised voices. Somebody is protesting.

"No, you can't see him now, he is busy."

"Never mind, we have to see him right away."

Two uniformed customs officials, the agent's clerk and Eliezer Rosen are standing in the open doorway.

"I am sorry, sir, to disturb you." (How wonderfully civilized these Dutchmen are!) "But this man was caught in a smuggling attempt."

The captain is still smiling, but it is a frozen smile, a contraction of facial muscles, kept with a conscious effort. He may explode at any moment.

"Three bottles of Scotch, four cartons of cigarettes."

Eliezer looks hurt.

"The booze and the cigarettes are my property, Captain. I bought them in the slop chest on board. You can ask the cook, sir. Yesterday, I bought them."

The captain speaks slowly. "Ever heard about customs, Eliezer? Eh? Customs regulations, things like that?"

"Nobody told me what the Dutch custom regulations are, sir."

"Your first time in Rotterdam?"

"No, sir. I was here in '71, and in '70, and before that, but you know how these customs people are; like ours, back in Haifa, changing their fucking rules constantly. So this time I didn't know what's allowed and what isn't."

"You thought you can smuggle out three bottles of whisky and eight hundred cigarettes?"

Eliezer shrugs. "I thought they wouldn't object."

The customs officer turns to the captain. "We must confiscate the goods, naturally, and there is a fine on the ship. But considering this man is being repatriated, as the agent tells me, it will only be fifty dollars."

"I'll give them a check for that amount immediately, sir," offers the agent's clerk.

"No, thank you. I'll pay the fifty dollars cash from my pocket, but I don't not want to see this man again. Please make sure I don't see him again, agent. Take care that he doesn't jump out of the plane in the very last moment before take-off."

Eliezer says, "Well, Captain, thank you. I hope you'll be all right, and you'll forget the whole business. After all, there was quite a lot of guilt on your side."

"On my side?"

The captain's big hands close convulsively into fists, but still he keeps perfect control, his voice is low and quiet.

"Sure. You shouldn't have left that safe key with the other keys. The safe key must be kept in your pocket. But forget it, you treated me fair, so don't blow up this business of theft in Haifa. And remember, I returned the money voluntarily. I cooperated."

"Take him away, please."

When they disappear, the captain says, "I knew that if I heard one more word from him I'd scream. So now, finally—touch wood—*L'chaim!*"

Exit Eliezer Rosen.

Exit from the ship, from the total experience of this voyage and exit from your life. Poor chance you'll ever meet him again. There is no doubt he will continue his life more successfully than you. His is a royal adherence to a straight line he has chosen, and a self-assurance of monstrous dimensions such as you have never dreamt of. Unshakeable confidence.

Eliezer eats when he's hungry, fucks when he has an erection, and thinks exclusively in terms of how to improve Eliezer Rosen's situation. He has never heard and never used the word morality: wars, revolutions, cataclysms do not touch him. And when his immortal soul is in need of transcendency, he sticks a hypodermic needle into his arm.

26.

That evening he goes out alone. He is sick of seeing the same faces at every meal, of having the same conversations. He is sick of drinking with them or drinking alone. He does not want to see his ship; he is not sure if it is his second home or his second prison.

"Listen, dog," he says, "I love you as always, I have nothing against you, absolutely nothing, but I must go out alone now. Can you understand that?"

For a moment it looks as if she does. The black, moist tip of her nose quivers slightly. The golden-yellow eyes look straight at him. Nothing but unlimited love and submission. Why does she have to have eyelashes as well? Do other dogs?

"Listen," he says in desperation, "I shall come back to you. I promise. I love you and I'll be back."

She jumps, puts her forepaws on his chest and starts licking his face.

He slams the door shut and puts on his raincoat outside. Goddamn it and once more goddamn it!

The raw cold air strikes him in the face and he inhales greedily. The asphalt of the quay feels hard under his feet, and that, too, is good. Out of the port gate, he stops and looks back. A forest of port cranes, masts, and derricks as far as the horizon, shops and ships and sheds and stacks of containers like gigantic matchboxes. On the other side of the canal they're pouring trains of ore into the holes of the *Thomas B.*, while other cranes load with grabs from the long, low barges moored alongside the ship.

Thomas B., a huge ore-carrier, long and sleek, and her seven-story superstructure are flood-lit from dusk till dawn. She has been loading for three days round the clock, she must be bottomless. Just behind her *Chew-Fong* is waiting on anchor for her turn, as huge as the *Thomas B.*, perhaps even bigger.

They could have taken us easily as a lifeboat, he thinks. Ten minutes walk to the bus station. The street is quiet. Occasionally, a heavy truck rumbles by on the way to the port. Heaps of dry brown leaves rustle under his feet as he walks, late autumn in Europe. The lights in the houses are already on, the big front window revealing an identical living room, apartment after apartment: a television, a few armchairs in front of it, a table, some decorations on the wall, a big floor lamp. Millions of people living like that in this country, moderately happy and quiet, and not neurotic.

You could live like that if you wanted, instead of struggling with your pains and *Weltschmerz* in the untidy labyrinth of your Jewish conscience. What is wrong with living like that?

Nothing. You get up at seven-thirty, go to work, you come back at five, chat with your kids, glance at your newspaper in front of the TV, have your dinner, coffee and cigar, kiss the kids good night, screw your wife in the bedroom upstairs and go to sleep. That's it. Call it a way of life. Do not condemn it. There is quite a lot of envy at the bottom of your heart. But that is how things are, so you'd better turn your head and go your way, which is not theirs.

The bus—how spotlessly clean their buses always are!—arrives on time and leaves on the dot. None of the dozen or so passengers is an inhabitant of those identical cozy apartments he saw, all are foreigner dock workers, Turks and Slavs, and some Chinese or Malays, perhaps the *Chew-Fong* crew. The driver sells tickets, his face unchanging.

He sits down in the rear of the bus, near the window, and watches the ships and the barges, an unguided tour around the Waalhaven. One of Rotterdam's twenty ports and as big as ten other European ports together. Sometimes the bus stops and the door opens with a soft hiss; other crews join the bus' passengers. They speak French, Russian, Chinese, German, Japanese. The Turks seem to be the loudest. They shout, quarrel and laugh. The man next to him asks in heavily-accented English where he is from.

"Israel."

The man shakes his head. There is something wrong with the right side of his face, it is smaller than the other half: shrunk or scorched. One eye is half-closed. He shakes his head and says, "No good."

"No good? Why?"

"Always fighting: Poom! Poom! No good. War no good."

"Our neighbors are always fighting. No good."

But the man shakes his head and makes clicking noises with his tongue.

"You Turkish?"

"No. Not Turkish. Greek."

He turns his head. He does not want any further conversation.

How beautifully we communicate with each other! Fifty words and the human bond is established: Good. No good. Fighting. Poom. Dirty Greek. Dirty Jew.

At the bus terminus the crowd disperses; most run to the moving steps of the Metro. And from the stainless steel and glass Metro, which runs with smooth efficiency, most disembark at the second station, Chinatown, where there are old houses, dirty streets and whores, and they feel more at home. Outside it, the world has rushed decades ahead, leaving them and the places they have come from far behind. That is why they feel better here.

He goes on, disembarking near City Hall, and then walks the well-lit rich streets of the town for hours, glistening in the drizzle like freshly-cut stones of a jeweler, affluent and sterile. Only here and there can you still see the foundations on which this ultramodern civilization rose thirty years ago: older streets, crumbling buildings, obsolete shops, bars, and people over fifty, with tired faces. In parts of the port—because, after all, the town of Rotterdam is only a tiny annex to the monstrosity of the port sprawling over hundreds of miles—the new and the old mingle in a more balanced way. There are still at least as many old ships as new: barges, river ships, all kinds of obsolete craft. Twenty years more and only a trace of them will remain. They will disappear, like the old houses. Like old people.

A cold wind sweeps the streets under the low canopy of a rusty red sky. He thrusts his hands deeper into the pockets of his coat, lowers his head. He now walks along a narrow canal. On both sides, on the embankment, are giant office buildings: banks, insurance companies, shipping companies. Down here, near the black water, the street is paved with cobblestones. The barges, moored three or four abreast, are dark and dead.

If I had no place to sleep, he thinks, I'd break the lock and sleep in one of their cabins. It would be dark, and protected from the wind, and cozy. The only trouble is, in the morning the fierce fire-red sun would rise again, and the coziness would be gone: the port, the people, would recommence their activities, and I'd have to get up and go somewhere, do something.

On a parallel track, at this moment, people are still dug in among the sands of the Sinai desert (stars are lower in the desert, here they are barely visible even on a clear night because of the glow of the town) and on the road to Damascus. The fire is burning.

He knows that on board, the dog Mississippi, curled on the bed, is lifting her head hopefully at every noise: perhaps he has come back? No creature should be that dependent. But humans are, even more than that.

The whole length of the canal, nothing but dead barges, and street lamps, nobody to be seen. In movies and in cheap novels, at such moments, one meets somebody: another lonely man, or a woman. In reality, one meets nobody. And this is your moment of truth: supreme reality, supreme loneliness.

I'd like to have a drink right now. Ah, I'd love to have a drink. A drink would help me. A drink would alleviate whatever it is that hurts me now.

At the end of the canal, there's red light. He quickens his step. He passes under the low arch of a stone bridge. An old river excursion steamer is moored there. Red bulbs on a string along the deck. Private club. Welcome. Live show. Welcome all.

He crosses the plank and jumps aboard.

Welcome. Welcome.

The room on the lower deck is cozy. Anything would be cozy after that canal street. The bar runs along one side of it, opposite is a little stage covered with white bear skins. A small screen is on the left side, some chairs and a movie projector on the right.

It is warm: four electric stoves glow pleasantly.

The girl behind the bar has an ultra-mini blue dress and transparent black panties.

"Scotch please. A double."

When she turns to take the bottle off the shelf, he adds: "Better make one for my friend, as well."

She looks up.

"He'll come soon," he says.

That does the trick, it works. He downs it quickly, and then the other glass.

"Make me another, please."

"My, you are in a hurry, aren't you? We try to relax here."

"There are various ways to relax."

She shrugs and pours again into his glass.

A big dog comes slowly up and smells his knees. Smells Mississippi, probably. But he is an old, tired dog. Mississippi is young and carefree; all the same he pets the dog's muzzle. He looks around. Two men at the other end of the bar are speaking in Dutch. He knows they are drunk from the way one of them holds the other's lapel, the red glow on their faces.

The proprietor—or perhaps he is a bouncer—is busy with the projector. Two women are sitting at the edge of the stage: one, a teenager, the other, a peroxide blonde, thirty, perhaps thirty-five. One can never know for sure with whores.

The elder one comes over, sits down at the stool next to him and puts her hand lightly on his knee.

"Will you buy me a drink?"

"Sure. What'll you have?"

"A martini."

"And another one of these for me."

"Why don't you start?" One of the drunk Dutchmen is talking to the bouncer. "We paid for it, didn't we?"

The door opens and a couple walks in. They are in their sixties, a very solid looking couple. She wears a round hat over her gray hair, a shy surprised smile on her pretty old face. One would expect her to put on a pair of steel-rimmed glasses and take out her knitting the moment she sits down. Her husband has a red, healthy face with pale blue eyes and a net of fine wrinkles around the corners of his eyes. He pays after a short discussion, and the bouncer directs them to the chairs in front of the screen. The dog comes across the room, walking unhurriedly, and smells the old lady. She pets him and tells him he is a good dog.

Another man, in an expensive, well-cut suit, enters and sits down at the bar. He smells of cologne and has golden cufflinks. He smiles and says good evening in Dutch.

"Good evening," he answers in English.

The teenage whore takes the stool next to him. "Excuse me," says the well-dressed man before turning his head and attention to her.

"He is a real gentleman," whispers the middle-aged whore. "He is well known in this town. Plenty of money. Banking. Aren't you Dutch?"

"I am an Israeli."

"My, my! It seems you have a war there again! Always trouble with you!"

"Think," he answers, smiling, "what the world would be without that trouble." He could not remember that reverend's name.

"What? I do not understand. I speak English, but not so well."

"Never mind. Have another drink."

"You are really nice. I'll have another Martini."

"And another Scotch for me."

"What are you doing in Rotterdam?"

"On board a ship. I am a seaman."

"Why don't you start, goddamn you," yells the Dutchman from the far end of the bar. "Isn't it late enough? Did we pay thirty-five guilders for nothing?"

Instead of answering, the bouncer switches the projector on.

The film is called, simply, *Torture*, and no credits are run. On the screen appear flickering images of a naked girl impaled on a huge artificial penis. Her legs and arms are chained. Two men in black masks belabor her writhing body with long whips.

"You like it?" the whore asks.

"No."

"Neither do I." Her face brightens. She puts her hand on the inside of his thigh. "This is shit: love is love, and normal sex is beautiful, isn't it?"

He removes her hand gently. "Listen, I am the wrong man for you."

"How come?"

"I have no money. You are wasting your time on me. It makes me feel lousy."

She looks up at him, and there is disbelief in her eyes. When this kind of thing becomes a purely commercial proposition, he thinks, and no matter how drunk I am, and no matter where it happens, in the south even, and in summer, too, on hot evenings, it always emanates a strange chill around it, as if you were standing right in front of an air-conditioner. A very distinct, physical sensation. Her eyes are very cold now. He finishes his drink in one gulp to warm himself.

"Honestly, you have no money? I charge only seventy guilders for a short time. Here, upstairs, in the cabins. It is very comfortable there. It is not much money, just seventy guilders."

"Next trip when I come here, I'll go with you."

"When will that be?"

"Six, seven weeks," he answers, losing interest, whatever interest he had in her, in this place, and dreading the cold street outside.

The cogs and wheels behind her narrow face are moving, he sees them clearly, as if her face were only a glass partition.

"Do you want me to buy you another drink?"

"No, I still have some here."

"When does the live show start?"

Her face lights up a little. "They have no real live show here."

"It says so on the ad outside."

"That is only to attract the public. Now, I was a live-show artist in Copenhagen for a year and a half. Have you seen those shows?"

"Sure. In Copenhagen, in Gothenburg. So what is it here?"

"This is a backward country. In Scandinavia they are more

progressive. Here they have only, how do you call it in English? Ah, yes, a masturbation show. Do you know what it is?"

"I can imagine."

"Well, you see, I was a live-show artist, I cannot work in a masturbation show, it is a different art altogether. You need another approach, another temperament. It is like telling a sculptor to become a painter or a musician. It simply does not work for me."

She explains it to him seriously, and he, fingering his glass, without looking at the screen, thinks about how articulate she is in her explanations. This is the real art, this is the serious business of today, explanations. The dog is on the couch in the cabin, where it is warm and quiet, and the ship is not rolling or pitching; she is safe and dreaming dog dreams about food and bones and running in long, floating leaps in the sand dunes or in fat grass. She does not know they brought a dog hunter from Hadera with a shot gun to the kibbutz. And I did not read to her from the kibbutz weekly bulletin a letter in which a woman explained that keeping a dog is a sign of bourgeois decadence, out of place in a socialist society.

Six hundred and fifty-four dead boys, they announced officially two weeks ago, he thinks. The Syrians and the Egyptians must have come with fury, and *en masse*, with thousands of tanks and planes and missiles, and caught us unprepared, that's the truth of it; we called up the Reserves only when the attack was already upon us, and that's how those few boys that were on the borders were killed. What is 654 dead for the world? Nothing. Tens, hundreds of thousands perish in earthquakes, in more impressive wars: in Biafra, in Bangladesh. In Vietnam. Famine in Africa. Drought in Pakistan. Six hundred and fifty-four is no number today. And the world does not love us much. After all, guilty or not, right or wrong, we have triggered off that oil business."

She keeps explaining and he, returning from his world tour, from Sinai and the Golan Heights, bows his head, sympathetically eager to listen to it, looking hopefully at the shelf where the bottles stand.

"And so, I am out of business here. I make love for money for a living. It is not bad at all, I mean the money, if you keep your class. The main thing is the class."

He nods several times to show her that he understands her point. "Who does the masturbation show?"

"My colleague," she says, pointing with her chin to the teenage whore who is leaning with her whole body on the real gentleman. Banking. "She is young, but very good. In her field, of course. I do not know if she could make a good live-show artist, though."

"If you don't start the bloody show right now," yells one of the drunk Dutchmen, "I'll start a scandal such as you've never seen in your fucking life. I'll call the police!"

The film clicks to an end, and the bouncer jumps on the stage. "Ladies and gentlemen, let me present to you, Lady Sylvia!"

Those sitting at the bar turn around on the high stools, and the banking man applauds vigorously. The benevolent smile on the old woman's face broadens, and her husband's jovial face remains unperturbed.

The record player whines, and the barefooted girl on the bearskin starts her performance. I have seen a striptease many times, he thinks, and it never excites me very much. I'm too absent-minded for that, was always weak on the power of concentration, even on dark triangles concealing mysteries. His thoughts wandered aimlessly. Please don't put the blame on too many whiskeys, because, on the contrary, they only smoothed the way on these excursions, out of the striptease realm. Excursions performed in a swinging way, like Tarzan in early movies travelling in the jungle from tree to tree. From Mississippi to an ancient Roman oil-lamp to the burnt out tank in the desert to the onion-shaped domes of Orthodox churches in Moscow, though a broken pipe in the bilges of the engine room from which water gushed like blood from a body from which the head was severed, to the puerile body of the teenage stripper on the bearskin.

When she is completely naked, she sinks to her knees and masturbates with long, slow strokes. There is now complete silence in the room, even the tape recorder has clicked to a stop. The smile on the old woman's face vanishes gradually, and her mouth falls open when the girl on the stage climaxes. All of a sudden the girl leaps to her feet and lifts her right arm high, the forefinger moist, glistening: a triumphant proof she has not bluffed. The Statue of Liberty, torch-bearing. Wild applause.

"Bravo! Bravo!" screams the banking gentleman.

He leans over to him, confidentially. "Do you expect her to give an encore?"

The man blinks behind his rimless glasses as if awakening from a dream. "She is an artiste, this little one, no doubt about it, a real artiste. Seventy guilders, short-time," he tells the banker, nodding and collecting his coat. He walks ashore; it's raining outside, and he turns around and looks at the red lights. Private club. Welcome. Live show. Welcome. A love barge. A love barge is nothing new, for sure. They were floating up the Nile, slowly, the queen and her lover. Sensual delights when afloat, have, for some mysterious reason, more attraction than on terra firma. Black Nubian slaves were singing, the huge red sail would fill with the northern wind, the barge would move slowly, small waves lapping the ship's sides.

Would you love me for seventy guilders?

No fantasy this. Rock-hard facts. And the landscape and the smell on both sides of the river never changes: the smell of Africa.

The Algerian warship. Was it Algerian? He will never know.

They were fighting in Africa, of course. Not on the Nile, though. The love barge would sail on serenely and the lovers would not hear the distant noise of the guns. And now this old steamer anchored in the dead end of a Dutch canal with red bulbs on a string along the main deck. A record player instead of Nubian singers, a movie projector. They had, naturally, live shows in Cleopatra's times. Very ancient, like every art. Did they have a masturbation show as well? Most likely. If they were less progressive than the Scandinavians.

He was not finished yet, letting the steady rain drench his clothes, wet hair on his head and occasionally gliding on his cheeks. He leans against a tree, opposite the club. A red reflection on a wet stone at his feet.

Then there was this Bounty legend and again what was most

fascinating was that it all really happened once. You can read it in the annals of the Admiralty, not only in novels. The romanticism of huge white swollen sails against the sky was as much of a deception as the red lamps on this floating brothel. They discovered somewhere along the way how wonderfully photogenic these sailing ships were, and exploited it to the last drop, in movies, in ads, and tried to make this romanticism objective, real, and people get hooked on it, easily, without realizing what a lie it is: but the South Sea island rising one morning from the ocean with its plumed palm tops was real, and the half-naked friendly people there, and the women. This was real, he thinks, I know, because I have seen the Greek islands materializing out of the sea in the early morning under a flawless sky. All islands in the world do, in spite of human follies.

A sudden wave of despair: return to your ship and on the opposite side they'll still be pouring wagonloads of ore into the bottomless holds of *Thomas B.* or *Chew Fong* under floodlights, and they'll keep loading iron, aluminum, bagged fertilizers and machines onto your ship. No weapons, no munitions. Which is what you were sent out for.

And in the cabin, on the couch, a yellow-eyed dog is waiting for you to return. In despair? Possibly. But never giving up hope, because she doesn't know what hope is. Animals are so privileged in that way, and we are so stupidly handicapped.

But there is a bottle of vodka—minus two shots, he remembers—in the closet, and another one, untouched yet, of Black Label, and they'll help.

I am an old, experienced whore, he giggles, standing on the slippery cobblestones of the canal street, and I know many tricks of survival.

Ho ho! We are not through yet. I have learned a lot in the art of survival, more than that girl in the art of masturbation.

A surge of confidence: Mississippi, poor thing, does not have it, cannot experience it, because of her lack of hope. But things are happening to her nevertheless and she'll be wild with joy when I'm back, she'll jump up and down, lick my face, and hers will be happiness, unlimited. No suspicions, premonitions, none of that. That is their superiority over us and the prize for not thinking.

But before he moves on, a strange thing happens: in a sudden flash of enlightenment he knows one could experience only very seldom, he sees it all fitting into a momentary pattern, into a kind of global order, all these pieces of the jigsaw puzzle which a moment earlier were dispersed wildly, at random, in various segments of his experience and memory: the artist of masturbation and modern rock music; the naked images of unbelievable cruelty and suffering and violence on the television screens and in the papers, in horror comic books and in movies; the cynical, bland faces of the politicians and the dead stares of whores in the shop windows; the close-up of the face of a dying African woman "already too weak to turn her face for a drink of water," with a caption about how proud the photographer must have been of this scoop; the crumpled body of an Israeli soldier in the desert sand covered with a stained blue and white flag; the famous—and already obsolete—picture of a Jewish child with raised hands against the background of a burning ghetto; the wet smile of a sex queen; the glistening streamlined new city of Rotterdam and the twisted quiet gray streets of a Welsh miners' town. All this makes sense in one short moment of total perception, forms a complete picture for a fraction of a second, then explodes silently again into a chaos of jagged pieces receding into a blur against the persistent image of the naked girl with a moist finger raised high, and the huge yellow eyes of a dog. A unique moment of full understanding.

But it is not comprehension the world is after; the world wants everything revealed, explained. Driven by a desperate urge, they want nothing to be concealed: not the most secret corners of the soul or the body, and not the mysteries of galaxies, millions of light years away from here. The face of a woman at the moment of orgasm and the face of a man in the agony of death. A pathological curiosity, the curiosity of a child crushing a beetle to see what is inside. Propelled, pushed by the desire to be included in the general pattern, to be a part of it? Or the atavistic compulsion to destroy, to kill, to become all-powerful? Unrestricted, unlimited, absolute power; yes, this must be the real, most basic drive, the impelling force.

This is what we are after, he says aloud, standing on the edge of the black canal. But the moment of almost understanding has passed and retrieval is impossible. Nothing can be done about it. I have to live with my chaos and accept it. I have to live it out, it is my life.

He starts walking slowly to the Metro station.

27.

They continue loading the ship for some days.

"I'll tell you something confidentially," the agent's clerk says. "They made it very clear from your home port, that this ship has no priority any more."

"You mean, they don't care if we arrive a week or two later than intended?"

"Exactly. There are other ships with more vital cargo than yours."

"I see."

Another wasted effort. He hopes the disappointment does not show on his face. But in the evening the captain takes him aside.

"Something to cheer you up."

"I don't need any cheering up."

"Still, I thought you'd like to know."

"Shoot."

"We are sailing from here to another port. We'll load some munitions after all."

"Is there any country in the world still willing to allow munitions to be loaded on an Israeli ship?"

"There are, but very few."

He cannot conceal his satisfaction. "Well, at least we have this. I knew you'd be happy to hear about it."

"Thank you. Thank you for telling me, I appreciate it."

Next morning he jumps out of his bed and on impulse, opens

both windows. Cold wet wind strikes him in the face. The dog, surprised and disgusted, crawls deeper under the blanket.

He takes a deep breath, takes the sharp air into his lungs, ignores his own shivering. Outside, it is still dark, low clouds tinted red on their underbellies from the ever-burning fires of the oil refineries and petrochemical plants, from the high-powered port lamps. But the wind sweeps over all this, strong and young.

He has always loved this kind of wind. Not all winds are like this. There was, for instance, the treacherous, hot *khamsin*, which you hate. There is something degenerate, rotten, in the *khamsin*, especially with a full moon, when the night is filled with a very fine powder of dust so dense that no stars are visible, only a sick greenish moon. The air is so charged with electricity than you can hear cracks of electric discharge when you take off your nylon shirt or touch your cat. The poisonous wind howls throughout the night, only to tear away the darkness in the morning, and then a blood-red sun rolls up and unbearable brightness strikes the world like a search light. He has always hated the *khamsin*.

Then there are the soft breezes of spring nights, so heavily laden with orange scent that your head swoons. On board a trawler, when anchored even two or three miles off the coast, this erotic wind comes stealthily, with indescribable sweetness, over the surface of a motionless sea. You lean over the railing, listening to the secrets the sea whispers and you are lured to submerge yourself in the phosphorescent water, which seems as soft and sensuous as the breeze itself, promising hidden delights, forgetfulness.

But this wind now—a European autumn wind, strong and invigorating—helps you to forget your years, helps you to live, to do. This is another day of your life, and you are in this city, and can do a variety of things.

You can go, for instance, to one of their museums. The city has a few of them; no cathedrals—the churches are new and cold and dead here—but museums. At Boyman's they have Hieronymus Bosch. His people don't walk out at you with the full splendor of light and shadow like those from the *Night Watch* in Amsterdam, as if they wanted to shake your hand or check your papers, which you feel they might do at any second. But when you look at Bosch's people for a few minutes you feel your scalp itching and the hair rising on your head. You know them too well, you meet them too often.

Also, they have other good pictures at Boyman's.

Or, you might walk out and look at Zadkin's sculpture. Very few people stop there now, in front of that twisted iron man with his heart torn out. Back home you seldom go to museums. But you have books and records and you take long walks and find old coins and oil lamps and pottery, like on the day this war broke out. You love them, clean them. You picked up a coin in a field, and there were sheaths on it, or grapes, and Hebrew letters, and you knew somebody had warmed this coin in his palm two thousand years earlier. Probably somebody very much like you. You had a vague feeling of a link, of a continuation of civilization, a thing you liked so much in Greece, in Italy, in Spain.

And even here, where the new, glistening city is spreading rapidly over the old Rotterdam, you still see noble old houses, canals, and a few windmills, which were once the landmark of this country. He knows them well, he lived here once, long ago, for more than a year. A wave of memories, of heavy nostalgia comes in a rush, and he pushes it away.

You should forget, the old man told him once; that is what is written there, in the holy books. But does it apply to these memories, too? Perhaps it is not the number of years, but the total weight of experiences, that determine a man's age: if such was the case, the army computer might well have been right, after all: too old.

But aren't memories a part of you, inseparable? They are, they are. They are the ballast you have to carry. Every man's Sisyphean rock. Carry them, then.

28.

On the ninth of November the return to normalcy received an official stamp. Sparkie pinned the Daily News Broadcast for seamen abroad on the information board, and there he read: "Golda Meir will attend the International Socialist meeting on Sunday in London. The meeting will discuss the situation in the Middle East." "Israel's all-star soccer team lost to Hapoel Tel Aviv 1:2 yesterday at Bloom-field Stadium." "State soccer cup games will resume tomorrow." "The *Shirim ve She'arim* radio program will resume broadcast from tomorrow afternoon."

"Those eleven all-stars are no-good pricks," says the cook. "Because Hapoel Tel Aviv has never been such a hot team. If it were Hapoel Petah Tikva—*nu, meyle*! But to lose with those invalids? A shame!"

"I thought you were for Shimshon, all the Yemenites are. We had a Yemenite bosun once here, on board, and he did great propaganda for Shimshon, collected money from the whole crew. We bought them a nice ball for fifteen dollars, and everybody signed his name on it."

"I don't discriminate against you *Ashkenazim*," says the cook with dignity. "Of course, Shimshon is a good club, but I admit, Hapoel Petah Tikva isn't bad, either. Hapoel Tel Aviv is shit, no matter if they are *Shkenuzim, Sfaradim*, or Yemenites."

This war never was, he thinks. Nothing changes, nothing will change: learn that lesson well. An incident, an interlude. A thousand, perhaps two thousand dead, several thousand wounded. The American airlift probably saved us. There will be relative peace now for a number of years, in five, six, eight years, another war. With small tactical atomic warheads used on both sides, most likely. The Russians will deliver them gladly to the Arabs. And then another, and another.

In between wars, the nation will live healthily, normally. It will cheer the National Soccer Cup players, pop singers, and the Top Forty hits. Girls will present wonderful slim legs and the latest vogue and hairdos on Dizengoff Street. Smiling, energetic young men will drive Audis and Subarus, building contractors will get richer and richer. Kibbutzniks will work and envy and ape the bourgeoisie, safe and confident in the certitude that theirs is the right way, that their leadership is jealously guarding socialist principles from the middle of the last century. The people from the towns and villages will continue envying the kibbutzniks for their trouble-free lives. In summer, the beaches will fill with thousands on the dirty sand, drinking cola and sweating it out under the flawless Israeli sky, parking lots jammed with an endless sea of cars. Others will, as a matter of course, travel abroad, to join the millions jamming the beaches of Italy, Spain, Yugoslavia. The parties will quarrel, the religious will sell religion mixed with politics, the Histadrut Labor Union fossils will babble and pay their lip service to the 'working class' (who the hell is working class? Who is not?) There will be the usual quota of traffic deaths and there will be small- and medium-sized scandals and thefts to give the nation something to gossip about, to give thick black headlines to the evening papers. Nothing will change: life will go on.

You won't participate in the next war. You were too old for this one, you'll be much too old by then. So will the dog.

He looks at her sidewise. She has adapted herself very well to life on board, as if this were a dog's normal way of life. She sleeps quietly, her long nose reposing on extended forepaws, eyebrows twitching slightly, probably dreaming.

What a power of adaptation! Almost like a human. When she was a puppy, he remembers, she found it difficult to climb on the sofa in the apartment. She made countless unsuccessful attempts but never gave up, until, in despair, she'd cry for help. He would assist her gently, lifting her legs, and once topside, enormously satisfied, she would chase her own tail for a minute. And then she'd cry to be let down.

"What a puppy you were," he says. "But now you are a grown up dog, a bitch, and you're sailing with me in this war that never was and we have a very poor chance of sailing in the next one, dog. Both of us, you and I. If they do not exterminate us at home, in the name of immortal socialist principles, as an act of protest against our bourgeois backgrounds, you'll grow old together with me."

Well, that is also a life's aim, as good as any other. A limited, but valid aim: to grow old graciously, without bitterness, and without making yourself a burden on others. With dignity.

251

Another word out of use now, Sippi. Don't bother about dignity, dog. Once we return home, to normal life, we'll have difficulties maintaining dignity, human or canine, I warn you. He knows what it means to be exposed daily to the special flavor normal life has in his country, a mixture of oily Levantinism (always putting on a golden-toothed smile) with *chutzpa,* that peculiar Jewish brand of arrogance. A mixture merging into one homogenous mass, chewed up and then vomited into your face through radio and television and the press. No amount of showers and scrubbing can remove this stinking, sticky substance from his skin. The only palliative is a swim in the sea, preferably with closed eyes. But even in the sea the tar spots grow more numerous daily.

The dog on the couch changes position, and sighs a human sigh, a moan.

And yet, taking into account all this misanthropy, you still perform remarkably well among people: small talk and smiles, jokes and anecdotes. Anyone who doesn't know you well might easily think you were one of the guys. And even when you say that all your adult life you've only been afraid of one thing, and that is that you might actually become one of the guys, they would take it as another joke. Except that you are dead serious.

He takes a big drink, and another one, and goes on deck. They'll be in port tomorrow. He has been in this port before, two or three times. He likes this port, and the people. They have always been extremely poor, and possess that—ah, here it is again—that strange dignity that goes together well with being poor, but not screaming about it. They are still moderately proud of their glorious past of conquests, empires. And soberness of spirit. Have they preserved it until today, in a Europe that has changed so rapidly, so radically?

He smiles, recalling an extraordinary prostitute he once encountered in this port. You meet such whores only in stupid stories or cheap romantic movies; you know how whores are, especially port whores: hard as a diamond, cold as an iceberg, unyielding, hating. And yet once he met a girl here who proved that life often copies cheap fiction and stupid movies. What was her name? He has forgotten. Still trying to remember the girl's name, he walks upstairs, to the bridge. The name. A commonplace name. Maria? No, never mind. He remembers the gesture, the smile, the touch of her hand, the smell of the place. His own serenity then.

"You are happy about this place?" asks the captain.

"Yes. And I have pleasant memories, too. Long ago."

"You won't meet her again."

He laughs. "No, certainly not. But she is a pleasant memory."

"I mean we won't have time for anything. They can load all this stuff in three, four hours. Then we're out."

"I don't mind so much."

"Neither do I. What have we had on this trip? The Algerian warship, if it was Algerian; the shame of Bremerhaven, the gloom of Swansea, Rotterdam. Ah yes, we had Eliezer Rosen. Now, this last port, and home. The trip is almost over."

"Six weeks altogether."

"Yes. But if we do stay here in the evening, we should go and have a good meal together. They have excellent seafood here, you know?"

"Yes, I know. And very decent wine. Yes, let's do it if we stay overnight."

29.

The pilot does not know how long the ship will stay or what she will load. He only knows, vaguely, where to moor her. But he supplies—unasked—a variety of other information. He is young, resolute, talkative, a new generation for this old nation, a new generation of seamen. Those he had known before were not like this one. He also speaks fluent, albeit not very correct, English.

"In fact," he says, "ours is one of the most progressive countries in Europe."

"Considering all the others," the captain adds in Hebrew, "he might be right."

The pilot ignores this intrusion. "This, we owe to good luck. We have had two very good presidents. One is dead, alas, and the other is new and ruling well. They are very different, these two presidents, but both very, very good. Keep more to starboard. What is your course? Ninety-seven? Steer one-oh-two."

"One-oh-two, sir."

"Both good, each in his way. Mr. S.—that is the dead one—he did not like to spend money, he put all the money in the bank, all the money in the bank all the time. Now this new one, Mr. C., he has a different character, he likes to spend, so now he takes all the money out, out of the bank, makes investments, builds factories, builds shipyards, builds docks, plenty of money from what the dead one put in the bank, and now he invests all this, much progress, much work, very good. Much luck."

"I read somewhere that half of their money goes into that endless war of theirs," murmurs the captain in Hebrew. "But so does half of ours."

Aloud, he says, "Pilot, you're from a lucky people."

"Yes, sir. Certainly we have much luck."

The ship sails up the river. The river is magnificent, with angry brown water that swirls past the ship's hull with great speed.

They pass the town and are moored on a distant quay. The quay is empty, no dockers are to be seen. Only two gloomy policemen saunter up slowly, stout in heavy uniforms, and place themselves near the gangway. It takes an hour till a car arrives with an agent's representative and some port officials. But after another hour the first truck arrives. It is an army truck, and the driver and the man sitting next to him are soldiers. Then a few stevedores climb on top of the truck and the loading of munitions starts.

Curiously, all men on board stop working, and watch silently, as if they were witness to some strange religious rite.

Look, dog. She, too, stands quietly, close to his knee. Look well. That is what we sailed out for, a month-long trip, a few thousand miles on the log, and here it is, finally: oblong boxes with rope handles, with numbers written on them. See? We load them now, put them carefully in the ship's hold. The crown of our achievement. I doubt if they are of any importance now, Mississippi. To tell the whole truth, they might not be needed at all. Sober people back home—not like you and I, I mean constantly and consequently normal people, even during the last six years, even before, those who work hard day after day from six in the morning till six in the evening and later, who deal with ships like they'd deal with trucks or railway transport, who think in terms of capacity and loading factors, daily costs and freight prices, normal people, I say, dog—will shrug about this. The ship was originally sent to load steel in Swansea, then the war broke out, like rain may come on a cloudy October day, and they, the stupid guys from the Ministry of Defense, I mean, diverted the ship to load military supplies in Germany. And then it came to nothing, so we took over again, and sent the ship to where she should have loaded in the first place, and then, as far as we're concerned, the war episode is over and ships have to go and to come, to load and to discharge, we calculate the freight and the daily cost, business as usual. The company must make a profit, if the trip doesn't last too long, or loses money if it does take too long, or breaks even. That is the power of quantitative thinking, dog. Don't underestimate it, the world is being run on those lines. If you have any illusions about it, get rid of them, quickly, because otherwise you become an outsider, or a laughing stock, or both.

For diversion, dog, you shall have TV, the Saturday paper of over one hundred pages. Occasionally, but not more than twice yearly, a good crime or mystery book, some sport. Also comradeship, social evenings with people you like—normal people like ourselves—some social drinking (mind you, social, not the sick kind your master indulges in: John Barleycorn is a friend and you must respect him!) Decent meals in Oriental restaurants, Goldstar beer, moderate sex with our wives or the occasional fling now and then. That's it. Thus we promote progress, trade, industry, good accountancy, and can lead a normal life. Our Holy Grail is normalcy, mediocrity, and the Progress of Mankind. We work honestly: ours is the power of Positive Thinking. Numbers and sums. Common sense. Two and two will never make five for us.

He watches the last case from the truck being lowered into the ship's hold.

Come, dog, the truck is gone, and the quay is empty, I'll let you run here now, there is very little traffic here, and in this most progressive country in Europe, as the pilot said, there is no danger of a dogcatcher around the corner. We'll have time to worry about that when we get home. In China, they say, there are no dogs at all now, and very few sparrows. They have been exterminated, for people must be clean. And after you've had your run, I'll close you in the cabin, and go ashore, and have a very good and expensive meal with lots of wine and cheeses and coffee to top it off. And then I'll take a stroll, because I like this town and have good memories of it. Is it OK with you, Sippi, this plan?

She approves, because she is a loving dog. She only stretches her neck out for the blessing of a pat, then she is off in long, strong leaps, and disappears behind the corner of the nearest shed.

The next army truck arrives an hour later, and the next one after three quarters of an hour.

"If they load at this pace we'll stay here till tomorrow night, or more," remarks the captain.

"Are you in a hurry?"

"Oh, not really, but there is something indecent about this show."

"Anything you can do about it?"

Before he has time to answer, a car arrives. The longest, sleekest, blackest, most shiny American car. It arrives almost noiselessly and stops noiselessly on its thick whitewall tires. The two policemen instinctively jump to attention. The driver in the truck puts on his cap, the soldier near him fumbles nervously at his collar. Out of the car steps a little round man with a shining pate.

From the ship, they can only see the back of his well-tailored charcoal-black suit, and the tip of a big cigar protruding aggressively from the corner of his mouth, for he stands in front of the truck and addresses the soldiers there. He speaks a language the seamen do not understand, but it is obvious to all that he is not showering compliments on the two. In fact, it must be a torrent of abuse: the two unlucky soldiers get out of the truck and stand at attention, pale and mute.

The small man with the big protruding belly turns around slowly and looks for a moment in silence at the ship and at the seamen crowded at the gangway.

"You must excuse me," he says in English. "Are you the crew? Please excuse me, but my patience has also limits. What the hell does this fucking colonel think? Does he think he is in Africa, dealing with niggers? It has been agreed that the trucks will come fifteen minutes after each other. What the fuck does he think, the dumb idiot?"

His face is red and he keeps his hands in the side pockets of his jacket, puffing incessantly on his cigar. Abruptly, he turns around and walks back to his car. He pulls on white gloves. He slams the door violently and the car moves away with a swish of tires on the gravel.

After an hour, the trucks with munitions start coming regularly, every fifteen minutes.

"Stop shoreleave at midnight," says the captain to the chief mate. "We'll be ready by then. Nothing helps so much as a man with authority."

"Even of that size."

30.

We are now on our way home. Next time you go ashore it will be in our country. Do you understand?

This habit of talking to the dog will be difficult to get rid of. I'll have to get used to talking to people again. That might be difficult, the most difficult part of it. I have been drinking with people during this trip, but I have not talked much with them. Whom did I talk to? The Welsh pilot. The priest at the *Flying Angel*. The middle-aged prostitute in Rotterdam. A few people on board. The captain.

When I come back, people in the kibbutz will ask me, on the street, in the dining hall, Hello! How was it? You back?

But I cannot answer these questions. I can only say, Yes, I'm back, a seaman always goes away and always comes back. You tell them, Sippi. Barking. You can bark, can't you?

Sitting back in his chair, with the dog facing him watchfully on the coach, he says, I can tell them I had a fantastic meal in the last port of call. It was a great meal of shrimp and lobster and lots of wine. We were six men served by two waiters. The younger of the two waiters had a sad face, and was nervous. The other one had on him the stamp of quiet dignity that makes you feel that although he was serving food to you, you knew it was a profession as honorable as any other. He did his work very efficiently and professionally, without haste, and although he was serving and you were eating, you felt you were on a basis of equality with him and you knew he would never get familiar or vulgar with you. There was no servility in him.

This, he thinks, we seldom have in our country. I won't tell the people at home when they ask me, How was it? And yet, it was more important than the meal itself.

What else can I tell them? That the city was as international as ever, only more so, with crowds of foreigners on the streets, and in the cafés in front of the grand hotels, all kinds of foreigners, tourists, and displaced persons, businessmen and spies and agents of all kind and color and size, men and women. A rainbow of passions behind all the faces, a true fashion show of human passions. A real international city.

And that I gave a big tip to both waiters, and that the elder one bowed politely, without smiling, and said thank you, and the young, nervous waiter said thank you very much indeed, sir. That it was raining outside, but it was a warm, light rain, and the neon signs glistened and their reflections shone on the wet asphalt, and there were traffic jams downtown, where the broad avenues and squares are, but nobody honked or cursed. They just sat in their cars with the windshield wipers moving to and fro.

You can tell that to the people at home.

Some of them, the sillier ones, will ask about the quantity of the munitions, and what kind? And you'll tell them that is a military secret; there are a few military secrets in our country, and most of these are the wrong ones.

It is a strange society, he thinks. But would you expect a society of Jews to be a simple one? Troublemakers, Jews, as that reverend in Swansea said. The *sabras* will be different, perhaps, but it will take time till they develop their own personality, their mediocrity, to match the nations of the world. I am glad I won't be there to watch that spectacle. My children will, though. I hope they won't produce anything on the idiotic, infantile, clownish line, which is so much in vogue now, like Amin from Uganda, or the other one, Qaddafi, from Libya. If they avoid that, and I hope they will, for there is after all a certain biological heritage, they'll only have to be pragmatic, and hypocritical, like the Nixons and Kissingers and Podgornys. To match them. Perhaps, with time, they'll produce real men of an outstanding format and quality without ever becoming slaves to a leader.

31.

The sea is smooth, like a mirror. You can break your head looking for a more suitable metaphor and you cannot find one. You can say a table, a pane of glass. You always compare it to something man-made, and there is something of desecration in it, but you are powerless to do anything else: it really is like a mirror.

On the right, far off, suspended between the sea and the sky you can just discern the shades of Crete's mountain tops, faintly bluish against the blue of the sea and the haze of the sky. Sometimes you are not sure if they are not clouds, vapors, rising from the sea or descending from the sky. Deckhands are chipping rust and painting, they are half-naked in dungarees, the sun is very hot, the gray of Rotterdam and the lead sky of Wales are only a memory.

On the horizon, far off, two black spots. The ship's course, the ship's blunt nose, points exactly between them. In this kind of weather, you can see objects on the surface that are very distant. In one hour, which means eleven or twelve miles later, the objects are near. A steel-gray warship stands like a rock in a motionless sea: opposite her, a mile or less from it, her supply ship, a freighter of sorts, but you can easily see it is not a simple freighter. There must be workshops on board, fuel tanks, stores. The cruiser's superstructure is a complicated mass of antennas, radars, tubes, masts, and missiles pointing at the sky at a sharp angle.

A motor launch is behind its poop, and sailors sit there with rods, fishing: they are half-naked, like our seamen. Others, on rafts, are slowly painting the cruiser's side with rollers tied to long sticks. There is a red star on the cruiser's rakish bow, and you can read, without glasses, her name on the stern, the name of a Russian town. The supply ship has no name, only a number. Our course passes between the two Russians.

Searching with binoculars, you see on the cruiser's decks, on her bridge, several men, watching us.

"Here they are, the Russians."

The deck hands abandon their work to look at the gray monster. The men in the motor launch stop fishing, and look at us.

"The Russians, curse their mothers' cunts."

"Really? I thought they were Brazilians."

"You're a clever one. A spit from one of these little tubes, and you're in heaven."

"With your grandmother and grandfather."

"My grandfather is alive and well in Tiberias, don't curse him."

"I only curse the bastards."

"They can't know we're carrying munitions."

"They know everything. With those dishes they can hear you talking now."

"Very well then, let them know what I think of them: perish, you motherfuckers!"

"Ha, how brave you are!"

"What the hell is their business here, thousands of miles away from their country?"

"They are always here, near Crete, and further north. We always see them lurking around the islands. They watch the Americans, who have their bases around here."

"I'd give a hundred dollars to see an American right now, just to boost my morale."

The cook, in a dirty apron, vapors of whisky escaping from his mouth, keeps repeating: "What the hell do they have to sit around here for? Who invited them? They have no fucking business to be here at all!"

The dog, on the boat deck, looks around intensely. She lifts her forepaw and is all tension.

"Quiet, Sippi. They haven't interfered with our ship so far, have they?"

They interfere with our lives, and how, he thinks. Every one of the boys killed back home was killed by a Russian weapon. The criminal, insane, idiotic, age-old dream of the Czars for a warm, smooth sea, pursued with maniacal obstinacy by the present stony-faced rulers. Nobody can persuade them to give it up. Drunk with power, they dream of a world empire, and nothing less. The mere sight of this ship must give them an enormous boost. Hitler loved to inspect his battleships. I saw his face when on board: proud, arrogant, smiling. A battleship is a mighty thing, better than a plane, or a tank.

Amidst the tension and hatred, a strange twist of thought: remember Malmaz? That other Russian? He also left his cold country and came to this warm sea—when was that, a hundred years ago?—and you were thrilled by that sweet music through your whole childhood and youth. You thought there was nothing more beautiful than the Sheherezade. Was it really true he wrote it after that trip to Algiers? Perhaps. It could well be. A Russian sailor in the Mediterranean.

There may well be another one like that among the six hundred or so crew of this cruiser. Poor chance. One can imagine music under a swollen main sail, but hardly in the shadow of a missile. The cruiser, like a real rock, remains behind, in the wake of the ship.

His hatred momentarily weakened, he walks away to his cabin, the dog trailing behind at his feet.

Anyhow, they are here, along with their accursed weapons and their accursed dreams and ideology. They remain on board for months and months, they cannot go ashore in this part of the world: perhaps only in Yugoslavia. But they do not even do that. It must be hard for them: the ship's routine, crowded bunks or hammocks within this huge steel box. Political meetings, lectures. How they must hate it! Still, they obey. They have been perfectly trained to obedience. They have a long tradition of obeying. But Russian seamen were also the first to revolt, the pride of the revolution, they were called.

He remembers another Russian sailor now, a big, middle-aged fellow in a blue-striped T-shirt, with a huge handlebar mustache. Right after the German collapse in '45. He had come over from one of the three minesweepers in a small German port. The ruins were still smoldering, and they sat on a destroyed harbor crane that looked like the skeleton of a dinosaur, and the Russian said, solemnly, "Well, you have a free Poland now. But remember: make it democratic! Guard your democracy!" And the word sounded strange from his mouth, for you'd think the man had never heard the word. He pushed his brimless sailor's hat back on his head, and said, "Comrade, have you got a bit of spirit by any chance? Even a hundred grams of spirit, eh?"

Which reminds him to get up and pour himself a drink. You miserable old alcoholic. All the same.

But there is a commotion upstairs before he lifts this drink to his lips. The door opens with a crash, and somebody shouts, Come, come upstairs, quickly, something is up!

He puts the glass on the table and runs out, the dog barking, running after him. The Russians, he thinks. On the bridge, almost the whole crew has gathered.

"What's happening? The Russians?"

"Maybe. Nobody knows. There are two of them."

He takes the binoculars from one of the men.

Two war vessels are coming at them at high speed. From the distance, all that can be seen is a huge double bow-wave on each of them, carved out of the molten-lead sea, and the fragile single mast with a dish-like radar aerial.

"Speed boats, or torpedo boats."

"Missile boats, perhaps. NATO?"

"Or Russians. Do they have any? I don't know."

"We'll see very soon. It won't take much time." The two ships fly like projectiles over the shimmering surface.

"If I did not know where we are," says the captain hesitantly, "I'd say they were…"

"Cherbourg boats, eh?"

"Cherbourg boats, absolutely."

"Impossible, here!"

"Look, look at them!"

One of the boats takes a long, gracious curve, and while the ship rolls slightly in her tremendous wake, she comes to a stop alongside, a few yards away.

The blue and white triangular flag of the Israeli Navy on the mast, young people on the bridge, some of them bearded, smiling bashfully and raising their hands in salute.

A huge lump in his throat, choking. Is it excitement? What is it? All around him the crew is cheering and shouting, the drunken cook lifts high an empty bottle, and the second mate keeps yelling,

"My brother Moshe is there, with the guys, call him, please call Moshe."

"He is asleep," say the boys from the navy. "Wait, we'll call him for you."

"How are you?" asks one of the officers.

"Oh, we're well."

"How long have you been out?"

"Forty, forty-two days."

"Well, we'll escort you from now on."

"The Russians?"

"Oh, we know, we know."

And then Moshe arrives, barefoot, rubbing the sleep out of his eyes: "Where? Where?"

"Dan! Danny!"

"Here, Moshe! How are things?"

"OK…Malka had a son!"

"No!"

"Absolutely! Four days ago!"

"Guys, I'm an uncle now! Let's drink to that!"

"Better give those boys something to drink!"

Bottles and cartons of cigarettes are collected hastily, everybody contributes gladly, the big package is secured and thrown overboard in a nylon bag. People from the missile boat pick it up.

"I would like the bastards from customs back home to see it," says the electrician. The second missile boat joins the first one, at a certain distance from the ship.

"I prefer to wonder what the Russians would say if they could see this spectacle."

"They can see it extremely well on their radar, don't worry. They can't be more than twenty miles away."

The boats now take their position further away. The three vessels are sailing serenely on the same course, for Haifa. A munitions ship and two navy boats. Quite a homecoming.

We will be home in a few days, he says to the dog, and I must sum up this trip. No, silly! Not an official report to the company, which lists neatly the Work That Was Done, Maintenance, Accounts, Spare Parts, Crew Performance and Work to be Done during the next trip. No. That is done easily, routinely, I've done it a hundred times. What I mean is, my personal summing up.

I have an urge to do this. It is a necessity. Because, after all, life in our country in the future will not be exactly as it has been till now, during the last six years. Mine won't change much, I guess, perhaps a few more things falling under the heading: Not To Be Done or Cannot Be Done. Or Too Old. But basically people of my age don't change for a decade or two. I'll continue living true to my conditioning and to my inheritance.

Remember, Sippi, that I'm a Jew born in Poland. That is the country in which I was educated and lived till the age of twenty.

I know it sounds very funny, but the species is running itself quickly into extinction: in twenty, or twenty-five years there will be no more Polish Jews left. If I live much longer I'll acquire a certain museum value, like that of an Australian aborigine, or of an Amazonian Indian. Strange, isn't it?

What? What was that emotional surge when the missile boats came? Ah, ah, my dear dog, you don't understand the situation! I'm an Israeli, as good an Israeli as anybody else, and it is only natural that I should be happy and proud finding myself under the protection of the Israeli Navy. In our bad times, a defenseless being is lost: you should know this better than anyone—don't you cling to my knees when somebody or something is threatening you? A simplification, you say?

Not at all, my friend, not at all. I want you to register it carefully: up till 1939, I was a Pole of the Mosaic faith. They invented such a thing in Poland under Pilsudski's rule. In 1939, I stopped being that, and became a Jew, period. There was no ambiguity then and there: our political and religious political leaders could learn a good lesson from that, if they weren't so stupid, for they're quarreling right now about who is a Jew.

In 1942, I became a Stateless Pole.

In 1946, I became Stateless only.

In 1948, I became a citizen of the State of Israel; nationality—Jew.

And what makes me a Jew, you ask? Well, what makes you a dog?

It is true, sometimes you imagine yourself, or you desire to be something else: human, for instance. Many Jews are subject to the same psychological urge you experience, but that does not make them stop being Jews even for one moment. But my destiny is to live out my days as an Israeli Jew, carrying with me, as I told you, the permanent ballast of the heritage of my European-born ancestors, and of the Western Civilization they acquired, a mixture of Jewish and Western moral values. Behavior. Style and quality of thinking. Period. Enough of myself.

What?

Yes, you'll get your liver in half an hour. At least six people on board don't eat it, and the cook throws it away. Yes, I'll bring it to you. I promise.

32.

"Did you see this on the TV? Did you see how tanks in Athens crushed through the university fence and rolled over a crowd of students?"

"Yes. I did. Terrible. It's shocking."

"Mind you, in the country where democracy was invented."

"So what? Have you seen what the students did at the university before the tanks came? Have you seen the graffiti on the walls?"

"I cannot read Greek."

"I can. Among others 'Down with American imperialists, colonialists, and their supporters and servants!' You know whom they mean?"

"You won't convince me ours is a democratic country!" Paul the Sparkie gets angry.

"It is more democratic than Greece, Spain, Russia, Poland, Hungary, Libya, Egypt, and Kuwait. Not to mention Abu Dhabi, Chile, and Iraq."

"It could more democratic! It depends on us!"

"More democratic than it is? With us Jews? I doubt it!"

"Then we're lost. We really are servants of that rotten capitalism!"

"We can, even as servants of that rotten capitalism, preserve standards of individual, personal decency."

"That's another idiotic bourgeois phrase."

"Stop quarreling," says the electrician. "I'm sick and tired of your fucking ideological discussions. This is the last bottle of vodka, the last in the slop chest, the last on this trip. Do you understand?"

"I am one hundred per cent with you, Albert," says the cook. "These men are crazy!"

"You want to build a society on individual decency?" hisses Paul. "Look at your politicians, your leaders."

"They are no more mine than yours."

But he feels sad, depressed. "Albert and Israel are right," he says. "Let's annihilate this bottle."

Drink with them while you can, then go out, on deck, and enjoy the last hours of this trip. You do not know when, or if, your next trip will be. You've kept that poor dog confined to this ship for six weeks, you've caused sorrow and deprivation to your woman, to your children. And all this in order to participate in the great feat of bringing in a few hundred tons of munitions, which probably nobody needs now. Only to satisfy your ego, that you could say, I was in it.

I could not have done otherwise, he whispers, God knows I could not have stayed home. If it happens again, touch wood, I'd do it again. How can I stay outside of it, when they were, they still are, fighting for their lives?

Night descends on the Eastern Mediterranean. He sleeps fitfully, wakes up several times, hears the dog pacing the floor.

The Longest Trip

It is definitely a serious fault of mine, as a kibbutz member, but I absolutely lack any urge for togetherness. Thus, I excuse myself from activities like communal dining, marching on Labor Day, participating in various committees or even in the weekly General Assembly. I am also absent during weddings, circumcision celebrations, and on Friday night when all our members (including children) dine together in our big dining hall. Funerals are a different story. I never miss one. It is difficult to be alone on a kibbutz, a society based on togetherness—difficult, but not impossible.

In search of solitude one morning, I chose a small table near the window in the dining hall. After five minutes, a young woman approached me. "Do you mind?" she asked, pointing to the empty chair. I shrugged. "Go ahead," I said.

Through the window I saw big ships anchored opposite the power station. "What does it do to you to sit here and watch the ships out there?" she asked.

"Nothing," I said.

"Does it break your heart?"

"I have no heart. As time goes by, the heart stops reacting. It is a normal process."

"No regrets?" she asked.

"What regrets? I have sailed a lot in my time. Regretting is foolish. It is like crying that I have no feeling in my right hand, or that my vision is blurred. I look at the ships and think of a particular voyage. Now, among other things—and there are a million other things, believe me, for sixty years is a very big chunk of time, and that is how old I am—I remember this trip well, because it helped me to understand certain things, to interpret some things which I previously took for granted in a different way. After I met Noah, I stopped relating to the Bible and its various commentaries with too much seriousness. Mythology is right, but the reality beneath it is often much more fascinating.

"You know, in many respects this voyage was like any other. We took the usual cargo to a few little Mediterranean ports, and we had to pick up cargo from others on the way back. I had been sailing on that ship for two years, and it was routine. But then, during that trip, some things happened that were not routine and were worth remembering. You still want to hear?"

"I want to hear," said the young woman.

"The second engineer pointed it out to me as we were entering the port with the Turkish pilot on board. 'What is it?' he asked. 'A boat, or a joke?' A piece of wooden bark, standing high in the water, with a single raked mast and a big blue eye painted just below the anchor in the prow. This strange vessel stood right behind the place on the quay where the pilot said we were going to moor.

"'Careful, don't touch it while maneuvering, the thing may disintegrate,' laughed our captain. 'Disintegrate?' grunted the pilot. 'That thing is indestructible!' When the harbor tug pulled us round it, we read on the stern: Ark, Piraeus. I failed to notice what flag this Ark was carrying.

"I met Noah next evening in a waterfront tavern, and we had several drinks and a long talk together. Still interested? What did we load there? Tobacco and figs, of course. Why 'of course'? Because there are raw materials or products specially connected with some locations: coal with Newcastle, mustard with Dijon, samovars with Tula, oranges with Jaffa: thus, figs with Smyrna.

"The first thing that struck me about Noah was that he looked older than anybody or anything I've ever known. Well, in a way it stood to reason: the story, the myth, must be 4,000 years old. Perhaps older. Still, somehow I had not expected him to look that old. His skin was like onion-skin paper that has been exposed to fire—thin, crisp, and yellow. It was so thin that at any moment one expected it to tear and expose flesh; well, not exactly flesh, but the bones beneath it. He was almost bald and the skin on top of his round skull was as dry and fragile as that of his face. His beard was very white, but I won't say snow-white, because there was nothing snow-like about it. The hairs of his beard were as thin as the silk of a spider's web. More about that skin of his. It was as tightly drawn on his face as the panty hose masks terrorists often use. Can you imagine that? The oldest part was his eyes, very deeply set, pale gray, surrounded by a net of wrinkles. But there was an immense courage in them, a flicker of something you knew was indestructible.

"I ordered Arak for both of us, and he took his drink undiluted, breathed aniseed straight into my face, and said, 'You know, there is a legend that I invented the stuff.' He tapped the bottle delicately with his bony finger. 'A lie,' he said. 'It is much older. True, I brewed some after that trip, but invented? No! I claim no credit not due to me. Booze existed before I was born. My old man drank it. What puzzles me is how people develop a myth out of reality, and thereby twist and distort it to suit their purpose. For example, the story about me inventing booze.'"

"Talking about drink, what about another bottle? It's refreshing, isn't it?"

"'Where are you from?' he asked. I told him the name of our ship. 'Why, you're moored right next to our old bark. A nice, modern ship. I saw it when you arrived yesterday. Nothing compared to our old tub. Whenever I climb our gangway I always recollect the Ark of the old days.'

"He recollects! But it happened, if we are to believe our Bible, some four thousand years ago!"

"'So what,' he said. 'Since then, you can say, I've sailed a thousand ships on a million trips. I can tell you, confidentially, a few things have changed, but the basics are eternal: the sea, the stars, human beings …' He drank again and covered my hand with his bony one. 'Memories,' he said. 'You think the slate is wiped clean when you are born again. No, sir, you take this luggage—or at least part of it—for eternity. That's why I remember this thing. And never mind four thousand years. The polar star is still there, more or less in the same place. As to my age, my young friend, remember: Old seamen never die.'

"From his pocket he produced a small metal box and opened it. There were four little white pills in it. 'Be my guest,' he said. I hesitated for a moment, and swallowed one of the pills. He took another one. 'These, too, are very old,' he murmured, more to himself than to me. 'Did I say that the sea never changes? Well, it's not so, exactly. It did change a bit before that trip with the circus. It retreated three miles before coming back again. You don't believe it?

"'No,' I said. 'I believe anything you say, but the circus?'

"'Of course it was a circus. What did you think it was? A Jordan river ferry? But let's begin at the beginning. All right, then. A circus to be brought from Jaffa to here, to Izmir. Freight prepaid, of course. It was not an easy cargo, you know. We had trouble with some animals. The pterodactyls insisted on hanging with their heads down from the upper beams. The hippos and the rhinos wanted to wallow in the bilge water in the lower hold, and the elephants refused to go down from the tween-deck. Have you ever tried to get an elephant into the lower hold?'

"He stroked his beard and continued his strange story as if the events had happened only yesterday. Thera had exploded and sunk a couple of months before. You heard about it from history or mythology, I presume,' continued Noah. 'Since then, there have only been a few catastrophes like that in the world. Krakatoa did the same a hundred and fifty years ago. Pelée, on Martinique, tried hard in 1902 and almost succeeded. But only almost. Then, in our most modern times, the man-made destruction of Hiroshima and Nagasaki. Well, let me tell you, when Thera exploded and sank it was like a million Hiroshimas happening simultaneously in all parts of our venerable globe.

"'Remember, God regretted having created the world, and decided to get rid of it. It was a bad mistake, He thought. Sorry. So the sky blackened for a few months, and the air we were breathing was mixed with ashes. The sea, as I've already told you, retreated and then returned, submerging huge chunks of land. But the total darkness was the worst. Try navigating when there are no stars in the sky! No sun, either; the air ceased to be transparent.

"'All I can say is, we were keeping the general direction: sailing north and not knowing if Izmir was still there. How did we do it, you'll ask. By instinct only, whatever that is. All the time the sea was very rough, and you can imagine how all those poor beasts suffered—the lions, elephants, camels.

"'My sons, who signed on for the trip as my mates, worked like slaves, feeding the animals. We had, naturally, stones for ballast on the ship's bottom, but tender as she was, the pitching and rolling were considerable. As for myself, I never left the bridge. Well, it wasn't really a bridge as you know it now, but I kept watching the world outside going berserk for forty days, from shore to shore, no maps, no stars, no sun, and I already felt that the shoreline must have changed greatly during that tremendous earth- and sea-quake. And so we sailed like a bunch of blind lunatics.'"

"What were the pills you took?" she asked.

"I don't know," I answered, "but Noah said they were very old and I didn't care. I was then at the age when one is willing to try anything once. And I trusted the man. I can only tell you what they did to me, more or less. Again, it might have been the joint action of the pills and the drinks, but the result was that when he spoke it was like watching a film and living it, or like watching things happen and experiencing them."

I tried to explain things to the girl who had broken my solitude in the dining room, and was not sure I was successful.

"At this stage I was well aware that he was holding me under a spell with his narrative, and I chaffed against it. I did not know if it was his pills, the quiet music of his voice, or his fascinating personality that created the spell, but I rebelled against the sensation of being forced to live the reality of the story, of participating in this crazy trip. He, too, must have perceived it, for the tone and the rhythm of the story changed.

"'Now, this is how it goes,' said Noah. 'First, a legend, then a myth which has been manipulated. And with each transformation the distance from the reality grows, you understand. We think that beneath every myth there must be a reality of some kind. I'm not so sure anymore. Look, it says there, in the Bible—the greatest compilation of myths that ever was—that there were giants on the earth then. I'll tell you frankly, I don't know because I never met one. Maybe there were, maybe not. It also says that sons of God saw the daughters of men, that they were fair, and they chose wives from among them:

And the sons of God came in unto the daughters of men and they bare children to them; they were the heroes of old, men of renown.

"'I don't even pretend to try to understand what is meant by that; perhaps angels or those giants mentioned before? I, too, had daughters, though not mentioned in the Myth, but I can assure you that they didn't screw around, not with the sons of God, not with the giants, and not with the sons of men. For my wife and I watched over them jealously (even if it is difficult for a seafaring man, being away from home most of the time, to watch over his children). Whoever composed the Myth omitted the daughters. They were not important. But he mentioned my three sons, so that later, when they rewrote the Myth, they could distort it to suit their purpose. Shem, Japhet, and Ham; Ham was presented as the villain of the story. But it was not so. In fact, Ham, the youngest, was the most diligent of the three, and a good seaman. I hoped he'd take over the family business when I'd be too old to run it properly.'"

"You never told me what he looked like," said the young woman facing me. It sounded almost like a complaint. "You mentioned his skin, his eyes, but what did he look like?"

I said, "He looked like a very ordinary Mediterranean seaman: medium height, long arms, slightly bent legs." Then I forgot her completely and dived back into the memory.

"'Now, what do you do,' said Noah, 'after an exacting, terrible voyage of many weeks, when the anchor—sorry, the anchor stone—finally goes down? Naturally, I got drunk, gloriously drunk. Who can blame me? I think I remained drunk for a few days. And believe me, I couldn't care less if my sons saw me or not, if they averted their eyes piously or stared. But the Myth, the rewritten Myth, makes a big deal out of it. Who cares? After all, the Almighty, who it is said was on excellent terms with me during this adventure, created us naked.

"'Where did all this happen? In the nearest port, of course, at night, in a tavern very much like this one, full of dancing girls and whores. As a matter of fact, I think it was Ham who found me there. He must have told the other boys: Dad's in the tavern, *Under Two Harpoons*, dead drunk; let's go there and take him home. And so they did. They wrapped me in a blanket, and I woke up three days later in my own bed.

"We drank again; I stopped counting the empty bottles. And then I said: 'Yesterday, when we arrived here, I went to the whorehouse section of town. I was body-searched at the entrance by Turkish soldiers who made sure I had no knife or revolver on me. Then I walked down the main street of this quarter. I wasn't looking for a girl; it was very dirty there, and I'm a married man and was scared I could bring home some bad disease. Simply out of curiosity, I just walked and looked. And there was that whore, stark naked on her bed out on the street. She asked me if I could give her a cigarette, which I did. It was a stifling evening, and it was a weird sight, a naked woman on a bed in the middle of the street smoking a cigarette. By the way, did you know that here they shave their pubic hair?'

"'Yes,' said Noah. 'It's a custom, but not as weird as you think.

Temple prostitutes of the Great Goddess did the same; they lay in front of their temples—minus the cigarette, of course—to attract worshippers, or customers, if you prefer.

"'But let's return to my sons. So the Myth made Ham the villain, probably keeping in mind the future relations between the Israelites and the Canaanites. All I can tell you is that I never cursed Ham and blessed the other boys. Ham was, as I told you, the best second mate I ever had. But never mind that. Just remember that the people who wrote that Book, still considered by many the mainstay of our civilization, were human beings like you and me, subject to passions like hatred, greed, and envy, not to speak of political and national considerations. Morals and Ethics have changed many times since, and the Book was rewritten as many times as the great Soviet Encyclopedia today. But as I told you in the beginning, human beings are unchanged; they are now as they were then. Also, evil passions and follies remain to this day the real scourge and curse of humanity.'

"Noah continued: 'I want you to understand me properly. I told you the story not because I want to fight the Myth. Not only what we perceive by our senses is real. Dreams are part of reality as well, and so is myth if digested by your mind and absorbed by your soul. If it penetrates that deep it becomes as real as anything you see and touch. But on that condition only. Later, people called the soul by various names: ego, super-ego. All these are intellectual concepts, but the soul is not. Suffice it to say, it is deeper than the senses and the mind, and it is indestructible.'"

"Have you understood this?" I asked the girl sitting on the other side of the table. I looked up, but she was no longer there. Obviously, my story did not fascinate her as Noah's had fascinated me back in Izmir. A moment earlier I had been looking at her. Our eyes had met, and I had thought, but did not tell her, that hers were as blank as those of the Turkish prostitute who asked me for a cigarette so many years ago. Now she had disappeared altogether without my even noticing. The truth was, I had a grudge against her, for I resented having been disturbed in my solitude, which brought me to contemplate that trip to Izmir long ago.

Alone now, I wondered how Noah really felt about that longest voyage in his fragile craft with the improbable cargo of animals. He got the specifications and scantlings for its construction directly from the Almighty, perhaps in a dream. Didn't he say himself that dreams are also a part of our total reality? Did the moral implications of his voyage, stressed so strongly in all later accounts, bother him much? Likely he had no time for those thoughts. He was primarily a man of action, a seaman.

I turned my head toward the window. Outside was the vast expanse of glittering sea. There was also a very big ship, a bulk carrier, riding on her anchor. Nowadays, the ships are much bigger than those of my day. But it is not so much the size that counts; much more important are the people that man those ships.

I thought again about Noah and his Ark, and that trip to Izmir long ago—an integral part of my reality.

After the Stroke

I am a professional survivor, but sometimes I think I have overestimated my talent at that vocation (being a survivor is actually more of a vocation than profession). Apparently there is a limit to everything, and one must beware of exaggeration. For example, I had a cerebral stroke a month ago, which deprived me of the power of speech and the ability to write. Unable to communicate with the outside world, imprisoned, so to say, within my own skull, I spent my time trying to guess what chance I had of surviving the next stroke. I had no illusions: the chances were nil.

But the night preceding the stroke I had a dream, which I was able to remember the next morning when the damage to my brain had already been done. The dream was about an old friend of mine, Malachi, who had taught me a lesson in humility when his wife came to my cabin and said in a staccato voice, "Malachi is paying off today. I thought you should know."

I was chief engineer then and Malachi my second. A second is an executive officer in the engine department. We had returned that morning from a trip to northern Europe and Malachi was now inspecting the sump of the main engine, a dirty job that always marks the end of a long trip. I had sailed a lot with Malachi and we liked each other. We used to tell each other stories from our lives.

Over his bunk he had a motto from the Ten Commandments—Thou shall not kill—which he said guided him in his life. Consequently, when a civil war broke out in his native kibbutz, he left, moving to another kibbutz. But most of all, I liked to hear his story of how his career at sea started.

Malachi became a crewmember of the trawler *Tsofiyah*. The kibbutz he had moved to was engaged, like my own, in deep-sea fisheries. On his first trip he was helplessly seasick. "I lay down under the windlass and wished for only one thing, to die as soon as possible. Mind you, I didn't curse the hour I was born; I cursed the moment my mother first met my father. I wanted to die. After two days and nights of that torment the Almighty heard and broke the trawling wench and they had to return to port for repairs. And that was how I survived."

So now this woman, not at all bad looking, sat facing me, piercing me with her brown eyes, eyes like steel drills, and said, "This morning I told Malachi it is either the ship or me. He is quitting now and returning to his wife and children, where he belongs. You understand?"

I said nothing and she left, slamming the cabin door. Fifteen minutes later Malachi, in his soiled white overalls, sat in the same armchair his wife had vacated.

"I must pay off today. The sump of the main engine looks okay." Then he said, "What do you do when there is maneuvering from the bridge and suddenly you have no more air in the air bottles and the compressors don't work?"

We use compressed air to start the engine. I said, "I phone the bridge and tell the captain I can't maneuver anymore with the engine."

"That is my situation now," said Malachi.

I looked at him, thought a moment and said, "Okay Malachi. Pay off. I'll miss you."

He left the ship and I saw him only many years later, a vegetable.

Malachi returned to his wife and children and worked in the kibbutz factory, in the garage, and in all the kibbutz agricultural enterprises. He was welcomed on each work assignment for he was an excellent worker; moreover he was also a subtle, sweet man, able to work as part of a team with anybody, without altercations or quarrels. He was the first to volunteer for difficult or dangerous jobs and when a mixer in a fertilizer silo needed repairs Malachi jumped in to do the job even before they were able to provide him with a gas mask.

He was dragged out, unconscious, an hour later. When he regained partial consciousness, his brain, deprived of the necessary oxygen, never recovered.

A famous neurologist said he would remain a living vegetable until the end of his life. He could not move his limbs or speak or communicate with the outside world in any manner. He could not control the movement of his bowels or his bladder and there was no evidence he could hear or understand anything. I saw him watching a spider on the wall, his eyes were moving, but there was no coordination between the movement of the spider and his eyeballs.

The kibbutz spared no money or effort, consulting the best doctors in the country and abroad. When modern medicine offered no help, Malachi's friends turned to unconventional methods.

A famous healer, a woman called Melissa, was summoned from America at the cost of many thousands of dollars. Moshe Dayan, one of our national heroes, was among the people who recommended her. In America, leading captains of industry, bankers, presidents of international companies, film stars and senators were among her clients. Malachi being hospitalized in Haifa, Melissa was lodged in that city's most expensive hotel.

Malachi's friends asked me, for reasons I could not understand, to take Melissa to dinner and to be present at the first healing session with Malachi the next morning.

Melissa was a large, mature woman, of around forty-five, with dark hair held by a glittering head band which I thought was gold. I was right. There was a green stone in the middle with a similar stone, somewhat smaller, dangling in each of her earrings. A topaz hung from a golden necklace and when she marched through the aisle to our table every head in that hotel restaurant turned in her wake. I rose to seat her and was submerged in a cloud of very strong, bitter, dark perfume.

Our eyes met only after she had finished studying the menu. Bright green eyes, inquiring, penetrating, mocking: What are you up to? Why were you sent?

Then she said, "I know very well that Malachi's friends—that is the unfortunate boy's name, isn't it?—who have hired me at very considerable expense, want to verify my healing powers. Perhaps I should start by telling you the names of some of my clients."

"It's not necessary," I said, "I know your list of references. But I wonder if you could explain, in layman's terms, how you intend to help Malachi?"

"I want to transfer part of my energy to his damaged brain."

"How?" I persisted.

"By touching his head. You see, we normally use only half of our potential vital energy. My gift, my healing power, is that I use the other half and can transfer it to others."

"How?"

She was evasive. "There are many ways of transferring vital energy. You'll see tomorrow."

"What kind of energy are you talking about?"

"Vital energy."

"Is it concentrated in the brain?"

"A part of it is. But as I said, you'll see tomorrow."

I did. At nine in the morning, I went to the hospital. Malachi was in bed, his eyes open, but again he saw nothing. He would not react if you moved your hand in front of his face, not even blink.

"Does he understand English?" asked Melissa.

"He did."

This morning she was wearing a simple brown dress. There

was no trace of yesterday's jewelry. But when she extended her hand toward Malachi's head, I saw a big stone in a ring on her finger.

"All right," she said, "you watch now. Malachi, smile. Give us a sign that you understand, that my energy has penetrated your brain." Her hand hovered over Malachi's face, close, but never quite touching, and she kept repeating those same words, over and over, again and again. The curtains were drawn and in the semi-darkness, keenly aware of the bright sunshine over the spotless blue sky of the Israeli summer day outside, I watched her hand and Malachi's dead face and suddenly I felt how much I wanted to be outside this room on this lovely morning, to forget all about Malachi and Melissa and the business of transferring energy. And then Malachi smiled. Perhaps it was only an automatic contraction of facial muscles, but I swear he smiled. Melissa withdrew her hand, looked at me and said, "You saw it? You saw it with your own eyes, didn't you?"

I said I did and then she left the room. At the door, she stopped a moment and sighed. "I am exhausted. I must leave now."

I stayed. I said "Malachi, Malachi, please smile again. Smile just for me. Smile for your friend."

But his face remained motionless, a dead mask as before. I left him there and never saw him again. A year later, while abroad, I heard Malachi had died. Rest in peace.

Now, many years later, I had my third stroke while in America and when they discharged me from the hospital I still could not speak fluently and it was clear I needed therapy. We chose one of many recommendations and I arrived at the address on Central Park West. This was not my first trip to America—I was familiar with the elegant apartment houses with round-the-clock security and uniformed doormen who check you out before you are admitted to the elevator—but here I was also accompanied to the elevator by a black doorman who would not allow me to press the button to the thirteenth floor. "Excuse me," he said politely, "I get paid to do this."

Melissa was standing in the open doorway. "You probably don't remember me, but we met once before," I said.

"Of course I remember you. Malachi, in Israel, eight or nine years ago. And what brings you to me across the ocean?"

"It hit *me* this time. Not as bad as poor Malachi, *may he rest in peace*," I added automatically in Hebrew, but she seemed to understand.

"Is he dead?"

"Many years ago," I said, "but I remember your transferring energy to him and his smile."

Melissa also smiled. "There are so many ways of transferring energy." She smiled again. "And how have you been?"

"Generally okay, but a month ago I had a cerebral stroke, as you can hear, and some part of my brain was affected."

I looked at her. She wore a simple dressing gown and no jewels, but the gown was only half buttoned and beneath, she was naked. I also saw a white streak in her black hair. But her eyes still radiated the green light I had found so remarkable then. A black cat appeared from nowhere and rubbed itself against her legs. The apartment was large, with many pictures on the wall. There was a large reproduction of Bosch's Garden of Earthly Delights over the sofa.

After the session, we had a long conversation. I said, "Immediately after the stroke I could not communicate with anybody. I was confined, so to say, to the walls of my skull, for I could not speak or write."

What was the strange force that made me yearn so desperately for help, even from strangers? It is true that Melissa was a healer, or claimed to be one, but it was doubtful she would be able to be of help in my predicament. My problem was to know if consciousness was all there was? If such were the case, the mind, which I understood sits in the brain, practically ceases to exist. This was the problem I wanted Melissa to solve for me. I had imagined the brain as a kind of pulp inside the skull, and instinctively found the idea that this should represent me in my entirety, repulsive.

I also remembered the story my neurologist told me. Einstein, as it is well known, donated his body to science. When they bisected his brain, the professor conducting the post mortem exclaimed, "If this is it, what was it the man was thinking with?"

But Melissa was reluctant to deal with the issue. She said, "This is really not my realm. I am too busy to work on such problems. But I'll tell you one thing. Most men think they make love with their penises, but it isn't so. Fucking is done mainly with the brain. So there is one thing the brain is good for."

I left Melissa and took the subway to the Port Authority terminal. But being confused, I boarded the wrong train and found myself in Times Square.

Now New York is often described as a modern Sodom and Gomorrah. If this is the case, Times Square is the very bottom of the pit.

I walked along 42nd Street, encountering many whores and their pimps and people who offered to inject heroin with a syringe into my veins. "Come on, man, I can fix you right here, right here in this doorway." Or at least sell me coke or hash. A large troop of transvestites passed by and I wondered what makes men want to disguise themselves as women and vice versa. A large number of passersby were talking to themselves. I recollected the comment an American friend of mine had made on this phenomenon, that they're damn lucky they had somebody to talk to!

I passed the hot dog stands, the felafel stands, the knish stands, the pretzel stands and the stands of sunglasses.

At the entrance to the terminal, I saw a drunken Negro spread on the sidewalk. Two white cops were watching him but did nothing to help him or remove him, because he was lying close to the wall and did not obstruct the entrance. People stepped over him though it took a broad step, for the Negro was big. But I felt a strange compassion for this unconscious man, and could not help wondering what dreams he could be dreaming in his drunken stupor. Then it suddenly came to me, at least a partial solution to my problem: on the level of plain logic, on the level of the mind, or the brain, if you prefer, there was just a drugged or drunken bum spread on the street.

But my compassion for him was not in this province. It must have been something else, something unaffected by my damaged brain, something altogether unconnected to the brain. Then I boarded my suburban bus and stared at the darkness outside the windows as the bus moved slowly onto the New Jersey turnpike. But when we came to Port Elizabeth, I felt—I felt, I say, because I could not see then—I felt the ships there, under the huge container cranes of the Maersk line. And I repeat, I felt—for the element of visualization was entirely missing—the presence of the crews of those invisible ships in the engine rooms which were, I knew, warm and smelling of oil and fuel and well lighted; the motorman or the officer on duty making his rounds, and the chief having a cup of coffee in the pantry or a drink in the comfort and stillness of his cabin, thinking strange thoughts and feeling very lonely.

Momentarily there was an element of regret and self-pity because I knew that scene would never be re-enacted in my life. And the regret was futile, like all regrets. But most of my life I had belonged to a ship or a ship had belonged to me, or at least the ship's engine room, and that can be a kingdom, too. But now I belonged to nothing, and all I had was the awareness of being, and even that was not so strong anymore, this in a way a justification for regrets.

But on this day the awareness of being was strong enough to have compassion for many people rejected, and to be sorry for them. I also felt on that raw December night the solitude of the ships in Port Elizabeth and the loneliness of the men in them. I knew the journey was near its end and as the bus turned off the turnpike, entering the local road, I remembered again my former shipmate Malachi. In his spare time he used to work on a construction of a model of a *perpetuum mobile*, building it from discarded spare parts he found in the engine room.

I said, "Malachi, you've studied physics and thermodynamics and of course you know that you're wasting your time: there is no such thing as *perpetuum mobile*."

Malachi responded. "You can call me an idiot if you like. Of course in my mind I know perfectly well the *perpetuum mobile* is a logical impossibility. But I feel somewhere deeper than in my mind, and don't ask where, because I don't know where, that I must try," and Malachi grinned his irresistible smile.

And now, many years later and Malachi dead and in his grave, I accepted with gratitude his knowledge, that there are things beneath and beyond the mind, that our brain is not all there is to us. Praise God for this divine gift: for the yearning for the impossible, for sorrow, pity and compassion.

Kibbutz Sdot Yam, February–March 1985

Entropy

*To United States Army General
H. Norman Schwarzkopf, with gratitude*

I was sick most of the trip, without being able to diagnose what was really wrong with me. Without a doubt, my subordinates must have felt it right from the start. But it was only later, in Glasgow, that the second engineer suggested that a doctor would help. He told the captain, and the next morning the agent sent a doctor to see me. The doctor had white hair and white bushy eyebrows and red cheeks and nose. He examined me in my armchair, opposite the desk; he took my temperature, checked my pulse and immediately replaced the thermometer and stethoscope in his big leather bag. After that, I showed him my tongue. He put his hand on my knee and said, "Look here, Chief, basically there is nothing wrong with you, except that there is not enough blood in your alcohol circulation system. Take my advice and take it easy for a few days."

"Doctor, will you share a little shot of something with me?"

He extracted a pocket watch the size of an onion from his vest and shook his head. "Too early for serious drinking," he said.

"And when is the proper time for serious drinking?"

"Five in the evening, of course."

I didn't give up, I was so thirsty.

"One little tiny shot, doc, with soda?"

"Young man," he said, "if God intended there to be bubbles in whiskey He'd have put them there Himself."

I had my shot alone. I liked that doctor, thanked him, and he left.

But the next afternoon, he came back.

"I wanted to check up on my patient," he said.

"I'm OK, thank you," I said.

"I just wanted to check," he responded. "Besides I think we mentioned serious drinking yesterday."

I brought out the bottle and the glasses.

The fact was I had reasons for such drinking. This was not a regular trip. On *Yom Kippur*, Egypt and Syria had attacked Israel. The next day I went to Haifa to my reserve unit in the Israeli Navy. They laughed at me there. "Are you crazy? You were discharged from the navy five years ago because of your age. Do you think we won't be able to manage against the bastards without your assistance? Go home!"

I went home and worried about young soldiers fighting the invaders. I started drinking and prayed. Next morning my prayers bore fruit. I got a phone call: "Are you ready to volunteer? To take out a Merchant Marine ship to bring munitions and tanks from Germany?"

"When?"

"Tonight."

"I'll be ready in half an hour."

"A jeep will pick you up for Ashdod."

So that was the situation. From a professional point of view I was confident I could handle it. I knew the ship, I had sailed on her before. But my nerves were probably not in the best condition and so it happened that on the outward voyage I drank more than I had in the past.

The war news was not good. The Egyptians had crossed the Canal and we saw pictures on the TV of our soldiers being brought to POW camps in Egypt. They had slippers on their feet. "Completely surprised," I murmured to myself.

The Syrians attacked in the north. Fierce tank battles were fought. In the messroom and the private cabins my drinking companions were the cook, the electrician, and the radio officer, all of them junior, but I had never been troubled by that before and certainly was not now. But most of the drinking I did in the solitude of my spacious cabin. I was drinking and praying and often I didn't know the difference. The Germans booted us out of Bremerhaven and we sailed on, to Swansea in Wales, and then to Rotterdam, then to Glasgow and finally to Lisbon. By then the war was long over.

But before we arrived back in Haifa I did some hard thinking and said to myself in the mirror (an ancient habit of mine): "My boy, that was probably your last trip in this life."

Is there another one?

And then my stroke, this strange thing, happened to me; perhaps it was connected to my thoughts during the last week of the trip.

I have always had an aversion bordering on hostility to mathematics in any form. In middle age, that aversion was replaced by a keen interest and even sympathy toward all subjects related to mathematics. Consequently, I was thrown when, as a result of my first cerebral stroke, the ability to deal with even elementary calculations vanished from my brain. But I still remember that turning point, when distaste for the subject became sympathy. A man called Dr. Feingold was responsible for that event, for he introduced me to entropy.

To qualify for the rank of chief engineer of the Merchant Marine one had to pass several written and oral exams and one of the most crucial was thermodynamics, Dr. Feingold's subject.

After serving the required number of years onboard seagoing vessels, I was sent to study at the Institute for Officers of the Merchant Marine in Acre, to obtain a license, my so-called "ticket."

It was not an easy time in my life. I was unaccustomed to intensive studies. My bedside bibles were Reed's *Practical Mathematics for Marine Engineers* and Lamb's *The Running and Maintenance of a*

Marine Diesel Engine. I read and studied until steam poured from my ears. I yearned for that ticket. One day Dr. Feingold said, "Gentlemen, you have proven your wisdom to me by choosing a profession in which you spend days and nights in the infernal noise of these sardine tins, the engine rooms of modern ships. But that is your business. Mine is to teach you the principles of thermodynamics and I promise you, I'll teach you."

"How?" asked a man called Benz. He was not a relative of Mercedes-Benz and Feingold knew it.

"I don't know how; maybe you should repeat for yourself endlessly what I state in class, and so memorize it."

But Benz, whom I liked and who was a perfectly competent marine engineer, persisted. "Dr. Feingold, you tell me how; you're the doctor!"

"I am a doctor, but not a vet!" snapped Feingold. I thought he'd explode, but he managed to contain himself.

He said, "I'd like to ask you gentlemen to buy a copy of Callendar's *Tables of Superheated Steam* and study the second column of numbers in the publication and ignore the first column entitled ENTROPY." At that moment I asked, "What is entropy?" Dr. Feingold stopped talking and thought for a full moment before answering me: "Entropy is the availability of energy to work. It is a physical concept, bearing, however, important philosophical implications."

And at that moment I fell under the spell of entropy.

Under this spell I started writing on top of every page of my letters, and later on every page I wrote, the formula $S = k \log W$: The entropy S is proportional to the logarithm of W; the probability of the given state, k, is Boltzmann's constant.

Entropy is the measure of disorder. It is always on the increase. The entropy of the universe is always tending to increase.

Reflections on this sad, pessimistic message, and drink—in moderation as advised by the good old doctor from Glasgow—filled my days and nights for the rest of that voyage, which did indeed prove to be my last. But entropy followed me home; it was with me as I descended the last step of the accommodation ladder in Haifa.

At home, I began looking for parallels between entropy and the ancient Greek tragedies. After all, tragedy is what is as opposed to what could have been and never will be. What did Aristophanes and the other Greeks know about entropy?

Millennia later, an American writer must have had a glimpse of the truth when he put in the mouth of the Soviet General Goltz in Spain the following: *Rien à faire. Rien. Faut pas penser. Faut accepter. Nous ferons notre petit possible.*—We will do our little bit.

And so I have succeeded in living with my entropy for almost twenty years after that trip in October of 1973. It has not been easy. I have received heavy blows to my heart and to my head. And so I continue to live with my entropy, which serves me as a means to curb my futile old man's anger, the fury that whatever I do is transitory in its context, doomed by nature to wane, to decompose, to disappear.

I am able to gaze in the mirror when shaving and trace, as Borges said, the patient labyrinth of lines in my face and the thinning hair on my head.

As I write these lines there is a man not far from here, called Saddam Hussein, threatening to kill me with poison gas. As he is separated from me only by the range of modern missiles, I must take his threats seriously. But for me this is ancient history. Fifty years ago, another madman, Adolf Hitler, also wanted to kill all the Jews with gas. He almost succeeded. But only almost.

I recollect from the same period the speech of the American General Patton during a press conference. He said, "And when we come to Berlin, I will personally kill that wallpaper-hanging son of a bitch with this revolver as I would kill a snake."

And today I hope that another American general will have as much courage and determination as Patton, to save us from annihilation. It is said that the inventor of the concept of entropy chose to kill himself as a very young man, when the world refused to accept what he had discovered. But that was certainly not the solution. We must not cease to act, even when it is meaningless.

Kibbutz Sdot Yam, Caesarea Maritima, September 1990

Afterword

Yes, I am aware of the fact that writers nowadays don't put After-words in their novels and stories. But I think that as a writer I belong rather to the last century and not to the present one, and therefore do not feel myself bound to follow the modern trend. Following the instructions of my physiotherapist, I was doing my exercises on the lawn in the backyard of my house when it occurred to me with the suddenness of a final realization that it makes no difference in the world of entropy if I am standing on this lawn of mine or lying under it. Strangely, this realization made things easier for me for many days, which does not mean that I have discovered the means to conquer entropy. Quite the contrary: I understood at last that it was God's wish to remind us that we must find the terms of our contract with Him because our time is limited. And so, months after writing the above, I dedicate this story to American General H. Norman Schwarzkopf with gratitude.

Reflections on Life in the Last Decade of the 20th Century, in the Form of Letters to a Friend, by an Ancient Mariner

I never really believed in the theory that the ninth wave is stronger than the others, but now, entering the seventh decade of my life, I feel that there is a subtle change of attitude that can hardly be attributed to the passage of time, naturally open-ended in both directions but marked mainly by the inclination to nostalgia.

Look, for example at the little Chinese sailor in his junk-like boat, staring at me now as I write this. I remember buying him many years ago in a shop in the Chinese quarter of Rotterdam, as a present for my wife, Irene, saying: Here is someone who, like myself, will always sail back to you.

But she never liked the Chinese sailor. She said, He is not sailing back to me, he is sailing away from me! Soon after that she died.

Twenty five years later I gave him to my second wife, Nola, and I am happy to report that there was an immediate mutual understanding between the two. She placed him on her night table and I often see her gazing at him. They like each other.

For a long time, the Chinese sailor had an unlikely partner:

an old New England skipper whom I acquired at a garage sale in Boston. Unlike the Chinese sailor he has a beard and whiskers and is dressed in his best Sunday suit with four golden stripes on his shoulders and sleeves.

Dear Saul,

In this memoir or story I have presented myself as an Ancient Mariner and I shall present a justification for this claim.

My first ship was a very old steamer, *Marianne*, whose crew I joined after being brought on board by a policeman from Stutthof. I was in Straflager Stutthof for a month under the documents of Jan Krukowski, a Polish stoker, after they caught me one stormy night in a stolen fishing boat in Danzig Bay. Stutthof was a concentration camp for Jews and other *Untermenschen*, but it had served before as a simple punishment facility for minor offences of Germans and others employed in the Danzig shipyard.

The camp's two parts were strictly separate.

Some official in the camp office must have discovered that Jan Krukowski was a stoker by profession, perhaps more useful to the state serving on a ship than idling in the camp barracks, but *Ordung* must be, as the Germans say. They insisted on the procedure and so my signature figured on the ship's papers opposite that of one Carl Schmidt, Master.

The *Marianne* sank a month later. I was rescued. After a week in hospital I was transferred to the *Brigitte*, another ancient coaster, and still later to the *Stettiner Greif*, and to the floating crane of the shipyard, *Langer Heinrich*, and thus ended my service in the German Merchant Marine during the Second World War.

Dear Saul,

The first ship I signed on after the war was the ss *Banana* of the famous Swedish company Salén A/B in Trellenborg.

Unfortunately I had to pay off the next day, when informed that the ship was to sail to Poland, from which I had recently escaped.

My next sailings were for the illegal Jewish emigration to Palestine for the so-called Mossad Aliyah Bet.

This included sailing under the Panamanian flag *San Basilio*, Captain Nogure and a crew of Spanish anarchists—excellent people!—work on the *Ulua*, under Lova Eliav, and from Port Sete to Haifa on the ss *Guardian*, later renamed *Theodor Herzl*, under Captain Mocca Iimon. After almost a year in the British detention camp in Cyprus, I started sailing on the *Pan Crescent*, under Captain Ike Aronwitch. Then a period of work on the deep-sea trawlers, of Kibbutz Sdot Yam: *Ne'eman, Alisa, Chana, Franseco de Pinedo*.

Next the transfer of the trawler *Iamerhav* from Rotterdam to Haifa.

But I have written about these travels of mine many times. No need to repeat myself. The last ship I was assigned to was the old bulk carrier, *Negba*. I was a bit scared. I had never worked on a ship that size. But I never signed on, it was the vessel's last trip, and she sank in a bad tropical storm in the Caribbean Sea.

Dear friend, I realize that the history of my life reads like pure fantasy, but you have known me well enough to know that I don't lie or invent stories. And besides, as you yourself have said, we are accidents, we simply appear, not by our own choice. We make what we can with the means available. My Israeli Seaman's book has the number 0053 and in spite of the fact that I have never sailed on a ship larger than four thousand tons or at a speed of more than fourteen knots, I believe I have proved my right to the honorable title of Ancient Mariner.

The leitmotif of this memoir is naturally nostalgia, that strange longing to relive what has happened once again. This urge is not only strange, it is illogical, and yet it remains irresistible.

And so I recollect that once I took my son Adam, a boy of ten, to the sea and told him, You know, if you continue in this direction you will hit America eventually. Today, when I walk to the same spot, I see three Hebrew letters—Adam—floating on the sea, a memorial created by friends when he was killed in 1974.

Dear Saul,

The leitmotif nostalgia is defined by my big Websters dictionary as the suffering caused by the wish to relive the past, which cannot be relived. I have no reason not to believe my dictionary, which, after all, was compiled in times much more stable than our present.

Epilogue

Saul, I dedicate this essay to two people, to you and to my wife, Nola Chilton Auerbach, who sustained me with her love when I was tempted to give up the struggle.

About the Author

John Auerbach

J ohn Auerbach was born in Warsaw in 1922, and served as a soldier
in the Polish army at the beginning of the Second World War.
During the German occupation, he escaped from the Warsaw Ghetto
and worked on German ships as a stoker under a false identity. He
was caught trying to escape to Sweden in a stolen boat, and sent to
the Stutthof concentration camp. After the war, he went to Sweden
and worked on Swedish ships. Here, he joined the Mossad *Aliyah B*,
and transported refugees to Israel for three years. He was captured by
the British and was detained in a Cyprus camp for two years.

On his release to Israel, Auerbach came to Kibbutz Sdot Yam,
where he was a skipper of fishing boats. After officer's training in
Acre, he served as a Chief Engineer in the Israeli Merchant Marines
for fifteen years. Upon the death of his son in the 1973 Yom Kippur
War, he left the sea and returned to the kibbutz, where he wrote and
published twelve books of short stories and novellas (translated into
Hebrew). His short story, *The Owl*, was awarded First Prize in the
PEN/UNESCO Awards in 1993. He died in November 2002, as this
volume was in preparation.

The fonts used in this book are from the Garamond family

Other works by John Auerbach
also available from *The* Toby Press

Tales of Grabowski

The Rickshaw & Other Stories

The Toby Press publishes fine fiction,
available at bookstores everywhere. For more information,
please contact *The* Toby Press at www.tobypress.com